*A Tale
of Two Worlds*

OTHER TITLES IN THE SERIES

A Tale
of
Two Worlds

Vjenceslav Novak

Translated by John K. Cox

CEU PRESS

Central European University Press

Budapest ● New York

English translation © 2014 John K. Cox

Published in 2014 by

Central European University Press
An imprint of the
Central European University Limited Liability Company
Nádor utca 11, H-1051 Budapest, Hungary
Tel: +36-1-327-3138 or 327-3000
Fax: +36-1-327-3183
E-mail: ceupress@ceu.hu
Website: www.ceupress.com

224 West 57th Street, New York NY 10019, USA
Tel: +1-212-547-6932
Fax: +1-646-557-2416
E-mail: martin.greenwald@opensocietyfoundations.org

ISBN 978-615-5225-82-6
ISSN 1418-0162

"This project has been funded with support from the European Commission.
This publication reflects the views only of the author, and the Commission cannot be held responsible
for any use which may be made of the information contained therein."

Library of Congress Cataloging-in-Publication Data

Novak, Vjenceslav, 1859-1905.
  [Dva svijeta. English]
A Tale of Two Worlds / Vjenceslav Novak.
  pages cm. -- (Ceu Press Classics)
Includes bibliographical references and index.
ISBN 978-6155225826 (alk. paper)
  1. Musicians--Croatia--Fiction. I. Title.

PG1618.N64D8313 2013
891.8'335--dc23

                                    2013042102

Printed in the USA

Contents

Translator's Preface

Several years ago, during consultations with the wise editors at Central European University Press, I decided to try my hand at a Croatian novel set in in an earlier time period from that in which I usually work. The work needed to fit into the CEU Press Classics series, a very valuable and growing collection of literature in translation, but I was also determined to find a novel that I found both truly interesting and historically significant. Whether I succeeded in fulfilling either of those criteria, or in producing an enjoyable and responsible translation, only the readers can say. But I did want to take a moment to underscore the fact that this novel did indeed strike me in the original as telling an important story, and telling it very well. I'll cut to the chase: a lot of famous novels failed my "sniff test." Anyway, I hope the beginning makes the reader want to read to the end, and I hope the whole thing makes us all want to explore more Croatian literature, which contains many delights almost unknown outside the countries where BCS (Bosnian-Croatian-Serbian) is understood.

The source for this translation was the 1932 edition of *Dva svijeta*, prepared for publication by Slavko Ježić and published by Minerva in Zagreb.

*

As fine a writer as Novak was, his style, of course, has its eccentricities that are, perhaps, particularly noticeable, and sometimes exasperating, to a translator. Naturally some of these challenges, or calls for patience, stem from the constraints of the time period in which he wrote. But certain solutions had to be found, for instance, to the problems of run-on sentences, of dogged overuse of key words, and of the presence of older or more obscure words for which ready translation was tricky. Each of these issues has its own solution.

In the first case, as pretty much any translator would do, I broke up long, murky sentences; where I go a bit further perhaps than others is in the addition of some explanatory punctuation such as dashes or semi-colons to bring order and heighten clarity to sentences (the meaning of which do not demand disorder or opaqueness, of course).

For belabored words, such as *zanos, ushit, duša, bujan, buran, nježno, krasan, zatim*, and the myriad Croatian equivalents of "tremble, quiver, or shake," I used a number of synonyms for the general ideas, respectively, of ecstasy, exaltation, soul, lush, stormy, tenderly, beautiful, and such. There is more types of "glory" in this story than I could ever have predicted, and even more words for "and," and I placed my bets, furthermore, on the essential similarity of "thinking" or "mumbling" and "saying to himself." A bit easier was the way people "feel inside"—for where else do emotions originate? English is more than rich enough to provide vocabulary to lighten up these examples of lexical overload, but at other times, frankly, I wished that our language had more options for verbs of noise, from babbling through dins to intoning. Another interesting lexical issue, which might border on a substantive one of interpretation, is the frequency of Novak's use of birth imagery and the notion of ideas or emotions finding *form* or being *clothed* in certain conventions. These did not always come through in my translation but they may be of interest in the original text to Slavists and specialists in comparative literature.

Finally, in this somewhat old-fashioned book (for those of us who work mostly with twentieth-century texts, anyway) there were certain words, some of them more accessible through knowledge of Slovene or Serbian than standard Croatian, for which finding a concise equivalent was very difficult. Perhaps I should say a "precise" equivalent—of equal length. My approach ignored the strictures of parallel structure, in that I sometimes used two words to convey the nuances or vagueness of one in the original. Splitting one word or idea into two energizes the text and keeps things moving along and, most importantly, increases the range of meaning and feeling.

*

I owe many colleagues and friends my thanks for helping me through this project. First off, thank you to Linda Kunos, Krisztina Kós, and Nóra Vörös at CEU Press in Budapest for their patience, support, and great expertise that made my job much, much easier. Thank you to my friends for their linguistic and musicological help: Megan Browndorf, Camille Crittenden, Dora Komnenović, Dragan Miljković, John Moraitis, Larry Schwartz, and Aleksandar Štulhofer. A big shout goes out to John Palmer for writing the afterword to this volume. And, of course, thank you to the Inter-Library Loan staff at my home university, North Dakota State University, for their assistance in getting all kinds of materials for my research: Wendy Gibson, Rachel Goodman, Lorrettax Mindt, and Deborah Sayler.

*

This translation is dedicated to the late Edward P. Lowe, (1932–1999), the Dana Professor of Music at Guilford College, for his years of steady mentoring ("Opera is about the spectacle, Johannes!") and exuberant friendship ("Frrreilich!"). A more cosmopolitan soul, a more caring teacher, and a richer personality there never was.

John K. Cox

Introduction

From Dalmatia to Bohemia: Culture and Politics in Vjenceslav Novak's *A Tale of Two Worlds*

Novak the Man

Vjenceslav Novak was born on September 11, 1859, in the small coastal Croatian city of Senj. Croatia was then a part of the Habsburg (Austrian) Empire, having been absorbed first by Hungary in the distant Middle Ages (1102) and then into the Austrian Empire, based in Vienna, during the Ottoman invasions of the 1520s. Senj is a very old town. It was founded by the Romans and it is extremely well integrated into the multi-ethnic and culturally rich Catholic world of Dalmatia and the Adriatic. A number of famous writers hail from there, including Silvije Strahomir Kranjčević, Pavao Ritter Vitezović, and Milan Ogrizović. Novak's father, Josip, was Czech and had been born in Karlovy Vary. His mother, Ivka, was from a family that traced its roots to Bavaria in Germany, but they had long been residents of Senj. Novak's father died in 1868, when he was just a boy, and his mother died in 1884.

Novak completed his schooling in Senj and nearby Gospić, a somewhat larger town in the ethnically mixed

Dalmatian hinterland. It was then in Zagreb, the traditional capital of the Croatian lands, that Novak earned his first degree. It was from the pedagogical academy. He then began his career in his hometown, where he worked as a teacher. In 1884 Novak won a scholarship and moved north to another major center of Habsburg culture, Prague, in the Czech province of Bohemia. Here he earned credentials as an organist and as a teacher of music theory and voice. For the next nearly twenty years, until the end of his career, he would work simultaneously in many intersecting fields of literature, teaching, and music. From 1887 to his death, he was a professor at the Men's Teachers College, and for the first half of the 1890s he also taught esthetics and music history at the Croatian Music Academy. And he wrote and published an enormous amount.

The novel *A Tale of Two Worlds* (*Dva svijeta*) from 1901 is an excellent example of all three facets of Novak's professional interests: literature, teaching, and music. We shall discuss this novel in greater detail below. But this work, quite probably his finest and arguably the finest prose work in the important field of Croatian realism, was far from Novak's first publication.

He had published a set of poems in 1874. His first book, a novella entitled *Maca* (1881), was a romantic historical work about the fate of a Bosnian girl at the hands of the Turks during the Ottoman occupation of the Balkans in the Middle Ages. He became a regular contributor to literary journals and he published seven novels and nearly a hundred short stories, and a great deal of other material; his collected works, which might well not yet be complete, comprise fifteen volumes.[1] Among his more unusual writing projects were his pedagogical materials and music theory, at least five volumes of which appeared between 1888 and 1893. He also composed choral works, organ pieces, and art songs, but most of these works have been lost.[2]

The combination in Novak's life of poverty and prolific literary production left its mark in one of his short stories, the autobiographical "Crtica o Božiću" (Christmas sketch).[3] There is perhaps something Dickensian about the situation in this story, even though Novak's concern for the poor and social critiques arguably cut even deeper, and verged on naturalism, compared to those of the great British realist. Novak needed to supplement his income with everything from children's tales to articles, autobiographical journal notes, and music reviews. He published in journals such as *Vijenac*, *Hrvatsko kolo*, *Smilje*, and *Hrvatska vila*; and he edited the music journal *Gusle* and a newspaper, *Glasba* (Music). Novak's only drama, *Pred sudom svjetine* (Mob judgment or Rab-

---

[1] Maria B. Malby, "Vjenceslav Novak (11 September 1859–20 September 1905)," in Vasa D. Mihailovich, ed., *Dictionary of Literary Biography* (Vol. 147: South Slavic Writers Before World War II) (Detroit: Gale, 1995), 170.

[2] "Vjenceslav Novak," in August Kovačec, ed., *Hrvatska enciklopedija*, vol. 7 (Zagreb: Leksikografski zavod "Miroslav Krleža"), 764.

[3] Maria B. Malby, "Vjenceslav Novak (11 September 1859–20 September 1905)," in Vasa D. Mihailovich, ed., *Dictionary of Literary Biography* (Vol. 147: South Slavic Writers Before World War II) (Detroit: Gale, 1995), 171.

ble's court) was premiered at the National Theatre in Zagreb just three months after his death; it combined two very different and powerful themes: the fate of an unfaithful married woman and the conditions for Croatian sailors in the Habsburg navy.

Much of his work from the 1880s was short fiction about his home region of Podgorje, along the Dalmatian coast. This period included the major novel *Pavao Šegota*. The novel that is widely recognized as one of his greatest works, *Posljednji Stipančići* (The last of the Stipančićes), appeared in 1899. Our novel under examination here, *Dva svijeta* (*A Tale of Two Worlds*), belongs to his final creative period, in which Novak worked themes related to modern (if unsatisfying or corrupt) middle-class and proletarian life. Novak's final two novels, *Zapreke* (Obstacles) and *Tito Dorčić*, echo key themes of *A Tale of Two Worlds;* in the former a young woman teacher despairs of a career in her homeland and emigrates. In *Tito Dorčić*, published just after the author's death, we see a talented rural youth butting heads with the local establishment as he strives for education and a better life; the youth consequently sets out on a path that leads to a wreck of a home life and ultimate madness. As for the proletarian works, mostly short stories, he depicted "the milieu of the urban poor, the world of people who've been marginalized and deprived of their rights."[4] Some commentators have wondered about the religious implications of his themes and characters, but all in all, despite the mys-

---

[4] Ivo Frangeš, "Vjenceslav Novak" in *Enciklopedija Jugoslavije*, vol. 6 (Zagreb: Jugoslavenski leksikografski zavod, 1965), 306.

tical elements that crop up in his stories from time to time, he usually seems to be depicting emotional life, and seeking to develop improved conditions for the flourishing of individuals, in the face of inimical materialist concerns.

Novak suffered from illness for much of his life, and by all accounts he wore himself out with overwork against a background of the pressing needs of a large family. He and his wife had seven children, although information about them—and more surprisingly, about her—is hard to find. Late in his life, Novak published an interesting autobiographical piece from 1901 entitled "Sličice iz moje bilježnice" (Scenes from my notebook), from which at least something of his family life in Zagreb can be gleaned.[5] At one point, at least, Novak did a stint at a sanatorium in the Alps to try to improve his declining health; after a final, severe two-year round of tuberculosis, he died on September 20, 1905. He had just turned forty-six, and he died at his desk, editing one of his own texts for publication. Novak is buried at Mirogoj Cemetery in the northern suburbs of Zagreb.

[5] Unfortunately this essay does not appear in the otherwise excellent volume edited by Vinko Brešić, *Autobiographies by Croatian Writers* (Zagreb/Dubrovnik: P.E.N. Croatian Centre and Most/The Bridge, 1993). It appears not to have been translated at all but is found in Novak's collected works.

Summary of A Tale of Two Worlds

Jan Jahoda is the sixty-year old Czech music director in a rural parish in Croatia. One day walking into his church to practice he is surprised to find a little boy, who normally runs errands for him, playing beautiful, self-taught music on the organ. Jahoda had never had a pupil like him, even among the singers and failed choir members in this area supposedly so proud of its vocal traditions; Jahoda even says this boy would be a prodigy even in his homeland, the land that produced Smetana and Dvořak.

Jahoda shows the boy off to the local priests, to the pious parishioners, the mayor, and the local intelligentsia: what a find! His name is Amadej Zlatanić. The boy is twelve years old and wants to study music with Jahoda. The two have long conversations—with most of the reflecting being done by the older man—on subjects like the beauty of music and the meaning of devotion to it. The conversation becomes more like an interview or even interrogation. Finally, in tears, Jagoda exclaims that both he and the boy are simply tradesmen at the piano, and neither is an artist.

Amadej, undeterred, dreams for three days of selling his house (we learn later he is an orphan with a somewhat shady guardian named Plavčić) so that he'll have enough money for studies. Then a message comes from Jahoda: they will work together! And a close friendship develops via lessons and visits.

Then one day Jahoda tells Amadej that he's taking him to the gentlemen whose favor may hold the key to his future. Meeting with the mayor and other local nabobs in a *biergarten*, Jahoda remarks in a roundabout way how much he needs a successor in the church...only to hear the potentates say that he should be able to teach the boy whatever it is about church music that is necessary.

Plavčić is forever scheming, and he tries to derail the idea of Amadej's attending the conservatory: "Oh, that's not for our boys—we leave that to you Czechs!" The novel incorporates some information about daily life in this provincial town, but most of the story is registered in the thoughts and conversations of the characters. (The style is, fortunately, vigorous and fairly colorful, and definitely not boring...)

Jahoda's health is going downhill, but no one wants to step into the breach and help fund Zlatanić's study in Bohemia. Then, the teenager begins composing. His first work is "Adelka," a piano sonata to his sweetheart. Meanwhile, in long conversations Jahoda pours out his life to the boy, especially how he attended the conservatory in Prague during the literary and political renaissance in the Czech lands. After the 1848 uprising he wrote a pan-Slavic hymn called "Beneath One Banner" that met with wild success. He also heard the Croat writer and Illyrianist Ljudevit Gaj speak and was very impressed. And—he fell in love, madly and permanently, with a nineteen-year old pianist named Mařenka.

Mařenka was already engaged to a sympathetic nobleman, and to avoid conflict, Jahoda left Prague for Croatia. He held a number of jobs up and down the Dalmatian coast. Then, it occurs to him that this old flame, Mařenka, now married and wealthy and very involved in patronage of the arts, might well help Amadej if he can effect a meeting. But Jahoda dies, exhausted, shortly thereafter.

Amadej enters a contest for composers sponsored by the choral society "Croatia" and his work, "Kolo," comes in second. This convinces him that he must go to Prague. He turns over the rent from his family's house to Plavčić so that he can afford his studies for one year; he will then seek a scholarship. People repeatedly try to dissuade him. But he makes the long train trip to Prague, makes cold calls with his briefcase full of compositions at the conservatory, and attends many operas and concerts. He is ultimately turned down, but the professors state that he does have talent and they urge him to take private lessons to catch up on formal knowledge that he is lacking. Amadej is also filled with pride at the achievements of Slavs (in a world dominated by German-speakers) that he sees all around him. He wants to prove himself. He reminds himself constantly of Jahoda's favorite maxim: *per aspera ad astra* ("Through thorns to reach the stars").

Amadej rents a room from an elderly woman in the suburbs of Prague. He hires tutors for himself and, as he grows in musical knowledge, finds himself torn between the "rules of art" and the freedom of great artists. He comes to rely more on the latter, simply believing in the genius of people like Tchaikovsky and Verdi. After a year, he is accepted into the school. Zlatanić is optimistic—about his career, about his great love for his homeland, and about his future with Adelka. Poverty gnaws at him continuously, though, and he hocks nearly everything he owns. His finances are like a rollercoaster, pulling his spirits up and down.

A helpful letter from his hometown priest reaches him: Amadej should write to the new vice-mayor, who is very musically inclined, and repeat his request for funding to the Town Council at the same time. The cleric even tells him what type of (obsequious) language to use in the letter…Plavčić claims that the rental house is no longer a good investment, because it needs repair and the rents are set too low. But the Town Council gambit works, up to a point. They agree to send him 150 *forints* per year, dependent upon appropriate academic progress. But we know the details of his budget: he needs at least 30 *forints* per month.

One day on a city street he stumbles across the office of an attorney, Dr. Jan Lipovský. Aha! This is the son (also musically inclined) of the famous Mařenka! He again considers activating this connection. Meanwhile, his penury is so painful that he takes a job in a pub, playing dancing and dinner music. He gets paid in food, beer, cigars, and…a little money. Two weeks into this job, another musician stuck in the same rut, Antun Vesely, befriends him. He is worldly. His advice includes tips on getting tips (ask for them!) and the gloomy prediction that Zlatanić will soon be pushed out of the conservatory, as he was. In an analogue to Amadej's relationship with Jan, these two men in Prague have far-ranging discussions about life, education, and music, until Vesely dies suddenly (at age 28).

At the end of his fourth year in Prague, Zlatanić receives another letter from the priest: Adelka's mother has died. He writes a long letter to her, both comforting her and musing out loud what his role in her emotional world will be now…As he is reflecting on his great hopes for intimacy with her, he enters another composition contest. He's been composing a fair amount for over a year now. This composition, an *adagio*, is also dedicated to Adelka, and he wins a major prize. Everywhere he is praised by Czechs who hail him as a fellow Slav and, at the very least, a non-German talent! And the Lipovskýs do show up at the concert—everyone whispers to him that now is his chance to engage a maecenas—where he meets them but, not wanting to be seen as a bum, doesn't take their hints. When he tells them of his friendship with Jahoda, though, they invite him to their mansion and playfully criticize him for not stopping in sooner. And when he departs Prague for Croatia—for Adelka—they send him a lovely parting gift of a decorated tobacco case.

The rhythms of the rails on his long journey south release unheralded creative powers in the young artist. After four years, he is heading home, to "his Croats" and his beloved, sweet homeland! A warm reunion with Adelka ensues. Amadej is able to get a position in a church to the tune of 400 *forints* annually. Reviews of other performances of his works reach him from Prague; they, too, met with universal praise. And he tells Adelka: my greatest work is in the pipeline, and it is entitled "Hymn to Love," and it is dedicated to you, and I will see to it that it premieres in Zagreb!

They marry and begin a life together. But his works that are performed on Croatian soil meet with a lukewarm or even disparaging reception. At best, critics label them "immature." And financial problems return: just when Adelka gives birth to a delightful baby girl, Veruška, the couple learns that even Adelka's family was in debt to Plavčić. So they have to quit her house and move into Amadej's old family home. But Plavčić is still in charge of the rents there, too, and he in his hard-nosed way is now charging a hefty sum. He tells poor Amadej that there are plenty of other prospective renters lined up; the rental rate is a take-it-or-leave-it deal. The reason is that the railroad is coming to town. Not only are there lots of workers and engineers and officials passing through for a while, but property values are sure to climb as a result of the infrastructure improvement.

Amadej's professional pride is damaged soon thereafter, when the town officials call upon him to organize a musical tribute to a big bureaucrat's twenty-five-year service anniversary—someone connected with the railroad, of course. He must write music and a serenade—and precipitously train a choir of singers he has no hand in picking. The poem he must set to music is...infantile and maudlin. To add insult to injury, when officials listen in on the choir's practices, they interfere constantly, telling him to change this or that, because it is too sad or too slow.

One of the officials, Lešeticky, has a beautiful wife named Irma. Zlatanić becomes fixated on her and then nearly obsessed with her. At this point, two-thirds of the way through the novel, the narrative switches to first-person: Amadej's journal entries. This Irma has a beautiful Bösendorfer piano upon which she plays all the latest sheet music that she receives by subscription from Vienna and Berlin. Adelka is merely dismissive, not jealous, of this new relationship. But Amadej and Irma are very attracted to each other, and their conversations move from exploration of common interests to that familiar and ominous question: "But how happy are you really?" Finally she writes a beautiful poem and convinces him to set it to music...but he backs out, feeling guilty at last.

Although he decides to put Šenoa to music instead, Amadej still spends time comparing the two women. When he confesses and weeps in Adelka's presence, she thinks he's drunk and packs him off to bed. Now he protests to her all the time how much he loves her...but as the local poet Mesarić begins visiting to rework the Šenoa poem to go with his score, he notices that the Mesarić is flirting with his wife. Zlatanić's jealousy grows.

Irma has this habit of summoning Amadej to her by sending straight to his home her card with an invitation written on it. One time when she has him over for a chat, music, and supper, he plays "Hymn to Love" for her.

One day soon thereafter Amadej comes home from work to find Adelka in bed, sick. A close family friend (Veruška's godmother) is there and notifies him that Adelka has coughed up a great deal of blood. Dr. Prus, an old family friend, arrives to treat her. Amadej tells her that Plavčić has died, as wrapped up in business deals and controversy as ever. It becomes necessary for Amadej to raise money and send Adelka, along with the godmother and Veruška, off to Zagreb to consult with medical specialists. In those days, though, Amadej is losing pupils (and the money from their private lessons) to a new musician in town, a *tamburaš* named Rakovčić, so money is a big problem. The two men agree to work together to take a joint, high culture-low culture approach to awakening the musical sensibilities of the people, even though they disagree on many points of theory.

Amadej misses Adelka terribly while she's in Zagreb. He realizes that he loves her more than he loves his art. He thinks of all the things they will do together when she is well again, such as vacationing at the Plitvice Lakes or visiting the island of Lokrum. After (only) five days, Adelka returns, full of stories of how enamored little Veruška was of the excitement of the big city. She herself confesses that she did not actually see a doctor there, but she let a relative of the godmother take her to a kind of midwife or woman folk healer who treated her, and she seems to be recovering.

There follows a long gap in the coverage of the diary. One day Amadej returns home from practice and sees Mesarić just leaving. He resents this other man not just because of the poet's interest in Adelka but also because he is in cahoots with Rakovčić, working to undermine Amadej's career. Amadej mutters to himself that he will humiliate, and then murder, Mesarić for daring to come courting at his home. He immediately goes to find Mesarić in a bar, spits in his face, and challenges him to a duel. The mayor and others try to talk him out of it, saying, in effect, that this is a case of "the pot calling the kettle black." When Amadej threatens to sue for libel unless they explain themselves, the local notables remind him that he, too, has spent a lot of time with another man's wife.

Zlatanić returns to wrangling with Rakovčić over a new concert. He criticizes the folk musician harshly on theoretical grounds such as insufficient mastery of harmony and chords, holding up Chopin as a musical model; the primitive *tamburica* is incapable of serving as the vehicle for genius and sublime spiritual or intellectual reflections. Rakovčić, however, starts to beat Zlatanić in various competitions, and our composer is both offended and humiliated. He sounds ever more curmudgeonly and impotent when he asserts that Croatia must take its place among the *educated* and *cultured* societies of the world, so that no one has any excuse for hiding his Croatian nationality, but that this must all be done by contributing to existing high culture, not by reviving folk traditions alone. Croatian musical greats like Lisinski, Zajac, and Milka Trnina are blazing the trail for future generations, but still…Zlatanić's concerts receive only lukewarm reviews as audiences fail to "connect" with his works.

A letter from Berlin arrives, from Irma, and an elated Amadej feels that justice is coming his way at last. She played his "Hymn to Love" to a small group in the German capital and a publisher is now interested in considering his work. Sure enough, the publisher writes, too, requesting a sheaf of unpublished compositions. They might be published…for pay! There is, however, only one utterly disconcerting condition: Zlatanić's name may not appear on the works. He is devastated at this thought, but he decides to take the publisher up on another kind of work also discussed in the letter: piecework, doing instrumentation and orchestration of other people's works. The pay is bad, and the music is bad (and includes an entire opera that is a knock-off of Wagner), but the work is easy and the publisher likes Amadej's work-by-mail; he never gets used to swallowing his pride and hiding his name, however.

Adelka falls ill a second time. Desperate for cash, Amadej thinks of begging the Berlin publisher for a raise or the right to attach his own names to works that he would then allow them to print, but he blanches. He remembers the poet Preradović's maxim that "nevolja gola, najbolja škola" (bleak distress makes the best education), but he cannot get anyone to sign a promissory note and a Zagreb publisher he approaches also rejects his work. Grimly mouthing the realization that he no longer cared about his career and that obtaining money for Adelka's treatment is all that matters, he prepares a package of his manuscripts that he is willing to turn over to the Berlin company on their terms.

The doctors tell him that Adelka's condition is serious and she should be sent to a southern clime to recuperate. Away she goes again, and he is again forlorn and lonely right away without her, but he feels recharged with creativity and plans to set to work on new ideas. Then he gets news that she is going downhill; he is summoned to her bedside but before he can leave his town she dies.

Doleful beyond repair, Amadej wonders briefly what life means to him now and what the world can hold for anyone. He stays up all night at the piano, composing a *notturno*. He goes to Adelka's bed and hallucinates about her, and then about Jahoda. He weeps till dawn. Soon thereafter he tries to hang himself, but even before he carries it out, he has forgotten why he is doing so. The godmother finds him and the mayor puts him under guard—perhaps to prevent him from hurting himself but also to keep him from being a public embarrassment during the ongoing festivities. Rakovčić has written a waltz for the mayor's wife, and Amadej plays it; he imagines that his rival is present, and the godmother feeds both of them dinner. There are brief, poignant scenes with Veruška, who does not really understand what has happened to her mother or her father.

Now mad, Zlatanić wants to pack and go to the carriage waiting outside to take him to the train station, from where he imagines that he will travel to Berlin to seek justice regarding his compositions. He knows they will say: "What great but stupid people are born in Croatia!"

Then, he realizes he has been locked up in an asylum. He finds his fellow inmates boring and disgusting and generally dreadful and cannot believe he himself is crazy. As a reality check, the doctors ask him what he knows about his wife…and Amadej responds that she is alive. If she were dead, how would I be able to talk to her? And if she is dead, then you should arrest me and put me in prison instead of this mad-house, because I would be the one who had killed her. Amadej despairs of convincing the "dense" doctors of the truth of his statements.

The novel ends with a set of visions of Amadej underway through a beautiful, varied landscape to be reunited with his beloved Adelka. His love for her was the ultimate incarnation of his ethos: professionally and personally she was his motivation. (There is less talk now of the nation.) As he fords streams and skirts mountains, he revisits scenes from his life all the way back to childhood, and he sees Jahoda and Prague and his homecoming from that city where he imagines that he was greeted with a conqueror's laurels and a thundering rendition of his work "Hail to the Homeland." Sadly he thinks that Adelka never truly understood his art, simply because of the physical limitations of most human ears, insufficiently developed "organs of Corti." But he does sense, as he drifts off into the light and the long vision ends, the angelic essence of the poetry of their souls as distilled into his music.

Naturally there are many ways to discuss or begin to interpret a large, well-written novel like this one. A critique of Novak's style, for instance, would probably lead most people to describe it as accessible if not particularly innovative (although the diary in the final third of the novel charges ahead towards stream-of-consciousness writing in the Modernist vein). Novak is very readable. One might like this work, for instance, because it is interesting in terms of plot and characterization. Novak's style tends to elide major events; the narrative flow is so smooth that our emotions are not held hostage by the plot. This allows us to narrow our focus, which comes to rest on Amadej's thoughts and feelings in their late Habsburg context. Still, in terms of characterization, one should note that the increasing quotient of realism in his novels did not exempt Novak from the criticism that he paid more attention to the way the world was put together than the way good books are put together.[6] The author is sympathetic to individuals of emerging and under-represented social classes or groups (the urban poor, artists, independent women), but he does not always succeed in painting compelling psychological portraits of his characters.

Another approach to interpretation of this book is thematic. One could examine it from the point of view of gender relations, madness and power, or intellectual history and nationalism (see *History: The Evolution of Croatian Nationalism* on page lxv). But the symbolism contained in the title, "two worlds," is another deserving starting point for addressing the importance of the ideas in the novel. Towards the end of the book, Amadej writes:

> Now I sense in and around myself two worlds. One of them encompasses all the serenity, truth, and rightful value of everything that exists, not because it is but because it has to be. The other world strives against the first one; it is inconstant and incomprehensible in its inconsistency.

This binary, an idealism/empiricism duality, to which he clings during his descent into madness actually has echoes and parallels throughout the entire novel. One Croatian critic underscores the tension in *Two Worlds* between the "imaginary sphere of art" and intellectual life, on the

---

[6] See Slobodan Prosperov Novak, *Povijest hrvatske književnosti: od baščanske ploče do danas* (Zagreb: Golden, 2003), 260.

one hand, and the warmth of human relationships on the other. [7] Another observer has delineated a large, though not exhaustive, number of the dichotomies operating in the novel. There are, for instance:

> the conflict between the artist and petty bourgeois society, high art and popular art, true artistic creation and craft or trade, the world around Amadej and the world inside him, Amadej and his wife Adelka, who does not understand him, and between the retiring Adelka and the self-confident Irma. [8]

We might also fruitfully examine this novel from the perspective of autobiography, as some critics have suggested. As a love story, Amadej's temptation by and dalliance with Irma contrasts markedly with the evolution of his feelings for Adelka, while the tension between Amadej and Mesarić, based both on a love triangle involving Adelka *and* on important intellectual or political issues in unspecified proportions, calls to mind the masterful structure of a novel by Graham Greene. And a final approach is suggested by one of Novak's more exhaustive biographers, Marijan Jurković, who finds remarkable the degree of "concentrated hatred of the bourgeois social order, of each and every one of its lies" that our novel nurtures. Whether connected or not to ideological diagnoses or political prescriptions, this hatred turns Amadej

---

[7] Antun Barac, "Vjenceslav Novak" in Vjenceslav Novak, *Pripovijesti* (Beograd: Luča, Biblioteka Zadruge profesorskog društva, 1933), 26.

[8] "Vjenceslav Novak," in August Kovačec, ed., *Hrvatska enciklopedija*. Volume VII. (Zagreb: Leksikografski zavod "Miroslav Krleža"), 764.

into a martyr or bearer of subversion and the book becomes "a halo for a revolutionary of emotion."[9]

This Novel in Context: Novak's Other Works

Most observers designate either *A Tale of Two Worlds* or *The Fall of the Stipančić Family* (*Posljednji Stipančići*) as Novak's best prose work, or indeed as his best work overall.[10] This latter novel treats the decline of an aristocratic family in a period of great socio-economic change in the Croatian lands. It was made into an excellent film in 1968, in an adaptation by the poet Jure Kaštelan.[11] The

[9] Marijan Jurković, *Vjenceslav Novak* (Beograd: Rad, 1966), 15.

[10] Frangeš says simply that *Posljednji Stipančići* is Novak's best work (Ivo Frangeš, "Vjenceslav Novak," in *Enciklopedija Jugoslavije*, vol. 6 [Zagreb: Jugoslavenski leksikografski zavod, 1965], 204). Kaštelan notes that it is the most printed and most often read of Novak's works (Kaštelan, Jure, "Između agonije i rađanja." Foreword to Vjenceslav Novak, *Posljednji Stipančići* [Sarajevo: Veselin Masleša, 1973], 14). Barac maintains that *Posljednji Stipančići* and *A Tale of Two Worlds* are the best things he wrote (Antun Barac, "Vjenceslav Novak" in Vjenceslav Novak, *Pripovijesti* [Beograd: Luča, Biblioteka Zadruge profesorskog društva, 1933], 26).

[11] This spare, haunting film, which has a few experimental sequences, depicts the increasing loneliness of Lucija, a young woman, and her mother; the family patriarch has just died and Lucija's brother, rambles aimlessly through Europe and finally adopts a Hungarian name and settles in Budapest. In the increasingly international economic and cultural environment portrayed in the film, every European language seems secure, except Croatian, and the family's remaining female members are left suffering from loneliness, disease, and poverty in a backwater they call "Illyria."

novel strikes this observer as similar in theme to Thomas Mann's *Buddenbrooks*; at any rate a connection to the more regional history of the Habsburg Empire is apparent, though, because in the novel Novak alludes to the fact that the family's decline comes as a result of a political decision made in Budapest. For the coastal hub and port of the expanding Hungarian railway system, Rijeka was chosen over Senj, guaranteeing that the latter city would face economic decline. What is more, Rijeka was chosen after its reclassification (probably unconstitutional) as a city under direct Hungarian sovereignty rather than under the intermediate rule of traditional Croatian authorities.

Some of his short stories are on intriguing topical themes. In "The Social Democrat" (1894), a chance encounter between a conservative priest and a strange, almost mad city-dweller. The man demands an audience and declares himself to be a social democrat:

> Yes, that's what I am, but not one of those social democrats who have lost their minds and rush off with a mad head to destroy the church and state and whom the people on the far left call anarchists or nihilists...That goes against the teachings of the Christian and Catholic church, whose loyal son I am..."[12]

After reassuring the priest that he does not drink, and that he has read theological works in German from Döllinger and Ketteler, the visitor tells the priest his life story. His parents had died and he had lived the life of a

[12] Vjenceslav Novak, "Socijal-demokrata," in Branimir Livadić, ed., *Izabrane pripovijesti*, vol. 1 (Zagreb: Matica hrvatska, 1925), 97.

poor adventurer, but religious feeling, inherited from his dear mother, had pulled him from the path of wickedness. He embraced social democracy and

> on this and that occasion I explain it to our Croatian peasants, whom soon a global wave from the anti-Christian sea is going to hit and who will then be carried away into the perilous open waters of its dissolute and immoral principles."[13]

While working for a set of surveyors who were building a road in the coastal region of Primorje, he impressed his employers and fell in love with a poor, devout girl from the local area. When his boss assigned him to a team of workers far from the town they were lodging in, he sought out his beloved fiancée to say goodbye. He finally came across her—in his boss's hotel room. In a fit of blinding rage and dizzying despair he attacked them and believed he had killed the young woman. But she was only wounded, and after serving a month of jail time he began to wander aimlessly through the South Slavic lands for years. He made his way to Zagreb and, while looking for work, rescued a woman and her sick child from the street. As he was literally carrying them around on his back, they finally recognized each other as Nikola and Marija—the couple that had been engaged years earlier. He forgave her and now was approaching the priest on behalf of this new, nascent family. The priest silently obliges by giving Nikola an entire silver forint, causing him to promise:

[13] Ibid., 99.

Other paupers live, and so will we...and by the time the little boy grows up, the principles of Catholic social democratic thought will come to prevail in human society—and then there will be neither paupers nor beggars."[14]

Modernity, Novak might add, comes at a cost. Gone are the days when modernization is viewed by historians as a linear path or unadulterated good, and Novak arguably always endeavored to capture that process in its ambiguity.

"Scenes from My Time as a Soldier" (1895) is a lengthy, day-by-day account of a two-week tour of duty for a group of rural Croatian soldiers in the Habsburg army. From the induction and distribution of uniforms to the unenviable sleeping conditions and great boredom of long turns of waiting, the first-person narrator describes the ups and downs of the colorful group of reservists. Some of the men in his unit are peasants, but many others are professionals such as teachers, attorneys, officials of the tax office, etc. The thumbnail sketches of individual soldiers are memorable and the language Novak employs in scenes of their training and socializing is fresh and detailed. They learn to march and shoot, try to come to terms with capital punishment, they trade drinks and stories of far-away loved ones in the canteen.

The attitude of the narrator towards the army is clear from the start:

[14]Ibid., 104.

Compared to the vast progress made by the human spirit; compared to the heights to which the sciences and arts were climbing; compared to all of that, waging war came across as a legacy of more brutal and less enlightened times, and the profession of soldier, apart from its exterior shine and gleam, was an evil one, which it would be better to eliminate sooner rather than later.[15]

Still, the characters are not Schweikian in their alienation from military life. They are unconvinced but obedient, and the narrative is realistic but not naturalistic in detail and less focused on a picaresque flow of events than on the careful, quiet elaboration of personalities of the characters. Naturally, nationality comes up. And the subject of one soldier's nationality receives quite a bit of attention halfway through the story.

Although this officer was a native Croatian from the rugged old province of Lika, the conscious recognition of his own position had impelled him to demonstrate how—shedding his home-made moccasins and rough-knit black cap at the military academy—he had cast out of his soul the memory of the house to which he was born and had made his heart discard the love for his father and mother, brother and sister, kith and kin and neighbors and village and that far-off province and that whole distant land and its entire people, which had produced him itself and above all for itself. And he forgot as well the delight of his mother tongue, which as a sweet and innocent suckling he had imbibed so that his tiny lips worked the sweet droplets of its milk.[16]

[15] Vjenceslav Novak, "Sličice iz moga vojnikovanja," in Branimir Livadić, ed., *Izabrane pripovijesti*, vol. 2 (Zagreb: Matica hrvatska, 1926), 116.

[16] Ibid., 134.

In the "Imperial and Royal" (German: *k. und k.*, *kaiserlich und königlich*; Hungarian: *cs. és kir.*, *császári és királyi*; Croatian, *c. i. k.*, *carski i kraljevski*) army, then, this officer had allowed himself to become de-Croatianized. Novak, not a hard-core nationalist but a keen observer of society who understood well both the importance of national identity and the contemporary increase in the number of ways it was being propagated in society, went on to say one more important thing about this officer: when one of the soldiers lines up incorrectly for drill, the officer

> lit into him in Croatian, a Croatian that was possibly intentionally mangled and distorted, because his small brain had deceived him into thinking that his faintness of heart and the poverty of his soul would disappear if he showed that he had forgotten the heroic language of his homely and ingenuous nation.[17]

In Novak's view it is as counterproductive for this youngish officer to hate Croatianness as it is for him to nurse a "cowardly antipathy towards the civilian intelligentsia."

Finally a kindly captain named Luka plucks the awkward Croatian intellectuals out of the larger unit and provides a separate drill sergeant for them:

> Take note: these men are not corporals, and they're not friars, and consequently they are gentlemen. They do not know our drills, but they know other things. Their hands are intended for the pen, not the rifle...Now, you remember that! ...A bit of training and then some rest...You can swear, but no blaspheming or abuse.[18]

---

[17] Ibid., 134.
[18] Ibid., 140.

The many divisions among the soldiers in the Habsburg army are not whitewashed in the text. But nationality is not alone as a marker of identity: religion is mentioned almost as much, and class, regional, and vocational distinctions merge in a powerful pair of designations of various soldiers and ranks as *kaputaši* and *kožunaši*. This story, like the screen version of one of Novak's novels discussed below, does not treat national consciousness or nationalism as simple or monolithic forces. A language-based sense of nationality co-exists, or nests, with other important forms of identity, and regional origins and affiliations remain very important. Such portrayals dovetail with the history of the slow growth of political nationalism in the Croatian lands. They also support the somewhat newer modernist interpretations that do indeed see nationalism as a construct but one that comes to be politically hegemonic on account of activity at the grassroots level as well as among elites. When peasants and working-class people begin to *practice* their national consciousness differently, then we have a nationalism supporting process based on political programs and high culture (operas, novels, architecture, and even, for the most part, public education) used by the elite to *propagate* corollary.

The strange little story entitled "The Tale of Marcel Remenić" (1905) at first seems like a droll commentary on a late nineteenth-century version of a metrosexual man trapped in the provinces. A local man, part of "good society" by dint of the money he inherited and his proclivity to show up at most public social and civic functions, has been chosen to escort the governor's wife to a soiree in town. Marcel is obsessed with fashion—avoiding politics and regular newspapers, for instance, but subscribing to fashion journals and constantly showing off his new acquisitions, from shoes to neckties—and he orders special clothes from a famous tailor in Vienna just for the occasion. On the afternoon of the ball, however, his ancient housekeeper spills greasy soup all over his new outfit, and Marcel, crushed, actually "dies of a heart attack on the same evening that would surely have been the crowning glory of his life."[19]

What keeps this story from being just an account of a frustrated provincial or a fussy perfectionist is, above all, its use of the concept of "modernity." Marcel seeks out the most modern clothes, but this is more than just vanity. Novak takes care to note that he is a *"privatijer,"* or a *rentier* who lives on inherited money. A version of the pan-European "superfluous man," his pathetic, brittle insistence on the modern as his one accomplishment in life lays bare the problematic mechanics of the adoption of external ideas in a provincial (or, perhaps, East European) setting. But Marcel does not stop there. He brags, in the local cafe:

> Science! Without a doubt, science has done a great deal for the advancement of humanity. But art, art has not fallen behind it in terms of its achievements. Take this pair of pants, for instance...what unity of line, what vibrancy, what bounce, in this genuine masterpiece![20]

[19] Vjenceslav Novak, "Pripovijest o Marcel Remeniću, in *Pripovijesti* (Beograd: Luča, Biblioteka Zadruge profesorskog društva, 1933), 49.

[20] Ibid., 48.

Marcel dies, ambiguously, as a hapless herald of a new era or as a vestige of a period of development passing almost silently. Nationalism, of course, is nowhere to be seen here except in the abstract workings of cultural borrowings, adaptation, and (aborted) convergence.

"Salamon" (1888) is the story of an awkward country tailor. His real name is Mijo, and he was raised by his elderly mother; he was ugly and none too bright, but kindly, and after his father's death at sea in his youth, he met with rejection in one trade after another as he was coming of age in his coastal Croatian village. He finally decided to become a tailor, and the townspeople thought a great deal of his work, but everyone made fun of his—impaired or ignorant?—mental state, because he claimed constantly that the sun moved around the earth and not vice-versa. Indeed, this phrase became his characteristic greeting and conversation piece.

Salamon longs to marry Mare, a beautiful but haughty local girl. She has only scorn and abuse for him, marries Nikola the sailor, and has a baby girl. When Nikola is away at sea for long periods, Salamon plays with the baby and offers Mare help to get through the winter—and both gestures are misinterpreted and answered with rudeness by Mare. But when their family is truly suffering one winter, Mare and Nikola decide to take Salamon up on his offer of help. They move into half of his house and then progressively take more and more advantage of him, squeezing him into the kitchen, where his health fails, and then having a large party when he is very ill so that everyone can listen to him assigning all of his property to their daughter in his last will and testament. When, at the end of the story, Mara tosses dirt onto his casket and declares that he was a good man, we have no idea whether to believe her or not.

The brief story is full of psychological insights but its emotional impact comes from its lovely, lyrical descriptions of human habits and needs in the face of material want, material greed, and conflict. "Poor Mijo" is yet another of Novak's unassuming, overmatched heroes who meets a terrible end.

"From the Underbelly of the Metropolis" (1895) is a departure for Novak. It takes place in a crowded working-class district of Zagreb, and not in the countryside or along the Dalmatian coast. The main character, Mika, faces a life like that of a character from a quintessential Ivan Cankar story or Emile Zola novel. He has only menial, backbreaking labor—in this case, wood-chopping and firewood delivery—that he must share with many other hungry, despondent men. He and his wife and their gravely ill daughter Evica live in a dark warren of rooms, shared with many other people, underneath a building; only a ladder affords access to their cave-like dwelling. Mika regularly drinks up much of his pay and fights constantly with his wife. During the day he is haunted by images of foamy blood trickling from his coughing daughter's lips. He curses his poverty, because it makes him feel contaminated and untouchable. After their daughter dies of her illness, Mika reflects on his own guilt and inadequacy, which he terms his "cruelty." His father was a digger on a canal project near Zagreb, and he recalls being beaten nearly to death by him for no good reason:

Mika was ten years old then. His father...commanded him to bring his lunch [to the work-site] precisely at noon, because he, as workers are wont to do, looked forward more than anything else about his job to the pipe that he would get to puff away at after eating; he would get to lie about some and doze. But on that day the schoolteacher detained Mika until noon, because he had not completed his homework the night before. And Mika had not done that homework because there were no candles or lights in his house... So when he took his father the meal, his father grabbed him unexpectedly and begin beating him in front of both the men and women workers. Some of them urged him a number of times to let Mika go, but his father struck him even harder as if to boast of the fact that he knew how to handle his own child. God only knows where so much ferocity and rage came from, until finally some women intervened and pulled Mika away from him.[21]

Mika recalls these events with both pain and shame. And afterward he simply longs to sink into the earth along with his daughter.

The story "Dissonances" (1906) contains a surprising mix of elements. It is above all a touching story of a mature, if challenged, marriage between two thoughtful and sensitive individuals. (And it has a happy ending!) But it contains a number of reflections on and of the *zeitgeist* of the modern era that also make it very thought-provoking. Virgil and Marija have had two children, a boy and a girl, and are now drifting apart in their marriage. As he watches her repair children's clothes, night after night,

[21] Vjenceslav Novak, "Iz velegradskog podzemlja" in Branimir Livadić, ed., *Izabrane pripovijesti*, vol. 1 (Zagreb: Matica hrvatska, 1925), 246.

Virgil feels impatient that she spends all of her brain-power on this one menial task. He is torn between boredom with Marija and a solemn and very historically concrete recognition that society has failed to educate women properly over the centuries and that they have traditionally been exploited by their own fathers and brothers. He tries to discuss Goethe and Schiller with his wife and her friends—for their generation does indeed have the rudiments of an education—but he sees that their understanding does not match their intelligence.

Virgil is a civil servant. He does well for himself, and one of his promotions takes him and the family to Zagreb. There he reads Bebel's book on women and socialism, and his hatred for the still widespread "Oriental" and "Eastern" approaches to the "woman question" grows—even as does his boredom with his wife and his appreciation for her calm, sincere, and nurturing nature, which he only gradually realizes is the result of the "regressive idea" of isolating her soul from the "blows to the brain" that men receive in modern society. Finally, his thoughts begin to distill into a sense of distance, a gap, between him and his wife. It is this alienation that will finally bring him clarity and peace. He is a very complex character.

Unsure of how to proceed at first, he joins a social club as a reason to spend time outside their home in the evenings. He is puzzled by her "irrational" unwillingness to ask him not to go to the "Club of the Content," even though it is patent that his absences grieve her greatly. He finally realizes that she understands—that she is sad because she understands—about the gap between them.

She understands a great deal, despite the fact that "even in the period of human prehistory woman had been a servant in the home, a slave to her lover, and a saint as a mother." Women, Virgil muses, give love and life, and men traditionally are given control over children's minds, even though their intellects and those of women are quite comparable! This is one of the sources of the gap, of the dissonance in modern life, but one that Virgil hopes can be overcome. In his way he hopes to bridge the gap by tenderness. The kisses he gives Marija are abundantly joyful because they are full of understanding—and yet, how few men have reached this conclusion? Few writers, a reader might go on to ask, presented such a nuanced view of feminism in Novak's day and age?

This Novel in Context: Croatian Literature in the Late Habsburg Period

The novel *A Tale of Two Worlds* has added at least two distinctions to Novak's reputation. It was, we know now, "the first attempt at a novel about a musician in Croatian literature." [22] In addition, critics and literary historians are far from unified about Novak's success in creating psychologically compelling characters, but he did deserve the epithet of "the moral historian of his times." [23] In terms of Novak's artistic evolution over the course of his career, it is commonly noted that he

[22] Frangeš, 205.
[23] Ibid., 205.

began under the influence of Šenoa's romanticism and ended as a great realist, bordering on the territory of naturalism and modernism. This novel in particular has been compared to the work *Radmilović* (1893) by Ksaver Šandor Gjalski (1854–1935), about a visual artist, but *Dva svijeta* is widely judged to be more successful in artistic terms. Gjalski also wrote an intensely critical, even cynical, political novel, *U noći* (In the night; 1886), which could be read as a companion piece to Novak.

Discussion of Novak's works is not exactly commonplace nowadays, especially in English or in English translation. But the Croatian novelist and literary scholar Dubravka Ugrešić includes *A Tale of Two Worlds* in her recent essay "The Spirit of the Kakanian Province." Here Novak shares an important recurring theme with other important Croatian writers, such as Gjalski, Milutin Cihlar, and Miroslav Krleža: the Habsburg variant of Turgenev's "superfluous man." We have in similar works by these writers an "over-sensitive, educated misfit or outcast"[24] who generally meets with dissatisfaction or disaster. In the Croatian context, that of "Kakania," a satiric term for the Habsburg Empire, this means that works like Novak's have a specific thematic relevance today (apart from any esthetic or biographical considerations). First, the "return to the homeland" sought by characters such as Amadej is really a return to the periphery, and it is a dis-

---

[24] Dubravka Ugrešić, "The Spirit of the Kakanian Province." Translated by Ellen Elias-Bursać. In *Karaoke Culture* (Rochester, NY: Open Letter, 2011), 277.

play of a self-pitying, colonized mentality.[25] Second, we should all ask ourselves, after the decades-long polemic of nostalgia by writers from Konrád and Kundera to Brodsky (and Ugrešić, not to even mention Miłosz and Kiš) about return of or to "Central Europe" at the end of the Cold War, which Central Europe do we mean to valorize? One can be constructed or advanced on the bases of the admirable cultural values these writers have memorialized, but another—that of pathos on the periphery, and isolation and inadequacy—also existed and might be lurking in the folds of the same flags.

Croatian literature in general is still little known in English-speaking countries. Of the works of the great Miroslav Krleza, perhaps one-fifth have been translated, and most of those books are out of print. There is a modest, if steady, flow of contemporary (i.e., post-Yugoslav) Croatian literature into English, but nothing like the amount going into German or, especially, French translation. For fundamentally important works of nineteenth-century Croatian literature, this is an even greater problem. As deserving of translation as some of these works are—the historically important *U registraturi* (In the registry office; 1888) of Ante Kovačić and the eccentric, psychologically modern stories of Antun Gustav Matoš come to mind—anything approaching effective coverage of this era seems a long way off. In order, therefore, to give an idea of prevailing themes and forms of Croatian literature around the time of Novak's life, three books are presented below as material for com-

---

[25] Ibid., 285–286.

parison and enticement to future translators. These books are not the canonical ones (as are the deserving works mentioned above), but are meant to show just how much intriguing Croatian literature is yet to be made available to anglophone audiences.

The first interesting but lesser-known work is *Prosjak Luka* (Luke the beggar), written by the great Croatian Romantic August Šenoa in 1879. Šenoa (1838–1881) is widely hailed as the first modern Croatian writer. In this medium-length realistic novel, a village beggar—actually, a foundling from Zagreb who escaped institutionalization and became a kind of village loan shark—seeks to establish a respectable life with family and property. Unable to secure the affections of the one woman he loves, the main character, Luka, retreats to a forest hideaway, returning to the village only to kill himself by throwing himself in the Sava. The somewhat melodramatic ending is more than compensated for by the intriguing plot and the detailed yet still fluid descriptions of village life with its pub, Gypsy camp, corrupt political campaigns, fractious legal disputes, and outbursts of envy among peasant neighbors. The narrative structure is basically linear, with a couple of major, productive flashbacks (such as the one to Luka's childhood in the "care" of the municipal authorities in Zagreb). There are enough references to government institutions (the courts, the army, the tax collectors) for the reader to place the Croatian village Jelenje in the Hungarian half of the late Empire.

Besides Luka, the main characters are: Mikica Ribarić, a local clerk who poses as a lawyer (*fiškal*) and engages in constant, mercenary intrigues both for and against Luka;

Ugarković, a Roma hired by Ribarić, who is himself often in the employ of Luka; Mato, the "real beggar" who bequeaths to Luka his nest egg which in turn allows him to start buying up mortgages and other collateral; Andro Pavleković, a simple peasant youth who relates his military experiences from all over the Habsburg Empire and is engaged to the beautiful local peasant girl Mara; and Martin Lončarić, Mara's father, a stalwart and sober peasant who is attacked and undercut by his neighbors, especially by Luka, who also longs for the hand of his daughter and tries every nasty trick imaginable, from cattle plague to barn-burning, to force Lončarić into a position of dependency upon him.

Šenoa based this novel on actual events; he had met and interviewed several of the persons involved, including the source of the main character, Luka. Šenoa is certainly famous for his prolific publications and numerous intellectual engagements, but his devotion to realism here is as noteworthy as his humanism: peasant life, he says in his own preface to the work, is as rich and worthy a repository of subjects for literature as any other realm. And peasants, he and his characters assert on several occasions, are people too! The tragedy-stricken Luka, after all, despite all his games with documents, deceit, and numbers, just wanted to be accounted a human being.

Next we will recount in some detail synopses of two works, unavailable in English, by Mara Ivančan (1891–1968). In her day, she was less widely read than the prolific and generally more traditional pioneer of Croatian women's literature, Marija Juric Zagorka (1873–1957).

Ivančan's first novel was *Uskrsnuće Pavle Milićeve* (The resurrection of Pavla Milić; 1923). This was Ivančan's first novel; only one other by her exists. The two could easily be paired in terms of length and subject matter; such a pairing would also show her development as a writer. Her third novel, which seems to have existed only in manuscript form, has been lost.

Ivančan's second novel is often rated more highly by critics in terms of innovation and technique, yet it is also more abstract; the plot of *The Resurrection of Pavla Milić* is at least as gripping as that of *A Wondrous Tale*, and the frank depictions of sexuality and emotions (and, yes, compromise) make this tale in some ways more engaging than the later novel. Iconoclastic views and socio-political realia are certainly present here, too, as in the figure of the elderly uncle, the rural elite's views on the modernization of Zagreb, and the Pan-Slavism of the main male character, Feodor.

The narrator, Pavla, begins by explaining that a man named Feodor Ivanović, who was once her lover, has no idea that she is writing this text. The early days of her love for Feodor, she muses, were "the most beautiful ones of [her] entire life" and she feels the need to have the reader recognize that the "springtime" of this love was "more pure than a mother's kisses," and that "the first kisses that my young flesh sensed...[were] as fresh as a rose in the morning."[26] The "embraces...[were] sweeter than the fruits of autumn, and hotter than...rays of sunlight."

---

[26] Mara Ivančan, *Uskrsnuće Pavle Milićeve* (Zagreb: St. Kugli, 1923), 3.

By age 20, Pavla had finished her education; she knew how to speak four languages, play the piano, and run a household. Although she lost both of her parents at a young age and lives with her uncle, her only relative, Pavla is warmly and stubbornly optimistic about life, beauty, and love. In her peaceful, well-ordered, and benign world figure only her elderly uncle, her cat Miško, and the family cook, Kata, and a profound love of nature. Spurred on by friends' comments and by poetry, Pavla becomes convinced that she needs to fall in love. One day, as she is despairing of meeting the right man and considering hurling herself into a life of utter renunciation, she receives a letter from an unknown man. He had been given copies of some of her poems by a friend, and he was writing to return the poems to her and to give his assessment of her work. These cannot be published, he writes, for they lack sufficient passion and maturity. She resents his flip judgments, but after a while, shocked by the sight of her withered and indifferent neighbor, Neža, who is miserable without love, she looks for an excuse to write Feodor back.

She tells him of the beauty of rural life, mentioning also that people in her village enjoy exchanging opinions with city-dwellers because these latter are so worldly and progressive in their views; she asks him in particular what he thinks of the "woman question," which is all the rage in England these days. Feodor writes back immediately, rejoicing over the contact and praising her style of writing. He goes on to mention his profound attraction to "authentic" village life, his admiration for Russia, with its plain, healthy living on the steppes, his mistrust of the institutions of Western civilization, and his enthusiasm for Balkan songs and styles of dance.

Seated at a small table in the main room of her house, Pavla continues her correspondence with Feodor, while her uncle plays cards by candlelight and the rest of the domestic, intimate life of the house rolls past her by candlelight. It is an "exquisite pleasure" to bare her soul to her correspondent, and "no one could ever imagine someone better at making confessions" than she was.[27] Days on which letters from Feodor arrived were like holy days, and she even dressed up in fine outfits to receive his letters, wanting to create an appropriately dignified atmosphere for their exchange. She poses, to herself, sophisticated questions about the nature of their attraction for each other, speculating that it is their very unavailability or remove that is the basis for their ever stronger sentiment. She claims an utter disinterest in whether Feodor wears French shoes or American ones, whether he is tall or short, etc., just as she asserts that he must be totally uninterested in whether their friendship will ever develop into something different.

Their exchange is a lively one, full of taunts and jokes, and talk of love and experience edges in. As the correspondence heats up, and Pavla's romantic interest rises, her uncle offers words of wisdom; this interesting character is quite wise, and progressive for his age, but he remains on the margins of the tale, offering only practical advice and emotional support to Pavla. Gradually the two young people come to express their love for each

[27] Ibid., 15.

other in increasingly passionate letters. They write for months, working through various misunderstandings and vexing misunderstandings from a distance, as Pavla experiences "a spring that is lovelier and hotter than any other in her entire life."[28] At last words alone cease to satisfy, and they arrange a meeting through an exchange of telegrams.

With quaking knees and her blood rushing to her head, Pavla gets ready to "taste the delight of all delights," her first kisses. Feda's estate lies about half an hour outside Zagreb on the main road. He lives in the city and, and only when city life enervates him does he return to the house where he was born and raised. Farmwork has largely ceased and parts of the property have been sold, but Ivanović plans to renovate the buildings when he retires. It is the middle of spring and everything is in full bloom.

Feda has warned her that he is somewhat eccentric; hoping that his odd behavior will not put her off, he promises that their embraces will tell the full story of his feelings for her. On Holy Saturday, then, the independent-minded Pavla arrives at the train station in Zagreb and hires a coach to drive her out to Feodor's house. Along the way she passes many peasants in traditional clothing, returning from church services, carrying baskets of blessed Easter bread, and planning the night's revelry at bonfires in the countryside. She arrives at the estate just after dusk. She first sees Feodor as a tall, slender, slightly stooped silhouette in his doorway; she

[28] Ibid., 32.

finds his home "idyllic" if modest. Most importantly, she feels deeply moved and deeply comfortable around Feodor himself: "All my tenderness, all my joy for life, these were the flowers with which I wanted to crown his forehead—the brow of my husband."

Ivanović installs her in the room next to his, but tells her that the house is hers, as well. She should make herself comfortable and not fear the arrival of any curious or meddlesome staff. They exchange very modern and witty jokes, about registering as a visitor on the premises and signing a written agreement about the rules of the house; other jokes are more flirtatious or intimate. Pavla repeatedly expresses her concern that he be "satisfied" with her, and he is, but Ivanović shies from expressions of perpetually enduring love, despite her wish to categorize their relationship as similar in potency to the conviction of the Christians around them at Easter that their crucified Savior would rise again. At any rate, their evening is "holy," and after dinner they spend it in each other's arms lying on a sofa.

Pavla can hear him moving about and striking matches in the adjoining bedroom, but neither seeks the other out until dawn, when she goes to the door of Feodor's room and peers in. She goes over to him, and he pulls her into his bed, where a passionate love scene ensues, uniquely captured by Ivančan's prose and accompanied by the tolling of Easter bells outside.

Later that day, the lovers enjoy the beautiful sunshine outside and continue their flirtatious teasing. Pavla has a long imaginary conversation with a daisy about the fragility of the love that is all around them, but then

Feodor reminds her that it is not time for "such lugubrious thoughts."[29] Every day they go into the city for lunch, and on the fifth day Pavla stops by the telephone office to call her uncle and tell him she is prolonging her stay. Instead she learns from Kata that her uncle has suffered a stroke.

Pavla goes home by train the next day, after a strange parting with Feodor; she feels gloomy about their future. Her uncle makes his last will and testament, and both Pavla and Kata are provided for, with Kata getting the lion's share of real estate. Her correspondence with Ivanović resumes. She toys with the idea that this ardent exchange of letters is her honeymoon, but she grows increasingly irritable because of the separation.

Her uncle suggests that she go somewhere on vacation, in order to recover her health and high spirits. She returns to Feda's country house, where after three days she receives the sad news that her uncle has indeed died. Her thoughts during the preparations for the burial incline again toward the pagan or pantheistic, albeit poetically and disarmingly expressed.

She decides to sell the fields and vineyards after one more sacred round of "harvesting, threshing, mowing, and picking." Milić will then take up residence in the city, though not too close to Ivanović, who tries unceasingly to convince her that their work worlds must remain unmixed and that they should not even meet all too often. In this way, he claims, their love will stay fresh and they will not burden each other with trivialities. For two years

[29] Ibid., 45.

their relationship continues in this way, but Pavla only truly feels happy and secure in Feodor's embrace; outside of his arms, she finds that she requires more than passion and romantic intoxication. She seeks "conversations, shared worries, and common work and struggles."[30]

She expresses her invincible love for him in almost physically agonized terms: "Rip off my clothes, rip open my chest, and pull out my heart, and I will still love you. Slice open my veins, drain them of blood, and I will still love you."[31] While Ivanović merely states quietly that he hopes she will never push for an actual marriage with him, because then they would be destined to lose what they have.

City life is noisy and fast, full of crowds and automobiles, but Pavla's growing insomnia has another cause: she feels she must find a way to work herself into the fabric of Feodor's daily existence. But they only see less and less of each other. She finally calls him to account, and he takes the opportunity to say that he will never be able to give more and that he is no longer the same person he was three years ago. Pavla's trust and her happiness are undermined; having given herself to him for years, she is now shorn of all the types of love for him that had germinated within her: "husband, lover, friend, brother, father, and child."[32]

After the first and last time that their physical intimacy was without warmth, she moves back to her coun-

---

[30] Ibid., 59.
[31] Ibid., 61.
[32] Ibid., 65.

try home. She hopes to save the guttering flame of their love. Two weeks later, Feodor announces that he is leaving for Russia. For six weeks she reflects on how easy and enchanting it is to fall in love, despite the doom that awaits and the mud and rot that lie beneath the gilded surface.

Then, however, Pavla suspects that she is pregnant. She is overjoyed at this thought. A new world of joy seems available to her now; she will not tell Feodor of it, but she dreams of their happy reunion when he returns from abroad and learns of their child. Shortly thereafter, however, she feels "that usual thing that she feels every month"[33] and her illusion is burst. She remains alone. In the middle of the night, feverish, Pavla descends into her cellar, taps into a barrel of wine, and drinks herself into unconsciousness. She is found, freezing and ill, the next morning by Kata, who brings in a doctor. He is the young Milan Nikolić, whose father was once the village schoolmaster.

Pavla's joints and lungs are inflamed and she is ill all winter long. She senses just how hard it is going to be to live from memories, an attitude that means anesthetizing herself, being deliberately deaf and blind, dying a slow death, "lying down alive into a grave and from their singing the praises of the shining sun, the break of dawn, and the beauty of moonbeams."[34]

Pavla and the doctor share childhood memories, and it becomes apparent that he is fond of her. Pavla cyni-

---

[33] Ibid., 69.
[34] Ibid., 72.

cally remarks that now Milan's mouth, too, is watering for her purity and her youth"; in desperation she then claims that anybody could have her now, anyone, and without all the doctor's sentimental talk…and if a woman falls into despair or debauchery, it is always the fault of her first love. Nonetheless, Milan asks for her hand in marriage; Pavla refuses, saying she still loves another, but she wonders at the bitterness inside her. Soon she spends another night in the cellar, staring at the moon, drinking wine, and pouring drinks for Miško the cat, and conversing with her deceased uncle. She winds up again ill and in the care of Milan, leading him to the conclusion: "You need to sell your wine business!"

Over the long run, Pavla returns to health and stability. She maintains contact with Milan, also inveighing against the hypocrisy and cruelty of people who force women to conform and even perish due to "a thirst for life." She contemplates a return to an urban existence, despite Milan's offer of a life of mutual understanding, support, protection, health, and purpose. Pavla carefully and realistically considers all her options. She and Nikolić embrace, and Pavla feels an explosion of sensual delight after three years of deprivation, and then afterwards she feels guilty and continues to long for the return of Feodor Ivanović.

Her contact with Nikolić grows more frequent and more intimate, until finally he shows her a newspaper article about a cultural association of South Slavs in Moscow. It mentions a lecture by Ivanović, who is newly married to a Russian woman. Pavla cries out to her deceased uncle for advice; instead of tears she emits a horrific scream as she lets go of the past there in the room in which her love had first sprung to life. She feels that the blood in her veins has turned to lead, and she considers burning down Feodor's estate or killing herself. A long and fascinating chain of thoughts leads her to the conclusion that her "suffering on the installment plan" was useless and that so are the career paths open to her: teaching other people foreign languages, typing in an office, or keeping the accounting books for some company or government agency. These are trivial tasks, she decides, conceived by people to kill off or at least debilitate the weak among us. She speaks in a pantheistic or very abstract manner about beauty, nature, and the battles men fight to preserve their privileges.

She finally decides that Nikolić will give her what Ivanović never would. A year and a half later, in the book's concluding scene, Milić has just given birth to a boy. She is elated and deeply fulfilled. She and Nikolić feel not only that the child unites them but also that the baby is proof that in nature there is "medicine" for spiritual as well as physical pain. Milić quotes a proverb: "It's a misfortune to be a woman, but it's great luck to be a mother." They freely discuss Feodor, how he awakened the woman in Pavla but how Milan awakened the mother. They plan to write to him with the news, and they plan to have many more children. Finally, when Milan says he must attend to another mother and her newborn daughter, Pavla remarks that there is now "one more Pavla Milić in the world!

The second novel by Mara Ivančan, dating from 1924 and recently reissued in Croatia, is *Čudnovata priča*

(A wondrous tale). Indeed interest in Ivančan's work is currently undergoing a modest revival in Croatia. This short novel in twenty-six chapters is a frank assertion of early feminist themes and, for its day, is experimental in form. The words of Elza, a young factory worker who admires the protagonist Marija, contain a powerful assertion of the need for bold feminist literature: "If we [women] did not have sharp tongues, you men would wolf us down."[35]

The point of view of the narration changes drastically during the book, and a number of chapters end with poetic sequences with repeated phrasing that drive home important points. Also of interest is the socio-historical background of industrialization on the one hand (with its urbanization, huge steam-powered threshers rolling down the street, electrical buzzers in the factory announcing shift changes, and need for English translations) and the details of the Croatian-Habsburg war effort after 1914 on the other.

At the beginning of the novel, we are introduced to the life of a twenty-six year old woman named Marija Katić; this is Zagreb in the throes of industrialization. She works in the office of a steel mill and lives in an industrial suburb with her sister Ana. Marija is described as beautiful, capricious, and given to bold statements and unconventional views. Ana rents a house on the edge of the city, amidst remnants of the old estate owned by the Reiner family, now taken over by urban growth, building

---

[35] Mara Ivančan,*Čudnovata priča*, edited by Marko Plavić (Zagreb: Mlinarec and Plavić, 2004), 27.

supply depots, and squalid working-class housing; Ana had left her drunkard of a husband ten years earlier, after the death of their three young children.

One day at work, the usually vivacious Marija is overcome by nausea and collapses. Old women in the office exchange knowing glances as they assist her. At home that evening, Marija confides to her sister that she finds their orderly, staid home as joyless as a grave. A cricket near the stove, chirping away loudly in a symbolic touch that recurs right up to the last page of the novel, is considered by Marija to be an omen of change. She then tells Ana she's pregnant. Ana reproaches her for being a drunk or a puerile dreamer.

The two women then have a long angry exchange that includes the philosophical and the personal. In short, Marija rejects Ana's carefully ordered world view built on calculation, duty, and conscience. Both women have insomnia that evening and come to the same conclusion in their thoughts: that Marija had been too young to witness all the grief that Ana was experiencing earlier, and that "youth is the great seducer that gives people rose-colored glasses."

Marija is not at all attracted to the idea of marriage, which she associates with mending socks, doing laundry, and a lifetime of listening to her husband shave and brush his teeth. But she has been attracted to the engineer named Nikola Križan, indeed—and she is frank about the purely physical nature of their attraction and the rapidity with which the liaison became sexual. Her sister calls her sinful, superficial, and short-sighted, and says that things (the freewheeling relationship, the child born out of wedlock) just cannot be this way. Marija's strong, self-confident response is simply: "For my sake, it has to be this way."[36]

The atmosphere of the novel heats up at this point. Marija describes her courtship with Nikola and how she almost instantly felt an "eruption of feelings" in his presence. She cannot go back to a typically feminine world of "candles, butterflies, spring breezes, women-folk, the chirping of birds, laughter, tears, worry, and trembling." She links this world to men who are clerks and petty officials with inordinate fondness for their number-filled desks and with crooked necks and hemorrhoids. She wants powerful, elemental men, like sailors or locomotive drivers.

The next day Marija goes to the boss of the foundry to tell him she is pregnant. She first gets him to admit that her work performance has been excellent, and then she says she hopes he doesn't believe that motherhood and proper comportment are at odds. But the director believes she will be exposed to much abuse from the other workers, and in the interest of the factory he suggests she go away in a month or so to a village somewhere to have the baby and then return to work. She rejects his "humanism," and he tries to placate her, saying she is overwrought. To this Marija delivers another verbal barrage: "A nervous breakdown is always necessary for a great idea, and perhaps that is the misfortune of the whole human race." She then has to counter the argument that an extramarital child will face a life of suffering: she counters

[36] Ibid., 20.

by saying that the value of a human life exceeds its chances for "a separate nursery, a governess, sleeping on snowflakes, and scooting around on plush."[37]

The women in the factory decide that "Uncle Maksim," a respected older man, should serve as the baby's godfather. But a major argument then unfolds among the women themselves over the issue of freedom and equal rights, pitting mostly the older, married generation against the young, unmarried ones. The women start a fund for the baby, and rumor has it that someone wants Uncle Maksim to adopt the baby.

In the office, Marija senses that she is being given more work than before as part of a plot to make her inefficient or commit mistakes. She grows nasty and defensive to all, and behaves "like a wounded wild animal."[38] At home, Marija is increasingly drawn to the outdoors, to the world of vital, noisy work, with all its volume and motion, while her sister's interior world of orderliness, lace, pillows, poverty, passivity, and peace reflects Ana's condition of "having had enough of life, being tired of suffering, tired of taking care of the sick."[39] She is very worried about Marija.

On July 26, 1914, orders are given for military mobilization. Music, bustle, and clamor overrun the city. A mood of pessimism hangs in the air. Nikola, Marija's lover, takes his leave with only a telegram. Marija is no longer working and she suffers from insomnia, swelling

[37] Ibid., 26.
[38] Ibid., 32.
[39] Ibid., 33.

in the legs, and many other discomforts of the final weeks of pregnancy. But the house and her sister Ana await the birth in perfect composure and silence. Finally, Marija reports seeing a strange, haunting man at her window and hearing "funeral music for millions"; she is thus afraid to sleep. Ana seals off the doors and windows for her so that nothing happening in the outside world can make it into her room. She hopes, as her labor pains begin, only to hear the cricket beside the kitchen stove again.

Now the narrative switches to the first person, in Marija's voice. After a painful delivery, she feels a sense of compassion and well-being like she has never before known. Her son's growth and needs become her chief preoccupation, and a second highly unusual poetic passage in the text follows, conveying Marija's newfound love for the social pariahs and victims of our world. For example:

> I love the blind man who stands at the church doors, and I ask him for his wretch's blessing. I love him, because I do not know if the eyes of my son will ever open to the beauty of this world. I love the prisoner being led out to forced labor. I love him, for I do not know what passions will buffet the soul of my son.
> I love the adulterous woman, for she may someday commit adultery with my son.

This profound empathy for the emotionally damaged and marginalized, combined with Marija's prescience about war casualties, constitutes a major counterweight to the chauvinism and militarism typically coloring presentations of 1914; Marija says that the word, and the attendant condition of consciousness, that represents the complete power to understand and heal the world is: "motherhood."

Her twenty-six-day old son soon seems to be literally drinking in the setting sun's fiery blood-red rays, a fitting reflex for "our proud century." This sun represents the same "bloody sweat and howls from hell in which our brothers, our sons, and perhaps even your father" are dying, she tells they boy.

At ten months, the boy can already walk and run. A mysterious stranger brings him home once when he wanders off, and Marija is shocked to see that it is the same man who had previously spooked her at the window. He is the steward in charge of the barn and fields next door, and over the next months and years he comes to spend a great deal of time with her son, showing him the animals and tools and carts of the farm. Marija feels acutely that she is losing her grip, or emotional monopoly, on the boy, and it rankles even more when he starts referring to the mysterious man (who also wears a muffler of purple, a color that Marija abhors and associates with death) as "Grandpa."

As the war goes on and on, life becomes harder. Many things needed for the family are in short supply, and Ana has started taking in sewing. But Marija observes that "I do not want my child to help fill in that devastating column in the statistics, showing that the children of mothers employed outside the home are the most likely to die in the first years of life."[40] So she gives up many things she used to enjoy, such as new dresses,

[40] Ibid., 42.

hats, and visits to the hairdresser. There are numerous references to rationing, war profiteers, "Jewish black marketeering," the wording of death notices for long-absent husband-soldiers, rituals associated with funerals (wreaths, government-supplied coffins, mumbling priests), endless queues, Red Cross stations, and trachoma. The country's future is repeatedly called "gray," and the interests of the whole society that are considered superior to those of the individual are degraded in her mind by their violence, deceit, submissiveness, and inhumanity.

While Marija waits interminably in lines, she imagines her son in a variety of mishaps at home. She feels terribly nervous and guilty. Her son—whose name is still unknown to us—is four years old when he meets Lily, the daughter of the landowning family next door named Reiner. Lily seems nearly to fall under his spell, the same way the boy is under the spell of the mysterious stranger, but her governess, Miss Sophie, forbids her to play with Marija's son, whom she considers vulgar.

The man employed next door remains a big part of their life, but Marija tries to explain to her son that he is not really related to them. She encourages her son—who is never named—to finish school and then he can buy horses and a farm of his own. In a set of odd encounters we observe the elemental bravery and adventurousness—and even the sensuality—of the young boy, qualities much admired (in men also) by his mother.

Looking into the mirror one day, Marija feels old, and she ponders the fate of women who "fall under the yoke of work" and lack the money for fine clothes and the time to "primp."[41] "Old age knocks quickly at their doors" and "the freshness of their skin, the brightness of their eyes, the color and fragrance of their hair, the elasticity of their bodies, and the vivacity of their spirit" all start to fail, resulting in a loss of suitors and the infidelity of husbands.

When her son is five, he confuses a cinema with a church, and his "Grandpa" tells him that the former is actually the devil's temple. Having also seen his Aunt Ana coming out of the movie house, his mother initiates a conversation with him about good and evil, heaven and hell. Heaven, for instance, is not found in church, where people go to deposit their sins. Heaven is wherever good people are found—where there are no bad consciences but rather only peace, honest, and purity.

As the novel winds down, Marija's mental state is more and more unsettled. She is pregnant again and sees the color purple—her nemesis—everywhere. Even the local shopkeeper sells her a scarf with flowers that she sees as skulls. One day the old man working next door falls from his ladder and, close to death, is brought into her house and installed in Marija's bed. In a final conversation she learns accidentally that he is Nikola Križan's father; so, in fact, he is the boy's grandfather.

Marija hallucinates and screams through the end of her pregnancy. Neighbors and co-workers come by to offer comfort and help, but the young ones see "all their enthusiasm for motherhood drown at the sight of the

---

[41] Ibid., 52.

strain that wrecks a woman's body when she gives birth"; something is agitated in their hearts that "breaks the power of their ideas and all of the rapture once felt about maternity."[42] Marija delivers a healthy baby girl and has a nervous breakdown. A doctor is called in to treat her case of "hysteria."

She dies shortly thereafter. And Ana, torn between bitter disappointment and hopes and prayers for a new life, lies down on the bed to comfort the "new Marija," the new-born girl.

History: The Evolution of Croatian Nationalism

The political scene in Croatia during Vjenceslav Novak's lifetime was stable and relatively peaceful, but it was also marked by increasing intercommunal tensions and anti-government agitation. Croatia was part of Hungary at the time, and Hungary was part of the Habsburg Empire, which, before 1867, had its sole capital at Vienna. The population of the Empire, as well as of almost all of its constituent territorial-administrative units, was very mixed in terms of language and religion (and, as eventually comes to light in the eighteenth and nineteenth centuries, ethnicity and national identity). This mixed demographic scene is by itself not a political problem, but a social characteristic; there are plenty of other potential arenas of conflict in the Croatia of Novak's day, as well, from industrialization and urbanization to the role of women to foreign policy.

[42] Ibid., 64–65.

Croatia in the Middle Ages, during the time of its history as an independent state (peaking in the reign of Kresimir in the late eleventh century, who ruled most of today's Croatia and Bosnia-Hercegovina, although stretches of today's Hungary and Serbia were part of the kingdom at various times), was called the "Triune Kingdom" because it contained three distinct regions: Slavonia, the heavily agricultural area along the Sava and Drava Rivers; the hilly central region, sometimes called "Civil Croatia," including the capital, Zagreb, and the regions today known as Zagorje and Krajina; and Dalmatia, the mountainous, island-peppered coastal region where Novak was born. In 1102, by the terms of a mysterious (because now lost) agreement known as the *Pacta Conventa*, the Croatian and Hungarian thrones were merged, for lack of a better word; Croatia became, depending upon one's understanding of medieval *Staatsrecht*, either a province of Hungary or an equal partner under an expanded common crown. In 1526, by a parallel if not entirely similar arrangement, Hungary was in turn subsumed by the Habsburg crown after the huge victory of the westward-ranging Ottomans at Mohács.

The events of the Napoleonic wars and the revolutions of 1848 gave birth to nationalist movements among many Central European and Balkan peoples, including Croatia. Gentry-heavy Hungary, proud of its new Habsburg co-capital Pest-Buda, and conscious of the many distinct national groups living in its "trans-Leithanian" half of the Habsburg Empire, promoted its own national identity and interests at the expense of its own minorities as well as the formerly dominant Austrian-Germans. In the Croatian case, the usual group wariness or rivalry was heightened by the Croats' relationship with Slovenes in the Austrian half of the Empire, with all of the groups in occupied Bosnia-Hercegovina, and, above all, with the Serbs and Montenegrins, independent polities across the border to the south of Hungary.

Beginning in the 1830s, the Illyrian movement—named after the Roman province that had included much of the Balkan Adriatic coastline—stressed the cultural similarities and potential for cooperation of these related South Slavic peoples; somewhat later, in the 1860s, a Yugoslav movement, built on the same ideas and energy, emerged in the work and writings of the Bishop of Djakovo, Josip Juraj Strossmayer. By this time, the idea of Croatian-Serbian (and other) solidarity included political cooperation, redrawn internal and international borders, and, possibly, a separate independent state. (From this derives the eventual name of the post-World War I South Slavic state, Yugoslavia, or "land of the South Slavs.")

By the 1880s, the Croatian political scene was growing rather crowded. There were elections to the *Sabor* (national assembly) in Zagreb, to the Hungarian parliament in Budapest, and at the local level. There was a growing number of political parties, including the People's Party (founded in 1841 as part of the Illyrian movement), the Party of Right (as in "historical rights," founded in 1861 by Ante Starčević and Eugen Kvaternik), the Social Democratic Party of Croatia and Slavonia (founded in 1894), the Pure Party of Right (founded in 1895 by Josip Frank), and the Peasant Party (founded by Stjepan Radić, inter alia, in 1904). Each of these parties had its own newspaper and lined up differently on the question of the greatest crisis or adversary of the day; some were pro-Habsburg and some were pro-Hungarian, and some were anti-Serbian and others pro-Serbian. There was also the powerful position of Hungarian viceroy in Zagreb, known as the Ban. This official was nominated by the Hungarian prime minister in Budapest and confirmed by the Emperor in Vienna; Croatian self-rule, which was more or less real in the arenas of schools, police, justice, and religion, extended neither to the selection of the Ban nor to management of local taxes and finance.

There were two main political issues that exercised many Croats. The first of these was a territorial one. The traditional Croatian lands (defined either as lands where large numbers of Croats lived at the time or lands that had been part of the Trpimirović dynasty's medieval realm) were divided and so commerce, politics, and educational life were segmented. Slavonia and the central region were ruled together, but by the direct, and increasingly intrusive, hand of Pest-Buda; Dalmatia and the Istrian peninsula to the north of it were actually assigned, since the *Ausgleich* (federal compromise) of 1967, to the Austrian half of the Empire, in part so that Vienna would have direct access to major naval and port facilities such as those at Pula. Furthermore, Rijeka, the biggest port in the Croatian lands, was reclassified as a special district directly under the Hungarian government's control. This condition of fragmentation, in the era of industrialization, population growth, disputes over administrative and educational languages, and pressure to increase the voting franchise, left Croats exposed to greater and greater threats of assimilation. The dualistic *Ausgleich*, which was from the Hungarian point of view a victory for democratic and nationalist forces stymied by the unsuccessful revolutions of 1848–1849, created Austria-Hungary in place of the Austrian Empire, although it was still common to call the country, now with two capital cities close together along the Danube, the Habsburg Empire. The Emperor of Austria was the King of Hungary, and only a few government functions (especially military and foreign policy ones) were decided jointly. But the niceties of federalism meant little to Croatians. Despite a local version of the *Ausgleich*, called the *Nagodba*, promulgated by Hungary in 1868, the Croatian lands were now split irredeemable between the two halves of the joint state, and the platitudes issuing forth from Pest-Buda about autonomy and cultural and linguistic rights were unenforceable. Indeed, as one noted historian argues, dualism put Croatia on the road to complete "political collapse."[43]

The other main political problem was the creeping grip of Magyarization, or Hungarianization, in administration, schools, and economic life. As far back as 1847, the Hungarians had insisted that Croats use Hungarian, and not Croatian or the traditional Latin, for political communication with Pest-Buda, and Hungarian was

[43] Branka Magaš, *Croatia Through History* (London: Saqi, 2007), 436.

made a mandatory language in local schools. Then the year 1875 saw the ascendancy of a powerful new political party in Budapest, the Liberals; their first prime minister, Kálmán Tisza, ruled the country until 1890 and was followed by other Liberals. One of the main goals of this party was to create such great unity in their half of the now-renamed (as Austria-Hungary) Habsburg Empire that the ultimate aspirations for political independence for Hungarians could ultimately not be denied. They also worked hard to create a solvent, modern, centralized administration; the Liberal cabinets can be critiqued from a number of perspectives, but it is the policy of Magyarization that hurt Hungarians' reputation abroad and, more importantly, tipped off their constituent minority groups that a national competition was off and running.

Specifically, it is the reign of the Ban who held office from 1883 to 1903, Károly Khuen-Héderváry, a Hungarian nobleman from Slavonia and a relative of Tisza, that cast a real pall of crisis over Croatia. He pursued the Hungarianization policy vigorously, also raising taxes and undermining the authority of the *Sabor*; he also partly suspended the practice of jury trials and manipulated the selection process for the patriarchs of the Serbian Orthodox church. The political scene in Croatia was at times volatile. In 1871 radical Croatian nationalists managed a three-day uprising in the village of Rakovica. Another crisis was caused in 1878 by the Austro-Hungarian military occupation of the Turkish province of Bosnia-Hercegovina; Croats, Serbs, and Hungarians already in the Empire disagreed over whether this step was a positive one and how the new regions were to be run. In 1881 came another crisis, occasioned by the dissolution of the old military frontier regions, which had been useful in deflecting Ottoman invasions but which now introduced many more Serbs into Croatian society at large while also depriving all former residents of the frontier area of special economic and cultural privileges to which they had grown accustomed. There was also a peasant uprising in rural Croatia in 1883, for tax relief, and then a colorful anti-Hungarian student uprising in Zagreb in 1895 on the occasion of the visit of Emperor Franz Joseph from Vienna. After those demonstrations and the following arrests, many young Croatians sought education and careers elsewhere. Khuen-Héderváry often favored Serbs in economic and political life, and he promoted a sense of Slavonian separatism from the rest of Croatia. Labor unions were prohibited, and the Hungarian government attempted to restrict the right to vote of the largely Croatian peasantry. In 1905, for instance, only 1.8% of the people in Croatia had the right to vote. In the economic sphere, most industry in Croatia was in Hungarian or German hands, workers in Zagreb received far less pay than those in Vienna, and most large landholdings belonged to Hungarians.[44] There was a steady out-flow of capital (i.e., profits from industry and agriculture) from Croatia to Hungary.

Overall, the Magyarization policy of Budapest achieved at least one of its goals. From being only a plu-

[44] Ivan Božić, et al. *Istorija Jugoslavije*, 2nd ed. (Beograd: Prosveta, 1973), 322.

rality in their half of Austria-Hungary, just as the German-speaking Austrians were, surprisingly, in their half, the Hungarians in 1900 constituted 51.4% of the population of the Hungarian lands. That number rose further by 1910 to almost 55%. The change is the result of self-identification and assimilation, not primarily of birth rate differences. But Khuen-Héderváry's rule was so autocratic that Croatia was called by some a "Hungarian pashalik," referring to a fearful and mismanaged province in the (imagined) Ottoman style.[45]

The effects of Magyarization on Croatia had two important historical dimensions. One was the growing antagonism between Serbs and Croats in Bosnia-Hercegovina, central Croatia, and, especially, Dalmatia. These tensions should not be viewed as manifestations of any "ancient ethnic hatreds"; nationalist conflicts, and violent group conflicts of any sort, they do not haunt the Balkans the way the popular stereotypes (and fear-mongering political hacks) would have us believe. And there were some successful multi-ethnic political alliances that achieved important local results in this period. But the Hungarian administration, pursuing a policy of *divide et impera*, tried to push the related groups into conflict, because it feared their combined strength, especially given the cross-border implications of South Slavic cooperation.

The other effect of Magyarization was the accelerated growth of Croatian nationalism. The activities of the

[45] Branka Magaš, *Croatia Through History* (London: Saqi, 2007), 321.

Party of Rights, and the pressures and confrontations that resulted in its split, as well as the splintering of a number of other Croatian parties, is evidence that Magyarization had anti-Hungarian and also pro-Yugoslav effects. But it is in this domain that Novak's novel also offers important historical insights. Novak is not writing to promote a particular political platform of his day, even though his hometown was a bastion of the Party of Right; indeed one of Novak's biographers stresses the fact that his works originate in a "dark and cruel time for his people" and that Khuen-Hedervary turned Croatia into a "prison."[46] Thus the musical nationalism in the novel depicts a very real stage in the evolution of Croatian nationalism.

One might say that the idea of a secular, linguistically distinct, historically attested people known as the Croatian nation was at first a product of "the mixture of aristocratic and bureaucratic nationalizing forces."[47] But Croatian nationalism will obviously evolve into a mass phenomenon over the course of the twentieth century, and Novak's book helps to show us how. In addition to being descriptive in that way, one could even argue that it is normative, also: the book aided the spread of Croatian nationalism by the very fact that it treated nationalism as a coherent and recognizable subject in daily life, even though Amadej's rebelliousness has personal roots,

[46] Marijan Jurković, *Vjenceslav Novak* (Beograd: Rad, 1966), 3–4.

[47] Peter F. Sugar, "Roots of Eastern European Nationalism," in Peter J. Sugar and Ivo J. Lederer, eds., *Nationalism in Eastern Europe* (Seattle: University of Washington Press, 1969), 53.

and a disastrous end. In 1983, one of the great theorists of nationalism, Benedict Anderson, introduced a concept called "Census, Map, Museum" in his seminal modernist work, *Imagined Communities*. In explaining how nations are created or evolve, and how nationalism spreads from the ranks of the elite to the broader population, Anderson very insightfully looks at the prompts and expectations in modern institutional practice, in short, at external stimuli, that habituate people to identification with a certain demographic norm, to national homogeneity or, in the eyes of nationalists, "unity."[48]

We do not know in precisely what years Novak has set the plot of this novel, but the premiere of Gounod's opera Faust, mentioned in Chapter Eight of Part One, means that it might be 1859 or shortly thereafter. It is early yet in the development of the Croatian "national renaissance," or as modernists would have it, early in the forging of a modern Croatian identity. Hence the confu-

---

[48] The principle in operation here can perhaps be illuminated by two examples from literature. In a short story from 2009 (*Und hieb ihm das rechte Ohr ab* [Göttingen: Wallstein Verlag], 9), the Austrian writer Clemens Berger notes, "The border had been drawn, first edging this way and then that, and both the one and the other group of people had found reasons to feel superior to those on the other side of the line in the Atlas"—even though initially nothing strikes the uninitiated observer as different on two sides of most borders. The Italian novelist Claudio Magris (*A Different Sea*, transl. by M.S. Spurr [London: Harvill Press, 1993], 91) puts it this way: an old-fashioned man notices that the machinery of a modern state is labeling and molding him: "Enrico is afraid—not of people, but of papers, documents, statements, census forms, declarations that he must continually sign, and of taxes too."

sion of the peasants in one of the most telling scenes in the book:

> "Why are you crying?" asked an old peasant woman sympathetically. She had boarded the train along with the other peasants. "After four years, I am now back on Croatian soil, in my homeland, and my swelling emotions are producing unstoppable tears."
>
> The peasants looked at him. They said nothing. Did they understand him? Is this something one has to learn from a book? But then one of the older peasant men said to him with conviction: "Every person loves the place he was born, the most."
>
> Then one of the younger peasant women, who had been watching Amadej with sympathy in her calm gaze, struck up a conversation with him. As soon as she learned that he'd had no family to call his own since he was a little boy, she asked him, with pity in his voice:
>
> "So who is it you are so happy to see, if you don't have any blood relatives to greet you?"
>
> "All Croats are my family!" Amadej told her in an effort to explain what he was feeling.
>
> "But this thing you are talking about—isn't it just a private matter for you?" he was interrupted by this question from a peasant woman.
>
> "He's among his people," her neighbor explained further to her.

Amadej's peasant interlocutors in the scene above, from a rocking rail car cutting across the countryside of the southern reaches of the great Habsburg Empire, think of Amadej's loyalty as something private, and something natural. One loves the place he grew up—what's the big deal? The peasants are testimony of attachment to a country, or countryside, a landscape; at first, in the modernist take on the construction of nations, this might lead to patriotism but it stops far short of the mass secular identity necessary for political nationalism. Very tellingly, the peasants wonder if whatever wild idea is in Amadej's head has to be "learn[ed] from a book"! How prescient! The nationalism of the elites has not reached the peasants. But Amadej, because he moves in the exterior world of Zagreb, Berlin, and Prague, and knows international currents of music and politics, has moved on to a more modern sense of loyalty and belonging. By the end of the book (Part Three, Chapter One), in a sentiment not mad but modern, he feels a connection to far more territory and people than he has ever laid eyes on, to a Croatia that exists in his mind:

> I remember, you know, how I used to sit by the brook that flowed near our hometown back in the first days after I returned from Prague. People, houses, trees, every little village, every stone—all of it, everything to be found on that holy ground, my native soul, it all had soul, goodness, gentleness, sincerity, and I loved this soul and it loved me. I trembled and cried in front of you at the feeling of magnificence, that inhabited me whenever I took my place on the banks of our little stream on whose waters my childhood flowed.

It is also no accident that a historical glossary of terms likely to be unfamiliar to the Anglophone reader would consist almost entirely of terms relating to national identity or a national movement:

Ban: the Hungarian-appointed governor or viceroy of Croatia
Dudaš: a popular, and particularly Croatian, variant of *Hirtentanz*, or Shepherd's Dance, often played around Christmas

Introduction

Dvořák and Smetana: Antonín Dvořák (1841–1904) and Bedřich Smetana (1824–1884) were two Czech giants of Romantic classical music famous for espousing "nationalism" in their work—that is to say, like Russian, Scandinavian, and other composers of their day, they challenged traditional conceptions of serious music in the post-Beethoven era by embracing nationally specific songs and motifs derived from the folklore and ethnography of their respective countries

Thomas Eisenhut: German composer who lived from 1644–1702 and specialized in choral music

Professor Gaj: Ljudevit Gaj (1809–1872), Croatian linguist and journalist, the leading figure in the Illyrian Movement aimed at reviving Croatian culture and developing cooperation with other South Slavic groups in the Habsburg and Ottoman Empires

gusle: folkloric Balkan musical instrument with one string, used to accompany the recitation of epic poetry

"Kolo" Choral Society of Zagreb: popular patriotic musical institution established in 1862 and named after a group circle dance (similar to the *oro* or *hora*), prominent in folklore across Yugoslavia; instrumental in, and indicative of the spread of nationalist sentiment, as were reading rooms and newspapers

Lisinski: Vatrosav Lisinski (1819–1854), composer of the first Croatian opera in 1846 and co-founder of the Illyrian Movement

Matica školska: the School Literary Society

Prague Slavic Congress: an impressive, but brief and inconclusive, Pan-Slavic political gathering during the stormy revolutionary year of 1848, focused more on nationalism than on other contemporary revolutionary trends such as constitutionalism or workers' rights; a self-conscious parallel to the Frankfurt Assembly in the neighboring Germanic Confederation

Preradović: Petar Preradović (1818–1872), a polyglot Croatian-Austrian army officer and poet, active in the Illyrian movement, grandfather of famous Austrian poet and novelist Paula Preradović

Introduction

Šenoa: August Šenoa (1838–1881), popular Croatian historical novelist and patriot

Slavija: not a goddess but a term for Slavs and their territories as a whole, or an artistic representation thereof

šljivovica: plum brandy, one of a number of related alcoholic drinks popular throughout the Balkans

tambura, tamburica: traditional Balkan stringed musical instrument of the lute family, having a variable number of strings and often played by whole ensembles in folkloric fashion

Milka Trnina: (1863–1941) internationally famous Croatian soprano

Lav Vukelić: Lavoslav Vukelić (1840–1879), poet of the Croatian national renaissance, born near Senj

Zajc: Ivan Zajc (1832–1914), famous Croatian composer, professor, and conductor, advanced many Croatian musical institutions and wrote the opera *Nikola Šubić Zrinski* about a famous Habsburg victory over Suleiman the Magnificent in 1566

Amadej's high standards, vaulting ambition, and disgust with the philistinism of his compatriots have, in the eyes of this observer, a particular nationalist cast. He longs for fame above all within his own country: to write great Croatian pieces of music, for instance. One of his most prized artistic projects is to set Šenoa's famous ballad "Petar Svačić" to music (Part 2, Chapter 3); this poem recounts the end of independent medieval Croatia by telling the story of the country's last king in the 1090s, just before the Hungarians took over. Amadej also wants to be conductor of the national theater in Zagreb and cannot understand why the capitalist booksellers and publishers in the capital do not want to promote his honest and original music, preferring cheap dances and marches to works in touch with

Europe's sophisticated high culture that demonstrate what the Croatian mind and spirit are capable of doing. Even the love songs he writes with Adelka in mind honor his native soil as much as they do her womanly heart and soul.

The obstacles Amadej encounters in moving towards these goals show more than just generic uncouthness. The priest in Amadej's village speaks of "national educational goals," and nationally-tinged classical music and choral societies are just fine, as long as they do not challenge people's sense of esthetics too much—hence the *tamburica* bands, the commission for Jahoda to counterfeit a Bohemian folks song for Count K., and the hack music composed and performed at the celebration for the chief railroad surveyor. Novak writes (Part II, Chapter 3) that "pianos spread to other families like some sort of communicable disease," and the local elites assert their power to be arbiters of culture:

> "That's the way you musicians think, but we are also allowed to say what we like and what we don't like," the mayor said. He winked conspiratorially to Mesarić and the priest.

The "demonstration effect" of imported nationalism precipitates in contradictory ways: pretentious local ladies refuse to speak their native Croatian in public, but people are "craving the opportunities to show their worthiness to the outside world," and even Amadej, fresh from a long rant against *tamburica* music and schmaltzy operettas, longs to find a partner with whom he can discuss Beethoven, Chopin, Grieg, and Goethe. The outside world is not just home to great trends and achievements against which strong Croatian hearts and minds want to measure their worth; it is also the source of example and acceptance, as we see in the warm Pan-Slavic embrace extended to Amadej by his "brother Slavs" in Prague. Only the lowlife Vesely barely knows where Croatia is; much more typical, and fortifying, is the encouragement Amadej receives to be proud and make a difference for his people.

Conclusion

Vjenceslav Novak can be praised from many angles in Croatian and European literature. He has been called "the most productive and comprehensive of Croatian realists,"[49] the creator of "the most complex and skillfully constructed female characters in all of Croatian literature,"[50] and the first Croatian writer to focus on describing "the spectacle of poverty" amidst rapidly changing economic conditions.[51]

There is some unevenness and, sometimes, a lack of psychological insight, in Novak's corpus, and perhaps he

[49] Ivo Frangeš, "Vjenceslav Novak," in *Enciklopedija Jugoslavije,* vol. 6 (Zagreb: Jugoslavenski leksikografski zavod, 1965), 305.

[50] "Vjenceslav Novak," in August Kovačec, ed. *Hrvatska enciklopedija,* vol. 7 (Zagreb: Leksikografski zavod "Miroslav Krleža"), 763–764. The characters singled out for this praise are Irma from this novel and Lucija from *Posljednji Stipančići.*

[51] Slobodan Prosperov Novak, *Povijest hrvatske književnosti: od baščanske ploče do danas* (Zagreb: Golden, 2003), 261.

overproduced; perhaps circumstances led him to write too much. But his introduction of proletarian imagery into Croatian literature and the fact that he is considered the best single portrayer of the Croatian petty bourgeoisie tell us that he was a gifted observer and chronicler who used innovative thematic choices to tell the story of his times. Furthermore, his compassion for individuals and interest "in the physiology of life"[52] enable him to write interesting, thought-provoking books that stand the test of time. Finally, Novak moved in his lifetime from imitation of his people's Romantic greats to providing strong intimations of and a bridge to the modernism of the twentieth century. It is for all of these reasons, perhaps, that the great literary scholar Antun Barac wrote in 1933 that Novak anticipated the work of Ivan Cankar,[53] one of Central Europe's greatest literary voices, who hailed from neighboring Slovenia. It would be hard to find a more meaningful literary tribute to the author of *A Tale of Two Worlds*. In our own day, and for our own purposes, Novak represents the kind of rich testimony on the evolution of nationalism, as well as on Croatian social and intellectual life, in which the many untranslated works of Croatian literature abound.

John K. Cox

[52] Ibid., 260.

[53] Antun Barac, "Vjenceslav Novak" in Vjenceslav Novak, *Pripovijesti* (Beograd: Luča, Biblioteka Zadruge profesorskog društva, 1933), 30–31.

BIBLIOGRAPHY

I. Works by Novak

Dva svijeta. Edited by Slavko Ježić. Zagreb: Minerva, 1932.

"Disonance." In Vjenceslav Novak, *Izabrane pripovijesti* (Zagreb: Matica hrvatska, 1925), ed. Branimir Livadić, vol. 1, 266–280.

"Iz velegradskog podzemlja ." In Vjenceslav Novak, *Izabrane pripovijesti*(Zagreb: Matica hrvatska, 1925), ed. Branimir Livadić, vol. 1, 241–258.

"Pripovijest o Marcel Remeniću." In Vjenceslav Novak,*Pripovijesti.* Beograd: Luča, Biblioteka Zadruge profesorskog društva, 1933), 43–49.

"Salamon." In Vjenceslav Novak, *Izabrane pripovijesti* (Zagreb: Matica hrvatska, 1925), ed. Branimir Livadić, vol. 1, 77–86.

"Sličice iz moga vojnikovanja." In Vjenceslav Novak, *Izabrane pripovijesti* (Zagreb: Matica hrvatska, 1926), ed. Branimir Livadić, vol. 2, 116–155.

"Socijal-demokrata." In Vjenceslav Novak, *Izabrane pripovijesti* (Zagreb: Matica hrvatska, 1925), ed. Branimir Livadić, vol. 1, 94–104.

II. Works on Novak

Barac, Antun. *A History of Yugoslav Literature.* Translated by Petar Mijušković. Ann Arbor, MI: Michigan Slavic Publications, s.d.

———. "Vjenceslav Novak" in Vjenceslav Novak, *Pripovijesti* (Beograd: Luča, Biblioteka Zadruge profesorskog društva, 1933), 5–31.

Čolak, Tode. "Vjenceslav Novak kao dramski pisac." In Vjenceslav Novak, *Pred sudom svjetine: dramska slika u 2 čina* (Rijeka: Pododbor Matice Hrvatske u Rijeci, 1965), 5–9.

Frangeš, Ivo. *Povijest hrvatske književnosti.* Zagreb: Matica hrvatska, 1987.

———. "Vjenceslav Novak." *Enciklopedija Jugoslavije,* vol. 6 (Zagreb: Jugoslavenski leksikografski zavod, 1965), 305–306.

Hawkesworth, Celia. *Zagreb: A Cultural History*. New York: Oxford University Press, 2008.

Jurković, Marijan. *Vjenceslav Novak*. Beograd: Rad, 1966.

Kaštelan, Jure. "Između agonije i rađanja." Foreword to Vjenceslav Novak, *Posljednji Stipančići* (Sarajevo: Veselin Masleša, 1973), 5–14.

Kovačec, August, ed. "Vjenceslav Novak." *Hrvatska enciklopedija*. Volume VII. (Zagreb: Leksikografski zavod "Miroslav Krleža"), 763–764.

Livadić, Branimir. "Djelo Vjenceslava Novaka." In Vjenceslav Novak, *Izabrane pripovijesti* (Zagreb: Matica Hrvatske, 1925), vol. 1, 3–33.

————. "Predgovor" to *Tito Dorčić: Pripovijest* (Beograd: Srpska književna zadruga, 1911), 3–18.

Malby, Maria B. "Vjenceslav Novak (11 September 1859–20 September 1905)." In Vasa D. Mihailovich, ed., *Dictionary of Literary Biography* (Vol. 147: South Slavic Writers Before World War II) (Detroit: Gale, 1995), 170–175.

Novaković, Novak. "Vjenceslav Novak (1859–1905)," in Vjenceslav Novak, *Dvije pripovijetke*, 3rd ed. (Zagreb: Školska knjiga, 1962), 5–7.

Prosperov Novak, Slobodan. *Povijest hrvatske književnosti: od baščanske ploče do danas*. Zagreb: Golden, 2003.

Ugrešić, Dubravka. "The Spirit of the Kakanian Province." Translated by Ellen Elias-Bursać. In *Karaoke Culture* (Rochester, NY: Open Letter, 2011), 275–298.

Živančević, Milorad. "Vjenceslav Novak." In Živan Milisavac, ed. *Jugoslovenski književni leksikon*. 2nd, expanded edition (Novi Sad: Matica srpska, 1984), 575–576.

III. Films

Lisinski. 1942. Directed by Oktavian Miletić. (Re-issued on DVD with accompanying program and essays, 2009).

Posljednji Stipančić. 1968. Directed by Eduard Galić.

PART ONE

Chapter One

T he old *kapellmeister* and organist, Jan Jahoda, running late in his preparations for vespers, received quite a surprise that Sunday afternoon when he strode into church. He heard, to his enormous amazement, unknown hands playing a prelude on the organ in the same style in which he had been habitually playing preludes at holiday vespers for many years. The elderly man stopped below the choir loft, rubbed his eyes, and looked around inquisitively. Am I dreaming? He wondered...Could this be a miracle unfolding, with me appearing as two people, one of whom is playing the organ while the other one listens to himself?

True enough, today I was a guest at the mayor's house. His little daughter has been taking piano lessons from me for two years now; before lunch I drank two bottles of genuine Pilsener, had a shot of delicious, aged *šljivovica*, and along with the plentiful repast had of course a bit more of the superb wine than usual—eight years old and from the mayor's private vineyard...All of that is true, and because of it I am a few moments late arriving here for work, but then again...And look at that—some mysterious personage just keeps on playing

1

those preludes in the manner of Jahoda himself. You can just hear, though, that his technique has not been perfected; the notes are not strongly connected, but then again this is only an improvisation—and a wonderful one! And thus, as agitated as he was curious, old Jahoda made his way up to the choir loft.

When he had the mysterious performer in front of him, his amazement faded away immediately and he was overcome by the feeling that had once impelled Archimedes to shout out his "Eureka!" On a little chair in front of the keyboard was seated a small boy, approximately twelve years of age, staring raptly at the keys as he picked out notes with his fingers. Jahoda had known this boy for some time, but that he was capable of this—well, how? He was the child of a poor family and seemed to spend all his free time up in the choir loft. Before Mass the boy could always be found in his spot, removing the curtain that shielded the organ from dust, lifting the cover above the keys, opening the register, dragging the chair over to its place, putting the sheet music for *"Genitori"* and *"Litaniae lauretanae"* on the stand, and then, if the sexton was busy with another task somewhere, he would go work the bellows. Jahoda would send him to purchase snuff and—when the worship service was on the long side—*šljivovica* in the modest little bottle that was kept in the cabinet with the church's archive of sheet music. Things had been like this for two years already. It was like the old man and the boy belonged together, as if they were linked by bonds of sympathetic feeling. They never thought about these ties and they did not even know each other's given names.

2

That this boy should actually have some sort of musical talent—old Jahoda would never even have dreamt this; indeed he stubbornly maintained that Croats had no real sense for the art of music. In his younger years he had worked in a parish somewhere in Primorje and, with his heart all aflame for his art, he had, naturally enough, tried at least to get a choral ensemble going in the church. But then he experienced something that did not lend itself to explanations by the general laws of psychology. People who had a good ear for music simply did not join his choir, and the ones who did come simply stuck it out for a week or so and then dropped it with no explanation. And, well, the ones who had no gift for singing insisted on doing it. Jahoda wore himself out working with them, and finally after much irritating and miserable work he dropped the idea. This is not for you people...Your ears are too accustomed to the sound of the waves on the sea—that's what is at fault, keeping you from distinguishing one note from another. It has made you deaf as doorknobs...

Here, in his new place of residence, he had heard how beautifully the peasants from the surrounding areas could sing, so he tried to form a choral ensemble from these folks whose eardrums had not been subjected their whole lives to the thundering of the waves. But each time he experienced the same thing as in Primorje; he would assemble the choir and begin instructing them, but the numbers fell as the weeks mounted. From twelve the first month, to ten by the fifth week, seven in the sixth, and then four, three, until there were none at all...They aren't worth this! Jahoda finally concluded, abandoning his fruitless labors. Well, now it's understandable why he was so surprised today, having discovered real talent in that small, poor boy, talent of the type one would hardly find even in his homeland, which had given the artistic world such geniuses as Bedřich Smetana and Antonín Dvořák.

Meanwhile, the youth kept on playing the organ. With equal parts attentiveness and enthusiasm his lively eyes beheld the keys that obligingly called forth the notes the way he—having listened to none other than Jahoda himself—bore them in his soul. And on his thin, swarthy face, the boy's spirit gleamed with such intensity and inspiration that Jahoda, himself enthralled, made no effort to get the child away from the organ. He was now more amazed at the singular beauty of the adolescent face, illuminated by soulful fervor, than he was at the fact that the boy was hitting the notes born into his musical imagination with an unexpected comprehension, as if his very soul—Jahoda's soul—were speaking...A peculiarly strong feeling swept the old man away: he should feel as if he had discovered something supernaturally beautiful, something that had been smoldering for a long time, far back in the depths of his life, something towards which he had directed unawares his improvised nocturnal musings at the piano, in those lonely, barren reaches of his apartment; it was something that in the same instant bore the traits of pain, and happiness, and tears, and his heart's laughter, and great and powerful and inexhaustible yearning that was stronger than any other sensation in his life, and any emotion, too...This great, mysterious something capable of burning his brain like fire and warming his breast like the sweet breath of heaven—This, then, was the kind of magnificent something that he saw before him now in this boy, and found in his large, black eyes suffused with ardor. For him, an aged bachelor, it was as if he had discovered youth that communicated with the voice of his own soul, a soul that would exist alone, on and on, even when his broken body was rotting beneath the earth. He felt himself to be a parent to this boy, not physically, but as a father to that which keeps the body alive, the part of him that thinks and feels...

The presence of several people who had gathered round for vespers tore Mr. Jahoda from his thoughts. They signaled impatiently to the boy that he should stop playing, since the priest up at the altar in his gold-stitched soutane was holding out the Eucharist and waiting to intone: *Pange, lingua...* The organ stopped, the priest started to sing, and the chords with which Jahoda would have instructed the congregation to continue singing erupted from the boy's fingers. To Jahoda it seemed that he had never heard a Croatian congregation sing that old hymn with such holy conviction.

Like always, there were the same voices, the same puny throats and the forceful ones, mixed together and celebrating the divine mystery, but today they seemed to Jahoda's sensibility to reverberate in an entirely new way beneath the church's vaulted ceiling. Emotion had found its way into the singing, along with both a sense of holiness and unaccustomed delight. Jahoda felt himself trembling inwardly under the force of the sacred hymn—and then he perceived in himself the strong and blissful desire to take in his hands the young performer's head and cover its dark hair with the kisses he had dreamt and thought about while improvising on the piano at night in his old bachelor's lodgings.

The concluding chord of the vocals and the organ poured into the church and remained, quivering, up high. From the bluish pall of smoke before the altar the golden gleam of the Host was raised up, glittering in the light of candles, and the church resounded with the endearing silvery tinkle of a small bell. Jahoda sank to his knees, devoutly bowing his gray head. The sparse white strands of his hair trembled in the manner of infirm old men, and when all the other pious folk were already back on their feet, he remained thus, head inclined and knees folded before the deity. His soul communed upward to heaven; he gave thanks for the great favor shown to him, transported as he suddenly was into a higher existence, from out of the sluggish flow of the everyday into which he had, long ago, fallen.

Then the bold chords that he had composed again came booming out of the organ, followed by the congregation singing its pious heart out: "Lord, have mercy…"

Jahoda could hardly wait for the Mass to end: he would assemble the priest and all these devout people in front of the church, along with the mayor and the town's entire intelligentsia to show them the boy: Here you are—and have I not discovered a real talent for you? What a find this could turn out to be! There would not be a single person in the town who wouldn't be discussing it excitedly! Then it would appear in the papers and reach the ears of the bishop and the *bán*—and the boy would head off to the conservatory, the director of which would report back, saying: "Listen, Jahoda, this boy of yours—one day the whole world is going to be talking about him!"

The congregation sang the final prayer in the litany and Jahoda went over to the gentleman who was leading the singing with a voice that was strong and determined (if far from pleasant). Jahoda touched his shoulder. The man, who was kneeling on the footrest and holding his clasped hands before his mouth, turned around crossly as Jahoda pointed his finger at the boy behind him:

"What do you say to that?"

"You taught him well," the gentleman said, and then took a big breath and squinted as he got ready to sing out: "*Genitori genitoque…*"

"Think so? But not a single note! He's learned it all by himself, merely by listening. Do you hear that? The boy—he's a prodigy, who must be sent away to study…"

The other man was no longer listening; the blood was already pounding in his face as the vessels in his neck swelled with the effort of overpowering the other singers in the contest of throats. God only knows, he thought to himself, whether those folks up there prefer it if you praise them more loudly than others do.

When the hymn had come to an end and the organ had fallen silent, a great aromatic cloud of blue rose again from the censer in front of the altar, with the gleam of the monstrance shooting forth from between the candles. The church echoed with the light tinkling of a bell, and the pious hung their heads low before the divinity and clapped their hands to their breasts in penitence. And old Jahoda knelt on the brightly colored handkerchief he had spread out; he bowed his aged head so that the longish tufts of his sparse, silvery-white hair slid onto his shoulders and over his wrinkled neck; he too struck his chest with his hand and closed his old, dimming eyes...Yes, there was something that outlives old age and death, something in life that is eternally youthful...But had he truly discovered in this insignificant, poor, nondescript lad the heir to his sensibilities and ideas?

Would that which he had built up with his soul really remain a part of life, and perhaps be tempered into something more beautiful and pure—as in his younger days, when he believed so, in an intoxication of spirit, and then he'd sit down in order to confide it to the keyboard or commit it to paper—but then it would disappear, get lost, fly off somewhere, as if it could not bear to be in contact with the material world...And now like a white shade it pushed its way to the forefront of the old man's soul, providing him with a reminder of the fervent love he long, long ago came to bestow upon Mařenka Lipovskova...

And with its inexhaustible strength, the thought once again cascaded over his soul that he had not been able to entertain either before or since: the thought of what kind of child he would have fathered with her, with the woman who was herself born to music, at a time when their hearts were enthralled and connected by passion and love?...This question, unencumbered by even the slightest scrap of base desire, had been crossing his mind over and over for a long time now, ever since he'd had to renounce the sole love of his life. Finally, with the advent of old age, this thought had ceased occurring to him, but a trace of it remained in his heart like a grave that reminded him at times of this dear dead thing that had never been fully born...But, behold—has not this magnificent idea appeared before him incarnated in this child?...All of this passed before his mind's eye in an instant: everything was as if he was now catching sight of a light-strewn landscape in its proper contours, one that had heretofore been revealed by flashes of lightning. Meanwhile the full chords of the prelude with which Jahoda usually concluded Sunday vespers was streaming, *fortissimo*, from the organ. The priest had disappeared into the sacristy and the public was crowding down towards the church doors; the full-throated man and the other pious congregants were going downstairs from the choir loft. Jahoda and his young man remained alone upstairs, save for the presence of the sexton, who was seeing to the organ the way the previous organist had trained him to do.

"You played well," the old man said, looking enthusiastically and kindly into the large black eyes. Those eyes were kind, and they were also lustrous and lively under their long lashes; they looked to be in perfect harmony with the expression on the boy's soft reddish lips and small mouth. For the first time Jahoda noticed that the boy was exceedingly pleasant-looking, and that his glance was being returned with the sweet, childlike forthrightness of a soul both good and melancholic. With his eyes, lips, and his entire swarthy but sickly face the boy smiled at Jahoda, credulously, joyously.

"Where did you learn that?" Jahoda inquired of him. He had the feeling that he had not yet hit upon what he really wanted to say.

"I watched you...and listened," replied the boy. His voice was thin and anxious, but he was obviously excited.

"Well, then...what is your name?"

"Amadej..."

The word *Mozart* flashed across his mind, and he observed the boy even more intently.

"Can you read music?"

"No, I can't."

"But you love music?"

"I love it...very much..."

"You love it...a great deal..." the old man repeated after him, lost in thought. And then he sensed all of a sudden that a new thought had begun to extinguish by means of its icy breath the warmth that this lad had ignited in his heart. This new thought was the doubt of an experienced man: was this truly a genuine talent? Or was the boy perhaps not the bearer of anything great and absolute in art—but merely native skillfulness, born of mediocre talents that would later disappear beneath daily drudgery? Never rising through his soul up into the sphere of pure art...?

Jahoda's soul had started to feel proud and fulfilled at the sight of this boy, and his sense of surprise had been supplemented by memories from his own youth. But now a dull, unpleasant emotion began to swallow up his enthusiasm.

"Hold on, now—"he said in tones befitting a teacher giving an examination. He called for the sexton, who was

10

waiting just out of view, ring of keys in hand, to come work the bellows. Then he moved towards the organ, lowered his right hand onto the keys, and, note after note, in a tender register like a flute, he poured out from within himself the musical thought on which he long, long ago had constructed his most beautiful composition...How was it that this melody was finding its way to his old fingers now, when the awakening life in his breast had long since gone numb? Why?... "L'Adieu" was the name of the composition...*adieu*...forever!... Something melancholic descended over the old man's soul, but beneath this feeling of dejection a desire was breaking forth, as if it all had not been so long ago: the desire to play through to its end this piece that no human ear had ever heard. He had written it down and kept it hidden in the same way that the word *Adieu!* had inscribed itself on his soul and remained there, groaning, concealed...

"Did you hear that?" and he turned abruptly to face the boy.

"I did."

"Try to play it."

The boy bounced over to the keyboard and pressed the same key with which the old organist had begun—and then played the beautiful selection through to the end, with no mistakes at all.

"That's beautiful," he said to the older man, now without any of the embarrassment he had shown earlier while standing before him.

"Beautiful?...You can feel the beauty in it?" Jahoda's wrinkled face was quivering with enthusiasm, and his moist eyes beheld the boy with great emotion. He placed

11

his trembling hand on the boy's tousled black hair. Then he bent down and kissed him on the forehead.

"Come with me," he said to him, and then led him back to his apartment.

They walked into a spacious room. It was rather dark, and the only thing that attracted the boy's attention amidst all the furniture, books, pictures, and other decoration was the old-fashioned piano in the middle of the room, with its black keys underneath and its white ones on top. The boy had eyes for nothing else. His soul hovered over those keys as they began to speak with sound produced by his fingers' touch. He was still living in the bliss of having been able today to fulfill his long-held desire, with an opportunity that might only present itself once, to sit in the place of Mr. Jahoda at the keyboard of the organ, something that had populated his sweetest dreams and, in the dreaming of it, given him a sense of what an invigorating and at the same time utterly precious existence it was, being in a position to devote himself, his body and soul to it, and doing so without pause, without the awareness of anything else, until his death...And now that seductive line of keys on the piano was dragging him its way once more, and it was about to resound with the most delightful blossoming of notes in the same way that he had played earlier, after the old man, on the organ. At last he could resist no more. As Jahoda stood taking off his jacket in front of the open wardrobe, the boy tip-toed over to the piano and in the room resounded the quiet, plaintive musical idea, full of mysterious beauty, that love had once before called forth from the heart of the musician Jahoda.

The boy lifted his hands from the keys and stared at the man with his wide, round eyes. His very soul was speaking out of him. "I had to do it. The piano drew me here, and I had to do it…"

But Jahoda said not a word. He just walked over to the piano and sat down in front of it, and his hands began to fly all over the keyboard as if they had wings. An arpeggio with beautiful harmony spread across the room, while the boy's dark, huge eyes beheld the old man as if he were a creature that did not belong on this earth.

"If you could only understand this!" Jahoda said, not raising his eyes from the keys in which he was absorbed. "If you could only understand this!" But then he lowered his old hands once more to the keys and his fingers began to make almost imperceptible contact with them, and the same sounds that the boy had produced just a few moments earlier began to arise magically to the accompaniment of a beautiful harmony. And then, like a nightingale's dolorous complaint, in tones deep and long akin to a sigh, as if the noble sound of longing were breaking forth, as if plying the silver strings of love, passionately and without restraint, forming a hymn to happiness, connecting notes in a pattern that resembled drops of his hot blood splashing across a moonlit surface: like that, precisely like that, like brilliant pearls the notes emerged from beneath Jahoda's fingers and landed on the boy, who stood there bewitched. He dared not take a breath.

This great, and holy, and sweet dolor of the artistic soul, in the very act of creation, when genius elevates it to its own heights, and the burden of physicality begins to press in—this pain ran down over his breast and his mind in radiant waves and merged in one singular sensation in him, with the notes, as if they were being born directly inside him and from there barely making it out through the wires in the old piano.

Time passed as fast as a minute, and as slowly as a century. The final note poured out into the semi-darkness of the room, and then, as if it were all an assembly of bright white ghosts, it disappeared slowly, moving farther and farther into the vastness of the universe. And the lad's spirit was vanishing along with the collection of notes into the indeterminate distance, until his moist eyes merged with Jahoda's. For a moment they were silent, and then the old man smiled and wiped his eyes with his big blue handkerchief.

"If you could understand...Back then I was twenty-five years old, and now I'm seventy," he added with a smile.

"If I could do it like that...I'd give everything I have!" the boy said with wild excitement in his voice.

Jahoda took him by the hand:

"Everything? What does that mean?"

"Everything..." the boy whispered, lowering his eyes.

"So would you like to study music?"

"I would!"

"So that you can play the organ in church?"

"That, too."

"And so that you'll get paid to do it?"

"They don't have to pay me as long as I'm allowed to play the organ."

The man unintentionally squeezed the boy's hand that was still clasped in his own.

14

"Then be my student," he said after a pause. "How old are you?"

"Twelve."

"Who are your parents?"

"I don't have a father or a mother. Both of them are dead. I have a little house with a garden, left to me by my father. The people in the mayor's office moved an old lady in there with me, and we live off the garden."

"If you have talent, and if you are diligent, then the city administration will send you, at its expense, to study music in Prague, where I was a student, too."

A smile swept across the boy's face like a bright reflection of his heart.

"But you will have to study a great deal, a great deal. *Per aspera ad astra.* That means, through the thorns to the stars..."

"I want to study. How could I want anything else?"

"So many grow discouraged!"

"I won't, though."

"They take it up with zeal, and they work with zeal, but when they get halfway through, to the point at which art starts to become the holy sacrament of the purest and most daring inspiration of the human spirit, and at which they see that they cannot be its priests, they withdraw, and defile it. They become artisans. It would be better for you to get a hoe and dig around in your garden! You see," the old man went on fervently, as though he were conversing with an adult, "from the bottom of my heart I wanted to have children...And when I cried the hardest for the joy that I was not fated to receive, it seemed to me that I was crying because there was no creature on earth that would be heir to her soul and mine...Behold, this magnificent idea," the old man, now completely flushed with excitement, played the main *motif* of the composition that the boy had listened to a few minutes before, "this idea conceived by her, since I was only able to create a work of art in collaboration with her soul. When we parted, the artist in me died, and what remained was a musical craftsman. Did you know that no one, with the exceptions of you and her, has ever heard this composition? How many would understand it? And you? Do you understand it?"

Amadej regarded the old man with confusion in his eyes; the boy could not figure him out.

"So why did I play it for you, eh? Why?... Aha, I know. This is no ordinary day; it's like I'm dreaming. Perhaps before I die my presentiment will be fulfilled: I'll find what I've been weeping for: the heir to my soul, the one who will resurrect in my soul the artist who has died...But of course you don't understand me either. People make me the butt of their jokes and think that I've got a screw loose whenever I'm overcome by pain and despair...And so I just laugh back at them as they satisfy their thirst for art with some waltz that I'm compelled to play. And you? Let me learn something about you."

Stern lines appeared on his face as he began to bang out a tempestuous dance number on the piano.

"And? Did you like that, too?"

"Of course I did. It was pretty..."

"That? Phui! Get away, please. Get away from me. Take up your hoe, go spread manure in your garden, and

16

plant those potatoes...Begone! I can tell from this that you are not what I thought you were. Go. Just go!"

The old man stood up from the piano and began to pace rapidly around the room. The boy smiled and couldn't help but think about the people who said that Jahoda was a bit crazy sometimes; he could not bring himself to understand why the eccentric was chasing him off.

"All you care about is music you can dance to," the old man argued, as if talking to himself. "And music that'll help you enjoy your wine...Just go away!"

The old man stood there before the astonished boy, inclining his head towards him; on his face, the individual muscles were giving little twitches: Go! Go! Your eyes deceived me. Amadej! Beautiful little Amadej!

And at that the boy burst into tears.

"All right then, what are you crying about? Did I hurt your feelings? This is an examination. I was trying to get a look into your heart and—wouldn't you know it—now I've found what I was afraid of finding. I thought that you were a born artist, a poet, but you aren't. It is what it is!...So what's there to cry about? It isn't your fault. For God's sake just get out of here, and if in the future you want to play the organ, then have at it. You'll become an organist of the type that is a dime a dozen in the world. But, for now, just go away..."

Amadej lowered his gaze, said goodbye, and left the room. He was in no position to comprehend what he had just experienced there. He had just felt the way a traveler feels after wandering around for ages in the night and then, glimpsing a reassuring light, when his heart leaps for joy, the light all at once disappears, and an even more dense darkness closes in on him. Where was it again? Where had he been going? In vain he reflected once more on the unusual thing that had happened to him...he felt a deep ache within, and he grew angry, though he didn't know why, at the old man whom he had admired above all other people because he was a lord, the king of all those sounds connected with the organ...

Over the course of the following days, the boy didn't go up to the choir loft in the church. He was ashamed of seeing Jahoda, and afraid of him, though he still did not know why.

Very well, then: the first time he saw his most dearly cherished dream coming true, that he would be able at any time he wanted to draw free-flowing musical notes from an organ—this splendid moment had passed all too swiftly, leaving behind bitterness. And the sight of a keyboard would now have hardly left an impression of magical power on his soul; that line of white and black keys no longer held sway over him with its intoxication and temptations; the keys were no longer some being that was known to him subconsciously from afar and could speak in the music of his heart...Now he would just crowd in under the choir loft for Mass and follow, with his pious eyes, the playing of old Jahoda, guessing how his fingers looked as they extracted sound from first the black keys and then the white ones. When the final chord had faded, he would stand by a column near the front of the church and wait for the old man with fearful and probing eyes: why has he found fault with me?...But the old man would not acknowledge him. Right in front of Amadej he would dip his fingers into the font, genuflect and cross himself, and then proceed with his little old-man steps out of the church.

The boy was forlorn. And he felt like some even greater secret bound his soul to the old man now that their relationship had suddenly, and for whatever reason, been broken off. Now and then he would look dejectedly at the children competing for favor in the town bell-tower, so they could be the ones to ring the bells in church; and he remembered that once he had been happy like that, when the bell would peal by dint of his efforts. But now he was astonished at how much pleasure he had taken in those bells, which always made the same monotonous sounds; and now he yearned for his soul to be able to speak in a clear language of notes like those that emerged from the organ or the piano of old Jahoda.

A majestic light went on suddenly in his heart, right in the midst of all these thoughts, causing him to tremble down to the depths of his being: if he sold the house, he would be able to use that money to buy a piano!...

With his childlike lack of understanding and experience he was not able—and in the final analysis did not wish—to probe the impossibility of such a bold undertaking. The idea was so strong that it was like bliss with lightning in it, so powerful that it dazzled his soul, the way the sun dazzles a searching eye and afterwards leaves everything else awash in murky shadows in which he could make out nothing. For three days Amadej elaborated on this decision of his, with all his inexperience and lack of comprehension, this plan on which the value of his whole life seemed to depend. Everything else in his imagination disappeared like something meek, commonplace, and unworthy when compared to the thought of what life would be like if it were always with him—that most lovely creature, that which emerged from the touch of his hand by means of the murmuring of notes and the longings of his whole heart. It was as if a part of his being were in these strings, and as if what were reverberating from these strings were in his soul causing trembling and quaking so that he lost his head amidst the delightful sensations of a bright, fairy-tale kingdom with its ineffably gentle creatures. With that he'd be capable of nourishing his ravenous heart continuously, using those notes. Without interruption or end. The things that his soul wanted to express, by guiding his hands across the white and black keys—these things would never be exhausted!

So for three days he dreamt of selling the house and buying a piano, and he hearkened over and over to the way his spirit rose into the realm of mystery when the magical sets of notes started. And on the fourth day he received a message telling him to go see Jahoda.

Jahoda received him while reclining on his couch. He was neither kind nor unkind. He let the boy know he had not been feeling well for some time, and he asked whether the boy would like to stand in for him with the church choir during his convalescence. Of course Amadej was thrilled to accept this offer, and all the more so when Jahoda added that he could, whenever he wished, come practice on his piano; he would give the boy pointers as well about what the choir would need to do for this or that church service.

From this moment on, the boy no longer felt like he lived on this planet. It was as if any other life for him had ceased to exist beyond the one that manifested itself in sound. Whatever he laid his eyes on, was poured out into chalices of notes; every thought in his head left him wondering what it would sound like expressed on the key's of Jahoda's piano.

The old man remained ill for just a brief period, and once he recovered he didn't bother—save on high holy days—to deprive Amadej of the joy in which the boy, seated at his piano, reveled with such authentic passion. One evening, when Jahoda returned from the inn, where he drank a couple of mugs of beer every day instead of having supper, he halted abruptly outside the door to his room. Like a fledgling bird that had just learned to fly, and settled onto a branch close to the nest, starting to imitate, in its still immature young voice, and with charming embarrassment and awkwardness, the song of its father—that's how Amadej was reconstituting, note by note, the composition that Jahoda had produced at that most portentous and memorable time of his life.

He's got spirit—the old man thought with great emotion. And whether it was on account of this composition, or because of his joy in finding someone, as he had craved for so long, to whom he could entrust the treasure in his soul, he felt at this instant the same sense of rapture and honest parental sympathy that Amadej had excited in him when he had surprised the boy at the organ in the church. After he walked into the room, he kissed the boy on the forehead and said to him, quietly but with great sentiment: "Be my family!"

From that moment on, the two of them believed that nothing could separate them except death itself.

* * *

Chapter Two

It could happen, especially during the rainy days of autumn, that a whole week would go by without Jahoda leaving his house. He would sit, wrapped up in his nightshirt, in a large easy chair, drinking warm beer and correcting, with eyes closed as if he were napping, Amadej's exercises on the piano. He quickly taught him how to read music, and then he forced him to play drills ceaselessly so that he would achieve technical proficiency and speed. But like a child who learns to read by tediously sounding out letters, and then rests and revives his spirits by looking frequently at the pictures in his primer, Amadej, made jaunty by the thought that Jahoda was not listening in his dreamlike state, would interrupt his dull drills and start to cast about freely for the notes with which his young soul was teeming. He would gather and collect them on the keyboard of the piano. Sometimes the sounds of compositions that he had only heard the old man play once would begin to rise up, willy-nilly, from the freewheeling melodies in his soul, and that's when Jahoda, opening his eyes, would incline his ear towards the piano and listen carefully to the notes that the young artist had received from him. They were unembellished, but the boy had obviously understood them. And, caught up in the flow of his own composition, which felt once more the way it had in his young and newly awakened soul, he would forget the duties of a conscientious teacher and help Amadej find the lost thread of the work. And when his old man's sense of fantasy got carried away with the thought that on the wings of these sounds the most powerful, the sweetest, and the most painful hours of his youth were being lived again, the conscience of the teacher would suddenly awaken. This teacher could not conceive of magnificent artistic goals without the harsh and difficult road that leads to the realm of absolute art. *Per aspera ad astra!* he would blurt out at Amadej...and warn him to continue practicing those dull, vulgar exercises from beginners' courses at piano.

One gorgeous Sunday in late fall Amadej, upon coming home from vespers, found Jahoda all dressed up in formal clothes. The old man was waiting for him, ready to go out somewhere.

"I am taking you," he said to the boy when they were in the street, "to see some gentlemen whose favor will determine your future. In the municipal gardens, His Honor the Mayor is holding court with several prominent council members, and I am taking you to them. It will soon be time for them to send you to the conservatory...See to it that you behave nicely in front of them. Answer freely if they should ask you something, but otherwise I'll do the talking."

And, indeed, they found the mayor, and a few town representatives, in the gardens. Making merry over their glasses of beer, they gave Jahoda a hearty welcome to the table. Jahoda took a seat and directed Amadej to sit down next to him. The boy was embarrassed, and he could not even take heart in the fact that his guardian, the shop-keeper and municipal councilman Plavčić, was in the group. The first to address Jahoda was the mayor. He was seated at the head of the table and had grown accustomed to certain gestures and a particular way of speaking on the strength of his job description and the realization that he was the first citizen among his citizenry.

"So, *pane* Jahoda," he began, drawing out his words in a kind of *weltschmerz*, and then tossing his head back, "I hear you are sick."

"Old age, Your Honor…I need to find a successor quickly." He then added immediately, pointing at Andrej: "Here he is! At last I found a genuine talent, and this fellow will, with any luck, be able to play differently than I do."

Amadej blushed and gave a pained look from side to side, but the gentlemen were all staring wordlessly at the mayor. It was up to him whether they applauded Jahoda or laughed at him.

"A talent, *pane* Jahoda? Well, that's nice," the mayor noted. "I've already heard a few things about this boy. They tell me he also knows how to play the organ."

"A great talent, sir!"

"Does he study with you?" the mayor asked. "Is he a hard worker?"

"He's a hard worker, but I'm no longer robust enough to be his teacher. It would be a shame to lose him, a real shame."

"Yes, but you can teach him whatever he needs to know for our church."

Plavčić, the boy's guardian, practically fell all over himself to echo the mayor's words: "To be sure! He can teach him whatever is necessary for our purposes!" His eyes bulged beneath his full head of dark hair. Jahoda had spoken with Plavčić earlier, asking him to solicit support from these friends of his, so that Amadej could go to the conservatory. But Plavčić had his own reasons for currying favor with the mayor. The local bull, owned in common by the town, had grown old, and Plavčić had been raising a younger bull on his own. Now he was anticipating the mayor's help in selling the community council his bull without the required formalities.

Jahoda had been decisively rejected by the boy's guardian in this intercession with the council, but he forced himself to maintain a calm exterior, saying, "For what our church needs, there is no reason to seek out some huge talent; and ultimately Amadej knows that himself."

"Look here, now," the mayor followed up, as if he actually cared about the matter. "Are you saying that it is possible for someone without real talent to play the organ?" He liked to seek out opportune times to demonstrate his ability to be a quick study on issues not falling directly under his purview.

"Yes, it's possible."

"Well, I'll be. That's interesting…"

"But this young fellow, Mr. Mayor, has a different kind of talent. He needs to be sent off to conservatory."

"Do you think he'd be in favor of that?" inquired the mayor in his man-of-reason tones.

"He would be. Decidedly so."

A moment of silence ensued. The first to gather his wits was Plavčić, Amadej's guardian.

"*Pane* Jahoda," he said, looking out of the corner of his eye at the mayor, "our children are not meant for that. We leave things like that to you Czechs."

"But why not, my dear Plavčić?" the mayor checked him gently. "For we too have had famous people in the world of music."

"Indeed...It's just that unfortunately we are poor. Now there's an obstacle for you..."

"Yes. Of course. We have to consider what it is that we live from. Bread is what we need. Luxuries like what you are talking about aren't our cup of tea," agreed the merchant Grubović with a yawn. He was a very well-fed man with heavy gold chains running across his round belly.

"Man does not live by bread alone," said Jahoda.

"But without bread, there isn't any living, *pane* Jahoda!" came Plavčić's smiling reply, with his eyes glued all the while to the mayor and Grubović.

The mayor did not withhold his final judgment for very long. He started, in a voice that betrayed the state of mind of the group of representatives from the town:

"It's true, my dear Plavčić. It's not in vain that the prayer runs thus: give us this day our daily bread...But people must also think about higher needs, spiritual ones...Yes..."

The mayor's state of mind was now reflected in his face, and some of the representatives made the effort to express their agreement. Grubović himself commented sagely: Certainly, certainly...

"And providing this daily bread is necessary," said Jahoda, "and everyone to whom God granted strong arms can have a hand in it. But geniuses, bona fide artistic geniuses, are rare even amongst larger nations. And when a great talent like this is found, then it is a sin that cries up to the heavens if it is lost. We are supposed to give him the opportunity to get an education—it's our patriotic duty."

"Well, yes..." the mayor drawled.

"In the case of the small nations—and that includes you Croats—such innate talent often fails due to poverty on the one hand and also to the lack of understanding on the part of the people who should be in charge of their education. You see, when God organized this world of ours, it came to pass that inspired artists are not always born into wealth. For any one person it'd be too great a sacrifice to take upon himself the burden of educating such a talent; but what cannot be done by one person can be done by several, by a club or foundation, or by a town. This, gentlemen, is the way it works all over the world. So why shouldn't we work this way too?"

The representatives were all staring at the mayor.

"Therefore you believe, *pane* Jahoda, that this boy could..."

The mayor propped his bearded chin on his hand, thought hard, and then said decisively:

"That is all very well and good, *pane* Jahoda...if...But this part of the deal—?" And he made a rubbing motion with his fingers as if he were counting money.

Then Grubović asked, "What does *pane* Jahoda think of that?"

"He thinks about it a lot," said the mayor, "but he has not asked...for...You think, *pane* Jahoda, that the town should send this boy off for his studies, don't you?"

"That is my view. That's how it is done in my home country and in other places."

The blood rushed to Plavčić's face. He stared with bulging eyes at Jahoda and shouted angrily:

"Other places! What do we care about other people as long as we have enough cares of our own? *Pane* Jahoda, you should mind your own business..."

"Mr. Jahoda has nice ideas, as I already noted...Yes...But we are poor folk. We have other needs..." said the mayor with a sense of his own importance.

"And what poor folk we are!" proclaimed Amadej's guardian to the mayor.

"*Pane* Jahoda thinks he's in Bohemia or Moravia," the town treasurer announced all of a sudden. Until now he had been following the conversation in silence, with a look of annoyance and ill-concealed boredom on his face.

"Well, then, sing something for us," and with that the mayor turned to face Amadej. "Let's listen to you."

The boy blushed and looked over at Jahoda.

"Well, what's holding you back?" the mayor repeated impatiently.

"I don't have a good voice," Amadej said, his face turning an even brighter red.

"What the hell kind of musician are you, then, if you don't have a singing voice?" the guardian shouted at him.

Everyone had a chuckle, and not even the mayor could resist a little smile.

"The boy is a mischievous sort!" said Jahoda. Amadej's predicament had adorned his face with both pain and anger.

"Yes, yes...so it is, *pane* Jahoda," said the mayor with a yawn; it was apparent that he would prefer for this discussion to be over.

"He who lacks money for school should not long for refinement," Plavčić stated with finality. His glance at Jahoda was cruel and scornful.

The old man said nothing, because the boy and he did not belong in this company. Nonetheless he was hoping to finish his beer in a leisurely way, and only then excuse himself. But the group expelled him from its midst sooner than he had intended. To wit: Grubović dropped the latest issue of the *Neue Presse* from Vienna onto the table, being unable to wait any longer to excite envy in his friends over the fact that his name appeared in big fat letters in this world-class newspaper.

Jahoda could not abide this paper, on account of its stance toward the political struggle of the Czech people and because of the articles and music criticism that Hanslick wrote for its pages—and with his philosophical meditations on "absolute music" Jahoda did not agree in the least. Nonetheless Grubović read aloud to the gathering the following announcement in German:

HAY!

Antun Grubović in the town of * in Croatia, of-
fers 300 cubic meters of clean dry clover for sale.
Located 7 km from the train depot. Cash.
Price negotiable.**

Jahoda had already stood up to leave when his
neighbor, Amadej's guardian Plavčić, took the opportunity to plant the following confidence in his ear with a
whisper: "All that clover was grown with the sweat and
tears of my gullible and exploited peasants."

"Why are you leaving, *pane* Jahoda?" the mayor said,
extending his hand with lordly benevolence. "Well,
then...Just have him take up some kind of sensible work,
so that he doesn't grow up as a loafer...And your home
country, *pane* Jahoda, will certainly see to it that we don't
go without musicians....Yup..."

The group laughed robustly.

"Let's go," Jahoda said to Amadej. "It's time," and,
with his gray head bowed, he walked out of the beer
garden alongside the boy.

*

Jahoda was ailing all winter long. While he was
wrapped up in his robe, drinking warm beer and dozing
in the big easy chair, he listened to Amadej practicing on
the piano. And he offered corrections. Amadej proved
indefatigable at the drills and made admirable progress.
The improvisations he could produce from his own

imagination had already grown more complete in terms of form. The old man realized that it was time for him to begin the boy's introduction to the theoretical side of the art, but he had to postpone this on account of his weakness and malaise.

"If you don't learn that side of things, they won't admit you to the conservatory," he would say to Amadej, for both of them were convinced that Amadej would still be going off to study music, although neither of them knew how they'd get the means for him to support himself in Prague for those several years. Amadej was hungrily looking forward to that schooling, which he always believed would reveal to him, like a key fashioned of gold, the deep mysteries of the art, and that he would then know everything about composing and committing to paper the notes that were coursing without abeyance through his soul, completely inundating him at times with their power; they wanted to burst forth, amaze the world, and bestow glory upon his name...He was sure that people who listened to the melodies from his soul would weep and tremble, the way he would start to quiver and cry himself when he heard their murmur within him. He believed that people would have to recognize his superiority and celebrate him when he revealed to them the genius that had ignited in his breast this quest for knowledge and fame.

Now he looked with bitter disappointment at anything that he plunked out on the piano in the search for glorious sounds, all the while scurrying around as in a frenzy and feeling overwhelmed, because he wasn't playing what was in his soul; it wasn't even an anemic, distant echo of what resounded there with gentle tears, thundering with splendid, poignant chords all the way up to the stars themselves—this impotence of his he ascribed completely and solely to his ignorance of the secrets by which one gained admittance into the holiest shrines of art. Once, when he was seated at the piano, depressed in this way, and glaring with envenomed feelings at the keys that could not or would not produce the sounds he heard in his soul, the boy said to Jahoda: "When I have finished training at the conservatory, I will know all the marvels and secrets of composing."

Jahoda understood what he meant.

"You want that to be the case; of course you do. But you will never be completely satisfied," he told him, touched by the naïve statement form this young artist.

One day in the spring Jahoda found, in a Croatian newspaper, an enthusiastically penned article from his parish priest. The headline was: "What Do We Need?" His discussion, full of fervor and patriotic fire, concluded with the words: "We need a living faith, we need ideals, and we need unselfish and energetic people who put ephemeral, materialistic, earthly wealth in the service of the spirit and offer it, proudly, for the realization of national educational goals..."

"Look!" Jahoda said to himself. "I hadn't even thought of him." And he donned his jacket and made his way, with his old-man gait, over to the priest's residence.

"Reverend," he said to the priest, "I have come to you with a request that I know you won't refuse."

"Indeed, *pane* Jahoda," the priest said to him with gusto, "how could I do such a thing to you?"

"This might be my final request...really. My last one, for I feel more and more like you'll all soon be singing the words for me: '*In paradisum...*'"

"Now, now, *pane* Jahoda!"

"I have only this ultimate wish. If it is granted, then I have lived in vain. You see, this boy who's substituting for me in church, he is, Reverend, a talent of a kind that is not born every day."

"He does play the organ beautifully..."

"An artist! He has spent all winter with me, and now I know his heart like the palm of my hand. He's gentle, enthusiastic, full of passion—it's a regular artistic temperament! If it goes to waste, Reverend, do you have any idea of what a precious treasure will disappear with it?"

"And why would it go to waste, *pane* Jahoda?"

"Because he is poor. He needs schooling. He should be sent off to the conservatory. I talked with the mayor and some of the community leaders about this, but they don't get it. If only I had as much energy left in these bones as I had a year ago, the boy would be my concern. So therefore, Reverend, intercede on his behalf! Maybe you could even help him some yourself. You'd be better placed than I to think up some way for us to send him off to the conservatory."

The priest smiled at him, and placed a sympathetic hand on Jahoda's shoulder.

"It could well be that he is gifted, as you say. But where would help come from, my dear man? Support him with what means? How?...We are poor, unfortunately. Poor. But do you know what? If he is diligent, he will learn enough from you to make a decent living."

"A living? That's not where my thoughts are leading. He won't perish of hunger, but he needs a different kind of sustenance so that the artist in him doesn't die. The musician. The composer. Reverend, I know I don't need to prove to you what you wrote about so beautifully and ardently in your article, 'What Do We Need?'..."

"I did write that...And those are my convictions...I shall come to the boy's aid. Let him continue to practice with you, and later we shall transfer him to the choir with a stipend of some sort, if he learns what he needs to for Mass and vespers."

"But that's nothing..."

"Nothing else can be done...Given our circumstances, what more, exactly, would you demand?"

Jahoda stormed out of the rectory, angry and saddened. How—he wondered to himself—was he to prove publicly, then, that a nation that's incapable of being thrilled by true art will be lost. With no chance of a better future. For there will be no idealistic energy lifting men and women to a higher life. They will be bogged down in the swamp of vulgar material concerns and they'll wear themselves out completely in the kind of struggle that is unworthy of a human being.

Thus passed a whole year, with Amadej standing in for Jahoda in the choir and also taking lessons from him. If training in music theory were still being postponed because of Jahoda's ill health, Amadej was nonetheless attempting to compose his own works in secret. Once he was brazen enough to show the old man one of the pieces he had written, in that insecurity and fear of another person's judgment that is the constant companion of natural artists who have not yet spread their wings to fly.

"What is this?" Jahoda inquired, moving the piece of paper farther from his near-sighted eyes.

"I wrote it..." Amadej whispered.

Jahoda read over it, frowning as he went. Then he handed back the paper and said querulously:

"You aren't allowed to do that!"

"But it's good, right?"

"No. Of course it's no good."

The boy clenched his teeth, set his jaw, and burst into tears. The piece of paper into which he had invested so much hope and joy, disappeared before his tear-filled eyes into an opaque, disfigured image.

Jahoda felt sorry for the boy, and he understood those tears.

"No, Amadej," and he spoke with poignancy, "that is something you are not allowed to do. It would be too easy for you to be lured away from disciplined study..."

At that juncture he began to relate stories about his own study at the conservatory, and he recalled the implacable strictness of his professor of composition, who would lash out with harsh criticism at even the most outstanding talents in the institute whenever they dared circumvent, or de-emphasize, in their assignments any of the hard-and-fast rules of the discipline. He would drill into us *chluku*—a word Jahoda had retained from his mother tongue, meaning young people of whom he was fond—endlessly the *Skizzenbuch* by Beethoven. That's the way true genius operates, re-forming, changing, embellishing continuously, never being satisfied, forever convinced that the composition in our souls was far superior to the one committed to paper.

But Amadej continued to write music in secret. At last Jahoda discovered the source of this compulsion in the boy's heart. It happened one time when, among Amadej's sheet music he found a thick notebook with a designation, written in the boy's hand, of "Adelka. A Sonata for Piano"...A benevolent smile of age and experience crossed Jahoda's face, and he opened the notebook to the first page. Under the numeral "1" and above the first notes was written the programmatic epigram for the piece. It was from the poem by Vukelić: "I love you, o ideal, as much as one can love the sea..."

Before commencing to read the notes, he remembered his neighbor, the impoverished widow Barbotić and her eleven-year old daughter, Adelka. Long ago Jahoda had enjoyed spoiling the little neighbor girl. She used to come over to his house every day, as soon as she heard him start to play the piano. She would stand right next to him and plunk out, to his immeasurable delight, the most dissonant notes while he was in the middle of a work. Once, when he made fun of her for doing this, she looked at him with her dark blue eyes—looking like a pair of violets, and not having any idea at first what he meant—and then exploded in tears. And away she traipsed. Since then she had never darkened his door, even though they had remained good friends. He said to Adelka's mother: —In the past I believed that someone who does not understand music can be neither beautiful nor good. But look at your Adelka, who is not given to music but is so sensitive! If I were a painter, I would not find that much gracefulness in any child's face, nor so much kindness in her eyes. Even if I were to paint an angel.

Jahoda, holding Amadej's composition in his hand, saw the gleaming world of his youth take shape before the eyes of his soul, illuminated by the powerful light of a long-lost love. Those distant, very distant memories began to circulate quietly in his heart. They weren't sweet or bitter anymore, but it was as if they had begun to live, rejuvenated and renewed, in the soul of that enchanted boy and dear little girl, as if they had started blazing afresh with a tempestuousness of life that he thought had died long ago in his heart...

Jahoda began reading through Amadej's composition. And, wouldn't you know it, this time the strict judge and conscientious teacher in him fell silent, and he took no offense at either the distorted expression of musical thoughts or at the abrupt, brazen leaps in melody and harmony, and not even at the throngs of grammatical mistakes. Reading on, into the exquisite confusion of these most daring musical imaginings, he remembered standing on a great crag along the seashore during storms, languishing for Mařenka's beautiful, artistic soul, keeping watch with a demon-like sense of solace as an enormous wave, swollen with water, came in under his cliff accompanied by a great clatter and shriek and sizzle, with a massive, crashing din, and with wild foam exploding from it, as if it were trying to fly up to the clouds and cover the universe with its splashing—and then it buckled under its own weight and streamed, seemingly exhausted, back into the bowels of the high seas whence it had come...That is the way the violent longing and unquenchable weeping for Mařenka had raged in his heart...

The first tempest in Amadej's soul—thought the old man, still holding the boy's composition in his hands. His first reaction was that this was something sweet and touching. But then another thought struck him:

With feelings like this at such a tender young age, this can only signify the awakening of a forceful creative soul.

One evening shortly after this, Jahoda was listening from his bed as Amadej began to interrupt his drills with a *fantasia* from his own composition that he entitled "Adelka." Now and then that *fantasia* would even cross over, unexpectedly but elegantly, into Jahoda's *impromptu* 'L'Adieu" that he had written for Mařenka so many years earlier. Experiences from long ago passed before Jahoda's mind with a vitality that he had not felt for Lord knows how long. Should he tell the boy the story behind that *impromptu*? ...He's still too young, the man thought. But he should begin to understand these things! Still...is it permissible for me to pour oil on these flames? ...And I, reasoned the old man, carried in my soul the poet's ardor, but it was only Mařenka's soul that was capable of kindling it...And why should I keep that a secret from him, when I might never get another chance in my life to teach him about it?...You cannot spare an artist anything! Let the flames dance high in his soul. The fire will singe him inside, but how much it will warm him! Such is the fate of artists—and the calling of art.

So Jahoda called Amadej to his bedside and began to tell him the story of his life.

Chapter Three

J an Jahoda finished the Prague conservatory as a young man of twenty-four. The year was 1846. After its literary renaissance, the Czech nation was coming back to life politically as well. The idea of the indomitable strength of united Slavdom filled the young Jahoda, just as it did his co-nationals, with fervid inspiration. Indeed, when the great Palacký called together the Slavic Congress in Golden Prague, and the enthusiastic Czechs opened their fraternal hearts to the Russians, and to the Poles, Slovaks, Croats, Slovenes, and Serbs, Jahoda's opening hymn "Under One Banner" won unanimous acclaim. Having received recognition of that sort for his creation, which he considered to be a confession of the stormy and majestic feelings in his soul, the young artist initially believed that he had fulfilled the main task of his life. This was not his vanity speaking. It was his goal for this flowering of his soul, this hymn from his heart, to ignite a holy struggle equally in everyone's heart, right down to the last Slav. He believed he was simply the one chosen by Providence to play the feverish chords that would resound all throughout the Slavic world and gather millions of people under the glorious flag of concord and unity.

While his heart was reveling in this grand opulence for the duration of the Congress, a man paid him a visit in his modest apartment. He looked elegant in his traditional folk jacket, but nature had given his body a stepmotherly appearance: short and hunchbacked, with a pockmarked face. He was around forty years old and introduced himself as Jaromír Lipovský, a wholesaler from the small provincial town of B———.

Jahoda's first sensation on being around this man, with his monstrous body and long arms, soon came into conflict with his sweet, intelligent face, with its energetic features and deep, dark eyes full of self-confidence and spirit. And with the robustness of his loud, strong, and manly voice, which made him seem more imposing than he was. For when Jahoda's gaze drilled into the deep eyes of this man—and especially whenever he'd start speaking with that elegance and tranquility of his, and with the power of his steely voice, Jahoda essentially had to forget the small, undistinguished figure that the other man cut at first. In point of fact, it seemed as if the visitor's stature had assumed the towering proportions that make it possible for one man to dominate another, and that awaken first respect and then awe. This man, one of the most prominent members of the Congress from the bourgeois estate, was visiting Jahoda in order to offer him the position of *kapellmeister* and music teacher in his home town. The things Lipovský mentioned, almost incidentally, about the excellent remuneration for the post in question were not as valued by the young Jahoda as the thrill the visitor caused by saying:

"Rest assured, good Sir, that we are in a position to appreciate your wonderful gift. We will stand by you in everything."

One month later, Jahoda performed his first official function there. Under the aegis of the most prominent and well-to-do citizen, he began to pursue his artistic work in the most favorable of circumstances.

Shortly after his arrival his patron took him to his house and made him an offer: to serve as the tutor for his wife. "My Mařenka," he said to Jahoda in the presence of the young lady, "has had occasion to receive some excellent musical instruction. But in view of the fact that she is so passionately taken by your artistry, we shall detail you, as an experienced art ist, to work for her at times as well as to be in service to your own muses."

Jahoda felt as if he had been transported to a world the existence of which he had hardly suspected. He felt inspired by its great lushness, elegance, and sophistication, and by its high level of education and genuine understanding of artistic ideals. It all seemed like a dream to him: he enjoyed the support of venerable, wealthy, powerful, and highly intelligent benefactors who, by dint of the innate gifts of their spirit and of their education, influence, and means, could defend art and could do so with real comprehension. Additionally, our young artist often had the opportunity to listen, at the Lipovskýs' house, to his sponsor's commentary on everything relating to the patriotic strivings and the future of the Czechs. And he frequently witnessed the way Lipovský supported, materially and with enthusiastic receptiveness, every movement of that sort, not only in his homeland but everywhere that Slavdom was showing signs of life. It was in this house that he heard Professor Gaj celebrated for the first time, and praised with so much zeal and love that Lipovský himself could barely distinguish between his enthusiasm for his own people and that for his kith and kin far off in the south.

The first time he saw the lady of the house, it was easy to recognize what Lipovský saw in her as a companion, if only on the basis of his brilliant mind and high status. She was barely nineteen, tall, and slender and supple as a young fir. When she approached Jahoda wearing her long, gray housecoat, with short, tender steps on the carpet, it seemed to him that she was a disembodied being, a marvelous artistic phantom, which one could not sense by touch. And when he accepted the hand she extended, which was tiny and soft, with long fingers, he felt in her touch that she was a human being of ethereal physicality. And a glance into her large dreamy eyes, greenish in color, made him think of Lipovský: how that man must be a refined spirit with a tried-and-true understanding of beauty, since he had picked as his companion this ineffably tender female creature with those eyes from which speaks an enigmatic amalgam of intelligence, maidenly naivete, understanding, and sweet, childlike devotion. When Lipovský kissed her fine, feminine hand and introduced Jahoda to her, he could see in Lipovský's moist, ecstatic eyes the total happiness of the wise man who is happy in love.

"She plays the piano splendidly, and she sings," Lipovský told him in a voice that, it seemed to Jahoda, was quivering with ardor. At that a smile appeared on her face, with its soft skin and delicate features, the kind of smile that angels have.

Indeed she did play the piano brilliantly. Jahoda realized from the first moment that she was an artist, owing to her understanding of the music, and to her execution and excellent technique. He almost had to wonder where this gentle, ethereal being had ingested so much force, because the *fortissimo* on her excellent Bösendorfer made notes pop and hum as if they were being produced by masculine hands. But he was also enthralled by the dreamy, elegiac poetry of her Chopin-like soul. From the side he observed the delicate complexion of her blushing face, on which had appeared light little rose-colored splotches the shape of cloudlets, and where the tiny, individual muscles around her small mouth trembled as she played. He could not imagine, though he tried with gratification, how this gentle, poetic Chopin-like soul was intimately connected to the rest of her entire being. That evening Jahoda, beguiled, wrote to his former director in Prague about the unmerited bliss that had come his way...

And this bliss increased. When the days came on which he was to go to the Lipovskýs' house and play a duet with her, or accompany her while she sang (she sang with particular understanding in her soft *mezzosoprano*), he would, when he woke up in the mornings, start to tremble with pleasure and excitement; on days when he did not have to go to the Lipovskýs' he perceived in himself a highly distasteful denial of artistic (so he believed) enjoyment. Then he would wander around on the outskirts of town. Notebook in his hand, he

45

would think of the way she played, and he would compose. At such times he was overcome by a forceful desire to go see the Lipovskýs. The house was always open to him, and both Lipovský and his wife would receive him equally warmly, but he did not dare go there outside of set times. And he had no idea where this pointlessly irrational and unseemly fear came from...Later he began to truly suffer from it all. Days on which he was not to go to the Lipovskýs', however, felt vacant and interminable, and they had something heavy and pinched about them, leaving him dejected.—In this manner winter came and went, and then spring arrived.

Once in the early morning Jahoda was taking a walk in the municipal park, notebook in his hand. He had never felt more capable of committing to paper a musical project this grand, this brilliant. He felt it inside him like this: a golden ray of sunlight appearing from a clear sky and traveling through the crowns of colossal oaks and lindens in bloom, the drumming of a nightingale, the exuberantly gay song of the blackbird and the sweet, bright cooing of a chaffinch...as well as the merry fluttering of all sorts of insects in the fresh clear air...the precious presence of hundreds of small flowers with droplets of dew on their petals and stamen...and much that was ineffable—things full, luxurious, sweet, and powerful, permeating the whole natural world on a morning in May. He interpreted everything as the solemn awakening of love in nature, and in all of it he caught a whiff of the soul of Mařenka Lipovskova...That is what he wanted to say with sounds, and his heart was carried away by the elegance of the thought that she would understand this composition...But when he took at seat on an isolated bench with the intention of focusing in on the right notes from amongst that welter of sounds, things did not go smoothly. Whatever he wrote down was alien, superficial, external; what hummed inside him seemed to remain beyond the power of his pencil. But he would not be deterred. In deep concentration he set out after the notes in his soul. And then, in a manner reminiscent of a tumble into slumber, he saw himself sitting with her at the piano. Now and then he cast a sidelong glance at her face, with its delicate and blushing skin....While playing, their fingers touched, and at every contact he felt his heart rock his chest from within...They played on and on...more...and Jahoda felt as though he had split into two persons: one of them was sitting with Mařenka at the keyboard, and the other was listening to what they played and jotting it down in the notebook. Then he roused himself and looked down at what he had written. Oh, enchanting ideas!...He leapt up from the bench, strode through the park with urgent steps, and in this mood of wanton presumptuousness he began to imitate the merry cry of the blackbird. And then he picked up his notebook once again and began to read, voraciously and single-mindedly, the musical ideas there...But all of a sudden he recoiled: everything he had written, note for note, was but a *motif* from Beethoven's "Adelaide," which Mařenka had recently played to his accompaniment, perfectly idiomatically...For a whole hour he had been writing down Beethoven's ideas as if they were the product of his own mind. In the end this unusual experience filled him with such raptures that he decided to go see Mme Lipovskova to tell her about it. And he was singularly happy that this had occurred, because now he could visit her outside of the scheduled hours.

But when he was just a stone's throw from the house, his courage began to abandon him. He sensed a block of some type, barring his path to Mme Lipovskova. This unnamed hindrance prevailed, and he sullenly turned off into another street. "Why am I not going?" he asked himself several times, and each time the intelligent and earnest face of Lipovský appeared before him: what would he say to this visit? And so Jahoda could not screw up the courage to go see Mařenka that day, nor the next, though he was tormented by the desire to be close to her.

In just two days it was time to go see her again. They sat at the piano for a full two hours, which passed, as ever, incomprehensibly quickly. They interrupted their playing with conversations about music, during which he timidly and uncertainly expressed his opinions. It seemed to him that her tastes were better defined and more pure than his. As they went on, he lost more and more of his independence to her; on a number of occasions he felt himself blush like a child when his judgment differed from hers. That's why he did not dare discuss with Mme Lipovskova the unintentional theft of ideas from Beethoven. Mařenka had outgrown him, and he could not let himself, not at any cost, come across as ludicrous or unreliable in her eyes. Now every one of his intentions was accompanied by the inevitable question deriving from her presence: What would she think of that? Would she like it?

Two weeks passed. Jahoda, who had glibly produced musical *motifs* for himself and his friends as a conservatory student, was incapable of setting down a single new idea in his notebook, nor did he touch any of the works he had already begun. But nevertheless he felt he had a great deal to say. These were things that could not be said in any way other than with musical notes. The condition of his soul was grim and unbearable, and it tormented him; he avoided people; without knowing why, his imagination turned to death and this left him with a pleasant feeling.

Once Mařenka handed him a small piece of lined paper with the inquiry:

"How, Mr. Jahoda, does this *motif* strike you?" Her embarrassment while posing this question was remarkable. But her light green eyes, with their delicate sense of intimacy, told Jahoda something that his very soul had been craving.

He read through the notes and stated with conviction:

"A lovely idea, *gnädige Frau.* There's a lot that can be done with it...This is your work?"

She blushed even more.

"My fingers just found it by accident, last night, when I was letting my imagination go...That's what my hours are filled with: evening improvisations. Your critical ear should never have to listen to me—and if I had any idea that a musician was within earshot, my imagination would flit away like a frightened bird. Oh, but despite all that—improvising in the dark, that is my passion!"

"You are an artist, *gnädige Frau,*" Jahoda told her in low, embarrassed tones. "Well, and this idea...the things that it would lend itself to! Might I be allowed to make use of it?"

"You're welcome to it," she said softly, throwing him a look that left his heart trembling.

Much later that same day Jahoda sat down to write, and write he did, the whole night through...When he awoke in the forenoon after a short sleep, he was very fatigued, but when his eyes fell on his work from the night before, he leapt out of bed and, clad only in a nightgown, began to read through the *Impromptu* he had written on the basis of Mařenka's musical idea.

He was quite satisfied with it. As he read through the work, he got the impression that someone else had written it, not he himself. He dressed in a hurry, grabbed the composition, and went over to the park to await the hour when he might call on Mařenka. It wasn't the assigned day to call on her, but he was well aware that today no fear was going to hold him back from this intention. The desire to show her this composition, to play it for her, was so powerful that he knew in his heart it would be impossible to still. Because the very waiting was intolerable, he went to the house even before the customary hour and asked to be presented.

Mařenka came to him in her long, light-gray dressing gown, which seemed to raise up her figure and cause it to float in the air. It seemed that she had never pressed his hand with as much firmness as today; he even seemed to detect happiness in her deep, greenish-brown eyes regarding his unexpected arrival. And when he told her, in a few words, that he had composed something on her theme, she leapt for joy exactly as a child would;

she took the paper and talked as if she had forgotten he was present.

"Ah, a composition on my theme?" And then, quietly... "How I would love to hear it!..." Her face flushed and she gave him the kind of look that set every last nerve in his body to quivering.

Today she seemed more beautiful and wondrous than ever. Under her light dressing gown her supple body was freely outlined in all of its contours and perfectly harmonious, womanly angles; and by her speech and the squeeze of her hand and the look in her eyes, Jahoda felt that sense of intimacy that so roiled him. Silent light crept through the heavy drapes into the richly appointed hall, where a solemn and heady sense of peace prevailed amidst the warmth and sophistication; Jahoda sat down at the piano and looked at her, nervous and overwrought, and then across from him she dropped into an armchair, her form as gentle and miraculous as a beautiful phantom born of an artist's reverie.

The introduction he played sounded wooden, like a schoolboy's assignment. But when he got to the *espressivo*, her theme came out clearly and sweetly, and his heart gave an enormous leap...He kept playing...on and on... deliriously now, as if his mind had disappeared into a realm of freedom whence notes came cascading back like pearls...No power could reign him in, no fear, no warning glances telling him not to say what was in his full, full heart. It felt like he was swimming hand-in-hand with her through immortal, glorious light. He still had not even looked down at the score...It did not feel as if these thoughts and emotions that he was expressing in sound were coming from him; rather it was like his fingers, obedient to a duty to a higher being, were simply flying across the keys. And the improvisation grew, and the resounding notes piled up and up as if they were not being born in Bösendorfer's instrument but on a colossal organ in some spectacular church; they spread in broad waves out of the dead silence in the hall, off into magical lands where blazing stars were strewn across the sky like midsummer bonfires, and the moon's thick, silvery light lay trembling. Like a specter the thought of Lipovský swept over to him...but then it disappeared just as abruptly, as if it had been consumed in the magical light...And out of the piano tumbles Beethoven's thought, like the ineffable and almighty voice of Jahoda's soul: *Ich liebe dich*....

When the final chord had died away in a distant *pianissimo*, Jahoda stayed seated at the piano and felt himself coming back to his senses, as if from a hypnotic state. He was in thrall to a blunt powerlessness, but vitality and consciousness were slowly returning...And then an oppressive, unpleasant feeling swept over him, something akin to shame and regret at a crime just committed...

"That's wonderful...," Mme Lipovskova said softly, giving Jahoda a look that made him melt. The look brought an inexplicable, harsh sensation with it, as though his heart had suddenly cracked open. In a dry voice, he said to her:

"It is nothing...A person purloins the thoughts of another and then deceives himself, too..." He stood up quickly from the piano. The effect of these words was like smashing an object of great value into tiny pieces.

"I've never heard that kind of playing before," she said, even more quietly. She lowered her eyes and the little pink clouds began glowing on her cheek.

"Beethoven's idea was tormenting me...It was certainly because of the beautiful way, *gnädige Frau*, you sang 'Adelaide'..."

"No, Jahoda, you are a great artist..."

"You gave the impetus for this composition, *gnädige Frau*. It was you. What I built onto it was from Beethoven...I am merely a machine echoing your thoughts, and those of Beethoven."

And the air seemed to close in on him in the splendidly appointed hall that he had entered a mere half hour earlier with such ardor in his heart. Somehow, unobserved, all the fine threads of sophistication and forbearance binding him to the feelings of heartfelt intimacy had been ripped asunder...

All day long he continued to think of Mme Lipovskova, and that night he dreamt the following: he was at the piano at the Lipovskýs', playing his composition, and she was standing in back of him, leaning lightly upon his chair. When he got to the finale, which included the *motif* from Beethoven's "Adelaide" ("*Ich liebe dich*")—she leaned over to him, wrapped her arm around his neck and locked her eyes onto his, so that the most complete climax of emotion that he had hitherto experienced in his life spread through his breast...Her breath flowed across his lips with maddening heat...His arm found its way around her slender waist...He pressed her soft, barely palpable body against him, and their mouths met in a protracted kiss....And then he awoke. As he opened his eyes, he thought he saw her form disappearing with soundless steps into the obscurity of the distance. He stretched out a hand after her, full of the longing from that dream and the swelling emotions that were choking his heart like the sea... "Her spirit—didn't her desire for me really bring her spirit here to stay with me?" he wondered, looking into the darkness where the phantom had disappeared, and he had to tear himself away from that thought at the nadir of his existence.

The following day, even in his wakeful state, he had to return incessantly in his thoughts to the moment when, swooning at the scent of her body, he had pulled her delicate waist to him and a long, smooth, perfect kiss had united their lips...

The incident was now fifteen days behind them. Jahoda was in love with Mařenka and sometimes he believed that she loved him, too...Their hands touched more frequently while playing than they did before, and after nearly every touch they would lose their place in the score and have to repeat the passage. At such times their eyes would hunt for each other, and Jahoda would notice every time that the blushing roses would break out on the skin of her face...

It finally dawned on Jahoda that she might be reproaching herself. The first time he entertained this idea, he recoiled in fright at the product of his own mind, and she continued, all the more strongly, to envelop his entire being the way an octopus subdues its overmatched prey. The awareness of Mařenka's husband trailed unavoidably along behind these thoughts. Jahoda knew about his great contributions to the Czech national cause, and he felt the repugnance and baseness of his intentions. Was he really capable of deceiving Lipovský in a manner this vile?

Nevertheless that seductive hour of oblivion arrived...In the midst of playing, while her long comely hands floated above keyboard, Mme Lipovskova told him this:

"Today Lipovský is going away for a few days..."

Why did she say that?... Jahoda looked at her. There, on her cheeks, were more little clouds of pink, and once more her greenish eyes rattled him to the core of his being...

Was he interpreting this blush and this look correctly? He trembled. His hand made its way over to hers as if pulled by some external force that he could not resist...Mařenka did not withdraw her hand from beneath his...and a strong and precipitous decision, like the one a person makes in an hour of desperation to commit suicide, delivered him from the hands of that mighty force. It fought back against the blind frenzy in his soul. He said:

"I cannot...I would die that instant... I'm broken... I love you."

Opaque light, gray and yellow and reddish, coated the hall, and in that light his mind felt obliterated. God only knows how much time passed in this way...

Mařenka was the first to speak: "Jahoda!"

She stood there, passions aflame, eyes downcast. Jahoda sought out both of her hands and fell to his knees in front of her, the sacred object of his heart:

"I am miserable because I love you...but I do love you...and I am burning up with love," he told her as he placed kisses on both her hands.

"Jahoda...For God's sake...Oh, Jahoda!"

"I know that it is not for me to talk to you in this way...This is the culmination of my life. My soul has stretched out for it even though I knew that it would languish from this moment on, cast down and moribund...I knew all of that...I have struggled against it, but I cannot do otherwise, Mařenka. I cannot!..."

"Jahoda, I am a wife..."

"For just this one moment, leave that out of it. I will not be able to wrest you from him..." He was on his knees before her well-built, lithe figure. She was soft and delicate like a child, but so grand in his heart!

"Come down into the garden tonight," he whispered to her. It was as if he had lost his head. "Come, so that I can tell you everything, so I can pour out my heart to you, and then what has to happen will happen: repentance, acquiescence, whatever. I would take onto myself all the bitterness of a lifetime for this one moment."

She pulled away suddenly, walked off a few steps, and covered her eyes with her hands.

"Jahoda, for the love of God, what are we doing?"

"Come," he said to her, quaking, beside himself with infatuation.

"Jahoda..."

"Come down, just for two hours...Come!..." He clasped her hands tightly and peered straight into her reeling, confused eyes; the flames of a powerful passion from deep within danced in his gaze.

"Yes..." Mařenka whispered after a while. She looked like a madwoman.

*

Lipovský left town that day, but Jahoda didn't go to the garden. He struggled until evening, and his struggle, his question, was a spiritual one: is this permissible for me? In this he was like a man who wants to roll an enormous stone from his path, a rock much exceeding him in size. Ultimately, self-interest prevails. He knew he was burdening his soul with an unforgivable sin, but he decide to evade that difficult issue of "Is it permissible?"....Then it occurred to him that no brutal abomination should be allowed to stain this pure and ideal love,—and so he calmed down, ostensibly. Despite this, he only endured the rocky course of that day with great difficulty. He felt as though an eternity was going to have to pass before that magnificent moment arrived when all the rest of her world would die away and they would reach nirvana, where their souls, wedded in the sacredness of perfect union, would sail over the resplendent waves of a planet fallen silent. "There can be no sin here!" he thought, and this conviction restored his peace of mind once more.

Towards evening, still making an effort to feign peace, he went to the town reading room. Lipovský's name came up in the talk of a group of people there. Jahoda shook. Coward! he said to himself.—It's all over now, said the voice of the cynic in him, popping up the instant he felt he had lost everything...The assembled people kept talking about Lipovský, who had gone to a neighboring district where the Germans were stubbornly using force to prevent a demonstration in support of the Czech national cause. Lipovský traveled there to support the Czech fighters with his eloquence, his experience, and his money.

Jahoda's soul was troubled. He left the reading room and roamed about outside the city with all hell breaking loose in his brain. His eyes were awash in red and yellow light, his nerves tingled as if he had a fever, and his blood singed him with its flames. In this state he reached his home, flung himself into bed, and began to weep. On account of Lipovský and of himself. He thought himself the vilest human being who had ever walked on the earth. Then he took a seat and wrote Mařenka a letter:

No, I will not be coming. Yet how I yearn to confess to you the happiness and the pain that are in my heart. I am afraid of a meeting like this. I am afraid that this tremendous love of mine might find some outlet, even if only in a single innocent kiss. I would never be able to forget it, and I would never find the strength moving forward to release my soul from a connection of that sort, which would both bless and poison my life. Tell me, what could that exalted soul of yours possibly think of me once your initial intoxication passed? While he, the glorious warrior, goes out to fight for his, and my, most dearly held ideals, I come to deprive him of that which is most beloved and holy to him, aside from his homeland. Imagine: he is that sublime, and I am that base! Would the choice between the two of us really be that hard for you? My concession is painful, indescribably pain-

*ful and difficult. This sacrifice, though, is even harder, and
I must place it on the altar, but not the altar of moral
law—rather that of our Czech fatherland. Be a loving and
sweet wife to him. Such a valuable recompense he has
doubtless earned. And I will go away. Don't forget me.
May our souls meet from time to time in the tender conversation with which you and he edify yourselves. Is that a sin?
I don't know, but I confess here and now that my soul will
simply have to assume the burden of a sin of this nature...*

That night proved sleepless for Jahoda. A titanic contest had begun in his heart and soul: burning desire
against heroic renunciation. He left town, announcing
that his mother had suddenly fallen ill.

The struggle was a hard one. Everything reminded
him of Mařenka. She seemed to crop up everywhere he
looked, every time a noise attracted his ear. Wherever he
directed his thoughts, there he encountered her, and
longing made his heart surge like the storm-stirred sea;
its powerful waves rose up and swamped the countenance of Lipovský, who kept his earnest, intelligent eyes
latched onto Jahoda the entire time...Now and again the
radiant idea came to him, like a lighthouse by a tossing
sea, that with the blood of his heart he had redeemed
for the Czech nation the man who had put its enemies
to flight like a lion. But even joy of that ilk was incapable of washing his soul in any kind of full, pure, and
peaceful glow; blood had puddled in his soul, blood
from his wounded heart, which he could have elevated
into sensuousness and incomparable happiness with one
decisive move of his own will. Many times he wanted to

submit, to give free reign to his heart in this hard-fought and unending struggle. And then he would again come to his senses and bow, painfully defeated, to his own triumph.

Some time later he saw a request for applications for a position as *kapellmeister* in the coastal region of Croatia. Jahoda sent off his application and was awarded the position.

In his heart, desire now made itself felt once more: if only he could see her again! Ultimately it would be the decent thing to do, taking leave of Lipovský and his wife in person, he reflected. But once he had made all the preparations for his visit, a thought occurred to him: would he truly be able to release her from his grasp if it should come to—and it really could come to—an intimate farewell just between the two of them? I would take her—I would take her away from him! Jahoda told himself, taking his head in his hands like a man in despair at his imminent ruin. And he did not go. He penned Lipovský a letter in which he described his heartwarming enthusiasm at going out among these far-off brothers, whom he had never before seen, these chivalrous knights, sons of the great mother *Slavija*.

But this elation, too, along with the impressions of his new dwelling place and new people he'd met—none of it could hold its ground against the passionate craving of his heart for Mařenka. His life was but one uninterrupted meditation on her face, one ceaseless yearning for her beauty. It would come, but for now he had not in the desperate longing of his heart been able to extol his own virtues with the thought of that noble sacrifice of his own happiness for the benefit of the "founding father" and patriot, his countryman Lipovský; that self-sacrifice in his current mood of full-blown cynicism came across to him sometimes as insanity and at other times as weakness. Then he would descend into a fit of fury and despair, which would rage relentlessly in his soul like a typhoon. Frequently he would be lying on his back fully awake and would play out the following in his mind: Mařenka and he are sitting at the piano, from which their hands are coaxing beautiful compositions, one after another in a tumultuous flow. In the midst of this improvisation, she frequently did not know which musical ideas were his, nor did he know which were hers: but nevertheless they worked in harmony producing delightful creations...Or it also happened that he was seated at the piano with her standing close by. He would strike several chords, and she would begin to sing. The beauty of her singing grew with the unsurpassed intensity of her notes, and his accompanying music enveloped her as if both the one and the other were flowing from the same spring...

At times he would jump up out of bed and go write down what he was hearing; but whenever he put pencil to paper, he found that his soul was already empty.

I don't have her, and without her I cannot create! he thought to himself one day, and then he started to feel like he was hearing the resolute voice of a righteous judge: Mařenka belongs to you!... And this thought took root and grew in him, the way good seed does when sown in moist soil. He came to be more and more firmly convinced that Mařenka belonged to him—for she did love him. And new thoughts confirming this state of affairs were in constant germination inside him.

He would theorize: if Mařenka does not love him but me—then how can there be a just law in either the human sphere or the eternal one according to which the two of us, Mařenka and I, should be consigned to suffering...? But Lipovský...? If Mařenka prefers me, and we explain to him reasonably that this is a matter of the law of nature against which we cannot set our brow, he too will have to acquiesce in his fate, if he is rational and just. And now Lipovský began to cross his mind less and less frequently, and his countenance vanished in the midst of Jahoda's unbridled desire for Mařenka.

At last Jahoda hit upon a plan: he would write to Mařenka and tell her to abandon her husband. To follow her heart. He will wait for her someplace in Vienna, from where they will both send a written explanation Lipovský's way, stating that what had to happen, did happen.

After he had written the letter, in which he demonstrated by more cold logic and reason the justification of his intention, and his plan for setting about it, he thought of something else: what if she doesn't agree? What if that sense of womanly duty holds the upper hand, and she's one of those for whom pride in a husband can replace love in the heart?...The egoist came to the fore now in Jahoda, as he was stretching out his arms for his prey. Love is more powerful than anything, he thought—and so he wrote a second letter. He described with poetic fire and vibrant, colorful detail his love and the miseries he was suffering on account of his longing for her. Thus he threw himself blindly into his plunder; it was as if he were in the dark, not caring whether or not he exploded in fires of damnation. She had to be his!...

"I have experienced," he wrote in her letter, "what it is like to live with you, and what it is like without you. This is, simply put, not a life. Rather it is a terrible and unrelenting sickness that can probably not even be cured by death. If you feel this way, too—then come!" For ten days afterwards he held on, existing in a dull, mechanical groove, prepared to deal with anything. Nothing could prove worse than what he had already lived through—and the very worst of it all had been the letter to Mařenka. He lived like a criminal, still alive after committing murder during a robbery, but awaiting his day of judgment in prison...

Finally, her answer arrived:

For Gods' sake, Jahoda, where have your thoughts taken you? My soul is deeply troubled and I know not how to interpret this other than to consider it the ploy of some wicked soul, a plot by our enemy. Return to us, and we can live as good friends, side by side; I am not looking for anything more, nor should you...

"Is this the nobility of her heart, or a calculation?" Jahoda asked himself. "Either way, I shall leave!"

He had already commenced preparing for a return to the Czech lands when a letter from Lipovský reached him:

Count K. is a descendant of a very old and aristocratic Czech family. For that reason alone, but also by dint of his

*wealth, he enjoys great renown and great influence. Al-
though he is not an adversary of his people, he is also not
what he should be, as a completely developed man. He is
not inspired by the idea of rights for our oppressed people,
as would befit a real Czech. The unfortunate circumstances
in which Czechs live have alienated him. Despite all this, it
seems to me that with the good will of our people backing
me up, we could win him over fully to our cause. Something
that I never knew earlier is that he is a passionate composer.
Let us not speak of the quality of his compositions. But
when I heard that he had set a hundred German popular
songs to music, I asked him, as a Czech aristocrat, to set a
suitable song of ours to music for an upcoming concert. I am
sure you understand my maneuver. The count hungers for
artistic glory, like all dilettantes, so—why don't we use this
noble weakness for the benefit of our cause?...Our young*
kapellmeister, *your successor, almost ruined everything for
me. When I presented him with the Count's composition,
he rejected it, saying it was worthless. Immediately I
thought of you. Therefore I am sending you this work by the
Count with the request that you correct it, and expand it,
according to the precepts of your art. And, furthermore:
lend it a few feathers from your wing. Don't worry about
how the Count might react to that. At first he will wonder
a bit, but then he will swear that all the delights in the
composition sprouted from his own head. Rework the composition, then, as you wish. You are the expert and you will
know how to help even the Count's feeble thoughts cut a
flamboyant figure. For now, don't play the severe professional judge. Think about how this is all a gain for our na-*

tional movement. In this case the maxim is justified: the end justifies the means...

Why haven't you been writing me? How are things for you there? The literary revival of the Croatian people has scarcely gotten rolling, so I know that the conditions there for your work cannot be particularly favorable. Don't judge too sternly. Conduct your work with patience and love, even if people can't always understand you! They are our brothers! But if you come to the conclusion that your marvelous talent is gathering dust there through disuse, then return to us. We will greet you—as you know—with open arms. Mařenka for some reason has lost her predilection for music since you left. But she sends you her warmest regards, too, and wishes you all the best from the bottom of her heart...

Jahoda's eye remained riveted to the letter. It was as if the lines had assumed the genteel outlines of Lipovský's face and the forthright expression in his good-natured and intelligent eyes. As if the letter contained the receptive soul of Mme Lipovskova, and it was the soul of the whole Czech people, too...Jahoda's mind departed for distant realms, but his body stood there frozen above the lines like a corpse. Quite a while, quite a long while, passed before he snapped out of it with a great sigh and looked back at Lipovský's letter, splotched with his own tears. He returned from some distant, bright world where he had been watching the golden-red rays of the sun rise up out of the night. In his heart day was breaking. Far away, in the darkness of that night, stood undiscovered that other Jahoda who had been prepared to do evil. But he had proven incapable of diving back into that night. Tear after tear dropped onto the paper—and Jahoda pressed his burning lips to his own fallen tears and to Mme Lipovskova's name.

*

"And she....Mařenka?" asked Amadej of his teacher.

"Mařenka?...You see, *chluku*, now that is an idea! She lives in Prague and has a son who is very highly respected, a lawyer and a major figure among our national leadership. Mme Lipovskova and her son have a lot of property—and, well, I'll be—Amadej, that's really an idea! Tomorrow I'll write her a letter—her and her son. They will support you while you're at the conservatory...Plus, he is a great patriot," the old man said all this and then fell silent. Amadej waited and waited for more, but the old man was now sleeping peacefully. Around midnight Amadej left on his tiptoes and went to his own house.

Amadej sensed that Jahoda had entrusted him that evening with an inexhaustible source of treasure, which he could use for a long, long time to sweeten the world for his heart. He now had certainly felt, and understood, both the beauty and the love of Mařenka Lipovskova; he could picture her before him and compare her with his sweet Adelka.

And like a glorious wave of light he felt in his soul that he would one day gaze into sweet Adelka's angelic eyes, see the love in them, and say to her: I love you.

Then he fell asleep, trembling with bewitching images of love, the kind born of a young and innocent soul.

One of the images that came to him as he slept was of himself playing the organ at a large gathering for Mass. He meant to strike a certain chord as introduction, a brilliant one, but from his hands came only muffled and morose minor keys, like something he would compose for a funeral Mass. He tried to resolve the mismatch between the particular ceremonial taking place at the altar—surrounded by innumerable candles, which made the dazzling, gilded garments of the priests sparkle and danced like stars in the bluish smoke of the incense—and the sullen chords resounding from the organ...Then he began to sing, but instead of a beautiful "Lord have mercy" of the solemn type Jahoda would have written for his voice, he intoned against his will a dull "For the eternal peace of..."

Jahoda's servant, an elderly woman, awoke Amadej from this heavy sleep. Her face was barely discernible in the first light of morning, but she said to him: "This night our master breathed his last..."

Chapter Four

After Jahoda's death, Amadej was hired on with the church choir, as the priest had promised. Amadej was content. His main concerns lay in ascertaining Adelka's age and finding out at what age young people could marry. From his elderly landlady he learned that Adelka was fourteen, and after hesitating for a long time he mustered the courage to ask the notary about that second issue. However much he tried to prepare cleverly for it, by covering his question with a veil of indifference, at the decisive moment his certainty left him. His voice shook and he spoke so fast and indistinctly that the notary had to ask him twice what he wanted.

"Well, well, now. You seem to be thinking about marriage already," he said, understanding Amadej at last. "Little Adelka, eh?"

"How do they know that? Amadej wondered, for he had not said a word to anyone that would betray the secret of his love.

At the auction of Jahoda's estate, he purchased, for an insignificant sum, the man's piano, his books, and his sheet music, but he saw nothing else of interest. A chest full of Czech newspapers and receipts for payments to the *Matica školska* were bought by a collector of odds and ends; the owner of a second-hand shop acquired Jahoda's clothes—and with that, having used up the old man, they buried him.

Amadej played the organ and inhabited an inner world, an isolated fairyscape concocted for him by his youth, with its golden and pink rays of light, free of shadows. He watched Adelka, with her golden hair and blue eyes, in the middle of a luxurious hall, the one in which Jahoda's Mařenka had lived; and he played her enchanted melodies on the piano, melodies that streamed from the center of her being to his heart.

Jahoda and Mařenka were the only ones who were allowed to enter this secret world, where infinite happiness and beauty were enthroned. From these quarters he produced compositions for types of people the world had no idea existed; the echoes of their praise and recognition for this music reached him through his heart; this was music that filled Adelka's soul with awe.

A year after Jahoda's death, Amadej found an announcement in the newspaper about a competition, sponsored by the *"Kolo"* Society of Zagreb. It was for several new pieces of work. "I should enter this competition!" he thought—but this idea did anything but give his soul peace.

He worked his fingers to the bone on the compositions, day and night; sometimes he'd dream presumptuously of the glory that he was going to achieve in the eyes of his co-nationals, especially Adelka, and other times he would imagine he'd been rejected, and he would fall to his knees in defeat and shame in front of the people of Zagreb and the rest of his homeland. Among a hundred other compositions in several arrangements and copies he had one piece based on the words of Lav Vukelić: "I love you, my ideal, like the sea..." He wrote it up one summer evening sitting below the old chestnut tree in his little garden; beneath its spreading branches a kind of everlasting tranquility, as in a church, hung in the air. He worked at it for an hour and a half, but afterwards he was beset until late in the night by indelible images, as if his mind could not return from that place where it, beholding the beauty in Adelka's eyes, had listened to the notes of his song and with their help communicated freely his love to her. Afterwards he was unable to find a suitable garments in which to present his song. There was no human voice, no musical instrument, that was sufficiently adroit and sensuous to perform it the way he had heard it in his soul, where those soft and radiant sounds had been more tender than the extended call of longing in the song of the nightingale; and where the quiet, sweet notes reflecting the look in Adelka's eyes, pliable like the golden moonbeams, had come pouring through the slumbering foliage in the treetops amidst the mystery of a summer night in the fairytale grove.

Ah, how the world will be dumbfounded, when it hears, and senses, for the first time the true sounds of love! For nobody had ever experienced the beauty and love of a woman the way Amadej had...

Two months after he had sent his composition away to Zagreb, he received a registered letter bearing the stamp of "The Croatian Choral Society '*Kolo*' of Zagreb." Every fiber of his being trembled as he began to read the letter: "It is a delight to inform you that your composition 'I love you, my ideal...' has been awarded second prize..."

For several days he carried the letter around like a pledge or deed. He read it to himself and aloud. He was of the opinion that his fellow citizens needed to see what a deity looked like. Amadej Zlatanić—composer! He couldn't conceive of anything more rarified or honorable. Letter in hand, he also went to see his guardian Plavčić...

"Have a look at this..."

"I heard already...And people are starting to laugh in your face, with the way you are crisscrossing the town and all...Two ducats isn't bad...But how long did you have to work to earn that much?"

"Half an hour. Not even that long."

"You're lying, little cousin. You're lying. Other people would join those musicians too if it were that easy to come by the ducats."

"I'm not lying..." Amadej responded, offended.

"You aren't lying? Well, then, little cousin, go work two hours every day for two ducats, and you'll live like a king..."

After Amadej's work was performed at a concert in Zagreb, the newspaper carried a brief story about it: among all the winners, the song by the hitherto unknown young composer Amadej Zlatanić really turned people's heads. Seeing his name in print for the first time, among those being fêted, meant that there was no power on earth that could keep him now from going to the conservatory in Prague. To this end he arranged for Plavčić to send him four hundred *forints* over the course of the next year as a loan, with the house as collateral.

Amadej's acquaintances—and that would include all the inhabitants of the town—neither approved of his plan nor tried to dissuade him from it. Some of them even remembered out loud that Amadej's grandfather on his mother's side was a dark man with Roma-like features; from that they concluded that Amadej had Gypsy blood in him and thus could never be content staying in one place.

Naturally, before he left, he went to bid adieu to Adelka's mother. She was an elderly woman, small-boned and angular; she had a worried look on her face and eyes that gave off a nervous, pained look from constantly asking that probing question shared by all old women: how much is the girl worth and where will she be of the most profit and use? And of course she could not help but notice that the boy was passionately in love with Adelka. She herself was a widow, with a meager pension from a minor official in some auxiliary government bureau somewhere, and on account of her bitter struggle for her daily bread from her earliest youth she estimated the value of every person and interaction according to the money involved. The fact that Amadej was leaving his own hearth to study music did not sit well with her. She viewed it as an act of youthful impetuosity. She believed that she had the right to oversee his every move, given his interest in her daughter, and therefore she decided to give him her two cents' worth about this business of travelling to Prague—admittedly to some degree, as well, in the desire of learning directly from him the exact tabulation of how much the travel would cost and how much profit could be wrung from it.

"They say you won't really do any work go there," she said, masking her true concerns with others.

"And who says that?" asked Amadej, energetically and with all the conviction of integrity and youth.

"That's how they talk...and for all I know, they're right!" she said, to challenge him. She did not take her eyes off the knitting in her hands.

"Ah, they are talking...But what do they know?" Amadej wanted to persuade her of the grandeur of the possibilities that traveling to Prague to study would bring within his reach, but he didn't know where to start. Meanwhile, Adelka's mother, emboldened by his embarrassment, piped up again:

"They say that you aren't doing the right thing... Somebody was totting it up this way: the church will be giving you twenty *forints* a month, and, over time, as the priest told someone, that will go up to twenty-five. That's no big deal, but, true enough, you won't need to worry about starving to death. Playing at Masses will bring in some money, and funerals will bring some, too, and you'll be earning a bit from giving music lessons. If you have a house and don't need to pay rent, then you can get by like that. You'll just have to tighten your belt and not waste money on things that aren't urgently needed. Yet now, I heard, you've sold the house?"

"I did not sell it. The first year I'm away, my guardian will lend me four hundred with the house as collateral. After that I'll get a scholarship."

"A scholarship? From whom? It's hard for poor people to get scholarships. And besides, I've never heard of a scholarship being awarded for music."

"They do award them! And how! Fame awaits me there...I just have to study..."

"All that's for rich people," Adelka's mother continued with quiet sarcasm. "And everybody knows what that Plavčić is like. He's still going to find a way to take that house away from you. And tell me, how do you plan to get that four hundred *forints* back into his hands? He'll be hitting you up for interest, repairs... and all of a sudden you will find yourself over your head in debt—and that house will no longer be yours. It'll be his."

This possibility left Amadej dumbfounded, and he was not at all inclined to reckon an experienced, ageing man such as his mentor capable of defrauding him like this. He understood nothing at all about buying and selling, but he did realize then that he was only going to stay in the old lady's good graces if he could demonstrate that he'd be able to pay off his school expenses without a hitch.

"But I daresay," he blurted out, quite flustered, "if I write just one opera, it could earn me thousands..." Then his face flushed and he added, in low tones: "The main thing is...I must complete my education."

"And who is it that's going to give you these thousands?" the elderly woman asked with malice in her smile.

"Who?...It happens out there that an opera can make twenty thousand forints for its composer..."

"Oh, please! Music—really?"

"There are also musicians who receive all kinds of honors, including the title of 'doctor.'"

"For music?!"

"Well, yes. Why shouldn't they get that for music?"

"Cross yourself, Amadej! I've had conversations with all sorts of people, with people who have traveled a lot farther out into the world than the two of us, but I've never heard anything like what you are saying. Before the late Mr. Jahoda came to our town, a man named Mato, whose nickname was Blinky, used to play the organ in church. He had that nickname because he was always blinking. He was a cobbler by trade. And, well, for doing the playing he got five *forints* per month. And when that Mr. Jahoda came, he got paid forty *forints* a month by the town council, with thirty more from the church. I know it because folks all over town griped about it. Even my late husband, who was a clerk in an office, got quite angry about the fact that a man who concerns himself with nothing but playing was receiving more pay than an official of the type he was. You be the judge—but you're talking about thousands?"

This examination grieved Amadej, and he was ashamed of what Adelka would think of this profanation of art, which he held to be the highest of all the pursuits of the human mind. But there you have it: the world sees it differently... How is it, how did it come to pass, that they cannot all at least get an inkling of what is magical about the world of sounds, the things human speech cannot express? Why is it that they don't sense their powerlessness in the face of music's message? Can it really be that their souls cannot ascend on the wings of rapturous chords up into the cosmic heights, where they would fly from star to star, listening to the speech of angels, and to the way angels cry and laugh?

"So how long are you going to remain in Prague?" was the next question from Adelka's mother, in a voice that indicated she had calmed down somewhat.

"Actually I am supposed to stay for six years."

"What the hell?" Now she was yelling straight into his face.

"There's a lot to learn there," Amadej said with a sense of self-importance and testy pride.

"Someone has pulled the wool over your eyes. Six years! In that time you could study to become a real doctor. But you already know that, damn it!"

"What I know about this is as good as naught."

"Well, how could you be up to playing the organ in our church if you don't know anything?"

"That's another matter."

"Another matter...Maybe you know something I don't, but I can't get my mind around this. Along with doing the church services, you could pursue something else here, too. You could, for instance, get a job as a clerk at the city hall. Because there isn't enough work in the church alone. But the person who idles is a loser on two fronts: you don't earn anything, and you spend what you ought not spend. I know this good and well because of the way things went with my late husband...At any rate, march to the beat of your own drummer but don't act in a way that you will regret later..."

Adelka listened to this conversation in submissive silence from the sidelines. Where her mother was involved, she had no will of her own. She knew that folks who have enough money live happily. In her own mind she found Amadej to be justified in deciding to go away to where he could procure fame and money. She was satisfied with this turn of events, but she didn't dare confess to her mother the contentment in her heart.

When the time came for leave-taking, however, Adelka's mother did not show even a trace of her earlier irascibility; she even gave him advice in emotional, motherly tones, about keeping up his health, being on guard around people he didn't know, and not spending money on superfluous things that aren't really necessary for life.

"You most likely won't actually be staying six years, right?" she asked abruptly, looking earnestly into his eyes.

"I certainly shall not; I'll stay three years, and after that I can study on my own."

"Three years..." the old lady said pensively, as if running the numbers on something in her head "even that's a lot. What do you think about the fact that things cost a lot in those foreign places, and the church is not going to give you a *heller* more after the one year?"

"But this isn't just about the pay. That's beside the point," Amadej smiled. But the old lady looked at him in consternation.

"It's not about the pay? Then what could it be about? Disavow these dreams of yours and stick to what keeps you in food. All of us—no joke—we all know what life is like when want is the order of the day. Your pay... That there could be something other than your pay!"

"Maybe it'll just be two years," Amadej said plaintively; he felt that this concession would restore him to her good graces.

"Well, but...that's still a lot for our town. I remember that now-dead cobbler named Mato, who maybe did not know as much as Jahoda, but, believe you me, the folks around here loved listening to him in church, as opposed to Jahoda.....And even I had to think: My hat's off to you, Jahoda, my friend, but when I hear you play it's like your inspiration is all dead and sad; but that Mato, he knew some note to play that would cheer your old heart right up. If you could learn about whatever note he used, you'd see how happy the people would be to listen to you. Even the late Reverend—he was quite a fun-loving fellow—he would say that he preferred Mato's notes to Jahoda's."

In the final moments of their goodbyes, the old woman indicated that she'd like to give Amadej a farewell kiss. He leaned over to her, and when he felt her kiss and saw the tears in her eyes, his own eyes clouded up. At that he gave his hand to Adelka and said, his voice full of sentiment: "Farewell!"

"Farewell," she responded quietly. She smiled bashfully and her face quickly turned red.

Amadej sensed that he had something more to say, a lot more, but it felt as though his lips were sealed and could bring forth no words.

"Write to us once in a while, and let us know how you're doing," the old woman told him, putting Amadej on the defensive, so that he replied with a bit of an edge in his voice: "I will. You know I will."

He went subsequently to take his leave from the mayor and the priest, on whom so much depended for a second year of funding, provided he made acceptable progress.

"I don't know how you'll fare out there..." noted the mayor. "You know, we have that saying, 'Ignore the tame one, but hunt down the wild.'...Ah, so it is!"

The priest was not in any better position to lend encouragement. "It's a wonderful thing, you know, for a young person to strive for advanced education, but—we don't know how to tolerate that yet. You'll work yourself to death over there, but no reward awaits you. The church has none to give, and the town is not going to want to pay you any more."

The next day, early in the morning, Amadej rode to the train station in a cart. As he passed by the little house where Adelka lived, he thought he saw her head through the partly open window. He waved his handkerchief in greeting and the window came all the way open and from the dark interior Adelka emerged. In the fresh fall morning she appeared to him as a wondrous angelic being. The exalted beauty of that face, sweet and pure, cast a spell on his soul.

Wherever am I going?—he wondered, fearful for the first time that he might lack the wherewithal needed for the colossal undertaking before him. He grew disconcerted; am I equal to the task I have started here?...It was as if he had just now fully realized that last night he'd held her small, warm, supple hand in his. And if he stayed, he could be with her every day. Weren't the priest and mayor right? ...After yesterday's goodbyes

Amadej now realized that he and Adelka belonged with her mother, and that they considered him one of their own. And life filled him with its forceful exuberance at the thought of that. In the east the sun was born, and its radiant red and gold disk rose up from the mountains. The pink meadows of the roadside tree trunks, on which mingled the green and red foliage and the withered leaves—they all appeared to tremble beneath the touch of the wondrous beams that unleashed such an abundance of voluptuous light. A symphony! Amadej remarked to himself, and he thought haughtily, with total confidence in himself, that he should sit down then and there and pen a full orchestral work called "Morning"...and the angelic sound of harps announced with tender, moving, sophisticated melodies the emergence of Adelka's profile...

"Quickly!...Quickly!...So we don't get to the train station too late!" he said to the coachman as he got carried away listening to the symphony that his soul was right then bringing into the world.

Chapter Five

In Prague Amadej noticed immediately that he vanished into the masses of people in the great city. He was alone—and without introductions or recommendations to anyone. And he also lacked the foundation and perspectives of a practical mind, which in such circumstances is our most trustworthy guide and reliable counsel. The unfamiliar panoramas and news of the metropolis were of only momentary interest to him; with sinking spirits he would ask himself why he had come here... And he was already starting to think that Adelka's mother was right, and the mayor and the priest, feeling that he had thrown himself—untrained in swimming—into the high seas during a typhoon. But then the image of Jahoda would start to take shape in his mind, and this image was always tied to the enchanted kingdom of music that he was now entering, to be bedecked someday with glory.

If only the lectures would begin already, if he could just make his way into them, then he would feel at home here, too, just like these thousands of people teeming in the streets focused exclusively on their own work and making way for each other mechanically, as if they were not seeing each other with their eyes but rather sensing other people's proximity through some instinctive awareness.

One thought served especially to brighten and fortify his soul: and that was the upcoming first meeting with his professors. He had always thought that these famous professors from his branch of the arts would read his soul with a single glance, discovering in him a genuine kindred spirit and gladly extending a helping hand to usher him, with enthusiasm and love, into the circle of the chosen ones.

Such a disappointment! He stood in a corner by himself while he awaited his turn, with huge crowds of younger and older people around; they had given him instructions on where to register, but after that no one took any further notice of him. It was as if they didn't even see him. In his hands he clasped his one recommendation—his compositions. All his faith resided in this one item. He waited. Finally it was his time, and he walked up to the wicket, behind which stood a desk.

"Your certificates?" a heavyset man asked from behind the lattice. He was the man in charge of matriculation.

But Amadej hadn't any certificates or school reports for his compositions. The fat man had a face that was not exactly unpleasant, but he was thoroughly bureaucratic-looking, plus he was evidently fed up with this kind of work. He took the composition and jotted down something on a form. Glumly Amadej awaited the man's judgment—and for the first time he feared that he would be rejected.

"Come tomorrow at 10 in the morning," the big man said at last. He casually inserted Amadej's document, along with the compositions, in a set of other papers.

As he left, walking uncertainly through the unfamiliar, long hallway, he noticed on the wall a large announcement printed in red letters. It said that today, at 12 noon sharp, the *"Hlahol"* Choral Society would be performing the premiere of the *chef-d'oeuvre* of *maestro* Dvořak: *"Stabat mater."* The composer himself would be conducting the performance.

I must go to that, Amadej thought happily. It was already 11:30, but if he hurried he could still make it to the concert hall on time.

The entrance fee was far from cheap, but the suspense generated by the large poster won him over. The river of people descending onto the Rudolfinum carried Amadej with it into a spectacular hall, where there were already a thousand people murmuring and creating a din of half-suppressed conversations. He immediately felt at ease here among so many faces showing sophistication and animated by joyous expectation and pride. The newspaper, clubs and societies, restaurants, coffeehouses, and private salons had all been spreading the word about Dvořak's masterpiece, and thus all the people there were beaming with happiness, conviction, and pride: the Czechs were once more presenting the world with a product of their mind and spirit of the sort that not even the Germans could demonstrate. This pride and sense of national celebration even Amadej had to share, and he wished that he were in a position to bring Adelka and her mother here to show them: so do you see now what kind of respect can be garnered by the musical arts?

A hundred musicians had already taken their seats in front of the stage. They were tuning their instruments, and Amadej's heart was filled with a strong, free-floating desire by the protracted notes of various types, and by the passages played by individual musicians as if they were having intimate conversations with their instruments in the final moments before the performance. Even the beats of the drums heartened him.

Shortly thereafter the platform began to fill with fine-looking women and men. They were attired in formal black. Some of them carried scores in their hands, and others did not, but they all had an air of importance about them, and they filled the space that seemed too small for such a massive assembly. The hall was still humming with the din of subdued voices, but everyone, including Amadej, was caught up in the excitement and expectations of something that was imperviously segregated from the whole of the outside world, the every-dayness of which would never reach these premises.

All of a sudden, as if by a magician's hand, the hall fell silent as a grave, and a man took his place atop a raised stand in the midst of male and female singers, a gentleman dressed in black, rather short and plump, with a full, tangled beard. He had barely appeared when the entire space thundered with the applause of thousands of hands and clamorous shouts of greeting to the composer, whose name filled the hall. Amadej, too, transported by the enthusiasm of the multitudes of people around him, put his hands together, and when he got up the courage to yell out the name "Dvořak!" himself, it was as if he were also being raised up to the throne of a grand Slavic genius. It caused his soul to shudder with ecstasy too great for words.

The great composer took a bow, almost as if all this uproar and glory were not directed at him. He raised his baton, thereby causing another immediate hush in the auditorium, which seemed to have been turned to stone by a single sorcerer's gesture. No one breathed. As still as in a photograph the vocalists all stood there, directing their eyes along with the hundred musicians' straight at the *maestro*. His hand moved, and an extended note, soft and full and warm, resounded in the hall, as if it were a gush of warm blood from a human heart. Then alongside it rose up a second, and then a third note, spiraling timidly, achingly, washing over the quiet of the hall in ever-expanding waves of sound like a river, which then made the air shake with a thunderous chord like an earthquake; then one after another the notes fell away again, until in the forlorn silence, so full of apprehension, remained just that one soft note, sounding of love and pain, and flowing on blood out of the heart of our most sublime Mother.

Amadej's mind was transported on these notes into a mysterious world where supernatural creatures made their presence felt in his body, called up by the power of the great Dvořak's artistic soul; and at his command they spoke their unearthly language. Right before Amadej's eyes, these thousand human heads, along with this splendid Prague hall, all disappeared, and somewhere up in the ethereal heights he could hear unseen figures proclaiming their pain in the language of music: *Stabat mater dolorosa*...But this dolor was exalted and holy, and his soul communed with it in emotion most magnificent. He yearned for it and floated with it in harmony with the universe.

Then robust applause, along with noisy enthusiastic shouts to the great artist, rattled Amadej. In place of the glorious, ethereal light, through which his soul had been floating, he beheld once more the hall full of people whose cries of acclaim knew no end. Dvořak, with a barely visible smile on his face, was obliged to turn around to the ecstatic crowd, whereupon Amadej tried to discern on that human countenance the genius that had conjured up such beauty. But he found nothing. A typical human face, and one wearing an expression of impatience at that.

The artist raised his baton anew, thereby silencing in an instant the boisterous hall that had been swelling and heaving like an ocean. The first chords of the second item on the program immediately pulled Amadej away with its hypnotic force to the site of another world, where he floated on the waves of notes until yet again that world faded like a phantom in the face of the shouts and tumult with which the enthusiasm of the audience burst in upon him.

In this way he spent an hour and a half of his life, in a marvelous dream, until the majestic finale of *Hallelujah* began to reverberate across the hall like the blaring of trumpets from a choir of angels. After that the auditorium roared with applause, squeals of delight, storms of enthusiastic praise—and on the stage the apotheosis of the artist had begun to play his role: they crowned Dvořak with wreaths of laurel, silver, and gold, to the unbroken accompaniment of unrestrained elation like that of a torrential mountain stream that catches hold of a thousand people as if they were one. Such an homage to genius Amadej was witnessing for the first time in his life; something ineffable constricted his breast, as if his own heart were squeezing the life out of him, and he was literally struck dumb. Then he began to weep. He was no match for his emotions, and they were transformed into physical pain.

The next day at 10 o'clock, when Amadej presented himself to the heavyset man who carried out the institution's administrative work, sitting behind his fenced-in desk, he was directed to betake himself to the auditorium where he would sit for an entrance examination given by the professors.

This bit of news unsettled him. He hadn't the faintest idea what they'd be testing him on, and, in addition, he felt like such a test was an expression of their lack of faith in his competence. He had never before considered the fact that a school for artists is a human institution, which also is concerned with the pragmatic goal of preparing people for life, and which therefore must necessarily take account of middling talents, or ordinary ones, and which cannot deal only at the level of the lofty and sophisticated. They are, to be sure, glad to discover a truly talented person here, but they do not count on his or her having a higher calling while in the institution's care; they keep such talents in the shackles of rule-books geared to practical ends, of frequently rigid and apparently superfluous regulations that date back God only knows how far into the past, and hector spirited souls, neglect individuality, and insist on their prerogatives with capricious obduracy.

Amadej had to wait an entire hour for the examination to begin. Dread of the test and impatience at the wait swelled within him. Look, he thought, at how things here are like the things in our town hall, or in our barracks—and he grew bitterly disappointed that even the freedom of the arts was fettered by chains of formalities that he had believed would have no place here, at least. And then he reasoned: there's not a single question coming up that I'll be able to answer. In point of fact, he had not yet learned anything at all. He had come here in order to begin his studies, and he had come relying on his deep and impassioned love of the musical arts; he was depending, too, on his will to learn and his native talent, for which the late Jahoda had vouched so many times in him. He considered all of that to be enough preparation to enter the conservatory. But they are demanding an examination of him. What will they ask?...An hour, stretching into infinity, had elapsed when the attendant told him it was his turn.

He took his place in front of a number of personages, whose faces he, in his considerable distress, could not clearly make out. He proceeded with resignation in his heart of the type that overcomes people with weak nerves when they are forced to take the plunge and make some decisive step or other. The examination lasted a full hour, after which they sent him back to the room where he had been holed up before the test began, so that he could await there the communication of the conclusions reached by the committee of professors.

Whenever he tried, during the waiting period, to think back on what they had asked him and how he had answered, or what they had given him to play, and how he had played it—he couldn't recall a single definite occurrence. The whole of the examination had passed with him in a kind of mental swoon, through which he heard some of the foreign words and names for the first time in his life. Now that he was conscious again, he felt once more ill at ease and grievously disappointed. He had anticipated that these stately arbiters of music, the artistic leadership, would recognize him at first glance and greet him with open arms and calls: "You are one of us!" But that didn't happen. Vis-a-vis Amadej they were cold, as unresponsive as corpses, nearly causing the disillusioned Amadej to put them in the same category in his mind as his rustic co-nationals, who were also incapable of understanding him.

At last the attendant turned up again and motioned with his head for Amadej to return to the room where he had sat for the examination. The professors were all sitting at the same long table, staring indifferently at him. One of the older gentlemen removed his spectacles from his face, looked Amadej pleasantly in the eyes, and began speaking, slowly, as if he were reading from the document that he was holding:

On the basis of your request to enter our institution, a committee of professors from the school of music has examined you on this day and found that, while you possess an indisputable musical talent, you have neither sufficient knowledge nor the necessary skill to guarantee that you would be able to make successful progress in this school. For that reason the committee, in fulfillment of its duties, concludes that it is not possible to accept you into this institution.

With that the room began to spin around Amadej.

I shall study, night and day, he said, holding out his folded hands imploringly toward the professors. Tears were forming in his eyes, and through them he kept looking at the fuzzy profiles of his inquisitors.

"We cannot go against the procedures of this institution," he heard one of them say. It was the same voice that had just slowly enunciated the previous sentence word by word.—"But, you know what?" continued the same voice after a pause. "Study privately for a year and then join us."

Yes, certainly. Private study. You have nothing to lose by that, another voice added—and then the scraping of the chairs was audible and, with Amadej watching through his tears, the professors vanished from the room one by one like a dissolving photograph. Amadej stayed there, alone.

What is to be done? A desperate Amadej put his head in his hands...Now what is to be done?

That evening he found himself once again in the theater. There was an opera performance: *Faust et Marguerite*—the first opera he watched and listened to. The music, however, remained the one kind of communication that he understood fully, and with his heart. As he reveled in Gounod's music, he forgot how terribly crushed he had felt. But now that depression returned, with all its bitterness and pain, bringing tears once more to his eyes.

"Why did they reject me?" he asked himself over and over—and his bitter realization that artists were people, susceptible in this life to the weaknesses common to all humanity, grew and grew... "They rejected me!" he said to himself, and in that painful interior voice the harmonies of Gounod's music were stifled, and the plot on the stage drowned in his tears.

For two more days he wandered about the city, undecided on his course of action. The recognition that he had in him an indisputable talent for music was the first point of light to start to appear in the gloom of his soul. This admission, from unimpeachably competent quarters, served to rouse him from his apathy, and he took the decision to study privately, as they had advised. He located a tutor and prepared to enter the predictable course of life of a pupil, with just one goal in front of him: lessons. And with just one chief thing in mind: to learn. Thus it was now time to rearrange his budget. From the four hundred *forints* put at his disposal by Plavčić, in accordance with their agreement, he now had, after various outlays three hundred and sixty. In order for this sum to last a whole year, he would allow himself to spend thirty *forints* per month. After a lot of ciphering, he finally wrote his expense estimates on a clean sheet of paper:

Apartment, lighting, and laundry .... 8 *ft.*
Rental of a *pianino* .... 3 *ft.*
Tutoring fees for 4 hrs/month .... 8 *ft.*
Midday meals .... 6 *ft.*
Tickets to theater and concerts .... 4 *ft.*

Total: .... 29 *ft.*

He thus had one *forint* a month for odds and ends. Amadej gave a quick grin; he felt rich; and he placed his budget on top of his cash as a kind of memento.

He found lodging at an old lady's apartment in an outlying district of the city; he had a room that was bright and pleasant, albeit small. To reach his room, he had to go through the kitchen, where the lady slept and, indeed, spent her entire day. But then he commenced working the way great talents do when they are filled with zeal, when they have set their sights on a great goal towards which they are goaded on constantly by the hot and vigilant spurs of their soul.

He adjusted flawlessly to his new life, and to the dryly mathematical side of instruction in theory, which seemed to have naught in common with art. He had believed he would find the golden keys with which to enter the realm of secret sounds and notes as soon as he journeyed to Prague, but there he was on the receiving end of lessons that were tough and bitter, for they were diametrically opposed to what with his whole being he had believed music to be. But, thinking of Jahoda and his words of wisdom, he bent to the will of his teacher: *per aspera ad astram...*

In addition he began to be tormented by hunger. The organism of this young man, an eighteen-year old, could not tolerate an interval of twenty-four hours between meals out. When sitting over his books of an evening, his stomach would remind him incessantly of its rights. He considered it, at first, a deed of heroism, of idealistic aspiration, that the sensation of hunger could not derail his work.

He had the impression that the kind, blue eyes of old Jahoda were fixed on him, and that he, satisfied, was nodding his head in approval. Later, whenever he was in the theater and would watch the commotion of people around the table of choice finger-foods, he started to feel embattled by an unpleasant emotion as well as the physical sensation of hunger: see the way they live! And how much of a support it would be to me if I could get just a scrap of bread every night...So, many were the times when, tormented by hunger in this way, he wanted to dip into his money, but, there atop his cash would be the budget, on its folded sheet of paper, fighting back like a living creature: Forbidden! But a healthy young man cannot fly in the face of a firm law of nature forever; he cannot stare at his money like a senile miser whose chief sensation in life has become the hunger for property. His budget protested and dug in its heels whenever Amadej considering focusing on money: Watch yourself! You are in breach of our agreement!...But one evening, when Amadej had analyzed a chord the way his teacher wanted, he went over to his suitcase, lifted his budget figures off the money, and delighted by the merriment in his soul began to talk to the piece of paper in a way that was certain to lead to eating: "Thank you, my friend, for your faithful service...but here is where we part ways. Forgive me, but hunger is more powerful than either of us..."

And with that he ripped the budget sheet, so rationally and conscientiously composed, into pieces. In addition to the budget, he had severed one other unpleasant connection, against which he had many times had to struggle vociferously. This had to do with visits to the theater and concert venues. Even if he were content with getting the last place in the theater, where he would stand there with the score in his hand and follow the performance of the opera, or with the last little seat in one of the concert halls, still the four *forints* vouchsafed him by the budget for such excursions barely lasted for the first half of the month. For him the opera stage and the concert hall were not simply a luxury and pleasure for his soul. Rather they comprised the real school where, with pure excitement, he would begin to discover the mysteries of how various artists create heterogeneous kinds of beauty from the same materials. What a tremendous difference there was between the school and his instructional materials, where the spirit of art was chained to dry, lifeless, cold paragraphs, clauses, and provisions. Is it possible that Gounod, Tchaikovsky, Verdi, and so many other geniuses and composers had to squeeze their spirit into the lethal corsets represented by these paragraphs? The countenance of old Jahoda would again pass before Amadej's eyes: the rules of art are the freedom of the artist. And Amadej respected Jahoda as a father figure who was incapable of lying—and therefore he would throw himself with redoubled energy and enthusiasm into swallowing this dry and acrid sustenance of articles and items sliced by a scalpel from the dissected body of the arts.

After a year Amadej passed the examination with flying colors and was accepted into the advanced class of the music school. He sent news of his success to the mayor by telegram, after having to change the last tenner of his stipend for the telegram fees. On the same day he sent a written request to the mayor, asking for his intercession with the town council, to whom Amadej had just put in a request for further support. Without it, there could be no talk of a prolonged stay in Prague, and he also proceeded urgently with his application for another reason: it flattered his youthful sense of vanity for those people who discouraged him from coming to Prague, because he supposedly already knew enough—for them to see that he'd had to toil away for an entire year just to acquire enough knowledge to be accepted into the conservatory! He believed that in his home town people wouldn't be talking about anything save his success on that exam. And above it all jutted Adelka's angelic face: he had increased in stature in her eyes, and become more worthy of giving her his heart.

But he himself indeed did not value what he learned from books, no matter how much labor it cost him to gain this knowledge. It seemed to him that he had known every bit of it at the time he came to Prague, but he just didn't know how to reproduce it the way it was written up in the books. For that reason everything that accumulated in him by dint of listening to concerts and operas constituted a priceless treasure-chest for him. In it there was incomparably more wealth than in all the books that he had acquired at great expense and plowed through with a groan. All that had been learned by the musical geniuses of the past several centuries took up its place in his heart like light that directs its rays straight into an enchanted temple of everlasting beauty and becomes fruitful.

His being was drenched with learning of that kind. In his books, where the unity of notes had been subjected to culling, cracking, and mincing, by way of choice arguments used to investigate why something is beautiful, he looked in vain for answers. Beauty found a way to manifest itself; he was aware of it and lived with it, but it protected its essence with secrets against every effort of esthetics to remove the otherworldly veil from its goddesslike body. That's the reason the books were boring to him, repulsive; they were created by speculative science to accompany and lay the foundations for the success of a work of art, to create the conditions for its origination—but he reveled only in works in which he sensed according to his innate artistic calling a powerful force of spirit, which grew in the hour of creation into a state of absolute freedom, where essentially the entire material world disappeared from his mind.

Six days later the mayor's answer arrived. He congratulated Amadej warmly on his successes. Regarding the assistance, he wrote: "...I will stand by you in this matter; at the very next session, your request will be on the agenda—and, for my part, I shall speak in favor of granting it." Amadej was pleased with this answer—and he needed to wait only a bit for the financial help. He was a familiar figure in the restaurant where he had taken his meals for a year now, and his elderly landlady knew him even better; he would only have to survive on credit, then, until that support arrived...And that is indeed how things went. The most unpleasant part of it for him was not having the means to pay for his piano rental. The owner, whom he apologetically sought out, said, "All right...all right..." in a tense voice, but his face stated rather clearly: "Just so you know, I'd prefer it if you forked over the payments regularly."

In this manner a month passed, in which he lived without a *fillér* to his name. Once again he had to dispense with suppers, and, considering the energetic demands of a young person's stomach, this was hard on him. His landlady started to ask him once or twice a day:

"So, Mr. Amadej, any money yet?"

"Nothing..."

"Hmmm...Well, I guess we'll have to be patient for one more day, then..."

"Maybe we'll even have it by tomorrow," he told her every day, feeling ever smaller, less worthy, and more depressed.

"Why aren't they sending it to me?" And he would try to reason things out, deluding himself with the sharpness of his intellect, which had been murdered by the paltry details and rigid formality weaving its way around bureaucratic offices like cobwebs several centuries old, in between the half-ruined walls of some medieval castle.

Then he began noticing the way they no longer served him in the restaurant where he was wont to eat with anything approaching the readiness and kindness that had been evident earlier, when he had been paying in cash. He would find himself obliged to remind the server several times to bring his food, and, when he would finally show up with it, it was impossible for Amadej not to notice on the man's face and in his sometimes insolent gestures that he was waiting on Amadej against his will. His sensitive soul was hard-pressed to endure this—but, alas, he had to eat at least once a day. So, Amadej thought to himself, "Just you wait. When I get my money, I will surprise you with such a lordly tip that you'll be ashamed of having acted this way towards me!" One afternoon, though, he waited in this frame of mind for a quarter of an hour while the waiter pretended not to see him and failed to bring his meal. Amadej hesitated to address the man; he felt that he had no right to make demands in a place where they were apparently feeding him out of charity. Tears of shame welled up in his eyes...If those people back home could only get it through their heads that life should come first, not bureaucracy! These thoughts were painful to him, but he called the server over to his table.

"Please," Amadej said quietly, "I still haven't gotten any soup." The blood rushed to his face.

"I've been instructed not to bring you any food," the server replied. And he gave Amadej a scornful look and moved away.

This was too much for Amadej's gentle soul. Never before had there been such a head-on collision between the world that lived and breathed in his heart and the world that he inhabited. He would surely break down when his soul felt this insulted, for it loved all people and believed in everyone. Could it be that not everyone recognized the holy calling within him? Is it possible that they could, with such implacable coarseness, spurn him—he who felt that he should be protected, adored, and received with exuberance because his heart held that which is greatest and most beautiful in human beings?

Amadej retreated from the city, far away, into the isolation of the high hills along the Vltava, where he sat dejected, with the river meandering majestically at his feet. What he was having to endure was not just the insult to his honor—they had after all said to his face "We don't believe in you." And it was even less about a man whose food had been taken away; he no longer felt physical hunger. It was the artist in him who was suffering, the person who always believed that the world venerated what he himself most revered; the poet-musician was suffering here, the kind that has less conflict with the everyday, material world through his or her art than any other artist. This was why he was weeping over his soul, with its holiness defiled and its nature misunderstood by others.

It was already the beginning of fall; and it was the type of day that is rare in the north at that season: the sky clear, with no cloud cover, the air agreeably warmed by the sun that was reflecting off the Vltava below him and flooding with light the enormous space above the old, old city. In his heart Amadej was transported back to the beloved region of his birth, back to the little

101

house of his parents, where he could still sense, through poignant tears, the warmth of his long-deceased mother's heart. How glorious were those autumnal days of his childhood, when at daybreak, in the cool of the morning, he and his school buddies would shake fruit from the trees into the dew-damp grass...He would place in the underbrush twigs smeared with lime to catch goldfinches, bullfinches, and other birds...following with his eyes great flocks of turkeys and geese as well as the peaceful cattle out to pasture in wide fields...and young boy and girl shepherds stoking their little fires amidst the bushes, to keep warm and cook their potatoes...A young shepherd with a turned-up little nose, barefoot in the dewy grass, barked something at him with irritable bravado, but then a young shepherdess, with large chestnut-colored eyes and smoothly brushed blonde hair, who evidently felt sorry for Amadej, offered him a baked potato: Take it. Don't be afraid. He won't do anything to you...And the shepherd boy approached him, and when the two boys stared into each other's eyes, they all at once became endeared to each other, without either one knowing why...Soon the sun broke through the fog, the lingering fingers of which then disappeared in the brightening air, and on the plains the dew began to coruscate like flung pearls...And then gorgeous melodies began to resound from the bells of the steeple of the local church...and Amadej drew away abruptly from the pair of little shepherds and the birds and the apples, and he flew up and over to the town so he could take his place in the choir loft before Jahoda...And everything in view around him quivered with the same tremendous happiness that had permeated all of nature and everything alive.

He was utterly beside himself with joy at the poetic idyll of his childhood, and for a while he completely forgot the harsh encounter his soul had had with the realities of our self-seeking world...Adelka! Oh, Adelka!—he thought—when will I be able to rest my weary, aching head in her lap, to feel her place that blessedly tender hand on my feverish brow, to look into her loving eyes that hold the cloudless skies of childhood and to hear her reconcile them with the world: It's a scourge and a trial, Amadej, but I understand you! The thought of this awoke in his soul the resplendent angel-mediator, a smile on her face cheering his soul by pouring into it the sweetness of the belief that he could not hope for any greater happiness than that which her words bestowed upon him: Amadej, I understand the sublime song in your heart...And he exulted in the feeling that Adelka's and his souls were harmoniously bound up together in a marriage of love and poetry. For had not Jahoda also felt this way in this very land—now sprawling before his eyes—when he knelt in front of Mařenka in the fever of his love? And he felt the old man's proximity, more so than ever; it was as if his spirit were biding with Amadej, stroking his brow and in his soothing, paternal voice, reminding him: Amadej, *per aspera ad astra*...

Peace returned to Amadej's heart. From the west the golden light of the sun spread over the smooth waters of the Vltava, while over Prague the smoke from the towering factory chimneys descended like clouds. A steamboat moved along the river, prodigally heaping up two piles of silver sheaves behind it, and from the top of its mast a flag fluttered triumphantly in the crystal-clear air. In vain did the waters resist, with involuntary force, the victorious progress of the ship; a strength from within the ship sliced with deliberate heedlessness through the waves that were smashing petulantly against its prow...Onward! Onward! This began to toll in Amadej's soul, where the light of assurance commenced growing, and where tossed and swelled the power that is born of belief in one's victory.

Chapter Six

When difficult days began piling up for him,
one after the other, the first thought that
would assail Amadej in the morning when he
opened his eyes, was: You have naught to eat...And
whenever he met her, the elderly landlady would ask
him now, in a voice ever more impatient: "What d'you
mean? Still no money...?" The piano's owner had already written on two occasions: I see in my account-
books that you still haven't paid the rental fee on that
leased piano for three months now, despite our written
arrangement that you would always pay one month in
advance...He had already hocked his watch and golden
ring, the memento of his father, and he had sold a Jewish dealer in second-hand goods everything that he
could sell from his modest supply of linens and clothes.
All of it was tipped into his hungry stomach, abandoning Amadej nonetheless to the dire uncertainty of not
knowing when there'd be an end to these insufferable
days that sent his soul reeling with shame.

At last the decision of the city council reached him:
"In its session, held on the—day of the month of —,
this Council found that your request, directed to us in

search of financial support for the duration of your studies at the conservatory there, is not acceptable..."

Amadej went numb. "What now?...People will be accounting you a swindler...and what are you going to eat? "And then, with stubborn insensitivity steering him completely, an sublime thought in him stirred with life all of a sudden: he would sell his house to Plavčić!...He told himself this in the spirit of quiet but inexorable resignation with which one's heart accepts the last available solution, no matter how repellent and arduous that way out had seemed earlier.

Then another letter reached him, this time from the priest.

Be consoled, and put your hopes in God. Just bear in mind that this is the destiny of talented poor folks among all the small nations. But I will give you some advice. They say that the new sub-prefect in our district understands and truly loves music. Address yourself to him by letter at the same time that you re-send your request to the City Council. The Council has a bit of money these days, because it recently sold off a large tract of forest holdings. If the sub-prefect were to speak on your behalf, the Council would certainly do what he wished. In the most recent elections I ran afoul of the mayor and most of the town councilors, and for that reason my intervention for you wasn't worth much of anything. It even worked against you, on their pretext that things should simply go counter to my wishes...Take care that you make that letter to the sub-prefect nicely worded and humble, and copy it over in nice handwriting. Don't forget to address him with the appropriate title: "The Honorable..."

Amadej immediately reworked his application to the city council and drafted a letter to the sub-prefect, but he had no means with which to buy either nice, clean paper or postage stamps. Help was not forthcoming from any quarter, so he would have to sell the property that he valued the absolute most—namely the compositions of Bach, Haydn, Mozart, Beethoven—by means of which he had, in his most difficult times, entered the consecrated world closely akin to the one built into his heart.

He wrote to Plavčić. Having thought the better of things, he asked him to lend him another hundred *forints* against the value of the house, at whatever interest rate he chose. Plavčić responded forthwith:

"...What in the world has gotten into you, little brother? Why would you write about my lending you more money against the old house? It's not even worth the amount that you've already received from me. Everything about it is old, it's in need of repairs, there are the taxes to consider, and the rent that I receive for it barely covers the interest on the former debt. Instead, the best way for you to solve your problems is to sell me the house. I'd give you another hundred *forints*, which I wouldn't do for anyone else, because it's not worth that much. Life here is tough. We work ourselves to the bone and have nothing for it. When you've finished your schooling, you'll get a salary—but me?..." And on and on it went.

The holidays were close at hand, and it was time to register at the institute. Amadej's only advisors were disgrace and hunger. And he sold the house to his guardian.

Two months later he learned of the decision of the town council regarding his entreaty. He was to be given an annual stipend of a hundred and fifty *forints* when he had real achievements to show, in the form of a certificate of acceptable progress at the conservatory. The first exam he could take was at the conclusion of the winter semester—how was he to get by until then?

He found comfort and hope, that indefinite hope that arises in creative but impractical people after apathetic contemplation of their future.

By the Christmas holidays he was once more penniless, there was no one to whom he could write, and it was still two full months till the first exam. He would get along for that length of time somehow, he thought, even though for that "somehow" he possessed not even the most tenuous guarantee.

Just before Christmas itself Amadej experienced something capable of suppressing, even if only for a brief moment, the everyday worry in his belly about bread, a worry that cost him half of his concentration when he studied. The students were being allowed for the first time to try their hands at independent compositions!

To be sure, Amadej's professors and classmates respected him as a very talented person who knew how to produce excellent contrapuntal compositions. But precisely because of the unbending rules of this subject, the pedagogical approach to composition appeared to him in a completely different light, and not as something lofty and inspirational as he had imagined before he entered the conservatory. The old professor who taught counterpoint, an experienced, sober, and learned teacher, did not truly understand the freedom of study in the way that the buoyant young spirit of Amadej hungered for.

He would praise all of Amadej's work, but in doing so he would make a hundred comments such as: "It's good like this, but you aren't allowed to work in this manner yet." Amadej couldn't comprehend this: it's good—yet nonetheless I am not permitted to do this kind of work! To his inquiry, the aged professor would have just one response: "The laws of art are the freedom of the artist..."

Amadej was, in the final analysis, of the opinion that this maxim had attached itself to the elderly professor and that he, like Ahasuerus, was now under a curse and must carry it around with him through the world until such time as death would deliver him from this evil...So it was that Amadej's first independent work—the topic was up to each student—won the full approval of his old professor, and of a majority of the students. Amadej composed a piece for *gusle* and piano and called it "a poem without words." In reality, it grew out of a program that he worked out one evening while strolling on the banks of the Vltava, which was throwing off the magnificent light reflected from a hundred street-lamps on the bridges and banks of the river. It made him think of his home region, and of his Adelka. As if he had mustered his entire soul into these simple words: "To you, Adelka, runs my mind's every thought, and my heart beats only for you."

In his soul these words flowed into notes, and that very evening he catalogued in writing what he had heard in his mind. The work was judged to be among the successful ones composed by the institute's young charges, and the old professor of composition listened to it with interest. Still, he was unable to refrain from comments of this type to Amadej: "It's pretty—if too free and uncontrolled. You're going to lose the reins, man—and then what will you do with those fiery steeds of your southern imagination?"

Once again those distressing mornings began to come one after another, calling Amadej to wakefulness with the thought: you have nothing to eat...And the hunger and cold and even the otherwise good-natured landlady—they all screamed threats at his aspirations like an angry monster against which he could not hold his own. He had sold almost all of his threadbare clothing and linens to the second-hand goods shop; he slept always in one of the same two nightshirts, from which he had cut out the backs so he could use them as handkerchiefs. He asked for more help from the priest and received as a reply a sympathetic letter full of paternal admonitions to work hard and not abandon his trust in the Almighty.

On New Year's Eve he roamed about the city, a forlorn man. Despair and resignation had crushed his soul. "I can't...I just can't...," he said to himself and tried to think of ways to get back home: hunger had finally clipped his strong, enthusiastic wings. Wandering across Vaclav Square, the sign on one of the loveliest of the palaces there struck his eye: Dr. Jan Lipovský, Attorney...and in an instant his battered soul rose up and he took heart once more as if that name and that name alone could lift him up out of his affliction and fortify his soul with hope. Sure enough, this was Mařenka's son, and it was possible that she herself was still alive. What it would be like to meet the woman whom Jahoda had loved so passionately! It would almost be like seeing Jahoda himself again. He was convinced that he had to go see her—and, because of the events of this single unexpected moment, he was saved. Saved!

Amadej paused not far from the front doors of the palace, in front of a shop window, to gather his thoughts. How should he gain an audience with this woman? First things first: if she should catch sight of him in this worn-out suit, reminiscent of some kind of wastrel from the streets of the big city, she'd be suspicious. But if he told her everything—and Amadej found himself transported, in the midst of his luminous thoughts, into a brilliant future that his opportunity was revealing to him. Jahoda's "*Impromptu*" came back quite clearly to him. Oh, what memories would awaken in Mme Lipovskova when he played her that composition about which Jahoda himself had averred that no human ear had ever been privy to apart from Mařenka's and Amadej's.

Meanwhile an elegant coach, with two liveried attendants at its flanks, came clattering out of the gates. Two women were seated inside. One was an imposing older woman with hair as white as snow and a stern look in her grey eyes, to which she raised her lorgnette from time to time. The other was a sumptuously dressed young lady.

Before Amadej could get a good look at the older woman's face, the coach shot away like an arrow, following tracks already pressed into the snow. Amadej sprang at a leap over to the watchman, who had saluted both ladies in military style, and he asked who they were.

"The mother and the wife of the attorney, Lipovský," answered the guard, looking dubiously at Amadej's outfit.

"Would the older lady's given name happen to be Mařenka? Do you know?"

"It is. Mařenka," came the guard's sullen response before he moved on.

"That's her then. For sure, it's her" Amadej said to himself, looking down the wide street towards the carriage rolling out of sight.—"So that's the Mařenka with whom Jahoda was in love...I'll bet she has the fondest memories of him! And that will mean help for me!" These were his thoughts as he determined to present himself to the elderly lady on the morrow.

At dawn the following day, he had scarcely opened his eyes when he was greeted straightaway by the horrific realization of a starving man: once again there is nothing here to eat. But then a comforting glow registered in his heart, because today was the day he would pay a call on Mme Lipovskova. He began in earnest his preparations for that visit, marshaling in his mind the various ideas and events that he should mention right off the bat. And his means of relating these things must be carefully chosen, because after all this matter has its delicate aspects, and they could produce, instead of his intended result, a fully negative reaction in the old lady. And wouldn't you know it—when Amadej arrived at this thought, a complete *volte-face* emerged from his heart. All of a sudden the sensitive poet was there, and he resisted staunchly the intended action. With a kind of cynicism he began to ask: what will I tell this lady?...Fine, I'll talk to her about Jahoda, and perhaps it will interest her to hear how he lived and died. But what then? She'll get a look at my ragged clothes and will think: I see, I see...You did not come here on my account, or on Jahoda's, but because you are looking for a handout...And she'll offer me alms and perhaps think to herself while she's doing it: it is what it is. Our Jahoda seems to have ended up among people such as this! Amadej felt the rage within him kindling, as if the insult were not the product of his lively imagination but had already been aimed at his people. "Nope, I cannot go there," he concluded. He remained in his bed.

But then hunger began to speak.

"What if you told her everything that Jahoda told you? How he found you worthy of his confidence and the secret of why he penned no further compositions. Not after being forced to renounce the woman who alone was capable of filling his soul with joy and creativity. What if you told her how he loved you, too..."

Then the poet in him entoned: "At that she would respond, justifiably, and with revulsion: Jahoda did not really know you, sir; he considered you a different kind of person and therefore he revealed to you things that he shouldn't have revealed to anyone...How much is it worth to you, Judas, to betray your teacher?"

And he was utterly convinced that he dare not pay a call on Mme Lipovskova.

On the eve of Three Kings he passed another whole day without eating. On Three Kings itself he found himself still lying in bed at noon, eyes wide open; the freezing room played host with mute indifference both to him and to the specter of hunger. He lay there listening to the terribly discordant chords drowning out, with demonic delight in their victory, the gentle, quiet song in his soul. These dreadful chords—they were hunger's composition. Just as the devil did to Tartini—so it was in his case hunger that dictated this harrowing piece of music. It would wake him up, and then it seemed to him each time that he had been dreaming of the melody and hearing it in his sleep. He would jump out of bed, grab paper and a pencil, and, retreating again under his quilts, would begin to jot down the terrifying dissonances through which the infernal melody wound. All at once he felt an unaccustomed weakness. His eyes fogged over, the pencil fell from his hand, and he was overcome by unconsciousness. "It's from the hunger," he thought to himself when he came to. And he cried out: "No, no, I cannot go on like this." From a church in the vicinity bells rang out, announcing Mass. The bright, full winter light illuminated his little room, yet he shrank from it: he felt he could still perceive the iciness of outside in it. "No, this is no way to live," said, and he called out for his elderly landlady.

Her gray head appeared in his doorway.

"Still in bed, eh?...Since yesterday afternoon! Let me guess: they still haven't sent your money?"

"I'm hungry..." He could say no more. He buried his face in his hands and wept.

"O, my God. Just look at that—oh dear God!" the old woman gasped, looking at him with sympathy. "Oh, this would be easy, if I weren't poor myself. With what you pay me I pay my own rent. When there's trouble in your world, there's trouble in mine...Why haven't your people sent you the money?...And, isn't there some way you can help yourself?"

"But how? I am a foreigner here, and unknown...But in two months I'll have a steady income again...I can show you the letter. Then I'll pay back everything."

"Nobody's going to give you money on the basis of a letter...You know how to play the piano, though, and tomorrow the dancing season begins. Why don't you play at the dances in some restaurant or other?"

"Absolutely! But where?"

"OK. I'll go ask around, if you're not up to it. See there? You would have starved to death and you didn't know where to turn, just to earn a bit of money..."

The old lady left for her kitchen and brought back a plate with several Christmas pastries on it.

"Take these and eat...I'll go see about things." She soon returned, and from the door she announced cheerfully:

"So, didn't I tell you? Get dressed. We'll go over together. They want you to make a dry run. Right here in our street there's someone who needs a piano player."

Amadej sprang up. In less than a quarter of an hour he was standing before his landlady, ready to go out.

The elderly woman led him to a small nearby restaurant with a colorful illustrated sign hanging above the doors: The Sea Crab. Inside the folks were just completing the preparations for the first dance of the evening. They were rearranging the stools under the direction of the heavy-set proprietor, who met Amadej with a suspicious, forbidding look and addressed him curtly. Experience had taught him to handle his piano men like this. After a short wait he led Amadej over to an old piano. Amadej took a seat, pushed back the lid, and warmed up with a short improvisation. The tavern-keeper watched his every move with a discriminating eye; from the preparations alone he wished to determine what sort of piano man this was, who had accidentally crossed his path. In addition the publican's wife was there with them, a short woman, with a wide, full body and a pleasant face—and the cook was there, too, a tall, able-bodied woman, no longer young, with strong, sinewy arms and legs on which the kitchen clothes rested weightlessly, as if they didn't belong there. And, last but not least, the waitress, a comely brunette of nineteen. And of course, there is Amadej's landlady, as well, in the role of marshal of the proceedings to decide on his worth. The waitress, truly the most competent member of the commission, names the dance number, and Amadej begins to play.

"Seems like he's got the beat down," the publican says to her.

"He plays fine," she confirms. Then she announces a second number.

"Well?" the publican cocks his head and looks at the waitress, and she also expresses her silent approval with a nod of her head.

"But if you're trying to dance, this isn't the best proof," opined the tavern-keeper, still eyeing Amadej with suspicion.

And he turned and went over to table where a young couple were seated. They were drinking beer.

"Hey, František, come take a couple of turns over here with your Karolina."

Casually the young man got to his feet: he was twenty-two, with a pleasant face but swollen, sleepy-looking eyes.

"A *tramblanka*," Karolina said, joining the young man on the dance floor.

Amadej hit the first notes and the two of them began to circulate around the large dance floor.

"He keeps time well," both of the young people said after flying twice around the restaurant.

"He plays fine," the cook said too, and she could feel it in her legs this time, even though she wasn't dancing.

"Eh?" the tavern-keeper asked once more. "Good then? And what do you say, František?"

"Fine. Really, it's fine," the young, drowsy man acknowledged peevishly for a second time.

"And it has a nice melody," the publican's wife went on, tapping her hands on her ample hips.

"Well then I'll take you," the publican ventured at last. "Let's come to terms immediately. Whenever there's a holiday, the dancing starts a 4 pm. Otherwise it's every day at 6. You have to keep making music on this piano as long as there are guests in the restaurant. If no one's dancing, play something they find entertaining. Compensation: every evening one supper, with meat; three mugs of beer, two cigars, and one *forint* in cash."

"Ja, ja—you see how easy it is to help oneself, when you know the lay of the land. When you know what's what." So spoke his elderly landlady, extremely satisfied with herself, when they returned home.

From this point on, Amadej did not get back home any night before 2 am. On Sundays and holidays the guests wouldn't leave the premises till dawn. Alongside all this work, Amadej did not fail to attend even a single lecture—he feared that the folks in the institute would learn of this job of his, which was strictly forbidden. But he was content. He no longer went hungry. He paid the monthly fees on his instrument. And he paid the old lady the rent that he owed. Of course he wasn't even close to entertaining the thought that he had started out onto a slippery slope on which many great talents lose their footing, never to rise again.

One evening, a bit after midnight, when the male and female dancers in the stuffy, smoke-filled restaurant were taking a break, Amadej sat dozing at the piano. He paid no attention to the noisy guests, who were now seated, red-faced and overheated, at tables laden with beer. Someone laid a hand on his shoulder. Amadej raised his eyes and saw before him a young man of twenty-four years, with a thin, dark face, and narrow, bright blue eyes with the watery look of a drunkard.

"Ho ho, colleague, are you sleeping?" the stranger inquired of him. He spoke in a hoarse voice and stuck out a skinny, bony hand with long, thin fingers and poorly groomed, black fingernails. "My name is Vesely. I'm a musician, like you. And what might your name be?"

Amadej told him his name, looking at the newcomer in bewilderment.

"That's a Slavic name. But not Czech."

Amadej shook his head no.

"So you're a Russian then?"

"No, I'm not."

"A Pole?"

"No."

"Therefore you are—Bulgarian? Or a Serb?"

"A Croat."

"A Croat?...Ah, yes! You are a compatriot of Stross-mayer?"

"I am."

"Doesn't matter. I don't set much store by nationality. I was born in the Czech lands by accident. And otherwise I am—to the extent they permit it—a human being. You improvise well; I was listening to you. But why belabor your *fantasias* here, or wear your eyes out with notes—for the benefit of this lout? You amaze me...Or are you just in especially high spirits tonight amidst all this mud-bespattered livestock?...I play not far from here. A place called 'The Happy Laborer.' My audience got into a brawl tonight—*cherchez la femme*, naturally. When glasses started sailing through the air, I decamped altogether of course. Came in here for a glass of beer. Hey, let's have one together. Karolina, two mugs." And the newcomer took a seat at the piano.

"So how long have you been playing here?"

"It'll soon be two weeks."

"Where did you play earlier?"

"Nowhere."

"How much do they pay you in cash?"

"One *forint* per night."

"And are the guests generous?"

"What do you mean?"

"I mean, how much do you squeeze out of the dancers over the course of the evening?"

"Not a thing."

"It's obvious you're a greenhorn. You are ruining our business. A dismissed conservatory student, eh?"

Amadej looked at him; the newcomer's face, pinched and somber, was wreathed in an excruciatingly disdainful expression.

"I am a conservatory student," Amadej told him.

"No matter. They'll kick you out sooner or later. I made every effort to keep it concealed so they wouldn't catch me at it. I hid the fact that I played the barrooms at night. But they have a special gift for ferreting out such quarry. I had no other way to live. They granted me an exemption, three times. Then they gave me the boot. Be prepared for that. The first time you fail to show for a class during Mardi Gras, their omnipotent minds, with one accord, will immediately conclude: that fellow's playing somewhere at night, and sleeping during the day."

"That's why I won't be cutting a single class," Amadej thought to himself. But Vesely kept on talking:

"How the hell did you end up coming here from so far away and landing at the conservatory in Prague? That's a distasteful way to earn a living, believe me. Well, no matter...You are my colleague, and you are wet behind the ears. You play for these cattle from sheet music. D'you know how I do it? In my sleep! For Pete's sake! I sleep there, with a cigar between my teeth, listening in my dreams to how they tromp around like horses, and I keep the beat for them. And not a single note more! I've got another piece of advice for you, too. For the amount of pay you are getting, you're playing too much. If you play as much as the innkeeper and these unreasonable blockheads want, the blood will come spewing out from under your fingernails. Take care, until the first couple has danced around the room twice. Then *basta*! Don't play for real anymore. They'll clap their hands, pound their feet, and howl more fiercely than a raging bull, but you should act like you don't hear them. Let 'em curse—what do you care? Then some guy will approach you arm in arm with his "mademoiselle" and offer you a glass of beer. Drink it up, but don't start playing. Wait till a second fellow comes up to you, and a third, and a fourth. Rustle up a cigar from somebody, and from someone else a cup of tea, a cognac, a coffee, ten of them—whatever! That, colleague, is how it's done, and there's more profit in it than in the tavern-keeper's pay. He expects you to do it, and so he doesn't pay musicians any more than the folks who sweep the floors."

At that point a blond boy of eighteen stepped up to the piano. He was too young for a moustache; but judging from the powerful features and pink skin on his face and from his bulging biceps, he was on his way to being a butcher. On his arm was a hussy twice his age. She was fat, and red-skinned, and had unruly hair, a large bosom, and a dissipated face.

"A polka!" the boy said to Vesely.

"Hey, friend—I'm thirsty," Vesely replied.

"A mug of beer for the musician!" the boy shouted, as he held his hussy tight and got ready to dance.

Vesely drained the mug in one go and turned away from the piano again to face Amadej:

"That was my twentieth mug. With this kind of smoke and dust around, I can't seem to quench my thirst!"

"So, aren't you going to play?" the boy asked him, still holding the woman around the waist.

"Coming right up."

Vesely's fingers flew across the keys, dashing off a few arpeggios, and then he dropped his hands to his side again. Meanwhile a rather old, tastefully dressed gentleman with intelligent features came over to the piano. He was leading by the arm a good-looking brunette, only about sixteen, with delicate but full features and a modest bosom. Her face was young, with a mouth that was still very girlish and eyes that were extra-large. The girl giggled slightly and regarded Amadej with interest. She definitely looked happy to be there.

"Paulina, what sort of dance do you wish to do?" her well-heeled companion inquired formally.

The girl's full set of healthy teeth showed from behind her small but full lips. She smiled again at Amadej and said merrily:

"A waltz."

"Sir, a waltz, please!"

But Vesely pretended not to have heard him; he wished to make quite plain the fact that he disdained the public from whose amusement he lived. He turned back to Amadej and continued conversing with him, paying no heed at all to any of the couples now pressing forward to the piano and requesting dance numbers.

"Where do you live, mate?"

Amadej told him the street and house number.

"So, on this street then. Very well. Tomorrow I'll come visit you."

"A waltz," the gentleman with the young girl still hanging on his arm said again. His tone was pleading, almost submissive, and he pressed some money into Vesely's hand.

"You'd like to dance to a waltz, and that fellow wants a polka," and Vesely pointed his finger at the boy who was resting his perspiring red face on the bosom of his dancing-partner, who was in turn cooling his face with a fan. "Therefore with one hand I'll do a polka, and with the other a waltz."

"This is the queen of the party," the gentleman said, fawning on his little dancer, who raised her eyebrows, turned her face towards Amadej, and unleashed a seductive smile at him. Her companion looked into her eyes in a nauseating display of lust.

"The queen? You'd never know it from this," Vesely responded, scornfully showing the man the copper coins he was holding in his hand.

"More rosin, eh?" And the gentleman turned crossly toward Vesely and placed a ten-spot in his hand. "And now, play!"

Meanwhile, more and more couples were pressing forward to the piano; it seemed that around Amadej gathered all of the commotion and din in the entire stuffy, smoky establishment. Everybody clamored, with deafening cries, for the dancing to commence. Vesely struck a few chords, the tumult died down, and the dance kicked off amidst mad galloping, clumsy stepping, and the boorish pounding of heels on the floor. Vesely played in exactly the fashion he mentioned earlier to Amadej: without thinking about what he was playing. His skillful fingers gripped the chords securely, sometimes with just one hand, because the other was busy holding a cigarette. In addition, he carried on a conversation with Amadej the entire time he played.

"So you really don't earn anything apart from that *forint* from the innkeeper? You're crazy. They're sons-of-bitches, these publicans. If they'd at least fork over a proper supper. You see, colleague, that's the pay our talent and knowledge bring in! Well, just wait. While we two get to know each other a bit better, I'll tell you more about this. Look at the way these cattle dance, like they're going insane...Ach, enough!" And he concluded the song abruptly with two chords.

The jam-packed couples swayed on their feet like travelers in a train car when it stops all of a sudden—and immediately worn-out throats began to raise a ruckus, accompanied by the clapping of hands, stomping of feet, and shouts: Go on! But Vesely just calmly finished his glass of beer and squeezed his hands between his knees:

"You see? That's how it's done, mate."

Several couples encircled the piano. A non-commissioned officer placed a cigar on the piano in front of Vesely, several laid coins in his hands, and others shouted hoarsely:

"Beer for the musician!"

"Do you see, mate, how the herd learns its duty?" Vesely announced loudly and resumed playing.

The dance lasted until three in the morning. For the most part, the dancers and their girlfriends had vanished from the restaurant by that time. Only a few utterly weary and befuddled couples remained sitting with their beers. The tavern-keeper paid little attention to them. The tables had been tidied up and Amadej was waiting for Vesely, who was drinking cognac and had just lit up a new cigar. Eventually they left together. Vesely walked with Amadej to the door of his building, and as they were saying goodbye he mentioned once more that he'd come by to visit later that day. Exhausted, Amadej fell fully dressed into bed, as he did on all nights like this one. He fell instantly into a deep sleep.

Before nine the next morning, Vesely knocked on Amadej's door; Amadej was busy getting ready to go to the university.

"Listen, mate," Vesely said, apparently surprised by something, "you live in grand style here. Do you really have this room to yourself?"

"I do," Amadej retorted, thinking that Vesely meant this ironically, for in his room, besides the *pianino*, were to be found only the absolute necessities, along with old, broken-down furniture.

"You have a piano...and books...and sheet music...Say, you even have some music published really recently. Would you allow me to stay here at your place and look through the publications by these newer composers?"

"As you wish. You can stay here until I return from the lecture."

"Ah, you're off to a lecture, are you? Of course. It had to be so. I know some gentlemen in this town who believe that without their wisdom neither Dvořak nor Brahms would exist. I was theirs for nearly four years, and when I take stock of what they taught me, I have to tell you it comes to: nothing...Just wait. We'll speak more about that later...So, then. With your permission, I shall remain here, seeing as how I have no work during the day—and since I haven't taken a serious look at new sheet music in ages. But, I beg you, mention to the land-lady that you and I are friends. She looked at me as if I were some kind of vagrant when I showed up at the door. Of course it's because people make judgments based only on clothes...But believe me, you live like roy-alty! I sleep in a basement, with these six sketchy indi-viduals. Each of us pays a tenner for the night—that much money just to be under a roof. Oh, go now—it's probably almost ten...Oh, hold on, mate—this belongs to you."

Vesely put his hand in his pocket and pulled out a fistful of coins.

"Take it. I forgot to give it to you last night after I collected it from that riff-raff...Just take it. I drank and smoked for free, but the money is yours."

Amadej balked but Vesely demanded he take the money, demanded it with a slowly emerging dominance over Amadej.

"Off you go now, and hurry. Have fun! No, really! Is that petrified Mr. Counterpoint still strutting around with his deep, wise sayings like 'the rules of art are the freedom of the artist'? That's daft! God only knows where he picked that up—but now he goes nowhere without it. Go, go! I'll wait here for you."

When Amadej returned home from the lecture, he found Vesely all curled up on his little couch, asleep.

"Oh, I just had a nice short little nap. This room is so good for sleeping!" he said to Amadej as he opened his eyes. "I went through some of that modern music; what's your assessment of it, colleague-to-colleague?"

Amadej didn't have the courage to tell him his opinion.

"You see, I have to agree with Rabbi Akiva that there's nothing new under the sun....What is beautiful is old, and what is new is not beautiful. I mean, really, look at this rhythm and tell me—who can understand it? Yet people maintain that it's beautiful precisely because we do not understand it. One is afraid to tell the truth: we don't get it. For then we'd lose the reputation of advancing with the spirit of the times. If there's some esthetic theory I do not understand, well, I know that it was some Kraut brain that cobbled it together, and I throw the book across the room. Depriving art of clarity, it seems to me, is like taking a person into a darkened room to examine a painting. Look how beautiful it is! But it's only the brighter colors that catch my eye—I cannot discern anything else. If they really thought at the level of a Beethoven, mate, then I'll be damned if they'd be able to write that kind of gibberish."

Vesely stuck around Amadej's place all day after that. In the afternoon, Amadej had no further lectures, and when he excused himself to do some work, since he was preparing for an exam, Vesely said to him, in a manner that brooked no resistance:

"Go ahead and work. I shan't bother you. By your leave, though, I'll just snooze here a bit on your couch."

Not until evening, when both of them needed to head off to play in their respective restaurants, did Vesely take his leave:

"Goodbye, colleague! If mine hit the streets before yours tonight, I'll come have a beer with you. Otherwise, see you at your place again tomorrow!"

Ten days passed in this way, with Vesely clinging ever more tightly to Amadej, who was not quite certain what to make of the other man. There was something of the demon about Vesely, whose overall look, combined with his views and his lifestyle, filled Amadej with dread. Yet in the same instant Amadej could feel the compassion occasioned by Vesely's appearance. It seemed that in his heart of hearts Vesely was a genuinely good man and a genuinely unhappy one too. He wasn't selfish, and he wasted every bit as much money on Amadej as on himself. He knew a great deal about a lot of things. Whatever he talked about, he talked about with crisp intelligence. He showed Amadej documents attesting that he had finished the *lycée* and then been a law student for a year. Following that he studied music up to the time they expelled him from the conservatory. About his studies, as about his life in general, he spoke with disdain and bile. He was, without doubt, very talented. Once he took one of Amadej's musical passages and reworked it on the spot in the style of the most famous composers from Palestrina to Dvořak. In addition he spoke, and wrote, perfect Czech, German, and French.—And Amadej's old landlady couldn't stand him, even though he brought pastries for her coffee break.

128

"That one could get you into trouble of some sort...Lord only knows who he is and where he's from. You mean you cannot see that he's an alcoholic and a bum?" she would tell Amadej.

Amadej himself did not pigeonhole him that way. In spite of his demonic sides, Amadej sympathized with Vesely's failures and told him intimate details of his life.

Once the two of them crossed paths with Mme Lipovskova and her daughter-in-law in their carriage. Vesely greeted them with a deep bow.

"Do you know those people?" Amadej asked animatedly.

"Aristocratic rabble!" Vesely replied with disdain and malice. "When I was a law student, I clerked for two months in the office of an attorney named Lipovský...That is his mother and wife. Ach, let's not talk about them. When I think about the upper classes, rage gets the better of me. Something stirs in me, like a wild animal getting a glimpse of blood."

Thus did Vesely begin relating to Amadej his terrible sentence on the faulty structure, injustice, and nonsensical organization of human society. "You see," he said to him, "right without might, and intelligence with no property—no longer counts in books, let alone in real life. Power belongs wither to stupidity and extreme impudence, on the one hand, or to wicked, soulless selfishness: don't you see this in your own life?"

Amadej nodded his head, and he was gripped by the fear that he might be coming to believe Vesely's teachings.

When they were seated that evening, each with a beer, after the dances, Vesely steered their conversation to a theme that Amadej listened to with dread. He had to admit that, despite all of its horrors, it had a lot of truth in it; and that, for example, even his own life could fall under it. With these thoughts running through his head, he started to explain to Vesely about Jahoda's love and about his inability to muster up the courage, after nearly starving for two days, to pay a call on Lipovskova's mother.

His eyes blazing, Vesely swallowed every one of Amadej's words, and then he said, full of enthusiasm:

"Well, colleague, this is really something! It is capital that really must be exploited. Hold it—we must think this through a bit more. Why didn't you tell me any of this earlier?"

Right at first Amadej did not grasp what Vesely was thinking. But he did sense that there was no way it would accord with the effects on his own heart of Jahoda's story about Mařenka. But when Vesely began to explain how it would now be possible to create trouble for Lipovský by sending him a letter threatening to divulge racy episodes from his mother's past—Amadej broke out in a sweat.

"Have no fear. There are newspapers that will print this, and thank us for it, too," Vesely said to him in a voice filled with conviction.

"You would do that?" Amadej inquired. He felt deep revulsion at this but was forcing himself to appear calm.

With delight! Who is looking out for you, mate? Your town council was on the point of abandoning you to a death by hunger...And who would have inquired after your well-being? Dog eats dog, and people are wolves to each other! Think of how much people amass, and Lipovský is still adding to his fortune today! Whom does he defend in order to satisfy his hunger for money? Clients? Clerks? Uneducated peasants or desperate widows? Go on! He is one of the richest men in Prague, and he plays a prominent role in public life, mate! From this little story of yours the two of us could live for a year! Just leave it to me. If we don't avail ourselves of this, we'll have made even bigger paupers of ourselves. You should sting that fat cat, poison him, even if only for a moment, darling!

Amadej was disgusted. For the first time he beheld before him a horrifying enemy of humanity, like a desperate avenger, who in his undying thirst for retribution did not recoil form the most wicked means to calm, just for a moment, the blaze scorching his brain. Vesely's fiery eyes, shaky hands, and hoarse voice, coming from deep inside like from the grave, filled Amadej with anxiety; he sensed that a serious crime was in the offing involving the two of them. His insides quaked and he felt like he was suspended from one of Vesely's hands above a fearful abyss. In the midst of his fear, he thought of something.

"Look, I have to tell you the truth, since this has gotten you so upset. I made up the whole thing. While I was starving in my bed on Three Kings' Day."

He said this calmly, and he was astonished at his ability to lie this way.

"Listen here, mate. If you concocted that, then you could write novels." On Vesely's face an abrupt change in his soul manifested itself in his painfully stiff features; his words sounded as if he meant to ridicule Amadej. But Amadej merely laughed.

"I do not believe you, however. At its core the story has too much of truth and clarity to be the fruit of your imagination."

"But it is."

"You won't be able to convince me of it."

"Why not?"

"How will you do it then?"

"Like this: in my hometown there has never been a *kapellmeister* at all; therefore there hasn't been one named Jahoda. "

"If this is true..."

"It is true."

"Who's in charge of the music?"

"No one. Before I came along, a cobbler played the organ at church, and now the teacher is playing till I return."

"So why did you think all that up with Lipovský in the middle of it? How do you know him?"

Amadej realized that the other man might be able to paint him into a corner by means of a long interrogation.

"I don't know him," he said calmly. "I read his name at some point on a house somewhere, and one other time I saw those two women you showed me today coming out of that same building in an elegant carriage...In a hungry man, the soul is flightier...I guess that's how I came to think up that story."

"If that's how it was, then you, my friend, have a vivid imagination. I'll believe you, then...but listen," Vesely went on immediately, his voice evincing doubt, "if you're deceiving me, you're making a big mistake. This is a way for us to squeeze a tidy little sum out of a money-bags like Lipovský, before he makes us even poorer."

"Indeed. If my story were true."

Vesely was lost in thought. Amadej could see that his story about Jahoda and Lipovskova was gnawing at him.

"I'm sleepy," Amadej said. "I'm afraid I won't get even an hour's sleep before tomorrow's lecture."

"Listen up, my friend," Vesely said back to him, as if he had missed Amadej's last sentence. "Don't take it amiss, but I still consider your story to be true. I'm going to attempt to write to her..."

"And if they have you locked up?"

"You wouldn't testify on my behalf?"

"You mean about things I invented in my mind?"

"Go to hell!" Vesely spoke angrily now, and got up from the table. "If you fabricated it, then go write novels. Your power of imagination is right for it."

They walked in silence all the way to Amadej's apartment. The cold was intense and both of them drew their cheap clothes up around their necks, but this offered little protection against the chill.

Vesely started in on him again as they stood before the door to Amadej's apartment building.

"I cannot get your story out of my head...Listen, friend, if it's true, whom are you trying to spare? You're protecting the wealthy man, who has a million properties and no heart...from yourself, who doesn't have a warm coat but has a big heart. Look whom you are guarding!...Now, whether Lipovský is a man of knowledge and talent or not—we won't go into that. Let's assume he is, and then you tell me: how has Lipovský been able to cash in on his talent, and how can you cash in on him? What sort of position in society has he come to hold, and what kind will you get?"

Amadej held his ground. He was thoroughly irked when he shook Vesely's hand at parting. But he felt joy at the fact that he had rescued his conscience from the very edge of a terrible precipice.

From that night on, anxiety grew in Amadej at the prospect of the other man's company, even though he couldn't hide from himself the fact that he retained in his heart a certain sympathy, born of compassion, for Vesely. It was roughly equal to his fear of Vesely's passion and hatred of the world and of people who occupied any kind of respected place in it. And then he had to note with awe the way Vesely would spend his last tiny coins on a penniless man like himself. He spoke about people from the upper classes with such furious animosity and vehemence that it seemed he would be capable of slaughtering them without a single pang of conscience; but once, when he was telling Amadej about standing at his mother's death-bed, he choked on his own sobs and was unable to finish his story because he was crying so much. He would say that his soul had no reaction to the tears of a rich man besides laughter; yet once when he was in a café, he read in a newspaper that a stepmother had been heartlessly tormenting her stepchild, and he hurtled the paper to the floor and wept out loud. Why do they write about such things? Do we really lack for misery and pain around us? Sometimes he would admonish Amadej earnestly, like an older brother, that because of the exam he should persist in producing merely some sort of boring schoolboy work, then the next time he would start to speak reproachfully, somehow provocatively:

"If you really have talent, you'll rise to fame without it. If you believe there's a Dvořak or a Tchaikovsky inside you trying to get out...But you study, even though it isn't going to help you much with this. What's inside is all you have. And schooling can ruin you, too: perhaps you are born to grow up like an oak in the liberty of the forest, but they are going to graft onto you a fruit that thrives only in the prison-like atmosphere of their schools. Then you aren't able to be this or that. All of them together are incapable of giving you a half-*fillér* more than what you have inside. Imagine for just a second: what do you learn in classes about counterpoint, forms, or esthetics? Merely mathematics with notes— empty, dead math, with art lying underneath it, breathing its last. And they teach history that way, too. A law of art! And who discovered and established this universal law? An iron net braided together with some acoustics, some mathematics, some philosophy—and there you have the law: which they then slip onto you independent artists like a straitjacket on a mental patient. Under the yoke of that law you will finish up at the conservatory and remain the same in values and capabilities as you are now. It's just that now they pay you one *forint*, and in the future they'll pay you two that's the difference. And then you will teach the 'laws' to others and fancy that you are creating 'artists' in the same way your professors imagine nowadays...And do you think it's better anywhere else?" Vesely continued, in apparently innate tones of malice and derision that matched perfectly the harsh and pained features of his face.

"There exist fools who in the sterility and impotence of their souls cram themselves full of these dead, undigested lessons in school, and the professors pass them with distinction. For such an infertile monstrosity, skilled in cattle-like submissiveness, high positions are certainly in the offing; where do they get the right to govern in things for which they are not equipped— matters of intellect and spirit? Do you understand, then, why certain people come in for my hatred, or why I cannot help but blow up when I see complete mental helplessness strut about with unfathomable bravado: we are the chosen ones...and spirit is a slave to those dead, unproductive chosen ones. They can't stand light, they cannot bear freedom, they tie the whole world up in their chains, and I am dying from the agony of being unable to break them."

Amadej got dizzy listening to all of Vesely's thoughts: they seemed to bring the kiss of death to his ideals, to his love and his art, and he experienced them as a kind of terrifying truth that would someday avenge itself on humanity.

From time to time, when he was sitting exhausted, elaborating a theme assigned by his professor, and he sensed that the unfettered operation of his mind, skirting all the mossy-backed rules, would allow him more easily and neatly to solve the problem at hand, he would give himself up with delight to the current of Vesely's words so that they could carry him away. He discovered the repulsive, the moronic, and the unworthy in many things—in lessons, in hunger, in many of the rules of human society, and especially in the incomprehension of the outside world that had already so crudely so many times traumatized the world of his soul. It seemed to him that right prevailed in life when people know what it is—nonetheless, in ways unfit for human beings but without vengefulness at the burden of injustice, millions of people continue to ache and groan, and in their tears, sweat, and blood swim egotism, violence, and arrogance. And life would go on all around him, hopelessly, obscured by darkness and filled with stifling air, while in him the conviction grew that Vesely was speaking the truth. And then it would seem to him that his heart would not be moved if the entire world began to run with streams of blood and tears of the people who in the noble guise of dignity and power kept injustice covered up...But such a state of mind he could not endure for long. The thought of Adelka, the beautiful image of his birthplace, transported his soul to the magical silent world of the artist who is a visionary and a dreamer. The entire world might remain foreign to him, and he might be unreachable and unintelligible to the world, and vice-versa—if only Adelka could understand him with her sensitive, feminine soul. From these thoughts a sense of victory and joy were born, and they triumphed over Vesely's sinister teachings.

If he was made unbearably uncomfortable by Vesely's presence, Amadej could nevertheless not find a way to get rid of him. There was something about Vesely's behavior and his manner of speaking that took hold like a polyp and could not be shaken off. One night, when Amadej came home from working a dance at The Sea Crab, he found Vesely in his room, asleep on the sofa.

"I'm thinking you won't be too miffed about this, mate," Vesely said to him. "There's space in this little room for both of us, and I'll help you pay the rent!"

From then on, Vesely showed up regularly at Amadej's when he needed to sleep, and to pacify the old landlady, who had started griping incessantly, although he was giving her money to make coffee for the three of them—and to buy fancy cookies. Amadej lost heart. He would do almost anything in the world for Vesely, but it was unbearable having to be in his presence. It happened a hundred times that he was on the brink of showing Vesely the door for good, but he simply couldn't figure out how to do it. And then all of a sudden Vesely himself piped up:

"I can see, my friend, that I am putting you out. Don't make any apologies! I know people. There've been so many times when I could tell word for word what you were thinking of me. I'll be leaving now. What right do I have to impose my company on you? From the moment we met, I found you likeable. I thought we'd become more forthright and devoted friends. You'd prefer to be sincere with people, but your heart's not in it. Thus, you see, you are weak, like all other people. We correct others, but we cannot abide it when they correct us. And we lie, all of us do—you, I, everyone. The lie is the supreme power; all of us are slaves to it,

one person out of necessity, one out of weakness, another from wickedness...We preach the truth—and we
all spit in its face. But that's just the way the world
works. When you observe it, it seems as if a great artist,
after thinking up the Venus de Milo, took a bunch of
decaying rock instead of the finest of marbles and
carved into it his idea. We can see what the contours of
his imagined world's beauty are, in all their genius and
perfection. But the materials are not according to his
specifications. Every feature and limb is deformed by
rot and structural cracks...But...I'll be going now. In
Malá Strana there's a dance instructor who's opening up
a new school, and I obtained the job of pianist with him.
Farewell."

At the end of February, Amadej passed his exams
with distinction. He didn't rejoice at his success because
of what it meant for his upkeep but because of the conceit, innate to artists, that other people would now see
what he could do. He believed that when the news of
his exam reached his home town, the people there
would talk of nothing else. And he was once more convinced that all people are good, that they all loved him,
and they esteemed in him the same things he esteemed
in himself.

After quite a while he ran into Vesely again one evening. Vesely acted very dispirited and complained of being sick. He was quite weak, his face was even swarthier
than before, and he was behaving like an old man, right
down to having difficulty breathing. He complained that
he couldn't eat, but he was smoking like a chimney.
They went out together for a beer, and while there,

Amadej carried away on a flood of his own feelings, forgot about Vesely's distress and spoke to him like a child about how the parish priest was at that very moment crisscrossing his hometown with a telegram in his hand, and how the whole citizenry would utter his name with awe.

Nodding his head, Vesely listened to him, and then he put his fingers on Amadej's hand. Amadej felt his fingers burning like fire.

"Man, you've got a fever," he said anxiously to Vesely.

"You bet I do. And you, my friend, you have a fever too. You have it—oh, but you do!...Tell me, mate, is it those countrymen of yours who all of a sudden now, after you suffered hunger for so long, after you risked your health and your life—are they going to give you fifteen *forints* a month so that you can continue your studies?"

"They are."

"And you believe, friend, that now, after this exam on which you place so much value, they are not talking about anything but you?...Perhaps they are talking...but about what! What they are saying is: Damn him, and damn those expenses he's saddling our town with!...My friend! If you had bought a steer yesterday for a hundred *forints*, and today you sold it for a hundred and ten, they would say and think the following of you: it's your profit, so good work! And as they were speaking that thought, it wouldn't let them sleep; they'd be envious of you; and they'd be afraid of you—because they have discovered one more rival in the competitive world. But that you got through an exam...Not that! Now, if you had written a Beethoven symphony, they'd keep sleeping soundly: let him go ahead and write; it does no harm to any of us. What do you think you are really preparing yourself to do? Bear in mind, friend, whenever you think in the future of other people, especially that so-called "general audience" in artistic life, you are to say: cattle...And show your contempt for them!"

Amadej managed a painful smile. At least he could stand such ruthless pessimism for the moment.

"You can talk to your heart's content," an overwrought Amadej said to Vesely. "You're entitled to your convictions. I don't care about other people. I know how to create a little world for myself and for one other creature who would rejoice sincerely at this test...From life I don't care to seek anything more."

"Who is it?" Vesely inquired of him, looking at Amadej with obvious mockery in his eyes.

"The girl whom I love in the same way she loves me."

"Naturally, if you have a fever, then it's one hundred times as dangerous as mine! Once, my friend, I knew someone who was, let's say, the kind of person you are. Maybe I was that kind of person myself...Ultimately it doesn't matter. So this man has a 'girl' like that and he contends that she represents intensified goodness and every noble trait that he felt in his own heart. But do you know why? He accidentally grew accustomed to her face, because he imparted to that face his own heart and soul and thus fell in love with himself...Well, and after that he totally came undone: he saw that his holiest object was an idol constructed of common, the most common, materials; but the holy object was greater to him that his own mother! Be careful that you are not deceived! You aren't building happiness on logical arguments, but on dreams. You will be disappointed."

He is sick and unhappy—Amadej thought to himself. Otherwise, he had no way of getting his mind around this much nauseating cynicism and disdain for other human beings.

However much he pitied Vesely, the comment about Adelka left him furious and offended. He would've allowed talk like that about his fellow townspeople, but with Adelka he was zealously convinced that he was pouring the vitality and happiness of his soul directly into hers.

Somewhere around the beginning of the summer, Amadej found in the newspaper on the lists of deceased persons from the city's hospitals the name of Vesely: Antun Vesely, musician, age 28, from tuberculosis.—He headed immediately to the morgue of the hospital so that he could see one more time the dead man with whom he had commiserated, and whom he had loved and whose presence he had feared. But when he got there, someone in the main hall pointed him to where the young medical students were hard at work: they had already dissected Vesely.

Other than this, a peaceful period for Amadej, in which he could devote himself full to his studies, had begun: in addition to the fifteen *forints* per month that he received from the town council, he took his meals in The Sea Crab restaurant, where he instructed the innkeeper's daughter in piano. He was completely content with this good fortune, which was only understandable to those people who in the end disentangle themselves from that abhorrent state of melancholy and depression that kills off sensitive people living in material want.

At the conclusion of the fourth year that Amadej had spent living in Prague, he received from the priest a letter apprising him of the death of Adelka's mother. The news unsettled him tremendously, but when he sought signs of grief in himself, he found none. And even his agitation seemed to have a completely contradictory source. It occurred to him that he was now the only person that Adelka still had on this earth, something that made him feel closer to her than he ever had before. This agreeable sentiment led him to start a letter to her with the thought of giving her comfort. And just then, when he pictured her, tearful and inconsolable and dressed all in black, he felt overwhelmed by pity and the heartfelt desire to alleviate her grief.

"How can I comfort you, Adelka, in your deep grief?" he wrote. "I know I don't really know what it means to lose one's mother. I lost mine at an age when true sorrow is inaccessible to the soul. Nevertheless to the degree that I can look back to those times via my memories, her face appears everywhere, her unclear but sweet face, smiling with love, beckoning warmly for me to come to her, and covering me with trusting kisses that nothing in the world could replace. When I tear myself away from that life, comparable to a dream, my eyes are always moist...and if I'm by myself I kneel and pray to my mother to get her to stay with me. I absolutely cannot think of her in any other way than as blessed among the select and able from there to protect, encourage, and guide me even better than if she lived with me in this world. And so you see, Adelka, that even a deceased mother is a secure refuge and bulwark against wreck and ruin. True love, and that definitely includes the love of a maternal heart, can never die. What is dead is what conveys the love to us here, and that is what we weep for. How shall I comfort you, Adelka, when the thing we've been left without is irretrievable? How else other than direct your attention to the One from whom whatever is eternal in us comes. Can you fathom, with your heart or your mind, that maternal love could perish, that it could be extinguished by death, against which it victoriously took up the struggle at the time it brought your life into the world? Can you imagine the thought of her not staying with you? Think of her suffering, far away from your tears, and rejoicing when you feel her at your side, soothing you, for all the days of your life. Real love is the desire for contact between two compatible and understanding souls...That's love that outlasts the grave, and exalts life, toughening it and lifting it up into the kingdom of spirit, where the filth of our selfishness and wickedness do not penetrate. Resurrect, Adelka, therefore, the faith in your heart, the belief that the dear departed is living with you, and alongside you. You will encourage, not bewail, the spirit of the one woman who loves you even now more perfectly than anyone else does."

Amadej meant to conclude his letter thus, but he couldn't bring himself to do it. He had to tell her something more...Tell it to her carefully, so as not to injure her heart in this exquisite period of lamentation for her dead mother. He continued writing:

"How happy I would be if I could replace just a part of what your mother meant to you! My thoughts and the desire of my heart abide constantly with you; and now, when so much grief has been visited upon you, I see your dear form before me, clad in the black of mourning, and would like to take all the pain of your heart onto myself. If the spirit of the deceased were to instruct me in what to do to clear the grief from your soul—this world knows no sacrifice that I would not make to see that happen! Through my feelings for you, ever since you as a young girl, still a child, really, first appeared before my eyes, like a well-behaved little cherub, all of my hopes, my fame, my happiness—they have all coalesced onto you. I can only conceive of happiness if I think of putting my life at your service, and if I think that I am beloved of you, because you understand me. In your soul, my soul finds more than all the rest of the world could give it. With declarations from my heart such as these, I would not make so bold as to approach you in person in this hour when grief for the mother you have lost envelops you like saintliness—if my emotions were not as chaste and holy as the pure impulse behind a prayer offered up by a pious heart."

Chapter Seven

Towards the end of his third year of studies at the conservatory, Amadej was allowed to engage in free composition. He had just begun to understand the old professor of composition, who forever had that German maxim about artists and the laws of art on the tip of his tongue when he critiqued the works of his students. His feelings about all those difficult and atrophied rules, which previously had villainously served to constrict his vibrant imagination, had changed; he now felt they were guards, unfailing in vigilance. They saw to it that no one strayed beyond the borders that they had designated for centuries as boundaries, ever since the human mind had been free to seek beauty; and they had not changed their stances, not ever, despite all the changes of taste and the evolution that art goes through as it develops within its various circles. The material that an artist uses to build had in truth never been this perfect, nor this rich: but beauty, which the human spirit had bestowed upon the modest voices of a Gregorian chorale, which Palestrina had put into his chords, and Beethoven into his symphonies, remained in and of itself unchanging and unchanged. Looking back now over the numerous compositions that he had retained since the time he had written in total freedom, in touch with the febrile, impatient mood of his soul, compelling him to write—he felt an agreeable sense of satisfaction at being an independent judge who could point out his own errors.

The first of his completely free works, then, that he presented to his professor was the "*Adagio*" for string quartet that he had entitled "Adelka." The old professor was very pleased with Amadej's work. A month before the end of the school year, people all over the institute were saying that at the upcoming public performance, given each year to showcase student works, the composition by the Croat Zlatanić was going to take first place.

This sent Amadej into raptures. "How immediate the incandescence of my love will seem to Adelka as well," he thought to himself, with magnificent self-assurance, "when she realizes that these notes came to me from my soul, engulfed as it is in flames of desire for her!"

This desire expanded with ever greater force inside him, because the time was drawing near when he would see her again and he'd be able to reveal himself to her without constraints. His desire for her became especially ungovernable when he, of an evening, spotted in a loggia in the theater not far from his seat a stylish young lady, clad in all black. He thought her face very much resembled Adelka's, and all evening long he studied her elegant profile, which, gracefully compounded with her fair hair, stood out with singular comeliness from the black of her dress. When the opera was over, Amadej hastened over to a place where the unknown young woman was sure to pass. And indeed she was a very beautiful girl, a blonde with brisk northern demeanor and sweet, coquettish blue eyes…but she was not Adelka, as Amadej had anticipated. That look on Adelka's face that so bewitched him could never be replicated, not even on someone who otherwise greatly resembled her. But when he stared at this twenty-year old girl, with her seductive curves, lissome as waves, descending from exposed shoulders to her full, firm breasts, he remembered that Adelka would now be eighteen herself, and that she would also be in the full flower of her maidenly beauty. At this thought his entire body was washed over with a feeling so rich that its strength caused his heart to lose its rhythm. And the short time that he still had before him in Prague seemed to him more trying than the entire four years that he had already passed there. He passed his exams with flying colors, and now the final day had arrived, with its graduation concert and his occasion to say farewell to professors and colleagues.

The roomy performance hall was full of sophisticated concert-goers. It was they who were going to pass judgment on Amadej's labors and they who would provide testimony about whether or not he had found his true calling in art. Even his elderly, soft-spoken professor of composition looked paler than usual today, and was patently agitated. Indeed he was also not at all sure how the verdicts of this outside audience would fall—the verdict pertaining to the whole institute and the ones on the individual students. And as the beginning of the concert drew closer, the performance in which his work would for the first time come before the public, Amadej himself became more and more flustered; inexorably he felt bearing down upon him an increasingly disagreeable feeling of his own incompetence, into which his energy and will were disappearing. In his powerlessness, self-confidence faded completely, and he was prepared to accept, with resignation unbecoming a man, the criticism of the public: see here—he thought he would surprise us with his so-called thoughts, but this is some kind of a slapdash job that any musical apprentice could throw together…And he saw his life in a tailspin, and how he would win neither Adelka nor fame with some tremendous victory. Pale and exhausted, he withdrew to the side of the room, to the young conservatory students in a corner, where he prayed fervently to his goddess of art to save him from the catastrophe he glimpsed before him…Was there any point to this prayer? he asked himself, though he resigned himself to it after he ran through it with efficient faithfulness. But didn't this prayer really mean: God forbid that two times two should be four?

"And what do you say to the fact," a lower-division student, unfamiliar to Amadej, said in German, "that this *"Adagio"* by a Croatian is the *pièce de résistance* of this year's concert?"

"Oh, please," his interlocutor replied scornfully, "I've listened to it three times. An ordinary school assignment with the requisite theatrical effects and a few Oriental *motifs.*"

"So why does the old ass cycle it through all the Czech newspapers?"

"Why? Because a Slav wrote it. I mean, it's out of hatred for the Germans. And then again, he's way past his prime. To think he's still in a position to make decisions in the art world!..."

Amadej felt his chest tighten. At first he thought that he was witnessing the envy of someone not likely to be an artist on the inside of the system, but rather someone vying for property and worth. But then he reconsidered: these two were talking so openly and matter-of-factly about their assessment of my work...They've heard it three times...Perhaps I am overhearing true conviction here...

The concert was just set to start with a *fantasia* for organ, a graceful work by a highly talented fellow student of Amadej, who was studying music as a minor field and had his true vocation in the study of philosophy at the university, when Mme Lipovskova entered the hall through the main entrance. She was with her daughter-in-law and a forty-year old man, tall and handsome with a serious, manly face, black eyes, and a thick black beard.

"Lipovský," a student near Amadej commented. Amadej turned to him and inquired:

"And who would that be, if you please?"

"Dr. Lipovský. The attorney. With his wife and mother. They are a very musical family. Patrons of Czech artists. You know, you'll definitely be introduced to him today."

"I...how so?" asked a surprised Amadej of the other fellow, who was much younger than he and had a likable look to him. Amadej recalled running into him around the conservatory.

"Since you're the composer of the '*Adagio*.'"

"You recognize me?"

"Why wouldn't I? A brother Slav—a Croat!"

Amadej was carried away by emotion.

"Thank you," he said to the young Czech, giving his hand a hearty shake.

Meanwhile the director of the institute himself had come up to the new arrivals and led them to first-row seats just in front of the podium. Amadej watched the elderly lady with curiosity: she had luxurious, if completely gray, hair, which she had done up high above her forehead like a queen. She was a vigorous, rubicund woman with an energetic air about her, and great nobility in her intelligent, dark-gray eyes. The director was conversing with her with obvious great respect, and Amadej saw again in his mind the scene, which he had vividly retained, from Jahoda's narrations about how he had kneeled before this woman and told her of his love...

And right at that moment the concert began: the swelling tones of expansive, deep notes from the royal organ thundered through the hall. It was the young composer himself, a man of twenty-two with a look of extreme intelligence on his boyish, unshaven face, performing his own *fantasia*, with noticeable skill and ease. From the rehearsals Amadej was familiar with his friend's delightful work, right down to its final note, but in his distraction and freshly reawakened anxiety he wasn't listening now. His "*Adagio*" was next on the program after this first item—and now his entire dread was focused on the Lipovský family: what are they going to say about his composition?—Nevertheless new guests were continually arriving in the hall. The young Czech, Amadej's neighbor, recognized them all, curiously enough, right down the line: there is the *Hofrat*, that one is a physician, he's a scholar, over there's an aristocrat...he knew everyone's name and rattled them all off for Amadej, who only had eyes for the Lipovský family, which was busy exchanging greetings and handshakes with all these new arrivals.

By this point the young composer had finished playing, and he was being greeted by squalls of applause from the audience. The director of the institute led him out to the first row of seats and his young face glowed with enthusiasm, joy, and excitement.

A group of four conservatory students were now already on stage. They took their places with their instruments, and Amadej, as if he still couldn't believe his eyes, looked again at the program and read:

II. *Adagio* for string quartet: "Adela."
Composed by Amadej Zlatanić

A powerful chill spread across Amadej's body, and, shaking all over, retreated farther into his corner. There was silence, murderous silence, and so many people's heads in their places before his eyes! A note long and soft, yet full and powerful, rose up into the silence from the cello and started to spread luxuriantly, as if it were going to fill the hall by itself, until the quiet chords of the other three instruments joined it, as if flowers were raining down lightly on first love as it came to life...But Amadej was unable to follow the opening notes of his composition. For him they vanished into a deafening roar; everything was muffled and veiled by the insuperable helplessness of his soul. Every second he could only think that it was pointless stupidity, a lie, delusion…and in every way he felt like the lowest person on earth, without any worth whatsoever…exposed to the derision of so many people who were listening to this presumptuous work, in which his soul, as he believed in days of yore, carried on a conversation with Adelka's…Right then came the second movement of the *Adagio*, a gentle, extended and enthusiastic *cantilena*, which he had written feeling that his heart was opening up and out of it was streaming—reverberating with the notes of that melodic line—his earnest love— and at that same instant whatever was making him feel suffocated and despondent vanished. Now he couldn't stand the thought of a critique coming from these people, because he felt that this melody was of a piece with his entire soul, that it was the prayer of his heart from when his ardor for Adelka had been the most torrid. As if he had forgotten that he had written down those sounds with his own hand, he felt as if he were someone else listening in on the magnificent poem of his soul, which so moved him with its mighty emotions that it wrested a tear from his eye.

The instant the final chord sank into silence, Amadej was buffeted by an uproar of applause and spirited shouts, emanating from all corners of the hall. His heart thudded madly amidst these signs of triumph, in honor of the poetry of his soul.

This splendid feeling lasted only a moment but it was as if he had broken from the material world and been transported to the world of dreams. Yes, just for a moment…but that moment was worth a year of ordinary life. The pupils standing in front of Amadej began to make way for him, and he caught sight of the director smiling and beckoning him. He was saying something but Amadej could not make out his words. The director led him out to the elegant figures seated in the first row, where he repeated Amadej's name several times. The ladies and gentlemen there congratulated him. In this way he came face to face with Mme Lipovskova. He bowed deeply to her, and kissed her hand, and she regarded him with curiosity through her *lorgnette* and then said to him, smiling with especial kindness:

"So, he's a Croat!…I'm quite happy about that!…I congratulate you, sir. Your composition is very beautiful. Full of poetry. That's the unanimous notion of everyone around me."

Her son also offered Amadej his hand, likewise congratulating him and declaring his satisfaction that Amadej was Croatian. "In our family," he said to Amadej, "the traditional respect and love for you South Slavs have been preserved. These feelings stem from my late father."

"I know about that," Amadej fired back excitedly. "From the late Mssr. Jahoda, who was my first music teacher."

"Jahoda?" said Lipovský, this time louder and obviously surprised. He took Amadej by the arm and brought him back before the elderly lady: "Mother, what a coincidence! This gentleman knew our friend Jahoda. He was even a pupil of his!"

"You don't say…He was my teacher as well," she said, fixing her eyes on Amadej with vigorous interest. "How I'd love to hear more about his life down there! He was my teacher and my friend."

"I was aware of that, *gnädige Frau*. He told me about it himself."

"Well, why is it that you've never paid us a visit?"

Just then chords from the piano reverberated across the hall. The third piece on the program had begun, so the elderly lady said quietly to Amadej:

"You must pay us a visit. We would be delighted if you'd be so kind."

Amadej promised he'd come by, and then he returned to his place at the side of the hall.

That means my composition was a success!—he thought happily, his heart rejoicing and his joy spreading like light. He had intended to say goodbye to everyone this very day, and leave town on the afternoon train for Vienna. But now he changed his plans. He decided to depart the following day on the morning train. Mme Lipovskova's invitation to visit her home pleased him tremendously. From it he was expecting the fulfillment of something inside him that had been making itself felt with great force since he had listened to Jahoda's stories; it seemed that he was about to experience first-hand the spirit that had inspired Jahoda to compose. Something grand, something mystical, was about to manifest itself in the intimate encounter with the lady whom Jahoda had referred to as Mařenka…

He was received warmly at her home, almost with jubilation, by all the members of the household. Once more they congratulated him on the success of his composition—and then the elderly lady started inquiring about Jahoda. She did so with patent curiosity, but the conversation never got around to that certain something that Amadej was keenly anticipating. It was as if the old lady had either forgotten it already or was deliberately keeping him in the dark about it. She did, it is true, repeat several times, speaking with clear respect for the late Jahoda, that he was a great artist, and in every regard a wonderful human being—an idealist, who could never be content on this earth; but for Amadej this was next to nothing. He had wanted her to supplement Jahoda's tale and bring to life that enchanting world of love that her heart and Jahoda's had shared. "Once more," he thought with some disappointment, "I have gotten to know some other new thing only in its external aspect"; he was remembering the now dead Vesely, who had shown him how people know the world only on the surface and are incapable of fathoming their own essence or that of others. Despite this conviction, and despite all the kindness with which he was received in this excellent house, Amadej was almost sorry he had come. Some wonderful illusions had melted away, and there had been no kind of exceptional or glorious experiences on his part. When he had gone up to the lady and announced, "I used to be friends with Jahoda, who—"it had been up to her to complete that sentence. But no, life went on in its normal, everyday, prosaic way...But when he recalled how they collectively deplored the fact that he had not gotten in touch with them precisely at the time when his life in Prague was anything but dazzling (and

Amadej during the core of this cross-examination made only a minor allusion to this state of affairs, while keeping completely silent about his hunger)—then he started trying to convince himself, with a pleasurable sensation of malice that he had acquired from imitating Vesely:

"They would have slammed the door in my face!...The bottom line is that the old woman has a very different Jahoda preserved in her heart and mind that I do. And Jahoda had once placed into the soul of this woman—as Vesely had done to Amadej's ideals—his world view, his ideas and thoughts—and then he'd fallen in love with her...If I had come to see them, they'd have labeled me a wastrel who was trying to worm some money out of them with this secret."

And he rued the loss of these illusions. He felt plagued by a dark pessimism, as if Vesely's spirit had coiled up around him...And Vesely's words came once more to mind: all people live on one and the same planet, but each inhabits the world of his or her own soul...And those worlds seldom touch each other.— And then he began thinking fervidly of Adelka: their souls could not help but inhabit one and the same mutual world, which contained everything that was superlative, everything most beautiful and most noble about humans...What was their reunion going to be like—it was a mere two days away now!...

Later that same afternoon, he had occasion to regret his rash conclusions about Mme Lipovskova. She sent him a costly tobacco box with the following words engraved on it:

A Tale of Two Worlds

To the young Croatian artist
Amadej Zlatanić
M.L.

A letter was attached, set down in an aged but still steady hand:

Please accept this bagatelle as, above all, an acknowledgement of the wonderful start to your artistic career—but also as thanks for reawakening in me marvelous memories of a man whom I esteemed, alongside my unforgettable husband, as the most noble of all people I have known. I wish you happiness, and all the best of everything, in your musical life, and may your work be, first and foremost, a blessing to your people, who are brothers to my Czech nation. And may you never forget the friend of my youth, your teacher Jahoda. What he taught you can only have been great and valorous, because in him lived both the divinely sparked artist and the honorable man, in perfect harmony...

Amadej read her letter twice, and this put the elderly woman in a new light in his eyes. He understood her; and that great something for which he'd been casting about the previous day, when he had responded favorably to her invitation, now revealed itself to his heart. He kissed her signature, completely transported by emotions sublime...And tremendous happiness shed its light into his heart...Now he saw himself crossing the threshold to a new and glorious life.—Off to see Adelka!—That was his soul's grand acclamation:

159

to Adelka! And blissfully he yielded himself up to his heart, which would in turn transport him to the girl he loved.

Chapter Eight

Amadej had never before felt in himself creative powers of the type he sensed as he traveled south in the railway car. His mind invested the rhythmic clatter of the train with an enormous wealth of harmonies and melodies; it was as if invisible beings around him were bringing them forth...By dint of the creative force in his spirit, he became enthralled by the noble vanity of the artist and by the thirst for glory, and in those exalted hours for his soul, it seemed to him that everyone should have to bow before the divine spark that resided in him...everybody, including even his guardian, that selfish man Plavčić. And in his imagination he watched as he enticed a tear out of that man's eye with the music he'd written, and then he saw Plavčić coming up to him: "Amadej, there's something divine inside you. Forgive me for not understanding you earlier..." And Amadej imagined further how he and Plavčić shared an embrace that encompassed all of humankind and raised him, like a brilliant light, high above the base desires originating in our material nature and in our hunger for bread, gold, and power. And even Plavčić was dear to him and everybody...everybody was!

His spirit was propelled by a great desire to engage the whole human family in this thrilling embrace...and his eyes clouded with tears from the overabundance of joy he felt in his wide-open soul.

In his delirium, he could see clearly how readily the execution of his artistic plans would increase appreciation for his work even in the last little hut of his hometown. His reputation and fame would spread to the very center of Croatdom until—voilà!—he could see himself standing before a sheaf of scores on a stand on the Zagreb stage. Two hundred singers, men and women, were lined up on the risers, with fifty musicians in front of them, and the house, chock-a-block with the most sophisticated members of the community, was waiting for him to give a sign that he was ready to unveil the composition that would make him famous. Amadej raised his hand, the first radiant chord flooded the hall, and then all the instruments and the triumphant song of human throats began performing the composition that, just a little while ago, his mind was teasing out of the rhythmical clacking of the railroad cars. On and on, more and more, as if out of an inexhaustible and abundant fountainhead, the magnificent poetry of voices poured from his soul...The music concluded with a brilliant finale...and the audience continued to stand there, mesmerized, as if the enchanted tones of his music had carried their souls away with them as they receded into the unexplored distance. And then—as happened with Dvořak—riotous applause arose, as did mighty cries, shaking the hall, of "Glory to Amadej! Glory!"... A feeling of enormous gratitude spread through Amadej's en-

tire being, while a thousand hands were stretched out
towards him with delirious cries of "Victory!" and
"Glory!"…But at the back of the first and most prominent *loggia* a diminutive, sweet female form sheltered,
riveting on him her divine, childlike eyes that were running over with tears through which shone her smile of
love and gratitude. It is Adelka! Direct your shouts her
way, to Adelka, and not to me! This is her work; she
formed it within my soul. But the public can no more be
made to settle down than the sea when it is whipped up
by a powerful storm: "Victory! Glory!"—though
Amadej yells "The Victory of our love!" and falls to his
knees before Adelka: "The victory of your spirit"—and
begins to weep from a superabundance of happiness.

He was convinced that this would somehow win her
heart…and now his entire being was filled once again
with love for Adelka. In every thought, in every intention and step of life in the future, her face would be
there with him; everything would be redolent of her
spirit and soul. And as for the beauty of these districts
through which his steam-driven train was now racing, at
times broad plains and fields with hillocks on which
white chapels gleamed, and elsewhere the majestic
mountain ranges of Styria and Carniola…It was as if
they were only beautiful because of her, and for her;
everything was consecrated to Adelka with that same
powerful feeling into which, like waters into the ocean,
all of his thoughts and other emotions ran: the feeling of
love. And when the train finally crossed onto Croatian
soil, and several Croatian peasants got into their car, he
felt as though in that moment something had been re-

turned to him, something of which fate had deprived him in the earliest days of his youth: his parents. He would have loved to embrace those peasants and bestow on them sincere, fraternal kisses of gratitude for the emotions with which their presence enriched his soul. Greetings to you, my beloved homeland, o mother mine! Hail, hail!...And Amadej, with a shudder of holy fear in his heart, lifted both of his hands towards the heavens, which gathered and met above his homeland and which blossomed through his tears into a hundred splendid colors; his lips trembled in blessed delirium as he uttered a wordless but exultant prayer and repeated with delight and bliss the verse: "Greetings to you, my beloved homeland!" It seemed to him that the lines of that great Croatian poet were emanating for the first time from his soul, like a spring finding its way from the inner core of the earth up to the light of day...And he continued to recite to himself that beautiful poem, and when he got to the words: "Accept my kiss..." he thought he felt tremendous emotion stabbing his chest...and he burst out crying with happiness, moved by his emotions and a sublime pain that sanctified the soul more than any joy.

"Why are you crying?" asked an old peasant woman sympathetically. She had boarded the train along with the other peasants.

After four years, I am now back on Croatian soil, in my homeland, and my swelling emotions are producing unstoppable tears.

The peasants looked at him. They said nothing. Did they understand him? Is this something one has to learn from a book? But then one of the older peasant men said to him with conviction: "Every person loves the place he was born, the most."

Then one of the younger peasant women, who had been watching Amadej with sympathy in her calm gaze, struck up a conversation with him. As soon as she learned that he'd had no family to call his own since he was a little boy, she asked him, with pity in her voice:

"So who is it you are so happy to see, if you don't have any blood relatives to greet you?"

"All Croats are my family!" Amadej told her in an effort to explain what he was feeling.

"But this thing you are talking about—isn't it just a private matter for you?" he was interrupted by this question from a peasant woman.

"He's among his people," her neighbor explained further to her.

"And I have," Amadej said ecstatically, "a fiancée!" and he felt his face blush immediately. And to think that Adelka and he were not yet engaged!

"Ah, of course, that's another matter," the older peasant lady chimed in. "You'll end up having children, and with them around you'll forget about having no father and mother. And so you see God gives everyone something to grieve about and something to rejoice over," she added before continuing to meditate in that same vein about human life.

Finally the train barreled into its final stop, and by the time he was seated in a wagon, darkness had descended on the land. Just another hour or two, and I will be close to Adelka, he thought, over and over, and he could hardly believe that this was really happening.

They reached the first little houses spread along the road, far from the center but belonging to the town. The driver turned to Amadej and asked: "Where do we stop?"

The question made Amadej uncomfortable. It reminded him that he no longer owned the house that, despite Amadej's many bad memories, had served since his earliest childhood as a reminder of his mother. As if her spirit had remained alive inside it...And now he was abandoning her, and it was as if the last trait identifying him as a local was disappearing, and now there was no reminder that he was the descendant of people who, like all the other inhabitants of the town, had struggled to build a life here. But not even that thought could mar his sense of celebration in the hour of his return to the place of his birth. It seemed that the bright windows of the houses, and the gardens surrounding them, along with the tall steeple of the church and the square in front of it, and the wide streets with their trees and benches...Everything was waiting joyously for him, with an eager heart, and it greeted him warmly and offered its help in brightening his mood...I'll offer Plavčić double his sum of money to sell me the house back, Amadej said to himself, instructing the coachman to stop at the first inn.

The next day, when he looked through the window, and the image of his hometown appeared before his eyes—an image planted deep in his heart and now brilliantly illuminated by the early morning light,—he enveloped it completely with his heart and his delirium, and with a smile on his lips and fears in his eyes he began to recite Preradović's verse: "Accept my kisses, oh country of mine!"…He could hardly wait for the moment when he would again join his people: never before had he felt that he loved them all, without exception, in this way, and they were all so pure and virtuous…In them he could find laughter and tears for his soul, and find reflected the struggles and aspirations in his heart…It was all engraved in the eyes and on the faces of these acquaintances and witnesses from his old life: in them he glimpsed both his history and the sweet ties of love binding them together. Not in a single one of the expressions of welcome with which they hailed him did he detect the slightest trace of any kind of convention or formality; it was as if they were just thinking up these words and pronouncing them for the first time, seeing him once more in their midst.

Joyous to the point of glee, Amadej bided his time until it was late enough to go see Adelka. That moment was sure to be the very sanctification of his soul, for after it would follow his real life, flooded with brilliant happiness as far as the eye could see…What was Adelka going to look like? Had she changed? Of course—for by now she must be a fully developed young woman…and Amadej grinned at the thought. How lovely she must be now if back at that almost childlike age she was already the harmonious perfection of maidenly beauty!

Before noon had come, he had crossed the threshold of her home with excited but uncertain steps. In the corridor he encountered an older woman who looked familiar. It was Adelka's godmother. She welcomed him humbly, but happily, and then she practically flew off to the bedroom and announced, at a volume to which she was herself unaccustomed:

"He has come!...Here he is...He's...arrived!..."

Amadej strode towards the open doors as if he were going into a magnificent shrine. An air of great mystery clung to him, as if this one moment, having arrived at last, was going to provide him the means to clear up a huge, fateful mystery.—And suddenly he saw her. She stood in front of him, all dressed in black; her head was lowered in despair over her shapely young body. When she raised her eyes to meet him, he recognized, with an ineffable thrill in his soul, that she had remained just as sweet as ever, with her child-like essence still finding expression in her calm, dark blue eyes. She is gorgeous, and he thought he would have to fall to his knees in front of her, for there were no words in any human language for his feelings.

"Adelka," he began to say softly, as she clapped both of her hands to her cheeks and started to cry.

As he stood there in front of her, he was in amazement at how she was grieving. Should he comfort her? In the harmonies that were flowing around her, dedicated to grief and love, any words he uttered were going to be full of grating dissonance. In her weeping, it was as if their souls were declaring anew that they were of one accord and belonged to each other—and from that feeling a wave of voluptuous happiness welled up through his whole body.

"Adelka, God wanted it this way...and we are alone now on this earth..." he said to her softly. Her sobs grew louder...Amadej came closer to her and took one of her hands in his. He stood there, spellbound by this contact, which his heart had magnified in its reveries to the peak of happiness for which anyone could wish...Is she mine now? he wondered to himself, and at the moment reality melted into something indeterminate and contingent, he placed his other hand on her shoulder and gently pulled her to his breast. His whole soul, his entire being, thrilled at that glorious instant to a magnificent hymn of victory.

And then, just as suddenly, there was no longer anything extraordinary about their encounter. It was obvious to him that their meeting could never have been any different at all.

PART TWO

Chapter One

A madej found a position in the church. It paid four hundred *forints* per year.

"That's enough to start out with," he told Adelka confidently. "We'll have lodging at your house, and later, when my work picks up the way I have it mapped out, you won't be lacking for anything your heart desires. Once my name gets into circulation out there, musical societies and publishers will be falling all over themselves to get their hands on my material."

He had subscribed to a number of professional publications from Prague, and they carried detailed information about the conservatory's end-of-year concert. About his particular composition, one observer had written: "...And now we turn to the second item on the program, a piece by the young Croatian composer Amadej Zlatanić. We would not venture to discuss this as a work originating in the constrained atmosphere that accompanies pedagogical discipline. One is, rather, obliged to employ in this case the critical faculties with which one examines works of art originating from the pens of full-fledged composers who already have carved out their places in the artistic world. This judgment of ours is justified by the original ideas behind the composition, their free but completely correct execution, and the profound warmth of the composer's poetic feeling." This assessment by the most competent of critics fanned the flames of pride in Amadej. His heart glowed, and he began to talk to Adelka about his dreams with the self-assurance of a person who sees no obstacles on the road ahead. Caught up in this enthusiasm, and on the verge of delirium, he blurted out:

"The greatest of my works...will...will be a a huge composition that I shall dedicate to you, for I never would have been able to imagine it had I not become so enamored of the sweet virtuous person that you are. The composition is going to be called 'Hymn to Love,' and it will be performed for the first time in Zagreb, and you will see how much glory will redound to us both! I have the whole thing ready and finished inside me, but when I once begin writing, I will touch it up and smooth it out every day, until there is not a single wrinkle or embellishment on it that could detract from the beauty that was a part of it when it was born in my soul. Adelka, it feels like my chest is about to burst with towering emotions when I consider how they are going to hail my name and what the newspapers will write: the composer exalts his homeland and himself with this work, in which the tale of his love is written with magnificent notes...And they will all respect us, and love us."

But then, as if he had said too much, he flushed with embarrassment and added: "I can talk this way with you, but not with anyone else..."

These plans were all but unintelligible to Adelka, for she did not understand what kind of work he intended to do. But his eyes were aflame with the fire of love, and she understood from everything going on that the fire represented the vaulting rapture of his soul, and the fever in the eyes of the young man—a man so virtuous and noble—was dedicated to her. This made her happy. She didn't understand him, but she felt his words carry her into the radiant distance somewhere among the pink clouds where he began to disappear as his soul made him soar to ever greater heights and with more and more daring...

After New Year's, Amadej and Adelka got married. They moved into Adelka's little house, which, as nondescript as it was, contained for Amadej more luxury and happiness than all the rest of the world. Not even his guardian Plavčić could enter this realm of dreams come true, trailing his vulgar cares with him, although he had pointed out to Amadej immediately following the nuptials that Adelka's little house was encumbered with five hundred *forints* of debt, money he had once lent to Adelka's father when the latter had found himself in dire straits.

Amadej's chief preoccupation was to establish a choral society, which, according to his plan, would serve as a seed from which would grow again a musical life like the municipality had once known...and this would be just the way for him also to proceed with his more far-ranging musical work. To him this plan seemed totally natural and quite feasible, since it was true that you couldn't find a single person in the town who would not be enthusiastic about such artistic offerings. But as soon as he tried to set his plan into motion, some unlikely obstacles popped up. He could not find even two people to stand by him and make a firm commitment. For the most part they belittled his designs and wrote them off as ridiculous or, occasionally, alien and exotic. The priest and the mayor, when he complained to them about this during one of their conversations, said to him:

"Your idea isn't for us...Of course it would be great to make this happen, but as you will see, all of your hard work is going to come to naught. Our people have more pressing needs..."

"You can count on the fact," the priest added solemnly, "that our people will always see in you their native son, whom they remember meeting on the street, and it will strike them as ludicrous that you are hastening to imitate foreigners in these great endeavors..."

And when Amadej started going around to the houses, one after another, for the purpose of rallying girls to join the choral society—girls being, in his mind, the easier half of the young population to inspire—he was faced with well-nigh insurmountable roadblocks. Everywhere he read on the faces of the mothers and fathers objections to his wish, even before he uttered it; one lady, from a wealthy merchant family, the mother of three daughters, even said to him brusquely, almost maliciously:

"What has gotten into you? D'you really think my little girl is going to sing on a stage in public, like a waitress or something?"

"They don't understand me!" he complained to Adelka.

Then he began thinking about Zagreb.

"I might wither and die here," he said to Adelka; "but there, even if I lived hand-to-mouth for a time at first, my rise would be rapid. I've decided on an excellent plan." He was speaking with conviction that betrayed the ease with which he believed his ideas could be realized.

"I have still not elaborated a single one of the compositions I've sketched out, but I shall send my *'Adagio'* off to Zagreb; after all it succeeded brilliantly in Prague in front of a most knowledgeable audience. When my name is known to the public in Zagreb, I'll travel there and make the rounds."

And he dispatched the *"Adagio"* to a *kapellmeister* he knew, with the request that it be performed in a prominent concert. Six months later he was still waiting in vain for news about his composition—after many more requests...and then he copied it once more by hand and sent it to *Kolo* Society in Zagreb. A short time later the program for an upcoming concert of *Kolo* reached him, and his composition was among those on the list. At the exact same time he received a letter from a music reviewer with one of the Zagreb newspapers, containing a request that he respond to the following questions:

When did he write the *"Adagio"*? What was the occasion for its composition? Does he have other compositions? Have they already been published anywhere? Where did he study music? And more inquiries of that sort—Amadej sent conscientious replies to the questions in the letter.

"In the end," he told Adelka when he was full of happiness, "recognition cannot elude me. Thank God, my day is coming soon...When the time comes and they mention my name with praise in Zagreb, then the circles that carry weight will be interested in me, and the distrust of me among our very own people will fade away."

And indeed it did happen that when Amadej's fellow citizens read his name on the program for the Zagreb concert, the esteem in which he was held rose. He could see this in their eyes and in their behavior, and he picked up on it in their conversations.

After the concert, he was in agony as he awaited the verdict of the Zagreb papers. Then one of them wrote: "A string quartet of our young musicians delivered a harmonious rendition of the '*Adagio*' by A. Zlatanić..." A second: "The third item, an '*Adagio*' for four strings, is creditable as a *bagatelle*, and pleasant to listen to..." The newspaper that wrote about his work in the most detail was the one with the music reviewer who had contacted Amadej by post and to whom Amadej had given those sincere answers: he had composed this piece when he was still a student in Prague, and it had first been performed at the conservatory with other student works in an end-of-year concert. He had wanted to append to the responses the review of the Prague paper *Dalibor*, but he had held off, thinking it would be too vain of him, an unseemly amount of self-praise, very nearly a sort of advertisement. This reviewer wrote: "The composition is correct, but in every measure it bears the mark of the stilted rules of harmony that leave the listener with the impression that this is more of a school assignment than an independent, unconstrained work of art that belongs in a concert hall. This unknown young man might prove capable of evolving into a good composer over time, but of course only with the continuous study of sound classic works, especially older ones..." And the fourth newspaper wrote: "A trifling schoolwork piece—as is evident upon listening—in which the *motifs* explored are for the most part already well familiar." In a fifth paper there was no mention either of his composition or his name, because the space dedicated to the report on the concert was consumed by naming the visitors from aristocratic circles and other weighty personages and by describing the *toilette* of their ladies.

This left Amadej embittered. He felt himself battered all at once by ignorance, injustice—and vulgarity. But at times he would start to ask himself: Am I not overestimating myself? I am so taken by this one piece of my work, and it's a good bet that I'll never be able to produce anything better...Perhaps, then, that means that this "divine spark" is not within me; maybe I am not called to be anything higher than an ordinary worker whom they pay just enough to live on; maybe my art is nothing special and I am nothing but a simple day-laborer!

These thoughts made him feel completely agitated and at a loss, but he withheld from Adelka the reviews from the Zagreb papers about the composition in which he had left his great love registered in notes...They had not understood those notes...But quick as wildfire the rumor spread around town that Amadej was very far from being what he had been building himself up to be since his return from Prague. They gossip even distorted the reviews in the Zagreb paper, and they did so with that kind of gusto that small people and small nations are given to, unconsciously but so whole-heartedly, and this was as good as telling Amadej to his face that he had not (thank God!) become what he had once thought himself capable of. And this gossip, sure enough, made it to Adelka's ears. Once, when after supper he took his leave to continue working on some composition, she said to him in her naïve way:

"If I were in your shoes, I wouldn't wrack my brains or throw away my nights like this. They already consider you arrogant...and claim you'd be living a better life, a more peaceful one, if you didn't trouble yourself with such things..."

Her words left Amadej feeling defeated. For the first time in his life, he harbored unkind feelings towards Adelka. Could incomprehension and aversion really be speaking through her—against the very things that had enabled him to win her respect and love?...He left the house—this time without a tender farewell—without kissing her or even saying goodbye. But he lasted only a few hours outside his home. Pain weighed on his chest like a stone. Why did people talk to her like that? Why did she believe them? Was she really in the wrong here? Did he have the right to insult her—he asked himself— especially now, when she acknowledged bashfully to him that the little house was about to be animated by the blessing coming from their love?...And he went home.

Adelka was waiting for him with a smile on her lips, but she could not hide the fact that she'd been crying...A heartfelt and tender scene of reconciliation ensued. Adelka retired for a rest, while Amadej remained at the table in order to work. But it did not go well. It was starting to seem that these were worse conditions for his artistic work than his hungry days at the Prague conservatory. The very air hemmed him in like iron, and he didn't know how to break through into freedom.

Adelka and he did, however, proceed happily into their new state of family bliss. But right away Amadej's straitened financial circumstances began to impose new concerns on him. When he had come back from Prague, he'd been able to say of himself: the only clothes I have are what's on my back. Because of his position among his fellow townspeople, and owing to the vanity of a bridegroom, he had to stock up on all kinds of basic necessities—on credit, of course. And now here came Plavčić with another admonition: no interest had been paid to him since Adelka's mother had passed away.

"Who's going to pay it?" he asked Amadej firmly.

"Why, I will," Amadej replied with conviction.

"So pay, little brother, pay! Everyone needs a cross to bear!...It's the same thing with this little house, on account of which I lent your late father-in-law, out of friendship pure and simple, five hundred *forints*, when it's not worth even three hundred! You can see yourself that this place is not even livable. The doors and windows are loose, the floorboards are coming up all over the place, and the roof leaks.—It's old, all of it, and falling apart. And who's going to fix it? I'm not going to do it, and you don't have the means. This house is so far gone that you'd be best off selling it. Out of compassion, I'd buy it from you. One Christian to another, I'd cancel the interest you owe, and give you a hundred in cash on top of that. If you think there's a better offer out there, fine, go get it. You see, I'm doing the honorable thing here."

The house isn't mine, Amadej mused. It's Adelka's, and she'll have to decide about this.

He and Adelka then discussed the issue for a long while. The inheritance from Amadej's father had long since passed into Plavčić's hands, and here hers was about to do the same. This thought pained them. But when they considered the reasons as adduced by Plavčić, it seemed he was telling the truth. The little house was located outside of town, and it was in pretty bad repair. And in the final analysis those hundred *forints* meant a great deal on the eve of the blessed event. In addition one other thing was enticing Amadej. Plavčić had taken Amadej's former home and fixed it up nicely; he had also promised to rent it back to Amadej in the event that they sold him Adelka's house. With completely child-like delight, he contemplated taking possession once more of what was his. Plavčić has no children, he said to Adelka, so it's no wonder that our having a child doesn't occur to him, and he'll sell it back to us at a good price. So Adelka gave her consent to everything that Amadej had decided. Plavčić bought her house and counted out one hundred *forints* into Amadej's hand.

What joy there was in the house when they saw what a vast amount of money they possessed.

"This money is yours," Amadej told Adelka. But she didn't want to accept it from him.

"No, it's yours. What would I do with that kind of money?"

"It's neither mine nor yours—but it will belong to...do you know to whom?"

Looking into his eyes, she asked innocently: "Whose then?"

He laughed at her naïveté, and then she understood immediately—but she would not let him say what he meant...How his heart reveled in her confusion and youthful embarrassment! It had been a long time since he felt in himself such a brisk flame from that sweet fire that engulfs the body of the poet.

He withdrew to the little garden behind their house, where he spread out on an old, half-rotten table a thick sheaf of note-papers bearing the title: "Songs Without Words." Here was written, in musical notation, the story of his happiness; he had been thinking of Adelka and writing this since falling in love with her back when she was a little girl—tiny cherub that she was. Three of those songs were already written: "Dream," "To Adelka's Side," and "You Belong to Me." He began reading through the last of these, and the farther along he got, the more fiercely his eyes burned with zeal and bliss. "Yes, you are mine, Adelka," he whispered into the solitude around him, paging through the composition to the end. He was completely transported by the sensation of divine fire inside him.—Above this particular score he had made the following programmatic notes:

Not through an embrace, nor through a kiss, nor by means of any words at all—or even with these notes, Adelka, can I convey to you how much happiness you have brought, with your beauty and your tender feminine heart, to my very soul!

Then he leaned over the sheets of paper and rested his fevered forehead in his left hand while gazing far out into the dark sky filled with stars, gently brightening the night with their light. It was the onset of autumn, and the trees were shedding leaf after crackling leaf, but the night was warm, and soft and peaceful; from the distance the feeble voices of crickets and other insects pushed up from the grass. In the room where Adelka had stayed behind, a cozy golden glow was visible. Adelka must be in there, occupied with the preparation of sets of little clothes; sometimes the painful expression on the elongated, careworn face of this young woman who was on the cusp of becoming a mother touched his heart with sympathy. There was something sad, ineffably sad, about her, and it poured lovingly into his soul, after which the first tentative,embryonic shapes of a new piece of music would announce themselves in the depths of his spirit. As if out there somewhere, far away, the sublime sounds were already echoing in all their glory, and he were eavesdropping on them; it seemed like the music was already famous—until he heard in it the first exuberant motifs of his "Hymn to Love," conceived so long ago. It will be the crowning piece, the climax of the cycle, Amadej thought to himself rapturously, and he returned to his work on what had been pressed from his soul in order to be born among us...Once more he thrust his overheated brow down onto his waiting left hand and stared into the night. An indistinct, but unaccustomed, sound began to envelop him, as if mysterious unseen creatures were congregating around him. Out in the darkness, the outlines of the trees were now bathed in the brownish-red light in which there glowed a small bright dot, which grew, and grew...until all at once there appeared from out of that point none other than Adelka, with an infant at her naked breast. The expression of maternal happiness on her youthful, maidenly countenance made her exquisitely beautiful, as did the singular, breathtaking look in her eyes—peaceful but ecstatic; that look alone could have brought forth the fruit of her passion.

The well-proportioned, fragile limbs of the child were like the incarnations of the kisses that he and Adelka had used instead of words when professing their love.

With trembling hand Amadej began to write: "God entrusted an angel with a gentle human soul so that it could gain entry to our world. The angel transported it carefully through the lustrous universe and sought, with a look of solicitude in his eyes, for clothing and form for this soul so that it would bear the aspect of our planet. He was watching from on high as your lips, Adelka, met mine in a kiss..." And then he wrote down notes, rapidly, nimbly, so that he could capture on paper the sumptuous torrent of sounds pouring forth from his soul. The first rooster had already claimed the day in the neighborhood when he put down his pencil and started reading back what'd he'd written. It was sound! he told himself. This was the way he always patted himself on the back when his satisfaction at having succeeded in committing to paper the things that had just thrust their way out of his soul was almost too much for words. In the window to the room where'd left Adelka he could still glimpse a light. He hastily collected all his music from the table and, beaming with enthusiasm, went back into the room. Adelka was still sitting by a candle, lacing little multi-colored ribbons through the myriad holes of the children's outfits.

"You must be chilled to the bone!" she said on a slight note of challenge. "I called you twice, but you didn't bother to respond."

"I didn't hear you. I was all wrapped up in this—but listen!"

Then he read to Adelka in an overwrought voice the programmatic notes and scheme of his composition.

"It's beautiful," she told him. "But you won't show it to anybody, right?"

"Why wouldn't I?"

"Because you know what people are like; God only knows what they'd say about it."

"People!" Amadej grumbled. He sat down at the piano. The hard, troubled lines in his face vanished swiftly under the flames of zeal that flashed forth from his eyes as he played his new composition. When he concluded with a powerful chord, which towered up to a grand height, buoyant and luminous he inquired of Adelka:

"What do you say now?"

Whereupon she met his look with her child-like eyes. She blushed and shrugged her shoulders.

"It's pretty, if you say it is. Because you know I don't understand this business."

He wanted to say something but the words stuck in his throat. It was as if his soul had been dragged by brute force from the radiant heights into the realm of vulgarity.

Something settled over his thoughts like a cloud, and without uttering a single word he went into the next room. Her voice reverberated all around him: "I don't understand...I don't understand!"—and clung like a grievous injury to his soul. The very thing that his love-besotted condition had enabled him to create for her, was an offering of his heart that she could not accept with proper understanding. Not even she!...Is even this felicity of mine destined to be wrecked? Didn't I once see only myself in her being, as Vesely once did long ago, and then later I believed that love would seal by matrimony the perfect harmony of our souls,—and now I am faced with a dead body before me, one animated solely by the coarse concerns relating to self-preservation?

Time in the house was unbearable now, so out he went into the street. But he hadn't gone more than a few steps when he heard her voice from the window behind him:

"Amadej!"

He turned around.

"Are you really angry with me?" she asked, crestfallen. He thought he saw tears on her face. He turned and went back home and found her standing, head bowed, by the table with its stack of children's clothes onto which her tears were now descending.

"Adelka," he said gently, lifting up her chin and looking into those peaceful, virtuous, blue eyes—eyes he loved so dearly!

"Forgive me, Adelka. Forgive me!" he beseeched her as he kissed the tears from her face.

They were now reconciled, but a leaden cloud continued to press on both their souls.

Shortly thereafter Adelka gave birth to a hale and hearty little girl.

Chapter Two

At this point the family moved into Amadej's old house. His former guardian demanded a hundred and fifty *forints* per year in rent; when Amadej made the observation that this amounted to thirty percent of the sum for which Plavčić had earlier purchased the house, the guardian—his face reddening precipitously—lashed out unexpectedly at Amadej. From the jumbled shouts that followed, a frightened Amadej was able to gather that Plavčić had made many repairs around the house with his funds and that since the town was on the verge of getting a railroad, the value of houses and parcels of land was rising considerably.

"If you won't take it, it'll be easy enough to find another tenant, now that all manner of workers and surveying crews are piling into our town," Plavčić concluded. Amadej acquiesced. He asked for forgiveness from his affronted guardian.

The whole town was talking about the construction of the railway. One day at the close of winter Amadej received a request to drop by to see the mayor in his office. The local priest was already there; both of them greeted Amadej affably, and the priest even offered

Amadej his hand, an honor he had extended to few people since taking the collar.

"You have to help us with something," the mayor began slowly. His tone was earnest but also sweet and even fawning. He was not wont to speak like this when interacting with other people who were dependent upon his indulgence in taking care of their business. "You'll understand directly," and he began to speak to Amadej about how, right at the start of spring, preparatory work was going to begin on the railroad, and it was to be overseen by the two of them in conjunction with one Leopold Lešeticky, Geodesist and Chief Surveyor. "As luck would have it," the mayor continued to elaborate, "this year during Holy Week will be the twenty-fifth anniversary of Mr. Lešeticky's entrance into government service, and on this occasion—as we have come to know from reliable sources—the Chief Surveyor is going to be presented with a major award. He'll be living here in our midst during that time, so it is incumbent upon the citizenry to shower him with the appropriate honors and display gratitude for the unmerited good favor and fortune that has come our way in connection with the railroad extension— something for which our town has been vying for over twenty years."

"The Reverend here," and the mayor pointed towards the priest, "he and I have worked out a provisional program and, among other things, we have decided that on the eve of the big day we will adorn the town with flags, and in the evening illuminate the houses with lights, and regale the Chief Geodesist and his lovely wife with singing—that is to say, with serenades, and a torchlight procession."

"That's fine...but who will do the singing?" Amadej asked.

"Well, now, that's our job. The Reverend and I will scare up the singers, and the new district assessor, Dr. Mesarić, will be our right-hand man in this. Your only concern will be to coach the singers and practice the performance. You could set a poem to music, a quite lovely one that the good Dr. Mesarić has penned for just this occasion. Of course the music will have to be something ceremonial...like...you know...formal...As a matter of fact, the word is that the Chief's wife is extremely musical. So...an opportunity. For you to win some recognition for yourself."

"On the day of the ceremony itself," the priest jumped in now, without giving the mayor a chance to finish, "we will celebrate Holy Mass in the church with a '*Te Deum*.' I need you to see to it that the choir chimes in with something pretty."

"A Mass! Why, gentlemen, that is seven pieces of music. How am I to pull this off with untrained vocalists whom—*nota bene*—we don't even have lined up yet?"

"You'll manage. All it takes is the will," the mayor replied.

Amadej was at the point of balking once more, but then it dawned on him that this celebration might be able to serve as the seedbed for the nascent project that was never far from his heart and mind: a choral society. And on that foundation it would be simple to go on to build a music society,—because the town council had recently sold another major tract of forest and used the proceeds to finance its contribution to the railroad enterprise—but they had also lent out the large remainder at interest.

"Very well," Amadej noted. "Do me the favor of assembling the male and female singers, and I shall take care of the rest of it."

"Now look here," the mayor said smugly. "This is the poem." He pulled out a sheet of paper and began to declaim, haltingly:

The iron horse's roar will unwind
as the way is broke by his mind
Across our region's inclines and valleys.
We'll be the link between the lands and seas!
With medals of gold decorating your days,
here'smore pay for your visionary work and ways.
To bathe 100 years more in glory—
these be our ardent wishes for thee!

"Well, what do you say? It says everything in a few words, eh?...And now you'll set this to music...you know...that kind of music..." As he spoke the mayor waved his hands about in the air but failed to find the right words.

Amadej stuffed the paper into his pocket and left the room. He was preoccupied with his notion of establishing a choral society.

That same evening Amadej was surprised by an invitation to come over to the parish priest's for a little chat. Usually the mayor went to the rectory in the evenings for such discussions (at least since he had made peace with the priest following a stormy electoral campaign for the local representative to the *Sabor*)—and also the district head, the assessor, the doctor, and a few gentlemen from the office of the *župan*, the district prefect, if they were in town. Yes, the invitation took Amadej off guard. But he quickly decided that it must be because his artistry was coming to be appreciated—and this notion blindsided him with a pleasant sensation not dissimilar to triumph. Around the table he found the mayor, the doctor, the district head—and the new assessor. This last man introduced himself with the following words;

"I'm Dr. Mesarić. District assessor and 'a poet of sorts.' This was how he was pleased to introduce himself to everyone, and he threw in a smile—but not one capable of overshadowing the seriousness of those words about being a poet...He was a youngman, energetic, twenty-seven years of age, with an attactive, strapping physique: tall, athletic, and muscular, with a full face and ruddy cheeks; and large dark eyes that bulged a little bit in their sockets, lending his entire face an expression of insufferable willfulness. This young doctor-cum-'sometime poet' had made the town his own in short order. Even his unbridled boastfulness, and the transparent lies he told about his origins, education, and experiences—everyone took them at face value. He liked to rule the roost and to use power to get his way, and his audacity stretched all the way to presumptuousness—though at least here he had not yet taken it upon himself to cuckold anyone, as some were saying behind his back that he tended to do."

From this first meeting forward, Amadej did not like Mesarić. To start with, their temperaments were complete opposites, and divided them: on the one hand, chaos, bragging, and impudent assertion of priority, and on the other Amadej's composed personality, with its modesty and interminable reveries about the ideals that tower above the whole of humanity. In addition there was the fact that, since their very first encounter, he had found Mesarić's boasting with regard to music and literature to be both insufferable and incomprehensible. Admittedly, Mesarić did know how to sing, from memory and with great affectation, several operatic arias in his powerful, unpolished baritone—but the things he said about Meyerbeer and Wagner and about the direction of modern music in general and about other things, using obscure words and odd phrases—this surprised him at first, but then it dawned on him that he had involved himself in a conversation with a man for whom the names of the above-listed composers represented the limit of what he knew about them. Amadej could not put up with such insolence and—whether they were going to understand it or not—Amadej made up his mind to tell the assembled group an anecdote: a man was inveighing against Mozart, who—so the man said—had written many operas only one of which, *Der Freischütz*, was worth listening to. Whereupon someone else said to him: "Why, it wasn't Mozart who wrote *Der Freischütz*, but Weber...So you see, the 'music critic' snapped back, how great was Mozart if he didn't manage to write that one either?"

That evening around the priest's table there was no further talk of music. And Amadej regretted his indiscretion. But to his enormous surprise Mesarić took him to a pub after the guests all went their separate ways. There Mesarić got him to toast their friendship and switch to a first-name basis.

"Rely on me! I'll help you in anything, however much I can," Mesarić said to him.

And Amadej determined to repair the offense he had caused Mesarić with his first improvident anecdote.

For several days Mesarić toured the town with another young man, a merchant, both of them in formal wear, to be sure; they went from door to door to judge whether the young lady of the house had a voice good and strong enough for singing. This was something new in town, and the young man's chest puffed out more and more as they worked the streets in tailcoats and tophats. This was the first time that an honor of this sort had fallen on him, and to think he was in such distinguished company! Whenever they showed up on someone's threshold, they thought they saw victory on people's faces, in their eyes, and in the very way they were received. The young merchant was at considerable pains to find a way of repaying this great honor, which was reflecting so well on him simply because of Mesarić, who was a doctor and an assessor. And he was a poet, and he was so amusing and dressed in such a tasteful manner! The two of them recruited twelve young ladies in this way, whereupon they were joined by twice as many men from the merchant class and officialdom.

Enthusiasm was the order of the day in the new club—and even the one woman, who at the time of Amadej's first request had not been able to conceive of her daughters' appearing in public and singing on a stage—even she said to Amadej the first time she brought her girls to rehearsal:

"Well, if anything nice is to be accomplished around here, it'll take an educated man from outside coming in and instructing us."

Feverishly but gleefully Amadej and the newly assembled company set to work. They spared no effort and worked the way people work when they feel they have both a calling and a longing to succeed. But how many problems there were to overcome, day in and day out! The "public holy Mass" that was to be held in the church on the day of the ceremony was well known in the broader musical world: it was by his former professor of composition. A majority of the choir spoke out against it, however, immediately following the first rehearsal, as did Mesarić in the midst of Amadej's and his circle of common acquaintances. They maintained that his Mass was too sombre for a celebration such as Lešeticky's, and that they needed to select something more joyful and rollicking. Amadej's stomach turned at the thought of treating art in this way. He felt like responding with the sharpest insults he could think of, and then just dropping out of the whole affair—but the old saying came to mind: *per aspera ad astra*—and with herculean effort he soothed the roaring lion in his breast. To placate the insurgent singers, it would not do to refer to his own taste in music; nor to rely on the renown that his professor enjoyed, both as a scholar and as an artist; nor even bank on the fact that this Mass had won a prize from the academy in Strasbourg in a competition with a hundred other compositions from France, Germany, and Austria. The only effective tactic was to show them the title page of the score with its dedication to one of the most famous members of the ruling house.

And he began to slave away; and his heart was quickly carried away by the beautiful work done by his teacher. He did not fail to observe a single hint provided by the composer for bringing the deep religious feeling in the work to its fitting expression, or a single clue designed to let the classically construed architecture of the piece shine through. The old master's ability to develop rhythms, melodies, harmonies, and the coloration of the notes was that marvelous! Through exhausting practice sessions he used his passion to inspire and goad the hearts of the singers who at first were impervious to his pickiness. And when he felt, as he did form time to time, that it would be impossible to give with this group a worthy performance of the works of his professor, he would say to himself: "No, ladies and gentlemen. Singing like that—it's a desecration of art." At one rehearsal he had to admonish the young merchant several times to sing more quietly; this was the same man who had recruited the choir with Mesarić and who had since that time miraculously sprouted angel's wings, but the merchant snarled back:

"You can't scream at me like I'm some kind of apprentice!"

"You must be willing to do what I say," Amadej reminded him firmly. "I am responsible for making this successful."

"Why do you think so highly of yourself? I mean, we read what they said about you in the Zagreb papers."

Amadej felt like he would have to drop everything and run away from there, screaming: "Leave me alone! This stupidity is suffocating me, this ignorance and this impudence!" But he managed to control himself. As if the beatific figure of old Jahoda had suddenly materialized in his mind—Amadej grew peaeful and told the young businessman:

"Forgive me!...Obviously I don't know everything but I beg you to try to defer to me as long as I am here. You and I and every one of us here—we are all equal participants in the coming success or failure."

When he would return to his home, mentally and physically spent following these rehearsals, Adelka would give him a sympathetic look and try to convince him to have done with unpaid toil such as this...And when he regarded the expression of warm compassion on her face, and their little daughter in her arms, he couldn't help but ask himself: will these superhuman efforts truly bring any kind of lasting success? But then he would wake up the next day as a man who had been entertaining sinful ideas: "What kind of a person would I be if I let myself get down? I cannot ignominiously strike the colors under the very eyes of my enemy; and my enemy is misunderstanding and ignorance."

"You'll see...This is not the way to establish something...You're tormenting yourself—and not for money!" she persevered.

At these words Amadej flew into a rage; as vexed as he was with his work, it was not difficult to push him into a paroxysm.

"Please, don't talk to me any more about this," he said to Adelka, "if you can't give me a boost, at least don't spoil it for me!"...Then he fled to the pub, but returned home shortly to find Adelka crying...In point of fact she had cried that whole time, thinking over and over: "What does he want from me?"

Nonetheless, fifteen days before Easter he was in a position to say to his singers: "Thank you, ladies and gentlemen. This is how we must sing!" That evening the practice went off as never before. Beside himself with joy, Amadej sensed in himself a mysterious power to control the will of the singers with his every move and his very glance. It was as if he had succeeded in imparting to every one of them a perfect understanding of this work of art, and as if they they had breathed life back into this work with a vitality originating in their souls, the way the mind of the old professor had created it. A single sublime feeling of unity hovered over the choir that evening, and Amadej looked at the young merchant with gratitude in his eyes for having submitted so pliantly to the demands of a higher will in which the laws of beauty were being made known. Mesarić did not attend the rehearsal that evening. Amadej blamed himself for this. Of late the two of them had not been on the best of terms, and there was a reason for this: Amadej had still not set to music the other man's poem of welcome for the Chief Surveyor, for the sole reason that the poem itself failed to inspire him sufficiently to want to craft a musical garment for it. In addition, Mesarić was proving to be repellent to Amadej in other ways. At the practices, for instance, he would sit all evening long beside the wife "advanced in years" but still spry—of the good-natured tax collector named Slivčić, whose eighteen-year old daughter, attractive but not exactly bright, was also part of the choir. Slivčić and Mesarić knew each other from the pub, where a tipsy Mesarić had drunk to their friendship and started addressing him by his first name. Inordinately proud of the fact that he was now friends with Dr. Mesarić, Slivčić took the other man into his home, and Mesarić had never shrunk from divulging to Amadej the vile plans he had hatched with the entire household of his dim-witted friend. From this gutter soul Amadej shrank with a shock. Whenever Mesarić would interrupt his whispering with Mme Slivčić and call out repeatedly, after a lousy rendition of some part of the liturgy, "Gorgeous! Absolutely gorgeous!"— Amadej could feel ire and abomination clamoring in his breast.

But this evening, basking in splendid success, Amadej's feeling of disgust towards Mesarić disappeared—and on the way home afterwards he decided that he would somehow find a way to set Mesarić's poem to music.

This was the most radiant evening of Amadej's entire life. He felt that all people were his friends; and in his soul the final traces of insult and heartbreak—so often inflicted, unintentionally of course—melted away. His contentment was reflected back to him from Adelka's face. She had already begun to anticipate with trepidation that the time would come when Amadej would once more grow unfairly indifferent to her and the child—and she would not know the reason why. She started biding alone in the house, considering whether or not Amadej was one of those people she had heard about who tire rapidly of family life and find themselves regretting the day they had gotten married. She would shake all over at the very thought of it. Back when Amadej was still in Prague, her mother used to speak about him to her as if he were already a member of their family. For that reason she almost loved him more as a brother than as a husband. Nonetheless she was thrilled and her heart rejoiced whenever he told her, in ardent throes of love, that she was the only woman in the world whom he could love in this way.

"You are my lucky star...my angel!" and whenever he would speak to her in this manner, tears would come to his eyes from an excess of emotion. Thus he was incapable of lying. But, still, days were coming when he would turn his back on her, maybe cruelly. "What was he going to want from me? What's wrong with him?" she would wonder amidst tears—all the while feeling that a terrible calamity was swooping down into her heart. In vain would a downcast Amadej appeal to her at the earliest possible moment to forgive him; in vain would the hours of reconciliation come, when he would tell her once more in the ecstasy of his powerful feelings how much he loved her and how she and the child constituted his only joys in this life. "I am unhappy, dreadfully unhappy," he would tell her yet again, at the end of his rope, "the people do not feel about me the same way I feel about them...if I am not afflicted by the pain and injustice directed at me, then i still suffer because of other people's pains and injustices. And the poverty of my homeland and the distress of all of humanity weigh heavily on my soul,. I am rarely, very rarely, happy... Only when I'm at your side, Adelka, and with our baby in this little house, do I feel like I am in paradise and capable of forgetting everything else..." He would go on pointlessly like this. She believed him, but she feared that at any time she could see the grim, harsh side of him and that he would flee from her and seek outside their home for what she could not give him. Ultimately she began to believe, with the relish of true conviction, that he must be unhappy in their marriage, and grief after grief piled up in her heart.

That evening after the successful rehearsal Amadej felt, for the first time after a long while, the urge to compose. So right up till midnight he worked on his "Song Without Words"—on the concluding section, actually, which he called "A Hymn to Love." Outside the early spring night was cold but gorgeous. All of nature was in the process of awakening to new life, and Amadej felt—aware of Adelka's closeness, and thinking of the embrace of her soft yet shapely body, of her kiss on his lips, and the sweet scent of her girlish body that so recently had taken leave of him and gone off to sweet repose—he felt as if he wanted to, and could, embrace and fulfill the magnificent poetic promise offered by his soul on this starry spring night. Mellifluous, powerful reverberations coursed through his soul and left him feeling that the world and the life that existed on it were attractive and good. Something mysterious, warm, and ineffably brightt began to heat him up from inside, and this in turn gave birth to his power of creation. He was surrounded by a perfect silence in which all that could be heard were the soft strokes of his pencil upon the paper. The cries of their child from the next room rousted him from this work. He sighed like a person jarred from a deep slumber, and he put down the pencil. Adelka began to nurse the child, and afterward she lulled it back to sleep with no further ado.

"Adelka!" he called to her softly.

And when she appeared in the door in her white nightgown, with her hair let down, her calm eyes, and a smile on her pale, hollow face, she seemed to him like an apparition from the other world, where his soul floated, creating poetry; she was like the incarnation of the notes of music he had just called forth from his soul.

"Listen," he said. He started to play his composition for her on the piano.

She bent to his will and remained in the room—but the sounds form his soul disappeared behind his youthful face, illuminated by the glow of artistic fire, behind his moist flaming eyes and the thick locks of hair tumbling down over his broad forehead.

"This is you, Adelka. It's your soul, my love!" He told her this as he passionately kissed her hands.

"Amadej, I forgot to tell you this, but while you were at the practice, Mesarić was here." She said this to him as if she did not feel she belonged to that gleaming realm of poetry into which his soul was cascading.

Amadej let go of her hands, and she looked fearfully into his eyes. His face was suddenly disfigured by a brutal expression. Gone was the exultation that she had just seen brightening his face with singular beauty.

"And you have to tell me this right now?...This very minute?...What business did he have here?" Amadej asked, his voice hoarse and trembling.

"He came by so that you'd make a musical arrangement for one of his poems for the Chief Surveyor."

"So why didn't he come to practice with the other singers? Why didn't he come there and tell me this?"

"How am I supposed to know?"

"Go away!...Go! Why do you do this to me?"

"What is wrong with you this time, Amadej?" she asked anxiously.

"Just leave me!...Now look at this!" he took the sheet of paper that had been at his place at the piano, ripped it to shreds, and hurled the pieces to the floor.

Adelka exited. She began crying in the next room. After a quarter of an hour Amadej came in to be with her.

"Forgive me...You're not to blame. People are to blame. I believed myself to be in heaven, and you dragged me down into the mire of their existence, even if you didn't know you were doing so. I'd prefer it if you kept me in the dark about his visit. Even more so if I've been deceived..."

"Amadej, why do you have to be this way? Tell me what you want from me!"

He was bitter. She sat there on the bed, covered in tears, like an innocent martyr with an expression of pain on her pale face.

"Forgive me, Adelka!...you're guilty of nothing. Forgive me!" And he knelt before the bed, once more kissing her hands, and she smoothed his wildly disheveled hair with strokes of her tender hand.

"I am not good to you...but I love you, Adelka. Oh, how I love you!"

"Your are good to me...but you aren't happy with me."

"What are you saying, Adelka?...I am happy...and yet unhappy. I wish that you loved me with a love so powerful it filled your entire soul. With a love that consumed your entire being—and I wish everyone loved me that way..."

He wept. She could not comprehend the reason why, and kept asking herself: What's going on with this man?

It wasn't long afterwards that the mayor, the priest, and the district head, along with a pair of high officials from the regional governor's office, came to a rehearsal. Mesarić stood with them listening to the singingfrom the side of the room, and after every piece he would applaud and then say: "Bravo! Excellent! Beautiful!" The assembled gentlemen could not help but follow his lead, and that rehearsal became a genuine triumph for Amadej and his ensemble. The mayor led the properly fired-up gentlemen to his house afterwards, and Amadej went along. Their little chat evolved into a proper example of large-scale, generous Croatian merrymaking, and it lasted till late in the night. Of course everybody toasted everyone, but Amadej emerged as the center of attention after Mesarić's toast. There were in the rich vocabulary of Croatian toasting traditions no high-blown words that he would shy from using to lionize this great artist, this wonderful human being, whose works were going to bring glory both to his name and to his Croatian fatherland. "When the fates stood over his crib, they saw that the genius of the Croatian nation had placed in his breast an ember of divine fire, and they destined him to become a priest of the art that, since the dawn of time, had been capable of casting a spell on people and bringing to life both wood and stone. Let us pay homage, gentlemen, to that darling of the *vilas*, the only person among us who can say along with the great Latin poet: '*Est deus in nobis.*'" — Mesarić drained his glass, went to Amadej and kissed him three times on the mouth, whereupon the company cheered adoringly and congratulated the speaker on his fine words.

"It's easy, good sirs," Mesarić continued, "to speak beautifully and passionately when the target of our talk is someone who has the power to inspire us. If my brother-in-spirit found in my stanzas some poetry worthy of his muse, then he must have been roused by it to kindle the fires of music creation in his own soul."

Amadej thanked everyone and concluded his own remarks by reporting that his musical setting of Mesarić's poem would be finished the next day.

Several days later Amadej invited Mesarić to come hear the poem. Mesarić brought with him the mayor and a few other men, and all concurred in their judgement that the composition had turned out to be top-notch. Mesarić explained to the men that Amadej had faithfully and nimbly used music to interpret his poetic thoughts, and the mayor added for Amadej's benefit:

"Indeed you did succeed in getting…exactly that— you know…like that" and he worked hard with both of his hands while talking to familiarize the others with his unelaborated notion.

With two weeks to go until the festivities, the chief surveyor and his spouse finally arrived. The first thing everyone noticed was the tremendous contrast between husband and wife. The Chief Surveyor, a man of fifty-five, was to all appearances already old: a tall, gaunt, stooped, and thoroughly listless man. His wife was at least twenty years younger, a vivacious woman full of strength and life, a bit too heavy—yet this stoutness of hers disappeared amidst her lively, flowing movements and the fiery, youthful expression in her black eyes. Everyone proclaimed her a very beautiful woman, and the mayor even went over and above that after their first meeting and declared that she was also a very witty and intelligent person with whom one could converse most pleasantly...But then again the mayor's people, sensitive to the point of malice to states of affairs like these, had begun, in the face of such an antithesis between the spouses, t concoct a variety of unseemly rumors until they were instructed not to take the measure of their own personal cleverness on people who could cause God only knows what kinds of problems in terms of the building of the railroad line.

The preparations for the activities for the evening before the festive day were carried out insofar as possible in secrecy. Everything had been finished and readied, and there was nothing to do but await the big day with growing impatience. But wouldn't you know it: the sky proved on that very day to be ill-disposed toward the celebration. From 7 pm right up till midnight rain poured down in what seemed to be one steady sheet.. By 8 pm the mayor was forlorn. He had been arguing with conviction that one of his properties was the most suitable spot for the erection of the train station. But he would have to win over the chief surveyor for that, and such was not possible unless the ceremony that had been prepared with such great care and sacrifice succeeded in softening the man's heart, known to be hard sometimes, and threw a veil over his eyes. The mayor thus got worked up into such a lather that evening that, like some kind of desperate military commander with his back against the wall, he wanted to lead his torch-bearers and singers blindly to the guest of honor's lodgings in the midst of the heaviest squall. The notary public—a rather clumsy man with bow-legs who was one of the town's leading functionaries but who was very concerned with his health because of his eight children—opposed this idea, whereupon the mayor launched into a series of furious and ear-splitting screams about making the trek with umbrellas. But when the notary went on to explain that torches and umbrellas don't belong together, the mayor's despair at the derailment of the celebrations was so great that he called the notary a stupid ass, right there in front of a large crowd of townspeople. But the insult was lost on them, and it was of no significance, because of the unrest among the torch-bearers, the singers, and everyone who was slated to participate in the festivities in any way. They looked at each other, pale and scared, as if some great, elemental misfortune or catastrophe were hanging over their heads; with anger in their voices, anger that verged on despondency, they talked of nothing but the intransigence of the heavens that serenely went on pouring rain into the already wa-

terlogged streets of their town. A few of them kept their
cool, however, and they boldly made wisecracks at the
mayor's expense, criticizing him to his face—something
the mayor could not be expected to notice in his current
state of excitement. Then the tumult of nerves abated
when, after 10 pm, the people lost all hope that the
ceremony would be held outdoors. The mayor, the singers, the torch-bearers, and all of the other functionaries
assembled in the large meeting room of the most
prominent hotel in town, the White Steer, and decided
to hold the ceremony there, insofar as possible. They
made haste to deck the room out in green boughs, flowers, pictures, and statues; the mayor sent off to his own
wine cellar for his very best wine and a table where the
guest of honor was to sit. Places were set with the most
expensive dishes that could be collected from the homes
of the mayor, the priest, and a few other wealthy and
prominent townspeople. The singers were shown to
their places, and the invited townspeople to theirs—and
finally the mayor felt a sense of relief: they had succeeded in rapidly preparing the hall for the ceremony,
right down to the lighting by means of great numbers of
candles stuck into silver chandeliers. He was convinced
that his speech was going to achieve the calculated effect,
and on that account he continued making the rounds to
certain people with guidance on when they should interrupt him with shouts of "Vivat!" and "Hear, hear!"—To
erase the stain remaining on his conscience from that
epithet of "stupid ass" that he had bestowed on the notary, he took it upon himself to whisper into the latter's
ear at an appropriate moment that he should submit a

request for financial support forthwith, even before going to bed that very night. The notary, you see, was expecting the ninth little blessing in his household. — The lighting, the greenery, the flowers, the rugs, the paintings and statues, and the buzz of voices among the guests—everything attested to unconstrained high spirits in the group, and soon enough the wine would be having its effect, too; for now it was sparking like gold, and flaming like rubies, under the brilliant reflection of the candles in the silver light fixtures. — When everything was ready, then, the mayor got into his carriage with one fellow citizen and they drove to see the guest of honor. Out in the hard rain in front of the inn, the *hoi polloi* awaited their return, drinking the house wine provided by the publican (at the town's expense) and preparing to greet the arrival of the guest with a tremendous cry of "Hurrah!"

Within just a few minutes the tramping of horses' hooves could be perceived in the muck of the street; then the light of the carriage came into view; and then the breathless horses drew up in front of the crowd, exhaling from their nostrils powerful bolts of steam into the rain. The notary, forgetting momentarily his precious health, strode as adroitly through the rain as the saber on his leg would permit, and opened the door of the carriage, whereupon a shockingly loud "Hurrah!" rose into the wet heavens. But the only person who got out of the coach was the unnamed townsman, who reported that the chief surveyor was not feeling well and had retired for the night half an hour before. The mayor had not even come back; he had set out in a second carriage straight for home.

But what the skies had ruined outside, nothing could ruin inside the church the next day. Shortly before the holy liturgy was to begin, the mayor showed up with the Chief Surveyor and his wife in tow. Together they all sat down in the first row, where the pew was draped in green cloth. Behind them the town representatives and higher officials were seated; they were all dressed in formal attire, and on their faces they sported tense expressions formal looks on their faces that they had picked up from each other on the misguided assumption that their position in society, and the roles they were playing in this event, demanded it of them. As soon as the official personages had been seated, the ringing of the little bell heralded the priest's approach to the altar; the organ roared to life; and the yellow glare from the wax candles fell on the golden robes of the priest and his assistants.

When the church service was over, Amadej expressed his gratitude to the singers: "Thank you. You all acquitted yourselves well." The mayor prepared to introduce the man of the hour to his well-wishers, but he was prevented from doing so by the chief surveyor's wife who told him very directly, if sweetly, that she thanked them most warmly for all these unexpected honors but that her husband, Lešeticky, was the kind of man who could not abide public pomp. He was, to be sure, grateful for this display of positive feeling for him that the townspeople obviously nourished in their hearts.

"How did you like the singing?" Amadej inquired of Adelka. He was waiting for her by the exit.

She smiled with her tranquil eyes and said:

"It was pretty...The apothecary's wife said though that all she could hear was screeching female voices." (Wouldn't you know it—her daughter was not part of the choir!)

"And the others?"

"Some of the others noted that it sounded morbid...that for such an occasion there should have been some happier singing."

Amadej had no wish to discuss this matter any further with Adelka. Indeed he felt those uncharitable emotions towards her begin once more to rise up in him: it was as if she were culpable for all of these misunderstandings that were now coming to the fore as conscious acts of malice.

After lunch the skies cleared swiftly and Amadej headed to the town park, where he knew he'd be able to find all the city fathers who'd been present in their official capacities at the ceremony. In fact, he was tugged their way by that noble vanity—with which no real artist can dispense—that insists that everyone pay unconditional homage to the same things he reveres. Under his direction, the singers had given an exemplary performance of a simple yet intelligent and majestic composition, which in Amadej's eyes was capable of moving anyone, just as one is stirred by looking at the simple but serious architecture of a place of worship of any type, seeing its clear and well-proportioned beauty and the dignity emanating from its lines.

In the garden he encountered the priest, the mayor, Mesarić, and several of the other town fathers; also present was his former guardian, Plavčić. Of course all the talk was of the day's celebrations, and the rain of the previous night and the curious disposition of Geodesist Lešeticky, who could not stand loud public spectacles.

"And our Amadej outdid himself," the priest was saying. "He trained them up pretty well on short notice like that!"

Praise of that sort did not sit well with Amadej. He wanted to hear just one word that was more serious and more relevant to the composition and the way he had interpreted it and the way the singers had performed it. Classifying the work as "pretty" meant nothing at all. Then the mayor had his turn:

"Nice...and fitting, given our circumstances." The chief surveyor's wife kept her head turned towards the choir the whole time. Amadej spared no effort; we have to give him that! For three whole months now my daughter's been walking around the house humming: "*Kyrie eleison, Christie eleison...*"

The assembled group laughed good-naturedly at that anecdote.

"It was all right," rejoined the priest now, "only—it seemed to me that the note that the music struck was too sombre for this type of ceremony. Would it have been possible to pick something more upbeat?"

Amadej felt the blood pounding at his temples.

"You know, Reverend," Mesarić said confidentially, "church music is like that for the most part, but maybe a somewhat quicker tempo would have been in order?"

"I noticed that, too," the mayor chimed in. "Yes, if it had gone at a faster...clip...that way, you know...But it is what it is. And what you all sang today can be used again when there is a need for a really solemn requiem, for instance, while for holidays you could work up something lighter with them...As the good doctor says, the *tempo*, you know...that's how it is..."

"It needed to be precisely the way it was," Amadej stated firmly, although his voice was shaking.

"That's the way you musicians think, but we are also allowed to say what we like and what we don't like," the mayor said. He winked conspiratorially to Mesarić and the priest.

That confidential gesture emboldened Plavčić, who had been very circumspect about expressing his opinions in the company of people smarter than he. He now intervened in the conversation about the Mass, saying:

"Zounds! I can hear like it was just yesterday the voice of dead old Matija the cobbler. My legs would start to jiggle in church whenever he was in the mood to strike up a merry note. And his *dudaš*, the one he'd play during midnight services—do you remember, Mr Mayor? The people would be dancing around all over the place. That, Amadej, is how you should play, too."

Everyone laughed, even as his heart cried for the ideals being wrecked by uncomprehending hands in their blindness. He was convinced that he must this very day rip into shreds all the sheet music that he had stayed up late in the night copying out for his singers, and then shamefacedly lay down his arms. I cannot fight this...

He had come here to engage in a discussion of the fascinating artistry of his teacher; and when they acknowledged the hard work with which he brought this

212

work of art to life with that ignorant and untrained choir, they also wantonly disseminated their conception of this work that had won so much acclaim in outside artistic circles. —So they are lecturing him and in the same instant dragging the genius of art onto the three-legged workbench in a cobbler's workshop and placing in his hands an awl, so that he can study with that lame old shoemaker Matija, who when he was half-soused used to profane the regal musical instrument in the shrine of the Unutterable, compelling the genius instead of a splendid fugue by Bach to appear in the wretched sounds of a *dudaš*! He couldn't think any more about it; hatred, pain, and lamentation tied up his soul. He couldn't bear the thought of being around other people but craved only the peace and quiet proferred by his modest home, which kept itself cut off from the world...If Adelka at least understood him, if only he could ascend in the company of her soul into the upper realms of his art! And now, feeling afflicted once more, he saw before him the figure of old Jahoda, his attentive face and his honest blue eyes and the smile of a reasonable man who sees and recognizes everything around it for what it is; he was holding one finger pointed upwards to the heavens and saying in his indulgent, paternal way: *Per aspera ad astra*! But when he looked at those people again, hemming him in and speaking with absolute conviction about the benefit that the continuation of the railroad would bring, the appetite for unseemly and flagitious revenge was being born in his heart. They carried on as if they had completely exhausted the topic of church music, and consequently Amadej believed that he should

213

be able to tell them to their faces: you are complete dunderheads! Why is it you feel no shame at pronouncing such mulish judgements about something you don't understand?...His late friend Vesely came to mind, and he felt like telling them about that debauched yet talented man from whom he'd heard, way back in the Prague days: They will envy you for buying an ox today for a hundred *forints* and selling it on the morrow for a hundred and ten. And should you write a symphony like Beethoven, Dvořak, or Brahms, they won't even look at you...How could Vesely have understood them this well? Probably because he had come across them in his homeland, too...for these people are littered about the entire world!

At this point the mayor's dog came rushing over to his master's legs; "Fido" was spindly-legged and had gray fur, a long snout, and a wise look in his eyes. He halted in front of the mayor, wagging his tale vigorously and looking up at him soberly: Don't get angry at me for turning up here! You know I love being with you more than anything!

His master understood the look in the dog's eyes and benevolently stroked Fido's head; then, to the great enjoyment of those present, he began to tell the story of a severe illness that the dog had overcome. He had had to send the dog off to Zagreb for an operation.

"Do you know, gentlemen," he concluded, "that this infirmity of his cost me a full fifty *forints?*"

The town fathers were evidently intrigued by the hound's illness because, for some of them, an operation on a dog was a real novelty, while for the rest of them, it was that the dog stemmed from the mayor's house where, as you can see, the very dogs have a right to diseases and cures that in undistinguished homes are the lot not of animals but people.

The mayor fielded all kinds of questions in a conscientious and matter-of-fact way, and afterwards he placed on the edge of the table a lump of sugar, which Fido only dared to grab when his master said to him: Go get it!

"What an intelligent dog!" Plavčić said with conviction. He was about to launch into more musings, on some topic or other, when the mayor breathed the words: "The chief surveyor!" He spoke in such a way as to make everyone around him recoil in fright at the weird and unexpected sound of his voice.

Indeed, Chief Surveyor Lešeticky had just come into the garden, leading his full-bosomed young wife by the hand.

On the faces of everyone in their group Amadej recognized agitation that could only come from some kind of irrational fear of this alien man and his wife.

"Make room! Make room!" the mayor said in an unaccustomed tone. He shoved the city fathers around rudely, whereupon everyone began jostling and elbowing everyone else chaotically, even swinging chairs at each other to make room at the table.

But the chief surveyor and his wife did not come over to their table. He returned their greeting, sat down nearby with his wife—who had carefully wrapped a traveling rug around her shoulders—and spoke to the innkeeper. The mayor waited in vain for the surveyor at least to glance his way, so that if nothing else he might be able to decipher some wish in that strange fellow's eyes. They mayor blanched, and in his vexation he mumbled as if unconscious: "He didn't come this way..."

"You could have just invited him over," opined the priest, and Mesarić agreed. This time even Plavčić ventured to say that, indeed, an invitation would have been the way to go.

While their table was awash in this kind of vexation and indecision, the chief surveyor actually stood up and began to walk their way. The mayor sprang to his feet to greet him, while the other townspeople stared at the newcomer; some of them wore an expression of naïve curiosity on their faces, while others tittered and giggled like sycophants. There was total silence at the table, though, as the two men stood nearby and began to converse.

"Holy shit, the surveyor's little woman is gorgeous!" Plavčić said, naïvely believing that this was a good way to pay Lešeticky a compliment.

"And she's rich," someone else said with an air of importance. Her dowry was worth a hundred thousand to him. "That's rich!" the three of them quickly blurted out in unison. They remained absorbed in this news, which actually wasn't new, because the servant girls and cooks had already been talking about the colossal wealth of the Lešetickys. then the chief surveyor walked the rest of the way over to their table, and they all stood up at their places; their faces beamed with happiness and propriety—with undertones of bittersweet obsequiousness and respect. The engineer did not shake hands with anyone, but he nodded his head at them after they bowed and then he turned back to the mayor, who was waiting for his orders.

"Please introduce me to this gentleman."

"Here he is," the mayor said, smiling ingratiatingly.

"This is our artist." He pointed at Amadej.

The chief surveyor extended his hand.

"It's an honor to meet you...If I may ask, my wife would like to make your acquaintance."

Amadej, somewhat taken aback, gave a bow.

"The choral music in church today filled her with awe. I don't know my way around such things, but she studied music at the conservatory in Vienna, and she can size up such things more or less like an expert. It is her conclusion that church music in such a serious style as yours is hardly cultivated anymore in our country's big cities. I hope you will not take her directness amiss—but she had not entertained any hope of finding it in a small provincial town in Croatia, either. Therefore, if you will permit me…"

He insisted that Amadej stay by his right side, and thus they proceeded to the table where the lady awaited them with an endearing smile on her face.

"Oh yeah. Take a look at that!" Plavčić, the first to regain his composure, just had to blurt out, in an expression of his surprise.

"That Amadej is a man of parts," Mesarić noted next, staring absently, along with the others, towards the table where the young lady was warmly shaking hands with their artist.

"A highly educated woman—I noticed that in my very first conversation with her," the mayor opined once more, rather pleased with himself, while Mesarić and the priest exchanged confidential glances and nudged each other's legs under the table.

The mayor, who was keeping a strict watch over the animated conversation over at the chief surveyor's table, was also a bit discombobulated and asked the priest if it would perhaps be the thing to do to call the other two over...?

After the priest and Mesarić both indicated that they shared the mayor's opinion, he said decisively: "Off I go!" and off he went.

The men made room once more around the table, squeezing their chairs even closer together. —The other two then actually did come over. The lady graciously returned the greetings of the burghers, who remained standing reverentially at their places, until, not paying any attention to the rest of them, she said to Amadej, in intimate tones, as if they were old friends:

"Please, *kapellmeister*, have a seat next to me." And without so much as a glance at the mayor, who was waiting behind a chair at the head of the table to offer her a seat at the appropriate time, she prevailed upon Amadej to join her, and she reached for an additional stool herself and pushed it his way.

Everyone stood there expectantly, standing by their stools, while from her fresh young face, and particularly from her dark, Gypsy-like eyes, irony shone forth along with a sense of her own superiority. Amadej regarded her fixedly, while the mayor introduced the members of the group to her. He involuntarily compared her beautiful face, refined and healthy, with lively black eyes, full of wit—compared it to Adelka's face, which contained not a trace of the forceful emanation of a critical mind, or of capriciousness or even obstinacy.

In the presence of the chief surveyor, the conversation gravitated to the building of the railroad, and in particular to the selection of a site for the eventual construction of the station. No matter how many burghers there had been in that crowd, you can be certain each one would've owned property at a site that was—they were each convinced—made to order for the depot!

Meanwhile the chief surveyor's wife was asking Amadej all about his muscial studies, and she went on to tell him that she had completed her vocalist's training at the conservatory in Vienna—and finally, in the kind of voice that women usually use when they are feeling sorry for themselves about having gotten married so young, she told him that she had only just turned seventeen when she wed Lešeticky.

"From the classroom to the altar." And then she expressed interest in all of his artistic work here; she asked him what he had written, and she promised him that she would sing for him in public whenever he wanted, as long as he could guarantee an appreciative audience. "When will you come visit me?" she inquired with warmth and directness, causing the company to marvel; they were irritated by the laconic responses of the chief surveyor, and so they had begun to eavesdrop on the conversation of our couple.

The lady was strikingly, compellingly, dominant. Amadej could hold nothing back when talking to her. They spoke about the criticism of the piece he had heard, and Amadej, in keeping with a weakness of artists, also complained in general about the coldness and injustice that had awaited him when he had returned to his homeland.

"What they don't know about you, my dear, is how sensitive the soul of an artist is, because otherwise they would not treat you so poorly," she said persuasively, in a manner of speaking used by old ladies but which seemed to agree with her perfectly. "It appears to me that criticism that is reckless and unfair like this, is, when hurled at an artist, is like a cruel punishment with which an unreasonable father, lost in his own blindness, chastises his own fragile child."

She looked fleetingly at everyone seated around the table, as if she were issuing a challenge. Then, ignoring the men's knowing nods, she continued talking to Amadej.

"All the good artists I've known have been pretty much petted and pampered like a little child. Maybe this is a weakness, maybe not. The poet bears in his soul compassion and love for every one of God's creatures, and he presents them in the forum of public opinion demanding fairness for them—so why should he not demand that the world treat him the same way?...Have you, my dear, been attacked? In the newspapers?"

"Aha, what does it matter, *gnädige Frau*?...That's how newspaper reviewers are."

"Reviewers!" the lady said with a smile. "Take heart, my friend. They do not spare even the greatest geniuses. Imagine how incredibly fed up with them someone like Goethe must have been, since he felt himself obliged to write the verse: '*Schlag ihn tot, den Hund! Es ist ein Rezen-sent!*'"

Everyone smiled dutifully at the lady's witty repartée, but Plavčić had to lean over to his neighbor, a retired major, and, forgetting to whisper, ask in a voice that all could hear:

"Now who was Goethe, if you please?"

"Do you think I know enough to explain music to you?" the major retorted angrily. Just a little earlier he had tried proving, in vain, that placement of the train station on property owned by his son-in-law would save at least three kilometers of track construction as compared to even the best proposals that had thus far been mentioned.

"Amadej, we have a saying," the lady continued. "Namely, that you can be a good man and still be a lousy musician. Take for example my husband. His mind is impervious to the meaning of musical patterns. He cannot tell an overture by Bellini from one by Wagner. At first I was amazed by this misunderstanding. I didn't comprehend, so to speak, that it was incomprehension. Then I got furious about it, and later I laughed about it, and now I just wait till he leaves the house before I let myself be whisked away into the world of musical language." Then she added quietly: "Lešeticky would like to leave now, because he doesn't enjoy staying out for very long in damp air. Also something seems to be bothering him..." Then she turned to face the chief surveyor, who was draping a blanket around his own shoulders:

"My dear, it's time for us to go."

"I'm ready then," he said, standing up from the table and taking his leave of the group with just as little warmth as he had greeted them.

They were all irritated after his departure.

"What an unapproachable man!" they said to one another, comforting themselves nonetheless with the thought that he was equally unapproachable to each of them. And when they went their separate ways, Plavčić pulled Amadej aside and said to him:

"Listen, she was giving you the eye...If you're smart about it, you can help me out. Tell her when you see her, and if you have the chance, that she should persuade her husband to build the train station on the spot where the little house I bought from your Adelka stands. For you she'd do anything...She's a woman. And, you know, it won't be for naught, as far as I'm concerned, if you can get this done for me."

Chapter Three

I think and experience things that do not lend themselves to expression in written form. It's been ages since I wrote down any kind of coherent musical idea. I sit down, try to force it out, write twenty bars' worth, read it—and tear up the paper. The desire—it's almost a necessity—to record my experiences has made itself known in me...But to what purpose? Perhaps I will find in my past whatever my sin was, and I can bury the artist in myself and be a man who prizes Adelka's heart.

It's obvious that she is fading, but she claims stubbornly that nothing is wrong. I ask her, but in vain, and she does not share her pain with me. I've already thought of all kinds of strange things. Once I even said to her:

"Adelka, I need to ask you something, on the condition that you will neither laugh at me nor get angry. Tell me, isn't it true that you are jealous of Lešeticky's wife?"

She laughed. I knew she was incapable of jealousy, but I wanted her to feel it...

Often I see her weeping. Why does she cry? She cries, and withers.

I will record what I am going through, and then maybe I'll be able to locate my shortcomings. I will burn and forget everything as long as it will make me be good to her.

*

Lešeticky's wife Irma understands me completely... nonetheless I could never love her the way I love Adelka. She is highly educated, and artistic, and passionately devoted to music. She says it's the only art that communicates clearly, even when all other means fail a person who is trying to lay bare his or her soul. When I played the first of my "Poems Without Words" for her on the piano, she spoke to me from her state of absolute reverie:

"Amadej...You are a great artist."

I intended to parry this claim, but I have to admit that her words set my soul on fire.

"Be honest," she said to me then. "You know it's true. Otherwise how would you be able to write these beautiful, visionary pieces?"

Making music together allowed us to feel such a sense of openness and intimacy that we became dear friends. Once she told me, placing both of her hands on my shoulders and looking at me straight on, holding nothing back:

"You are going to be a famous man...Many women put on airs by singing Chopin, seeking to indulge their tender, artistic souls, and that is exactly how I am going to boast about being friends with you..."

This was, I am confident, a victory of the greatest and most beautiful traits of humankind. She was the first person, since I returned to my homeland, who revered with her very soul the same thing that I revere—and therefore I consider her a vestal virgin in the temple of music. Everyone else humiliates me, calling my art a trade or a craft that one uses to earn a living.

She is continually receiving new compositions by mail from Vienna and Berlin, and she has a gorgeous Bösendorfer for her accompanist.

Her husband had not the slightest interest in music. Out of all the times I went to their house, he only peered into the *salon* once; there we sat, the two of us, making music, playing a duet on the piano or with her singing (her voice was not forceful, but it had a bright timbre and she was an excellently trained mezzosoprano) to my accompaniment...All that Lešeticky required of me was that I tell him every month the number of hours, and he pressed into my hand a stack of banknotes: exactly two *forints* times the number of hours I had calculated.

*

My soul took flight again under the influence of this friendship. I was very much taken by the desire to compose a ballad based on Šenoa's poem "The Death of Petar Svačić," and I had already jotted down a number of *motifs*.

After that I started to orchestrate my "Hymn to Love." It was my intention to send it off to Prague. Via Prague, or Vienna, it might return to Zagreb...and by that point maybe my own people would want to put a little effort into me. I boiled over many times at our child during my intense sessions of work, so I would frequently ask Adelka to keep the peace as I worked nearby. Once I lose my patience, it takes me a long time to be able to get back into the flow of my ideas, and sometimes I have to postpone work altogether. And then I'm peevish, and nothing can cheer me up. But Adelka has little pity for me at times like that. Once she was flabbergasted by the way I objected to the child coming into my room to play, even when the little girl was not crying. So I blurted out: "Lešeticky's wife—now there, you see, there'd be the woman for me! She would know how to cheer me up and encourage me in my work, something you don't know how to do. The only things you have on your mind are vulgar concerns about money, and you are forever hanging your worries on my wings like leaden weights."

Afterwards I regretted terribly having said this. She didn't let me see her feeling sorry for herself, but she couldn't hide from me the fact that she was grieving inside. I knew she felt very unhappy. This pained me. I don't want to get all philosophical about this; I just know that I'm culpable for her being unhappy. And yet I do love her...

My spirit feels invigorated and cheered when I am with Irma, listening to her sing Grieg and Jensen with such fine understanding. But then there's this example of what I still have to endure.

Ever since construction commenced in our town on this railroad, my fellow citizens have been craving the opportunity to show their worthiness to join the outside world. A merchant procured a piano for his daughter's name day, and then the acquisition of pianos spread to other families like some sort of communicable disease. All of a sudden I had received more engagements for private tutoring than I thought I could handle. But when I started teaching them as my conscience dictated, they were not content. They all agreed that I should not torture their children with scales and other annoying exercises that made their fingers ache; rather they wanted their children to know how to play ditties for social gatherings or dance music for evenings out. The shop-owner's widow, R., astounded me, then, when she let it be known that she was completely satisfied with my method of training. Well, now, you see, I thought. Sometimes you can find innate understanding even in uneducated people. But oh, how disappointed I was a little bit later on, when she said to me:

"I like it, you know, that for now she plays all quiet like that, because it wouldn't be fitting for her to play happy things, since it hasn't even been a year since we lost her father."

I could not debase my knowledge and my art to the level of these demands, and so once again I found myself without the income deriving from private lessons.

When I mentioned this to Adelka, she said:

"What does it matter how you feel about it, as long as they pay you?"

"I don't work for pay," I responded.

She gave me a look that I was not accustomed to seeing on her face. It consisted of both complaint and something approaching reproach.

"You are not working for pay, Amadej?...Then what are we going to live on?"

"You do not understand me," I said to her, moving out from under her hands, which she had placed on my shoulders in an effort to restore me to good humor.

"In what way do I not understand you? We already have this child, and you are not at all concerned about her. Every day we go deeper into debt, no matter how I cut corners..."

The look on my face must have told her a lot: she looked at me in alarm and abruptly turned away so that I wouldn't see her tears. Then she left the room. Numbly I looked through my music for a quarter of an hour, thinking about nothing but her tears. Finally I stood up and went into the room where she was. I found her at her sewing, her eyes overflowing with tears, and—and I begged her forgiveness.

We always buried the hatchet in this way...but for a long time afterwards I would recall with anguish her tears and once I said to her:

"If you only knew how much this makes me suffer, you would not cause such scenes between us."

Her response:

"Only God knows what I am going through..."

Her suffering was patent. She was sensitive, and she had a very tender and virtuous heart, something I adored about her...but still we were often unhappy. Was I the guilty party here?...To me it felt like our souls were two brilliant, unblemished stars with no kind of bridge between them.

Sometimes grotesque thoughts would plague me after scenes like this. She's so weak I could kill her...The possibility that I was already a murderer would occur to me, and begin to afflict my soul terribly. I would betake my-self out to an isolated field, far from the town, with all my senses paralyzed. I saw nothing, heard nothing—my brain burned in my skull and created this hallucination:....Adelka was sitting alone in the bedroom, sewing, and our child was with her. Adelka looked over at her with tears in her sweet eyes and said: "The two of us are responsible for the troubles and worry that your father experiences out-side of this house. All of it....Why is it that he has no friends in the town? When my godmother comes here to visit, she says that all the menfolk are lined up against your father. Whenever he puts something together musi-cally—if it doesn't pan out, he acts haughty and heaps scorn on them. Mesarić says that your father has too high an opinion of himself... Nevertheless I believe your father more than the others...But why doesn't he realize this? Why does he insult me? He is constantly upbraiding me with rude accusations: "You don't understand me...You are not the woman for me..." More than anything I want to say to him: "Oh, I understand you...You regret marry-ing me..." But all of this makes him suffer, and I feel sor-rier for him than for me...So we reconcile, but I would most like just to stay here alone with you so I can cry. I would prefer to die if you were not here. At this point you don't know anything about this, but your eyes are full of understanding of why I cry, and your face changes when I smile at you again...I would not burden anyone with my grief, not even if my own dear mother were alive. No one could understand how I suffer, not even Amadej, your father. This is beyond even intelligent people. So Mr. Mesarić..."

And my blood boils at the new thought that alighted on my mind. Nonetheless I allow my thoughts to continue, gulping down this poison for my soul.

"Mesarić almost always comes to me when your father is at the Lešetickys'. He says to me, 'Why shouldn't we have a little fun, since Amadej is having fun over there?' I do not know if he is joking about this, but the whole thing is hurtful.—I do not dare even mention his name to Amadej: he flies into a passion and is unfair to me, just like he is in everything. Not long ago Mesarić remarked to me: 'Your Amadej is replacing Mr. Lešeticky as regards his wife, so you should look for a substitute for Amadej...' 'Of course, of course,' she answered, grinning indiscreetly. And he continued: 'Here I am! I long for your beauty...' Adelka responded to this with one more indiscretion: 'And why shouldn't I?...'" Then Mesarić takes both of her hands in his and she feels him kiss her lips...

Here the hallucination ended. The blood rushed to my head and I flew home, blind as I was. The moment I found myself once more in the presence of Adelka and our child, I was ashamed of these thoughts.

*

Once, when it was already evening, I received a note from Irma:

"Come over, Amadej. I am alone, and I am very bored."

Right away I got ready to go, and, kissing Adelka goodbye, I asked:

"You saw that she summoned me, and she is alone...Aren't you jealous?"

"Just go...You men think of nothing but *amour*."

I looked with delight into those girlish eyes of hers. They were still, and full of melancholy and unexplained worries.

I would have preferred to see in her gaze flames, consuming her—

At the door of the house in which Irma lived, I met her cook and another girl from the neighborhood.

"Is the *gnädige Frau* at home?" I asked, the same way I usually did.

"Go right in," the cook said, making room for me in the doorway. And when I approached the stairs she added with a smile: "The *gnädige Frau* is expecting you...She is alone. The master left yesterday on a trip."

And both girls exploded with half-suppressed laughter.

"Crazy girls," I thought, angered by their vulgarity.

Irma sang by the set of open windows. We worked our way through an entire volume of songs by Jensen and were thoroughly carried away by the beauty of the poet from the north. Sometimes the notes struck us as unusual, or almost unintelligible; something mystical revealed itself through them...The further we went, the more we found ourselves in a new, unknown land of poetry and the more were in awe of novel, delicate combinations of rhythms, melodies, and harmonies. What had at first come across as dark began, together with the lyrics, slowly to lighten with the rare charm of musical colors, and we both caught the fever of the vital poetry that breathed more and more fully in those notes. As for Irma, she sang with supreme emotion.

At ten o'clock I took my leave of her. She was sad that the time had passed so quickly, as was I.

"And what is your wife going to say, Amadej?" Irma asked me, not releasing me after we had shaken hands.

"She's used to my coming home late. I typically hold choir rehearsals at this time."

"That's different. I mean," and she gave me a singular look, "that perhaps she might be jealous of me?"

"Ah, my Adelka does not suffer from that malaise."

"You don't think so? Then you do not yet really know your own wife. How can a woman prevent herself from getting jealous if she is really in love? Or am I just that safe?"

The next day I got another invitation to visit Irma in the afternoon; some newly published music had just arrived from Berlin. That day saw tears in our home once more. Adelka maintained that she needed a larger sum of money from me, above all for the purchase of certain items for our child. I was, to be sure, delighted with the thought that she wanted our beautiful child's very frocks to catch everyone's eye; she was forever making and altering things for her. But she descended upon me with this request at a time when I had no money at all in my pocket, and when I had no immediate prospects of getting any.

"Making our child happy is my only joy in life, and you are holding back on me even with that," Adelka accused me unfairly.

"I have nothing," I told her calmly. "Be patient for a while."

Then she mentioned the names of the mayor, the priest, and Mesarić, adding that it was their opinion that I did not take care of my family the way I should.

I felt insulted—at least as far as the mention of Mesarić went; when does she have conversations with him—about me—in such a familiar way?

On the way to Irma's house I ran into the mayor. I grew hot under the collar at the very thought of meeting him; I wanted to take him to task for making so bold as to inquire about the degree to which I was taking care of my family. Then it occurred to me that he must be the source of the tall tales that Adelka's godmother was telling her.

When I greeted the mayor, he halted and pointed an admonitory finger at me.

What is he thinking? I thought to myself, even as the loathing rose within me.

"Amadej, watch yourself!"

I cannot abide this man at all, because he is dreadfully stupid. That in and of itself would not be anything sinful or dastardly, but his arrogance and his vain assertions that he was intelligent were insufferable. It's his conceit that makes me furious, and the only reason I stop and talk to him is to check on just how moronic the man really is.

"What do you mean?" I ask.

"You better pay attention to the Ninth Commandment!"

When I realized what he was saying and scrutinized his face, I realized that all the wickedness of the world was stored up in that man, who was looking down on me, from the heights of his spiritual vanity, in a brazen act of supposed superiority.

"Listen here. You are an outrageously stupid and dishonorable man. Let this be a word in your ear," I said. I continued on my way. But he had made me think about things that had never crossed my mind before.

Compared to Irma, I always feel small and unimportant. Her striking beauty always stirs me as an artist, but somehow it's as if she lacks a tender feminine soul. And her sophistication and wealth, her pride and way of interacting, leave me with nothing but a feeling of inferiority. When she has sometimes come across to me as more humble, less proud, or a bit melancholy, when she has seemed inclined to allow me to have the last word and steer our friendship a bit, I have messed things up every time. I have not been accustomed to acting so independently around her, and so I have comported myself with great clumsiness. In her presence I cannot play the role of a man stronger and more vital than I am—rather the reverse. I would not be able to kiss her—not, for example, in the way that I sense a man can kiss a woman. Around me she is the stronger and more active one...and that sensation hinders in me the emergence of any kind of more tender feelings towards her.

On this particular evening, Irma was complaining that she was not in the mood to sing. We played a duet on the piano, after which she asked me to go down with her into the garden for some air. Her voice, the look in her eyes, her sweet demeanor that evening—they were such that I could imagine her being in love with me...But then I had to consider the possibility that this was only an echo in my heart of what the mayor had said to me...and I was in the sway of vague but extremely unpleasant feelings.

After a longish stroll we sat down on a little bench facing the full moon.

"Tell me, Amadej, are you truly so happy?" she inquired in a voice more soft and brooding than I was used to hearing.

"What do you mean, *gnädige Frau*?"

"Why don't you call me by my first name, the way I address you?...Tell me, do you love your wife?"

"I do."

"And does she love you?"

"I would say she does."

"And therefore you're happy?"

"I've never thought about it."

She was quiet for a moment. She directed her gaze upwards towards the moon, and I detected something theatrical in that. I could sense, close by, her voluptuous body and I was watching her face in the light of the moon: exquisite, but like ice.

"Ah, you see...I am not happy," she began speaking exactly as she would have done on stage. "I love my husband, and he is indescribably kind to me and loves me too. But despite everything, I feel in my soul a great emptiness...and I have for a long time. Maybe you understand what I'm saying," and her sentences became stormier; she took my hand and lay her head on my shoulder. "I would like to take a lover, a Platonic lover. My soul longs for it. I dream about it all the time...A love of that type is permissible. And not even my husband could begrudge me that kind of happiness."

I couldn't think straight after that unexpected pronouncement of hers. The first things I thought of were unfair: you are rich, you have no concerns in the world, you are childless...and this is nothing but wantonness on your part. Then I reconsidered: was I not doing her an injustice? Even I dreamt that my Adelka would love me to the bitter end with an immaculate love that only the soul, or a woman's nature, knows.

I told her this, and she gave my hand an exuberant squeeze:

"I sensed a long time ago that we were kindred souls."

She turned to me and looked straight into my eyes, a melancholy grin on her face. She placed both of her hands on my head and kissed me on the forehead like a child. And then, squeezing her eyes shut, she put her head on my shoulder.

My blood began to seethe. My throat clenched, and in the kaleidoscopic din of my thoughts I kept clutching at one question: do I dare kiss her? And my desire for this kiss was not the same as when I had longed from abroad to touch Adelka's skin with my lips...In this new desire was something brutal and cruel that I dared not act on...Would she still regard me as this impotent and indecisive if I reached for the apple she was offering?...My trembling probably sprang more from shame than from any other feeling...and then the mayor's face took shape before my eyes, and it seemed to speak to me, saying: Well, good sir, I guess idiocy edges out intelligence, eh? And everything wonderful that I had witnessed in Mme Lešeticky up to that point crumbled to dust. The warmth of her full, soft hands, the touch of her skin on my face, the feeling of her voluptuous body—it was all disgusting. More than anything I wished to flee, and the one word that my soul produced was: seductress. Adelka was born again in my heart, and I bowed contritely before her holy countenance...

All of a sudden Irma lifted her head from my shoulder. She stood up and ran her hands through her hair.

"Oh, heavens! Put this out of your mind...I do this sometimes..."

Surreptitiously I watched her face. Pain seemed to have possessed it...and I felt sorry for that woman.

That evening I did not go straight home. I kept going over and over in my mind this strange experience, and it began to seem less and less real. And then I began to feel, once more, ashamed and humiliated. I think that the vanity has started to awaken in me of a man who has wasted an opportunity by demonstrating to a woman that he does not possess the strength of character that she imagined resided in him. What would Goethe have done in a case like this? This bizarre question shows my weakness in its most naked configuration yet. My actions are those of a lifeless and wearisome man. Where does this weakness in me come from? I am not by any measure a moralist; I am thirsty for love, I hunger for it, and my thoughts and my eyes hunt for it constantly. So how could I have comported myself thus at that very moment—right in front of this splendid example of womanhood? It felt as though scorn would get the better of me for the rest of my life...until I began to think back over the entire period of my friendship with Irma, and I felt for the first time that there had always been in her eyes something demonic that caused me great alarm. And then my thoughts returned ecstatically to my Adelka, with her virtuous and peaceful soul that I love so. Was she capable of acting the same way as Irma? I wondered, overjoyed by the resolutely negative answer to that question. —Only one dissonant wave resounded in my soul: if Adelka loves me, then why isn't she jealous?

Three days passed, and I went again to Irma's house; she acted as if nothing had happened.

We played a duet, and she sang—until Lešeticky put in an appearance. Then she invited me to stay and have supper with them.

At the table Lešeticky's demeanor was cold. It's likely that he was all caught up, as usual, in his business affairs. That's how he is, despite his ill health. The townspeople, my fellow citizens, who are sensitive and derisory to the point of ingeniousness, made up a list of five different diseases from which he was said to be suffering, the most bearable of which hindered him from sitting, standing, or lying down.

*

Once, when I was saying goodbye to Irma, she begged me to come see her earlier than usual the following afternoon, for two local ladies, the wives of the mayor and the apothecary, respectively, had announced their intention to visit.

I caught both of these women unawares at Irma's. I don't know if other people have this, but I am possessed of an exaggerated ability to sense immediately what people in a group are thinking about me when I turn up. I just know, for instance, when we have visitors who want to be accounted members of the upper crust and who are most inconsiderate, not to say ignorant, in their behavior. They tell bald-faced lies, sniff around in every nook and cranny of our house, and ask idly about everything "Where'd you get that? Where did you find it? When? For how much? Cash or credit?" and even "What's underneath it?" If it's a curtain or coverlet...I cannot stand such nibby fools and I cannot hide the fact that I can't stand them; they make me angry and I either don't answer their questions or I answer by telling lies so brazen that even a child would recognize that I am deliberately bluffing. And they either don't get it, or they don't want to get it, and they keep sniffing about and interrogating us.—And when I entered the *salon* that time at Irma's house, and found those two ladies there, there was nothing to see but, I felt, by dint of this unknown faculty of mine, that they exchanged a lightning-fast look with their eyes: "See him? You know he must've thought she was alone!..."

Irma tried to get rid of them. I could sense this, but the two women didn't.

"Please wait just a moment, Amadej," she said to me. "We'll get started in just a tick." I was overawed by her energy, and it made her seem even more accessible and sweet.

I have noticed that in general I find Irma very attractive and likable when I see her in this kind of mood, direct and energetic and merry. The thing that makes me shrink from her, the demonic part, is only in evidence when I see her degraded or depressed, or when I imagine her the way she was in that evening encounter that played out in the garden.

Shortly thereafter Irma spoke to me again:

"Dear Amadej, please get the music ready...We'll be starting directly."

I lifted the lid on the piano and put out a volume of songs by Grieg. Every gesture Irma made betrayed the fact that she was merely waiting for the two visitors to leave. But they stayed glued to their seats.

Finally Irma stood up and gave me a look that elicited a knowing grin from me. This discussion carried out by our eyes could have been translated roughly thus:

Irma: This is unbelievable! I can't shake them!

Me: I can see that...Well, let's just start. But I don't find their presence agreeable either.

Irma: Don't you think I can tell that?...Anyway, let's do it.

So I sat down at the piano, and she sat next to me, wrapping her left arm around my chair. Once more I could feel their stares, and they announced:

"Scandal!...Such a display of affection, and right before our eyes!"

I was pleased that they were hot and bothered by this, and this also made me appreciate the enjoyable proximity to Irma's shapely body. I had never been able to abide those two women. First of all, the district head's wife, because she, like our mayor, was arrogant and conceited—and secondly because she never used her Croatian mother tongue in public, and thirdly because she never returned the greeting of anyone who was not of higher social status than she.—The druggist's wife was just as supercilious and also never spoke Croatian in front of other people.

When Irma had finished singing the first song, the women expressed their approval with halting gestures and uncertain words. Irma seized the moment to whisper to me, as I improvised a prelude for the next song:

"They have not the slightest understanding of music...What insincerity!"

Evening had already fallen by the time the two ladies finally took their leave. I intended to depart as well, until Irma, in a purposefully loud voice, told me right in front of the both of them:

"Stay just a bit longer, Amadej. I have something I want to show you." And when the ladies were gone, she sighed:

"Thank God! You cannot imagine how tiresome I find those two..."

We played and sang for a while longer, and when I was leaving she held out a packet of paper:

"Here you will find a printed copy of the poem I wrote. Read it, and it if speaks to you, then go ahead and set it to music. How I would love to hear a musical version of my work..."

At home I opened up the packet and found in it an issue of the German journal *Familienblatt*. I flipped through it a bit and found a poem, circled in black pencil, entitled: "Awakening to Perception, a poem by I. von L-y."

Here's the content of that little poem:

"...I thought him a child...a fair and wise child, the artist about whom my soul commenced dreaming in that distant girlish time when it awoke to life. I was under the spell not only of his beauty, but also of his youth and his tender poetic soul...yet he was a child, and I loved him as one loves a child. I made bold to take his hand in mine, and play with his hair...like an older friend would do, as guardian of his preciousness, when the outside world has no concept of its worth...Once I placed a kiss, without passion, and without an awareness of sin, upon his smooth fresh forehead...I do not know the name of the perverse spirit that roused me from my belief...I do not know how I came to see that this was not a child, that it was not for me to caress him, that I did not dare touch his hand or his hair or kiss his brow. It was this new perception that fanned in me the flames, the desire of a happiness that I'm not fated to find."

Because of these lines of poetry I found myself unable to sleep for an entire night. The poem, once in my blood, was turned into fever. Demon! Delilah! I said to myself, yet my thoughts rushed pell-mell to this demon and Delilah. Joined in an embrace with her statuesque body, my mind transported me like a cyclone across the most enchanting landscapes of our wide world; and love, happiness, glory, and wealth—we had all of it at our feet. I forgot about my homeland, my wife and child, and Irma's husband. Once ensconced in this luxury I encountered three figures. My wife, the child—and Jahoda. Adelka stood there before me, her head bowed, tears in her eyes, staggered by grief and shame; the child asked me by means of her reasoned glances: Why, father, have you abandoned us? And Jahoda gestured with his hand at the two of them:

"Why, Amadej, have you done this?"

My eyes were wet with tears—and by dawn, after a terrible battle, I was convinced that I would not compose the setting for Irma's poem.

I made my way to Irma's house and handed the poem back to her, asserting that I would not do the music for it. Oh, how much torment, and how much shame, it took to utter that sentence directly to this proud woman's face!

The color drained out of her face...and then she said to me in a strange, quavering voice:

"I knew you would not like it....Folly!..." I said nothing. The sweat of helplessness poured down my face. Irma apologized and said she had to go off somewhere on a visit...so I made my exit, full of self-recriminations.

*

I am much taken by the idea of composing a musical setting for Šenoa's poem "Petar Svačić." I sketched out a ballad in a grand style, of the type that would be suitable for the creation of a musical picture of this most tragic episode in Croatian history. The project excites me as much for the power of the lyrics and the rarified diction as for the subject of the ballad itself. The opening lines arrested my imagination the very first time I read them. Sometimes I envision myself as the director of the Croatian opera house in Zagreb: there's a baton in my hand, and there are two hundred singers in semi-darkness up on the stage, and around me extends the orchestra. I give a sign with my hand and the violins erupt into sound *con sordini*, like the rustling of dried leaves on a mountain, and then the mysterious, sluggish, and muffled plucks of the strings of the cello depict the steps of the wounded, star-crossed Croatian king. The form of a poem by Šenoa is not at all suitable for the development of a ballad in an extended format, with solos and choirs. Once, when I mentioned that to Mesarić, he offered on the spot to prepare a poetic work for my composition. He paid me a visit one day with this project in mind, at a moment when I had no inclination to chat because I was tremendously preoccupied with something that Irma had said and that was now stuck in my head.

What I mean is Irma's statement that a woman who loves must be jealous.—Adelka had never given any sign that she was jealous, nor had she ever said anything to that effect. Does that mean, then, that she does not love me? Like an off-pitch voice trying to sing in harmony, this thought kept crossing my mind over and over. Sometimes it seemed childish and ludicrous, but other times it hurt like hell....Insignificant events from my married life would come to mind that made me recognize how often I had been jealous. On other occasions I was unsettled by Adelka and a male acquaintance having a conversation that was a bit too friendly...at other times I would entertain unpleasant suspicions if I saw someone walk twice past the front of our house. At such times I actually felt real fear that she could love someone else in addition to me. Is that fear the same thing as jealousy? Where does it come from? Would I feel this way if I didn't love Adelka? Is this the same sensation he would have if it were some other woman whom he thought was running the risk of treachery and scandal? No. The dread that he felt in his insides about Adelka, when he considered the possibility of her loving someone else, grew quickly into fury, into a savagery that demanded revenge. But the dread he felt when he witnessed an unsuspecting innocent nature seduced into doing evil—this had nothing of that same savagery. Instead it brought great grief and pain, a bitterness which rained down all over my soul, he thought; it is identical to the pity that afflicts my being whenever someone is suffering from injustice, violence, sickness, penury, despair, or some other ill. The first is an unchained and insatiable frenzy of vengeance that leaves me feeling as strong as a wild animal...while the latter is an aching awareness of my powerlessness to protect and help those who are less fortunate than I. This much is clear. But does Adelka's heart ever ignite in this way on account of me? It seems like it never does...and that's when I hear once more the discordant voice that bewilders me ever more...I fell in love with Adelka as a child, and ever since that day I have felt the powerful desire to kindle in her, by means of my love, a longing both intense and passionate for our souls to be in perfect harmony, in unity, like flame and light. If I discover in her an indifference to that kind of unity, then my love is pointless. It would be unfruitful and forlorn, exactly like the warmth of the sun when it shines down onto an abandoned, arid stretch of land...So can proof of love only be delivered by jealousy? Irma is a woman—she knows...

After that I began making comparisons between Irma and Adelka. Adelka is, even if she is a mother, as innocent and inexperienced as a child. Her heart is virtuous, this woman's heart of hers, which in its purity can never push so far as to ask: would Amadej really be capable of loving another woman besides me? Her nature has shown itself to be sublime, peerless in its purity and integrity, with the kind of soul that I loved as a child with all the strength of my being.

But Irma, to the contrary, divides into two figures in my mind, into two beings: the artist, who knows how to overwhelm me with her earnest, vehement poetry—and the beautiful woman of the world, who is experienced but has no comprehension of that virginity that a married woman might preserve in her soul.

I kissed Adelka and told her to tell Mesarić, if he should come by, that I had errands to run. I still hadn't realized that I could leave Mesarić alone in the house with Adelka—comfortably, and without suspicion or fear—because even though he was used to stealing glances at her right in front of me, she would just smile at him—uncomprehendingly.

I was quite caught up in these thoughts and, when I showed up at Irma's at the agreed hour of seven o'clock, she wondered at my mischievous good mood. She sang Grieg, Jensen, Schumann and Schubert, and I improvised on the piano like never before. Marvelous phrasing flew from my fingertips, as if another's brain were guiding them.

"You're in an interesting mood today," said Irma, whereupon I struck up a new musical idea, one that she didn't understand: "Adelka Has Vanquished Delilah." On the way back home I brainstormed a new item for my work "Songs Without Words"; it would be entitled "Her Heart and Soul."

Adelka was already asleep; the poor woman was greatly afflicted and very weak. When I lit the lamp, she woke up and followed me calmly with her eyes. I soaked up a huge measure of happiness just from this gaze; going over to her, I gave her a hug and inhaled the sweet, childlike scent from her body. Then I strode to the piano and played a few chords. Adelka lifted her head:

"You're not going to play now, are you?"

"Listen, Adelka. It's dedicated to you. To your soul."

"Stop, Amadej. You might wake up the baby."

But I was truly on fire, and these were flames—when I composed—that consumed all feelings of the world.

"For heaven's sake," Adelka objected once more, "You'll have time to play tomorrow. You're going to wake our child...And what will people say if you are playing the piano at this hour of the night?"

"Listen, Adelka. Maybe by tomorrow this will no longer be accessible to me. It will have escaped to that distant realm of poetry whence it came to me." And I played on.

"Amadej, what's wrong with you today?" she asked me yet again.

"Quiet, Adelka. This is my song to you..."

She did listen for a moment, and then the baby woke up.

"Amadej, do you hear me? What's with you tonight? Maybe you were off somewhere drinking. But listen to me: let the piano be, and come to bed."

I stood up, trembling. I looked her in the face and wanted to say something, but the words stuck in my throat. And then she asked:

"Where were you tonight?"

"Adelka, I was with an artist who is able to understand what's inside of me. And you can't do it."

"Oh, darling, come to bed."

"I can tell. You think I've been drinking. Well, Adelka, I am intoxicated. My head is buzzing, but not from wine. I'd like to play some Grieg for you, but you wouldn't understand it. You don't even understand the things I am trying to tell you at this very moment. Say it—you don't understand—"

She repeated one more time, just as before:

"Oh, listen to me, Amadej. Come and sleep...You were out with friends somewhere, and you don't have much of a tolerance for wine..."

"Say it, Adelka: did you or did you not understand what I just played for you?"

"What's to understand, Amadej? It's night-time. It's when people rest. Just come to bed, my darling, and tomorrow we'll talk all about it."

"Tomorrow," I laughed acidly, achingly: "Adelka, you and your soul cannot ascend to the world my soul inhabits. We are going to be very unhappy."

She sat up in bed, and tears began to pour out of her eyes: "Why do you say these things to me?...You don't treat me right, and you can see that I'm not well..."

She had disarmed me. I actually am being unfair to this helpless, ailing woman who married me to find her protection and support in life...I had a sensation of the blood humming in my head and coursing rapidly through my body, as if I had consumed hard liquor. The pain of a grave impotence took control of me, and I had the feeling that I was fighting an unknown opponent and would end by bowing my head and acknowledging defeat.

"Forgive me, Adelka!" I said to her. My entire existence, from my birth up to this instant, seemed so somber, tangled up, blurred, and iniquitous that it is as if everybody around me is just babbling in some sort of drunken state. It's like we are all trying to get our hands on something that gives light, but it shrinks from us so that we are forever suffocating, terrorized, and weighted down with insurmountable worries.

"Adelka, forgive me. Oh, you know how unhappy I get sometimes. I come to feel like the whole world is one stubborn, open wound staring me unblinkingly in the face. I see no comforting figures around me, only free-floating sadness, misery, and hopelessness—so much so that even the thought of you brings no cheer to my soul. Be true to me, Adelka, for you do not know how often I am in pain, and I myself do not know why. You surely would be happier with me if I could banish from my soul this misery for which I can find no cause. I love you. I lied when I said that you don't understand me. The woman out there understands me, but I flee from her to you. The root causes of love lie deeper than level of education and beauty. Love abides even after death. I feel that with as much certainty as I feel that I am split: into one being with a bodily life and into another, the real me, with thoughts and emotions."

"So what is wrong with you tonight?" she said sympathetically. She stroked my hair as she often did. "Tell me, did someone out there insult you again? Why do they have to be like that with you? Why do they consider you boastful and deny that you have anything to boast about?"

"Never mind, Adelka...They don't understand me. But you, oh, if you could understand me—how happy we would be! I could create many many things, and I'd became famous, and people would celebrate me, together with you. Ah, you need to love me in a different way, so that you set my soul on fire, and so that it makes my brains boil, so that I rise unconsciously with my soul into the other world, from which all beauty makes its way to us."

"All well and good, Amadej...Just come to bed. I know you're going to be complaining of a headache tomorrow."

She acted like I was drunk. I pulled away and put my hands on my feverish head.

"Adelka, do you know where this inebriation really comes from? Do you believe that only someone who is drunk could say the things I'm saying? Oh, yes, I am intoxicated, but by other means. Something in me is rotten, and it is wrecking our happiness...I can see how distant we are becoming from one another...as if we are being borne on winds blowing in opposite directions...farther and farther apart...And I weep and stretch my hands out for you. Where is she, the Adelka who animated my soul? Far away...unattainably far off...It's as if she were dead...And without her my heart withers and is sure to be miserable to the grave."

"Amadej!" Adelka shrieked in an otherworldly voice that pierced my mind. She was alarmed at my behavior and had stood up. Now she was embracing me and starting to kiss my head and hair. Her hot tears plunged onto my forehead and rolled down my face. I looked up at her and saw her: diminutive and mortified in her thin white nightgown, with her hair tumbling down; her shoulders exposed, white as milk; her narrow, almost girlish breasts; and her eyes filled with sorrow and panic. She looked to me at once like an angel and a martyr. I slid down to her feet, clasped them, and began heaping ardent kisses on them.

"Adelka! How I love you!"

"All right, Amadej...But if you love me, do one thing for me: go to bed."

"I'm going," I said with resignation, fading fast from these exertions of heart and soul. "If you say so, I'll go...But we do not yet appreciate each other..."

*

I was working in my room when someone came into the other part of the house where Adelka was. From the voice I could tell that it was Mesarić. They chatted for a long time, but Mesarić spoke in such a low voice that I couldn't make out a single word of what he said. Why should I not be allowed to hear what he is saying to

Adelka? Is there an intimacy to their talk that shows they are already well used to each other? I was paralyzed with fear. I admit my weakness, my irrationality—call it what you will. Something traveled through my breast like a knife, and my heart was pounding and blood was thudding at my temples. I wanted to fling that door open but I refrained from doing so, for I realized that it would make me feel ashamed in front of the two of them.

So you see, such is jealousy, I thought. Why isn't Adelka jealous of me in this way?

Shortly thereafter Mesarić knocked on the door to my room, and I had to interrupt the thread of my speculations.

"I brought you my reworked version of Šenoa's ballad, like you wanted," he said cheerily. The he added, as he put his hand up to his brow: "I worked on this last night until three in the morning...Allow me to read it to you. I think I pulled it off quite well."

And so he began to read aloud. From the very first lines I was extremely irritated. He shattered the attractive musicality of Šenoa's verse, and that's not to mention his prosaic diction, which gave me constant offense when compared to Šenoa's flights of imagination; listening to Mesarić was like taking a walk from a set of tended gardens to some desolate alley where the poor gather rags and pick through tattered old clothes. But he read his lyrics with due pathos, interrupting his performance constantly with the remark:

"This part here came out really delightful!"

When he was finished, I tendered my thanks. I didn't have the strength to say to him: How dare you place your heathen hands on the work of a great man and profane it so?...

But he took my appreciation at face value and added:

"While I was writing this" (to hear him speak, you'd think he had picked up where Šenoa had left off on some aborted project) "I was considering everything, just like I was composing. If I only knew how to write notes, then you'd see what kinds of melodies I am capable of thinking up."

And then he began talking about himself. He said he had a clear talent for all the arts. In his dreams, for instance, he often saw pictures and statues that no one had ever seen in real life, and in the same way he listened to opera that no human ear had heard. "My spirit is free when I slumber," he pontificated, "and it has no need of the material means for giving my artistic ideas tangible form. All that is required for that would be the schooling, the technique—but I don't have that."

This elaboration struck me as completely specious. In our town Mesarić was definitely considered highly educated, and it was my impression that he knew enough to get by on these things. Moreover he liked to stand out as someone with philosophical training, and I was so impressed by that word "philosophical" that I did have the impression that all the obscure and puzzling hidden parts of human nature, concealed from us when we observed our own inner workings, were as clear as day to philosophers. And with these thoughts shooting through my mind, it occurred to me to ask Mesarić what philosophy can teach us about this: can love exist when there is no jealousy? I just didn't know how to ask it,

though. I feared that Mesarić, in the way of philosophers, would divine on the spot why I was asking, and I
did not want to sow doubts like that about Adelka and
me in anyone. Perish the thought! I wanted to put a lot
of distance between that question and my relationship
with my wife, so I hit upon this formulation:

"If you don't mind," I said to Mesarić, "I recently
read a poem by Vukelić, and I liked it so much that I
feel compelled to set it to music. The poem is called
'Doubt Is the Ruin of Love.' I would argue that the music itself needs to embody some kind of tone of jealous
feelings...Tell me, what do you think jealousy actually
is?"

But I blushed, and Mesarić searched my face with
quizzical eyes...He suspected something. I looked back
at him, even as wrath began to build inside me. Here's
what I was thinking: you are visiting my Adelka with
immoral intentions, her beauty appeals to you, and you
consider her stupid and inexperienced and you plan to
use that to exploit her for your loathsome ends. You
interpret my friendship with Irma in the same way as the
mayor, and you have come to the conclusion that nothing is more natural than for a woman who has been deceived to pay her husband back in kind...The scarlet on
my face, and perhaps the tentativeness in my voice when
I asked you about jealousy, have led you to this interpretation...so that now, right before my eyes, you are wondering to yourself if this is firm evidence that scenes of
jealousy between Adelka and me are playing themselves
out as must invariably be the case any time a man or
woman makes a false step. Such confrontations would

make it easier for a third party to triumph, and you also use them to explain her sickliness and restlessness, and the despondency that heightens the beauty of her eyes. Don't deny it. Just a little bit ago, upon entering her room, you complimented her on her looks...Then Mesarić responded:

"Jealousy..." he began, incoherently...

"Well, yes," I spoke up in a shaky voice. I could not control my excitement. "Is it necessarily found in conjunction with love in every case?"

"Well, yes and no," he said, looking as bewildered as could be. "There is a great deal that could be said about this, my friend. But let's come at it from the following starting point: first we have to ask, what is love? It is a feeling that is born in us of desire, of the longing to awaken the same kind of longing for us in a person of the opposite sex. When we have achieved that, there develops in us a pleasing sense of satisfaction of heart and soul that nature placed in us for its own ends. Partly because of these naturalistic goals, and partly because of our individual selfishness, we cannot imagine without discomfort that the beloved creature who returns our love could share this feeling with someone else also. The fear of that longing extending to someone else besides us is what is called jealousy. Do you follow me?"

"I follow you," I said, but he had not addressed the question regarding Adelka and me. Everything he said I already knew myself, even if I could not have expressed it in the way he did. He didn't even mention the thing that was eating at me.

"Can a man love someone and not become jealous of her?" I asked Mesarić again.

"Yes and no," he answered philosophically again. "It depends upon his temperament, how much he loves, and how much faith we place in the person we love."

"What do you mean?" I asked him. I was warming to the subject—that is to say, there was something in these last words of his that could put my mind at ease.

"Well, for instance, you love your wife, and in addition you are quite convinced that she could never be unfaithful, not under any circumstances, since you know that aside from you there could not be anyone on whom she would bestow her affection. She's just that way...and you know it. In that case you'd have absolutely no need to be jealous. But if you knew that your wife adores flattery, and that she deliberately seeks out the company of men who flatter her, in that case it would be different. Anyway," he added, "I'll bring you a book about that, and you read it!"

*

One evening Adelka handed me a note from Irma, asking me to come see her.

"It could be that she'll have me stay through supper again," I said quite deliberately to Adelka, keeping my eyes on her face. But she only began inquiring about what there usually was to eat at Irma's house, and whether it was true that she had very expensive dishes and cutlery and so on.

No! She is too virtuous and untainted to be jealous, I thought. This was followed immediately by the feeling that I would be much more pleased if she revealed herself to be jealous. The very thought excited me, so I made a provocative statement about Irma:

"That woman is gorgeous."

"She is very pretty," Adelka confirmed. She then started to describe Irma's eyes, her beautiful complexion, her stature, and so on.

So I took her by the hands and glared right down at her:

"Just tell me, what would you think if Irma and I were in love?"

"Be serious, please, Amadej," she replied. "Do you believe that women are like that? Just be careful and don't get mixed up again with a bunch of heavy drinkers on your way home. You're not used to that sort of thing...You know, you've been talking all kinds of nonsense lately, and it's got me really worried about you."

I let go of her hands and saw the reflection, in her eyes, of my monstrous face. No—she does not understand me. Nonetheless, along with all the heaviness now weighing on me, I still felt compassion for this good and steadfast woman. Why could she not have Irma's soul in her, a passionate and broad-minded soul with room for more than just our small, impoverished household, our child, and the trivial concerns of daily life? To me she seems just like our two-year old girl, only with a developed body...She only demands from life what a child seeks: a roof, food, and peace—with no sense of or reach for what is remote or grand, those things that I hasten after with all the power of my spirit.

So I kissed our child profusely and approached Adelka in order to say goodbye. When I brought my lips close to hers, in order to kiss her, she pulled away from me, her eyes clouding up with tears.

"Go! I can't tell you anything, even when I am completely in the right."

We are not getting through to one another!...And no, this is nothing even close to the kind of joy I had imagined having with Adelka. Although every flutter of my soul is immediately and unmistakably reflected in her eyes, I am starting to feel sorry for her. I have taken to chiding myself when I think of her perfectly kind nature. This makes me feel devastated, and grief and hopelessness break my heart; it is as if my élan has begun crumbling, my thirst for glory breaking up, and instead of feeling conceit at my artistic calling I am bitter inside, and I have the terrible thought that everything is mere frivolity, a pointless struggle for the unattainable, the yearning of a shackled eagle to disappear up into the sun. And more and more I am struck by the loathsomeness of my own life. I am seized by regret for the fact that I am about to be reborn as a new man by closing my spirit to light and freedom and locking it into preposterous inconsistency, selfishness, and the falsehoods of the material world.

But, once I was with Irma, these feelings of melancholy passed quickly. Her singing was transcendent, and I could not even tell the moment at which my soul cleared up. And then right at the moment when I noticed this new serenity following the gloom and anxiety that had accompanied me to Irma's place, I declared to myself: My God, what this music can do! If only Adelka could understand it too!

Irma's and my conversation was more open and intimate than usual. When she asked me about our child, I unburdened my heart and probably sounded like one of those young fathers whose speech becomes so childlike it all but borders on ridiculous. I explained to her how I, ecstatic over Adelka's gift, sat down by myself and wrote a poem and music. I felt obliged to relate to her the gist of my poem and then to play the composition. I played in a trance, completely transported by the poetry of my work.

"Listen, that is marvelous," Irma told me. "You have to write it down for me. Will you?"

I was told to play it for her again, and then once more.

"Is this composition from your song cycle 'Poems Without Words'?" she inquired. And then: couldn't I find some catchier collective name for the cycle?

"Hymn to Love," I offered.

"Hymn to Love," she repeated pensively. "Tell me, Amadej, are you a happy man?....I know I asked you that once, but I truly don't remember how you responded...I like pondering this point for everyone I know. I only want to know whether you are happy. I consider it the height of happiness when a person finds a kindred spirit who understands him or her and when the two of them are then united in love. Don't you think so? Tell me, Amadej, have you done something like this to celebrate your love for Adelka?"

"I've tried," I replied sheepishly.

"How happy your Adelka must be! I think the same thing about myself. Three months after our wedding, I came across a painting in my husband's workshop. He was going to surprise me with it. This discovery delighted me more than every other attestation of his love. Just think, Amadej! He painted himself, awaking from a dream at sunrise, and above him is a smiling angel—and that's my image."

"What a fabulous idea!" I exclaimed.

"But what do you know—he never completed the picture...I often rummage secretly through his papers and paintings in the hope of finding something that will testify to his love for me, but by the same token I am afraid that I will unearth the fact that he loves some other woman besides me...I never found either. You see, when I was a girl, nothing would have thrilled me more than marrying a poet, a painter, a composer, or a famous actor, and being fêted along with him. But you can see that my lot was husband who did indeed marry me just for love, and who is remarkably good to me, but who has not a whit of feeling for the arts. This has always stood in the way of my complete happiness. I have always believed that someone who is a poet or artist would love differently, and he'd have in his love a richer and grander palette of musical sounds. Your Adelka should be so grateful to have you!...But of course," she added with a self-conscious smile, "those are the intimate details of newlyweds, and not things people like to talk about."

In fact, as my surprise grew at the way her words interested me, I found myself less and less able to resist talking frankly about this very subject. The last thing in the world I want to do is air the discord that I have noticed between Adelka and me—but then I realized all of a sudden that all these questions were likely the product of the ironical nature of a talented and educated woman who has herself begun to notice something....and subsequently I sensed that demon in her that my soul so abominates.

At this juncture Lešeticky came in and invited me to stay for supper. He was not proving to be nearly as unpolished and bristly as I had constantly imagined him to be, considering the things other people said about him. He was actually quite kind to me, and whenever I asked him anything pertaining to his field of expertise he would explain it to me patiently, even lovingly. Otherwise he took little part in our conversation that evening, too. Based on his behavior towards Irma, it was impossible for me to judge whether he loved her or was indifferent to her—and, if he loved her, whether it was in the way a husband loves his wife or the way a father loves his daughter. Irma showed herself very obliging towards her husband, even putting the food on his plate herself and setting the traveling blanket to rights on his shoulders whenever it started to slide off. And she did this in such a way that he could only consider her pampering of Lešeticky to be the attentiveness of a daughter towards her father—the same way he interpreted what she had said earlier about her marital happiness. She did not conceal from him her sympathies for me. That evening she talked to him, with great zeal and high praise, about my "Hymn to Love," while he smiled and showed his approbation with the knowing looks of a man who understands but has no time for such things.

And that evening I learned that they would soon be leaving our town; the construction of the railroad line was approaching its conclusion.

When I returned home and gave my wife a kiss, she told me that Mesarić had come looking for me. He had left me a book.

"What book?" I made sure to ask her, in the hope that she might show some interest in what I was reading.

"I haven't even looked at it. There it is. On your desk," she replied.

She hasn't looked at it...She has no interest in anything. Nothing arouses curiosity or doubt in her. — And Mesarić...He shows up here again, knowing I'm not at home?...I was quaking in my boots, but I didn't have the strength to ask Adelka about it.

The book was in German and bore the title: *Love and Jealousy in Light of Physiology and Psychology.* —I gathered my strength and strove mightily to read the entire tome. Several times it made me angry and I tossed it away, only to reach for it again in the hope that I might still find in it what I needed. A lot of it was too hard for me to understand, and the parts that I did comprehend made me think how superfluous and crazy it was to write about a clear and simple truth as if you wanted deliberately to hammer it into a carapace, hard, heavy, and dark, from which it would later require great exertion to bring it back into view. Finally I got through the entire book—and learned absolutely nothing.

*

One evening, upon returning home from rehearsal, I found Adelka in bed. Her godmother was sitting next to her. She told me off-handedly that Adelka had been coughing up a lot of blood. I took great fright at this.

"Why does that make scare you so much?" her godmother asked. "It's a typical woman's illness. Have you seen me cough up stuff? And, what do you know, nothing's wrong with me."

That calmed me back down somewhat. Adelka was looking at me and smiling somberly but sweetly, like some kind of saint. She was in agreement that we should send for the doctor. Concern for her health was forcing my hand. For—if truth be told—my conscience was stinging me about my being responsible for all of this...Adelka was unhappy with me but she was hiding it...and suffering inside.

Our doctor was an old man, a Prussian by birth. He examined Adelka and joined with her godmother in declaring that there was nothing wrong with her. Nonetheless I was seized by anxiety about her well-being. The old doctor was an optimist. Here's what he said about Plavčić, when he was down with an illness recently: "Zere iss no furzer danger. Tomorrow or ze next day you vill trink beer togezer." But that night Plavčić passed away. And he died without a will, and all sorts of people descended onto his property from all directions. They divided up his estate, and then the beneficiaries took to fighting, and all said unanimously about the late Plavčić: "May the Devil rattle his bones!"

Otherwise, Adelka was in a good mood. She liked it a lot when I sat by her bed and doted on her. She ran her hand through my hair and smiled at me, and I recognized in that smile the desire to tell me something, but once again she bit her tongue.

"Adelka," I said, "why don't you tell me what's on your mind?"

"How do you know that I have anything to tell you?"

"I know. You can't hide anything from me."

"Then tell me," she said, drawing out her words, "what would become of our child if I were to die?"

Her eyes filled with tears.

This question fell heavily on my heart. But then she added quickly:

"So Mme Lešeticky is leaving you?"

"Why do you say she's leaving me?"

"Because you found it very agreeable to spend time with her..."

"I did, Adelka!...And when she leaves, I will miss her a lot. There'll be no one left for me to play music with, and she is a wonderful artist."

"That's true," Adelka confirmed, apparently in complete agreement with what I had said.

"I had thought, sweetheart, that you were, in any case, a bit jealous of Mme Lešeticky."

"Come on now!" she exclaimed with a laugh. "It's as if you men think of nothing but romance. That friend Mesarić of yours is the same way; it's all he can speak of."

This admission made my hair stand on end. I had noticed the quantum of love in Mesarić's eyes when he stared at Adelka, and the fact that he hid his glances from me.

I now looked Adelka straight in the face; her eyes were placid, gentle, and guileless like those of a child.

*

Irma departed. And what follows is a description of our goodbye:

I waited in the *salon* while she went to fetch her scrapbook so that I could write something in it. A *motif* in C minor full of dissonant harmonies popped into my mind. Her leaving irritated me...I was losing a major patron and a friend.

In the scrapbook I jotted down a few notes about the music and then wrote out the *motif* for piano, signed it, and added: "Our loves are nothing but infinite dissonance, interrupted at times by short-lived harmonious chords."

"My compliments, *gnädige Frau*," I said firmly. And I kissed her hand.

"Farewell, Amadej...I thank you for everything. It will not be so easy to forget you. Think of me now and then...You are not allowed to forget me even when you become famous."

"Ah, *gnädige Frau!*"

"Amadej, you are..." here she broke off her thought abruptly as a melancholy look came over her face. Then she resumed, in a livelier tone: "In my diary, I changed your name to Benjamin—and that is what I will call you forever. Don't take it amiss if you come to be known by this name in public. Whomever your talent belonged to would have the world at his feet..."

I understood her....and I was all the sadder at her leaving. I was losing a friend with whom I could be completely sincere...

*

Everything around me seems more and more like a wasteland. Now I really see what Irma meant to me... Adelka is sickly and irritable and she sighs a great deal. Occasionally I will say to her:

"Don't sigh, Adelka. Believe me: I lose heart when I hear you sigh for reasons that I don't understand."

"That's easy for you to say," she remarked to me.

Easy for me?

Then she started crying, and said nothing more. I fled, as if drunk with wine, out into a distant field. When I returned, she greeted me with eyes wet with tears, but she gamely tried to humor me. We kissed and picked up our child, whom we watched with amusement. Then Adelka broke the silence. She complained that life had gotten much more expensive since our town got the railway, but my income was decreasing steadily, because I had lost my few private lessons since Rakovčić had come to town. Everybody was frantically taking *tambura* lessons now.

*

This person Rakovčić, then, was a *tambura* instructor. He was a young, attractive man. He visited me and he behaved as if he were in the presence of a composer of great renown. This pleased me, and we agreed to work together with one accord and awaken in our people a feeling for the musical arts. I've always believed that people would be ready to sacrifice everything for the sake of music if they would just put some energy into understanding it. Admittedly I am not very taken by *tambura*-playing. Let our tradespeople have it, and other people who only like esoteric music, so they can have fun tickling their ears. Only do not introduce the *tamburica* into places where there exists the need for pure art as a requirement of higher intellectual life. My new colleague Rakovčić is in complete agreement with this view, and I'm happy about that. We will at least work for a common goal, and as a team of two we'll be stronger than if I were working alone.

*

Since Adelka's illness took no turn for the better, I grew despondent. Three days ago I heard her saying to our little Veruška in the bedroom:

"What will become of you, poor thing, when your mother dies?..."

This alarmed me to no end. So, I am indeed responsible for her worries—for the poverty we are enduring and everything bad that comes from it. Forlornly I went in to see Adelka.

"Tell me, darling, are you feeling even worse today?"

I embraced her, pressing her soft body to mine, and she whispered in my ear:

"I'm going to die, dear Amadej."

I don't know anymore what I said in response. But I did decide that I would teach any kind of piano lessons that my fellow townspeople desired, and that I would take up the tambura too, if it meant easing Adelka's anxieties.

"Adelka," I said to her resolutely, "you need to go see the doctors in Zagreb."

*

It took a great deal of doing, but I managed to get an advance on my salary of fifty *forints*, and I used it to send Adelka to the capital. Both her godmother and our child accompanied her.

So this evening I am sitting all alone in our home. Everything around me is barren, and this barren solitude bowls me over with an unbearable heaviness in my heart. I want to work on something, but there is no way I can. I have not felt for far too long that fire that can prod my mind into adopting the numb stupor where the essences of melody and harmony flow. Even if now and again some brilliant thought flashes through my mind, I cannot hold onto it or sail forth on its wings. I falter as soon as I have written down a few bars.

My thoughts return over and over to Adelka and Veruška. I found Veruška's little blue outfit that Adelka had sewn, and I saw in my mind the indescribable happiness on Adelka's face when she took our child out for a walk dressed up in it. Adelka's bliss was all the more evident to me now, in this wasteland, and I held the child's clothes up to my face; they were permeated with the scent of a baby's body. I felt an irresistible urge to cry, as much out of heartache as from the tender yearning for the two of them to fill the unbearable emptiness of this house. That made me feel better, and I took out once more my "Hymn to Love." At first I read through it with relish, as if I were reading a work from someone else's hand, and then I started arranging it for a large orchestra. Listening to my composition in my head as I wrote out the score, it occurred to me that no musical instrument in the world possessed either the force or the sensitivity to recreate those sounds as they existed in my soul. But I was convinced that this work was blazing the path to glory for me. Now things are going to be better for us...ah, Adelka, I would so love to see you happy! I love you tremendously. My love is immortal, and therefore I cannot picture her dying.

*

Today is the third day since Adelka's departure. I received a letter from her, and I am happy to see that her mood is good again and that she feels all right. May God hold her in the palm of His hand!

Mesarić has been promoted, so last night he invited a lot of his friends and acquaintances to celebrate with him. He invited me as well. At first I had decided that I wouldn't go. The man is odious to me. But then I realized that I might need his help, in the form of support or some intercession, and I began to relent. My income really is insufficient to live on, and I have to protect Adelka's health. Therefore I am backing away from my ideals; I am lost; I am in free-fall. And how I used to value my firmness, my good character!...Now I am well

269

down the path of justifying this weakness in myself: why not just go? I am making him out in my imagination to be an enemy, but perhaps he isn't what I think he is.

So off I went. We drank and made toasts. Everybody there had to say something in honor of Mesarić. Then it was my turn. This was painful for me. But I thought up a few words about the learned man, who was a poet and a patriot. When I had strung these words together in my mind, the way slaves are bound together by chains, I stood up and commenced speaking. I looked over at Mesarić, saw his eyes—and it occurred to me that he had beheld Adelka with those eyes, those brutish eyes with their filthy prurience...And I am standing here before them with flattery, with lies!—My thoughts abandoned me, as did my ability to speak. A frosty feeling of indifference came over me. I set my glass down on the table and spoke:

"Gentlemen, I cannot tell lies..." and then I sat back down.

No one spoke. At first I found what I had said distasteful, but afterwards I was glad. I reveled in my own fortitude. Then I left the gathering, imagining that the others were saying behind my back: "He's not in his right mind. Such a terribly neurotic man!"...

I set out on foot for home and crossed paths on the way with a soldier. He was leading a girl by the hand and kissing her constantly. Why can't I enjoy life that way— with wine, lechery, lying, and hypocrisy? Why do I create turbulence where others roll along smoothly, and why do I treat as bitter the things that others find intoxicatingly pleasurable and felicitous? Why?!

I sit at my table, with Adelka's and Veruška's clothes stacked in front of me. I press them to my face, and their identical scent leaves me intoxicated; I sense the sumptuousness, but also the pain, of what they mean to me. The two of them mean everything to me. Oh, holy is that smell, the smell of a child-like creature, before which my soul bows. Now I grasp the divine words of Jesus: "Suffer the little ones to come to me!" Small, isolated, pitiful, and miserable—such is my world. I shall suffer along with you wretches, as long as you maintain that sweet and holy smell of a child-like soul, which has no equal. While those people out there lie, and kill...

You are so dear to me, Adelka! Scarcely three days since we parted ways, and to me it feels like an eternity. I found in you the best and most beautiful things about human beings. The arts, science, wealth, honors—all of that is lifeless and hollow compared to your virtuous soul, in which the deity resides. I kiss these clothes with their youthful airy scent of your souls, Adelka and Veruška, and I am deeply moved; I kiss them lovingly, ecstatically. The breath of the divine! I spread my kisses and rue the fact that I was not always as good to you as you deserved.

*

Today Mesarić came to see me. He asked me to go on a walk with him and invited me to be his guest for lunch, because, surely, it was unpleasant for me to live in seclusion when I was used to having family around.

I did not know who was being shameless, he for talking that way, or I, for being silent.

"You must be thinking of last night's little *contre-temps*," he went on to say. "That kind of thing usually happens when someone is drunk, and last night's incident is already forgotten. Don't build it up into anything in your mind...It was so minor."

Drunk? Have I truly gone mad? I wish I were crazy, because then I would surely not have to endure this anti-life.—Now I sense in and around myself two worlds. One of them encompasses all the serenity, truth, and rightful value of everything that exists, not because it is but because it has to be. The other world strives against the first one; it is inconstant and incomprehensible in its inconsistency.

Maybe Mesarić is mad. Maybe everybody is...Ah, Adelka, I cannot find my way without you. Now at last I see what you mean to me, my sweet Adelka!

*

Adelka is coming to see me tomorrow! She wrote: "...I feel well again, thank God. I would like so much for you to be with us, if only so you could see Veruška, and the way everything in this big city intrigues her."

I read her letter through several times, filling in with my imagination the things she did not write about.

It is now two hours past midnight and I have still not been able to get to sleep. I am totally alert and therefore I decided to get up and light a candle so I could write in my journal. This has for some time now been the kind of work that is most dear to me. It feels as if this journal is the only friend I have who understands me completely and in whom I can confide everything weighing on my heart.

But, alas, I cannot even tell it everything that's on my mind. Lying on my back in bed, my whole life passed before my eyes. If only I could include in this diary illustrations of these thoughts of mine, the way they lined up one behind the other in my soul, then I would really see myself in this book, the way I am, and by that I mean what I have kept hidden from others and what others have concealed from me. Musical *motifs* swirled about in accompaniment to some of the pictures, and they aided me in giving form to my thoughts. And now that I am sitting here writing, I cannot do anything. It's as if everything was consumed in the flame of this candle burning so peacefully in front of me. I am reflecting on my life, the brightness of which seems locked away inside a heavy, black shell preventing it from connecting with the wide-open currents of freedom in the universe...How replete with abomination this life is! With filth! I believe that after death we throw off these earthly encrustations with disgust, as if they were soiled undergarments, and we clothe ourselves in purity.

For a full three-quarters of an hour I ambled around my room with all kinds of thoughts running through my head. So much inconstancy! I hate wealth and wealthy people for the simple reason that there are poor people on earth. And to think that I was imagining myself as a wealthy man! I thought about how Adelka and I could travel to the lakes at Plitvice to escape the summer heat. We'd have a beautiful villa built for ourselves there, and

Croatian poets and artists would come to enjoy our hospitality. A string quartet would reside there permanently—as would Irma. In my mind it is night. The moon is blazing above the magnificent, enchanting temple at the source of the Korana River. I walk silently into the shrine, sit down next to the cave and hearken. In the glorious silence delightful harmonies come down from the celestial sphere to be born through the gentle sound of the waters; somewhere out in the dimly-lit forest a quartet of *vilas* intones a beloved folksong: "Oh River Korana, those cold waters of yours."

Marvelous. Ah, just marvelous!

It's wintertime. The tops of the mountains are bedecked with thick layers of snow, and Adelka, Veruška, and I are seated in the still heat beneath centuries-old pine trees on the edge of the vast waters of the Croatian coastline—we are on the island of Lokrum.

Under the pines walk mysterious, invisible beings; I sense their movements, and I close my eyes tightly and watch a huge chorus of singers in their bright red caps assembling. The great Zajc takes up his position in front of them, and a thousand voices break out like thunder in his song "Arise from Your Dream!"...It booms like a tempest from the rugged Dalmatian coast, driving waves before it out into the open sea.—As we sit in silence under those century-old pines, Adelka is in the full flower of health; and her gaiety and smile and Veruška's honeyed babbling combine to refine and thrill my soul.

I take up my pencil and write the music to "Petar Svačić."

Dawn reddens the sky—today is the day that Veruška and Adelka come!

*

I greeted Adelka and Veruška with such happiness! All the bitterness and hardship that had enveloped me was consumed in the rollicking good cheer of my spirit. How long had it been since I had felt so happy?

Adelka talked and talked to me about things, telling me everything about our Veruška: how delighted she was by the big city, and how she hadn't desired to return home but wanted Adelka to write to me to come join the two of them there.

Both of them had the same amount of child in them, but nevertheless it also warmed my heart to hear Adelka's panegyrics about our Veruška's guileless soul, which she understood better than she did mine. Ach, let them have their buoyant, crystal-clear world. Why don't I cave in and be part of it? What could be more beautiful or satisfied than the soul of a child?

Amidst conversation like this I well-nigh forgot about Adelka's illness. So I remembered it and inquired of her:

"And what, dear Adelka, did the doctors tell you?"

Her pallid face grew red as a rose. She put her head on my chest, locked her eyes on mine and smiled like a little girl who has done something against her parents' wishes but which she, in her naivete, cannot conceal.

"Well, Adelka, does that mean things are all right?"

"Don't get mad, Amadej..."

"What?..."

"I didn't go see the doctor."

Adelka's godmother had located one of her relatives in Zagreb, and this woman had taken Adelka to someone who knew how to treat women's disorders. This woman had given her medicine—and Adelka claims that, after taking it, her condition was much improved.

*

I haven't made an entry in my journal for ages now. I will try to describe what has been happening...

One day while coming home I saw Mesarić leaving my house. And he noticed me, too, but he turned into a side street, pretending not to have seen me. That beast of prey in me was roused, the one named jealousy. But I maintained self-control. It's something else—not that—I told myself. Behind my back, and all around me, people are gossiping about the tambura teacher Rakovčić. They say he is overshadowing all of the self-admiring talented people in our town. At least that's what Mesarić said, toasting a drunk—Rakovčić.—So therefore it's true, I thought merrily with regard to the horrifying notion that he had been at our house because of Adelka. This was to my unmistakable shame...So why had he asked for me in my own home? Suddenly my blood pounded in alarm.

*

Adelka was completely covered in tears...I could scarcely bring myself to ask what had happened.

She walked out of the room, saying, barely audibly, "It wasn't anything…"

I went after her and took her by the arm.

"Tell me what happened."

"Nothing."

She was pretending, but her eyes, her tears, and everything else about her, save her lips, were telling me something else.

"You can't fake it…And why are you keeping a secret from me? Something has happened to you, but your silence mortifies me more than the worst possible news."

"What?....Ah, nothing I tell you," she said, raising her smile-wreathed face to me. But her eyes were filled with tears. She looked weak and pale, as if she were made of some transparent material, stretched too thin. But with this grief expressed on her face and the smile registering in her moist eyes, she looked as beautiful as an angel. I regained my composure and kissed her forehead.

"You are not capable of hiding things…You cannot do it, Adelka…Have no fear. Tell me everything."

"But what?" she asked anew. And then she burst out crying and pressed her light, tender body against mine.

"Adelka, what happened?"

"Promise me," she finally said, without lifting her head from my chest, "that you won't tell anyone about it."

I promised.

"It was…Mesarić."

My whole body began to tremble, but she said nothing further. A beast was raging inside me, convulsing at the sight of blood.

"You have to tell me everything. Do you understand? You have to!" I was shaking with the power and passion of my feelings.

Finally, in truncated sentences, she admitted to me that Mesarić had offered her his love, and she had run away in shame.

My blood pounded mightily in my ears. A hundred schemes went through my mind. I would humiliate him…and then kill him!

I retreated to my room and devised a plan. More than anything I was thinking of purchasing a revolver and then shooting him down in public like a dog…but that just made me feel powerless all of a sudden. My only sensation was one of being insulted. I wanted to cry, and this weakness made me ashamed of myself in front of Adelka. How dare he do this?…One moment I was burning up in flames of passion, only to fall into languid impotence the next…How could this blackhearted scoundrel, with his animalistic egotism, fan the flame of discord beneath a family's contentment? I had to discharge my misery to someone, or else I felt that I would be strangled by all that was happening inside of me. So off I went to the pub, where he sat with a group of friends. Red light streamed all around my field of vision like blood.

"You coward!" I called out, spitting in his face. "Bastard! I demand satisfaction. I challenge you to a duel…" I was out of control. I even grabbed a glass from the table and was prepared to shatter it over his head. But he withdrew.

This was a death wish, since I had never held a weapon in my life. Shortly thereafter the mayor summoned me, and I found him with the parish priest. The priest talked to me about the weaknesses of the flesh and the magnanimous spirit of forgiveness, and the ill logic of the idea that an offense could be erased by a duel. And how the Mother Church forbids such a thing.

The mayor bade me not talk about the incident. We're all human, and everything will be forgotten. "And don't you see, Amadej," he added, "how just God is? That which you would not have others do, you should not do to them."

"What are you thinking of?" I demanded of him.

"I am just reminding you...and you know perfectly well what I'm saying."

"Say it, or you'll answer for this in court, if the intent of your words is what I suspect."

"I won't say another word about it. You are, my dear fellow, one nervous man. Calm down. Think of your health."

He was in fact thinking about my friendship with Irma. Coward!

Two months have passed since then, and no one has spoken of the incident. But my soul remains wounded, with wounds that will never heal.

*

My mind is unleashing thoughts that could definitely never be set to music. And I'm not even having any musical ideas. Like a barren fruit tree, degenerating. Is it the soil or the air that doesn't suit me where I live? But I do

have some more stuff to get down on paper and I'll try
to do it calmly.

The tambura teacher Rakovčić has requested that we
do a concert together. He wants to make a public appearance with his group of players. True enough, the
young teacher hereabouts did tell me to be wary of
Rakovčić, for he is pulling the rug out from under my
feet. Not too long ago he called me a dunderhead in the
middle of a party we both attended. That young man,
although he is still very much wet behind the ears, is a
likable fellow, and once more I couldn't bring myself to
believe what he said. And one day, for instance, when I
was listening to all the members of Rakovčić's tambura
group playing together, I became aware of a very large
number of grievous mistakes not only in the arrangement of the parts but in the fundamentals of musical
harmony. After the rehearsal I notified Rakovčić of
these mistakes; his face turned deep red, and I felt bad
for his discomfiture. I took the score and corrected the
passages.

—How could he label me an ignoramus then? —For
that concert I transcribed for piano and harmonium the
"Adagio" from Beethoven's *Appassionata*, with the intention that Rakovčić and I perform it. My choir was going
to sing a lyrical piece by Thomas Eisenhut. Rakovčić
agreed to my program, but I had never been able to persuade him to come to rehearsal—and there were only
three days left till the production. Then that day I snuck
up on him in the auditorium and requested that we give
my transcription a trial run. At first he tried the excuse
that he had some work to do that he couldn't put off,

but then he shamefacedly admitted that he couldn't play any instrument save the *tambura*. At the last minute then I changed the program so that I was playing Chopin's first piano *Ballade* instead.

The concert was underway, and after the first *tambura* performance, the following thing happened: a pair of *tamburaši* came up onto the podium with Rakovčić, one of them carrying in his hand a silver wreath. The other gave more or less this short address: "With this wreath we are not only expressing our respect and gratitude for your artistry, your hard work, and your ardor, but also for the marvelous musical instrument of the Croatian people, which has such a glorious future before it, and which one day will rival the violin in concert halls, when our patriotic musical artists perfect it and elevate it to a fitting place in the same way in which, in other nations, musical experts have exalted their national folk instruments to the heights of artistic achievement."

After that the other fellow presented Rakovčić with his silver wreath, and the audience burst into applause and cheers.

I was deeply offended, and then the tears thronged my eyes...It was all I could do to hide them so that I didn't feel even more ashamed and victimized. But that Rakovčić proceeded past me acting dignified and obviously convinced that he was more worthy and accomplished than I. What heinous revenge for that which I had once tried to argue this way to some of our people who asserted—but without a whit of understanding of the musical arts—that we should prioritize and foster the *tamburica*: "Gentlemen—so I told them—you do not demand that our poets not break ranks with the decasyl-labic lines and traditional themes of our folk poetry; you do not demand that our orators and actors say their lines on stage the same way the proverbial blind old Croatian recites his folk songs to the sound of the *gusle*; you do not demand that Croatian painters and architects feel compelled to stick with the forms and shapes that the people created in their textile crafts and building styles; in every one of these cases, you insist on more. You want for Croatian writers and artists to offer up what not only what the genius of the common man has cre-ated but also what the genius of a highly educated and culturally developed individual person can do, of a man who is in contact with world events, with elemental movements in the human soul, and who is influenced by discussions of enigmatic issues ranging from psychology to social and political life, creating in the spirit of pro-gress that modern science has placed at his disposal. But from music—you require its alpha and omega to be the Croatian *tamburica*? And that *tamburica* isn't even ours, in terms of its origins; it was brought to us, God only knows when, from the far east by the Arabs; this in-strument, and others like it, are attested in the history of music of other peoples, too. You venerate such an in-strument as this, regardless of whether it was originally ours or is an ancient adoption; you esteem it as the means by which the people, in accordance with its set of skills, in their primitive aspect, asserts their artistic im-pulses. But, I beg you, refrain from thinking that the *tamburica* will be the interpreter of profound or dignified artistic thoughts of great genius! You have no understanding of music, and for you its minor primitive part, the esoteric, is its proper domain. Your kind stand firmly on that ground and don't believe in the value of anything that is not within reach of their critical faculties. Let us be patriots; let us honor and love Croatia, and die for it. Anyone who keeps his Croatian name secret is a scoundrel, but we dash off with this holy name into the world of the cultured peoples; we are striving to meet up with those others in the same circle, as measured by our culture, but that is a circle in which we will never capture a spot on the strength of our *tamburicas*. What a *tamburica* was a thousand years ago, it still is today. Meanwhile you take our full-throated Croatian girl, in whose mouth our wonderful folksongs are right at home, and as beautiful as flowers—you take her and deprive her of these songs and have her sing pieces written by musical geniuses from their Scarlatti to our Lisinski and Zajc, all of whom were intending them for voices elevated by formal training to virtuosity and for souls blazing with flames of passion, sensitivity, and agony, flames known only to people with a high degree of cultural refinement. The *tamburica* will never play what the composers wrote for any instrument in an orchestra, just as the loudest Croatian peasant girl will never be able to do what Milka Trnina does. The *tamburica* isn't, and never will be, a violin, in the same way that even the loveliest folk song about Kraljević Marko or the maiden of Kosovo isn't the equal of the vocal parts from Gundulić's *Osman* or Preradović's "Ode." In the same way that the most charming folk tale we have isn't the same as one page in a historical novel by Šenoa. The *tamburica* cannot rise above itself, just as similar musical instruments among other peoples have never been perfected to the point that they become suitable for higher artistic aims. The *motifs*, the musical ideas of the Croatian people, can provide the artist with material—look at how that titan, Haydn, was able to combine them into sublime musical constructions that awe us, whatever it is we marvel at the most—a clever, animated poem, a painting, or a sculpture. The mystery is how a great work is created from such inconsequential little *motifs*; the creators themselves may actually be in a position to say less about how this is done than can the speculative scholarship with which critics and aestheticians are outfitted. But I'd bet my very life that not even the greatest musical genius in the world could ever exalt that kind of creative construction with the help of the *tamburica*!

A young shopkeeper and *tambura* player, the one who had earlier worked with Mesarić to assemble the choral group, then posed an insolent question to me:

"Tell us—and be truthful!—whether you would speak out like this against *tamburicas* if you knew how to play one."

I did not intend to answer his question, but then someone else remarked:

"This just doesn't seem to fit: he bills himself as a patriot, but he stomps on the things that are national..."

They did not have what it takes to understand me.

Two days after the concert the newspapers from Zagreb reached us. They carried a notice about the concert. I'll copy out here just a few passages from it: "...Since the young musician Rakovčić has come here, considerable progress has been noted in the interest level among our citizens, both men and women, for the captivating art of music. Mr. Rakovčić, a merry fellow by nature and an adroit and very young trained musician, won over our populace immediately, established an ensemble of *tambura* players, and today, on the 8th of September, we reveled for the first time in the marvelous sounds of our national instrument. You should have seen our worthy lasses and our stalwart lads as they submitted their wills to the talents of the conductor—and you should have seen us, the way tears of joy bedewed our eyes..." And so on. At the end of the notice: "The *kapellmeister* and pianist, Z., dashed off a composition by Chopin that failed to excite the audience. Perhaps such things are excellently suited for the frigid north, but here in the warm south everything is more lush and heartfelt, and that includes the music!"

While reading this I laughed, and I grew angry, and I cried...Ah, wise old Vesely, how I call you back to mind more and more frequently now! You had a surpassing understanding of people!—And how many times do I now recall Irma...for do you know what her companionship now would mean to me? I treated that woman unjustly. She has the refined essence of a woman who feels things with such intensity that she cannot shy from revealing to a man her soul's hunger for a pure, Platonic love. But I am built of cruder stuff, I, who saddled her heart with this base product of my own soul, the demon of seduction!

Out of all my private piano lessons I had kept only two. And these two let me go, and hired in my place Rakovčić, for two reasons: first, because his lessons cost less, and second, because with him the kids played only jingles, marches, and dance tunes.

My income was falling as my expenses in the home were rising. Adelka was very weak and feverish, and we had to take in her godmother to help her. Something heavy, awkward, and mournful tinged our life. We bore the cross of poverty, but there was something else, something more, for which I cannot find words. It often occurred that we would sit together in the evenings, without talking, and with me at a loss to chart a course away from the river of sorrows where I was drowning. Often all that brightened the leaden atmosphere enveloping us was our sweet little Veruška, with her cheery disposition; she was our only joy.

From out of the houses where there was a keyboard of any kind you could hear marches, drinking songs, and schmaltzy melodies from Italian and German operettas. I listened to them and it was like they were there deliberately to provoke me. Ah, but that's not the case: this is the cultural harvest of my colleague Rakovčić, whose reputation and fame grow day by day. I grow furious and fulminate publicly against his ignorance. But in general I am getting more and more feeble, and I cannot conceal my irritability...Of my pride there remains not a trace.

*

Dawn is here! And good fortune can knock even on my door! At all events, ultimately justice will triumph.

Yesterday a certified letter reached me from Berlin. I open it up and glance first of all at the signature: Irma

Leschetizky, née von Irány...and I felt joy right down to my toes. She addressed me as "Dear Amadej"—and she announced that they were staying near Berlin with some of her husband's relatives. They often entertained company there, and there was much music-making. Not too long ago she had played, before a fairly large crowd, the excerpt of my "Hymn to Love" that I had given her when she lived here. Everyone liked my composition, and one of the people there was the director of a well-known music publishing house in Berlin, and he asked her for my address. She wished me all the best and looked forward to receiving published versions of my work soon. "Didn't I," she said in conclusion, "predict that you would turn out to be a famous man?"

This letter made me ecstatic. I did not know how to master my vanity, and I showed off the letter everywhere. The effect was immediate: everybody treats me like a new creature to whom they do not yet know how to adapt their behavior. I sense that I am growing in their eyes. At first I fell prey to an unworthy feeling of maliciousness, but I have already grown embarrassed by that. I can see they rejoice in my success. And anyway people are not as wicked as we imagine them to be, thinking only of ourselves, and forgetting that they have just as much right to think of themselves as we do. The moment someone obstructs one of our interests on account of one of their similar interests, we think they are bad, but we forget that we are bad in their eyes! "And are there really any people at all who have never felt the power of invisible kindness, and have not even the worst among us at some point been good in an unseen way?" When I read these words of the French poet the other day, they had a soothing effect on me, and today I am still marveling at the perspicacity of that man who knew how to plumb the depths of the human soul. Since receiving Irma's letter, I have no enemies.—And Adelka is very happy about the letter; for the first time she is actively interested in my work. So the day is dawning on all sides.

*

Now a letter has come from the publisher in Berlin. He wants me to send him more of my competitions. He'll review any that have not yet appeared in print. If they pass muster with him, he'll publish them; and he hopes that we won't have any problem agreeing on terms.

This offer elated me and tonight, after a long hiatus, I stayed up till three in the morning reviewing my cycle of smaller compositions for piano. I will tell you honestly—even if there is also some vanity in it—that I delighted in these works of mine. Many times my reading was interrupted by involuntary cries of "This is beautiful!" With these pieces I also included a précis of my orchestral work, of which I had made far-reaching sketches with the intention of writing a ballad to Šenoa's "Petar Svačić."

"The sun's coming up already," Adelka said to me when I came to bed. "You have to head to church early today. When will you rest?"

I kissed her passionately and remained sitting on her bed for a long while, talking to her about the respectable future that was headed our way. We were, both of us, truly grateful to Irma, and we were happy, very happy.

*

I could hardly wait for an answer from the publisher in Berlin. And yet just more disappointment!...Not even things that seem firmly in my column end up going smoothly and without opposition. I delude myself when I think that everything in life that is just and unequivocal has to succeed. So once again the two worlds: how it is supposed to be—and how it is. —And what remarkable obstacles! The publisher is willing to bring out my song cycle, and he is willing to give me a royalty of one thousand *marks* for the first printing of two thousand copies, as soon as I sign the attached contract—as soon as I renounce my name! Yes, my name, which is not yet known in the musical world, and which thus prevents him from advertising with it in the marketplace. I created that work in the happiest hours of my life, and now I am supposed to give up my name? I cannot do it.

"Our hopes have come to naught," I told Adelka. "I will not make excuses here, but it's not my fault. What they were demanding of me is not something I could do. In my view, if I agreed to it, I'd be no better than a common wastrel."

She remained silent for a long time and then said in a quiet voice:

"Nothing goes right for us...nothing!"

When I read through the publisher's letter a second time, I did find in it something of comfort that I had overlooked in my initial excitement. To wit, the man wrote: We can see from the passage of your orchestral work that you sent that you are a skilled orchestrator. Therefore we could provide you with some regular income if you are willing to arrange, according to our instructions, other people's compositions for orchestral performance.

"You see, Adelka, not everything is lost yet! This is wage-labor, and for that reason I need not be ashamed that my signature will not be on it."

*

From Berlin I received a flurry of random compositions, for the most part bad ones that seem to have been made in cookie-cutter fashion. Night after night I orchestrate marches, polkas, waltzes, and arias from all kinds of operas and operettas. Berlin is satisfied with my work, but the pay is lousy: for one hour of labor I find it impossible to earn more than a *forint*. But, well, I'll be satisfied if I can just get that much. During the day I can't get much work done. Even if it's just mechanical work, I nonetheless have to have absolute peace and quiet to do it. And our little Veruška is as spirited as a baby bird, and you can see her everywhere, and you can hear her everywhere—the whole house is hers. Sometimes I yell at her, but then I feel bad about doing that and I seat her on my knee and postpone working till the evening. In the nighttime I work for hours, now and then getting carried away when I put a little of my soul into invigorating some languid melodies first penned by God knows whom.

An opera in three acts came, and I was supposed to instrument it. The melodies weren't bad. To be sure it was, all in all, a cheap imitation of Wagnerian dramatic music, but it at least made sense. I have to turn it into something different. When I finish, I will get an honorarium of two hundred *marks* for each act.—What do you know—I think while I'm resting—I had to fall back on the protection of foreigners, of people unknown to me, and for their profit and glory I must suppress my name, just so that I can get payment by doing the kind of work with which musical apprentices occupy themselves. How did my puffed-up artist's pride just disappear? I work like a machine in the still of the night and mope about, feeling ashamed of myself, and ask myself in turn, with the cynicism of a half-wrecked man: Amadej, what became of your artistic pride? Where are your big dreams? In the end I am overcome by boredom and loathing for what I do, providing for prettier clothes for the pale, bloodless, and infirm spiritual children of an unknown German composer. And I think about how he is walking proudly down the sidewalks of his big city, about how he superciliously makes the rounds of his relatives who shower him with glory and champagne, and how he feels grand compared to me, the musician from an unknown minor nation. He considers me his slave, because I agreed to hire myself out as an apprentice on whose work he, aware of his prerogative, places his name. So where is it that your pride has gotten to, Amadej?

Then I pick up this journal and read. Will that fire ever again blaze up in me, after flying straight at me from page after page? That fire is banked below the ashes...Oh, the soul languishes that would ensorcel this world!

*

Adelka is not at all well. She lost a lot of blood again, so I decided that I would take her to the doctor's in Zagreb myself. We can leave our daughter with the godmother. We were waiting for her to recover enough to make the trip, which she did, thank God, but now we are faced again with the crude and execrable question of money. From Berlin I did indeed just get one hundred *marks* for work I sent in, but not much of it is left. I paid our overdue rent, and the rest went for Adelka's illness. I had the bright idea of appealing to a possible Croatian *maecenas* by letter. I told myself I would attach to my note copies of my compositions along with the letter from that publisher in Berlin demanding that I suppress my name. And I would describe my situation, and Adelka's illness. Initially this was a fabulous idea... But when I sat down to write the letter, quite a different image formed before my eyes. Will the man not ask, "Who is this fellow who is making so bold as to molest me with his entreaties?" And perhaps he will turn me down, or, even worse, he'll regard me as a man of no dignity who feels no compunction about begging. At that my soul clouded over. In a trice the radiance of my plan was extinguished. And once more I had ashes, and in them bitterness and disappointment.

But then I discovered a second, truly rational idea. Why don't I offer my compositions to some publishers in Zagreb, even if for smaller royalties? Good grief—let them place advertisements in the newspapers saying that a famous Berlin company was prepared to publish these works itself; if our public needs to rely on an outside judgment even on home-front issues, well, here it is! Another plan was complete in a moment: I will start up an IOU for a hundred *forints*, which I will pay back with the royalties from a publishing house in Zagreb. How inventive one can be when it comes to push and shove! "Naked necessity is the best of all schools," Preradović says.

*

Yet again I am felled by shame and rage. I asked five of our wealthy individuals to sign this promissory note for me, but not a single one would do it. I can't even remember who used which excuse. The majority just stated that they wouldn't sign "on principle." I came up with a more lucid translation of their words of alienation: I don't believe you. You wouldn't pay it back, and I'd be left holding the bag...Someone else said to me in helpful fatherly tones: Give up on the promissory note. They never worked out for anyone. You'll see that you can get by without it, and then the one hundred *forints* would be jingling in your own pocket..." A fourth man told me about his own woes. A rich man, a large landowner he was, a merchant and member of parliament, whom people estimate to be worth two hundred thousand *forints*, he lectures me: "Everyone has his own issues." But for him these frightful concerns about how to keep body and soul together do not exit; he is just concerned with preserving his stash and adding to his property. And he has the audacity to compare his woes to mine! Wasn't Jesus taking aim at people of this sort when he said that it's easier for a camel to pass through the eye of a needle than for a rich man to enter the kingdom of heaven?

I came home and despair got the better of me. My wife, the mother of my child, was going to perish on account of a hundred *forints*! Where do people get that article of faith, to which they pay lip service, that a maternal heart is a treasure beyond measure?—Yet when it comes right down to it, if one hundred of their *forints* are on the line, then they can see neither a sick woman nor the value of a mother's heart. They calmly and conscientiously cover all of that with their "principle." But my dear man, they all say, from behind their lecterns or in their books, one hundred *forints* is nothing to be sneezed at! And the love of a woman and mother, a human life—to be sneezed at? My mind cannot keep up...Does God forgive sins like this? If he does forgive them, then we truly cannot accept that He is good.

I shared my complaints with our young schoolmaster, and he said to me with a smile:

"Pass it here. I'll sign for you, as will one of my colleagues."

I felt like kissing the ground at his feet, not so much because he helped me in my time of need as because he showed he trusted me and in turn restored my faith in humanity.

*

Here we go then. In front of me are my published compositions in a big envelope that bears the address of that publisher in Berlin. And at the top of the pages my name is nowhere to be found. I will renounce everything—just give me money!...I do not grieve, I am not angry, and my conscience is not bothering me. I'm impassive, that's all. I feel nothing. I sold my name and with in the pride from my soul, and I remained as empty as a vessel made of common material from which the noble liquid has been emptied. I am dull, dull, dull-witted.

I will write this entry about what I went through in Zagreb.

Naturally the very first thing I did was go to the doctor with Adelka. He was, people said, outstanding in his knowledge of the field, a scientist and an artist both. His manly demeanor, the energy in the expression on his elongated face with its French goatee and pensive, penetrating eyes, his quiet ways and composure amidst the nerve-wracking hubbub (in his antechamber about twenty patients were waiting for him)—a little voice inside me told me all of this: "This fellow can, if he wants to, cure Adelka."

He gave her a scrupulous examination, prescribed medicine, and advised me to dispatch her next winter to some place by the sea with a milder climate. We would see, and if she didn't want to go, then we'd consult with him further. When he escorted me to the door, Adelka went ahead but he held me back. With quick quiet words, he told me:

"Your wife's condition is rather poor. It would be a good idea for someone to go with her if you send her anywhere."

I felt the blood solidify and contract in my veins, and I didn't know how to respond.

When we got out onto the street, I cast sidelong glances at Adelka and I thought I was seeing the ravages of disease on her face for the first time. I was afraid she would notice a change in me, so I said in a merry voice:

"What a pleasant and favorable impression that man left on me. I believe there are doctors who can cure patients solely by their gaze."

"Those were my thoughts, too," she replied happily.

In general, I found it heartening that she was starting to show real concern about getting well.

I dropped her off at a restaurant and went in turn to a publishing house with my compositions in hand. I told them what I would like to do.

They had no desire even to look at my music. The man turned me down while he talked the whole time with a lady who was purchasing books:

"We can't get mixed up in this. That sort of thing isn't done here. Unless you want your publisher to..."

I continued along to another one. This fellow leafed through my compositions disdainfully, with more or less spiteful negligence, shaking his head the whole time and pursing his lips... "Tsk, tsk, tsk." I felt as though I were standing on pins and needles before him, until he finally said, carefully: "We have no use for these. This kind of thing is not in demand. If you have a nice march, or something for the dance floor, or a humorous piece for singers, we'd take that off your hands."

"The things you want do not belong in the realm of music as art."

"But that's what moves."

I hesitated for a brief moment, mustering the courage to say to him, "I dare say you would be doing a patriotic service if your publishing house were to accept these. You'd be supporting a Croatian musician and furthering the spread of pure art."

He did not let me finish my thoughts.

"Ah, the way you talk! This is a business, and it has nothing to do with patriotism."

And he laughed right in my face. It was a laugh of righteous indignation and fury.

"That's true," I told him. My lips were still trembling, an unpleasant sensation that always comes over me in such circumstances. "But a company like yours can also function as a *maecenas*."

"*Maecenas*? Benefactor?" And with that he turned to another man in the shop, and both of them began smiling and mouthing the word "Benefactor?"

Out I went, holding my compositions in my hand, but I had been put to shame, made an object of ridicule—all because I walked in mentioning the word *maecenas*. Conclusion: material gain ranks above ideas. Matter over spirit!

I am losing the rudder on my life. The thought returned, having already crept seductively into my head so many times, that this is how our world is structured, and that every attempt to approach what is superior to it is doomed. Culture, progress, all of that is merely illusory. Everything remains stuck in its old ways. All that changes is the…form…Oh, God! Make me into something different, for I am falling apart!

I pulled myself together and went along to a third shop.

This dealer met me with a sharp look, experienced and suspicious, like a butcher eyeing a lamb to determine its weight.

I told him that I had come to offer him something, and I added:

"I'm willing to give you this for less money than usual."

"You're looking for a fee?" he asked in an abusive, mocking tone. He just handed me the compositions back without having read even the titles.

"Please, read," I said to him. "Please read this letter from a publishing house in Berlin. He is offering me an honorarium of 1000 *marks* to publish them, if I will just waive the right to include my name. But I won't do it."

This publisher was not even curious whether I was telling the truth. He just glanced at the signature and handed the letter back to me with these words:

"So just give them to that fellow. In these parts no one is going to pay you for them. I mean, really…your name? The main thing is the money."

When I stepped out into the street, I felt like crying. Could it really be true that I did not know this world into which I was born, and where I make my home? Do all ideas, all poetry, all exalted human thoughts, really only come into circulation after this much haggling, after "coming to terms," after such bickering and sniping, and possibly even accompanied by lies and deception? Are our writers and journalists lying when they say in print: "our patriotic and self-sacrificing publishing firms"… and so on?

I did not want to tell Adelka any of this. I pretended to be happy in front of her. She, who had supported me so little in my artistic world till now, picked up on it immediately whenever something major happened to me outside our four walls.

"Tell me, Amadej. Something's going on with you. And I guess I'm not allowed to know about it?"

I convinced her that my mood was altogether fine.

"Well, then, the doctor must have said something worrisome about my health, and you aren't allowed to tell me."

At that point, of course, I had to reveal the truth.

The next day I saw her off to the coast. So that she would not have to pass by home again first, but could leave straight from Zagreb, I jotted down her exact instructions about what items of clothing to send to her, how the household should be run, how Veruška was to be taken care of, etc.

Our parting was labored. One moment she wanted me to accompany her to Primorje, where she had never been before, and the next she bade me return immediately to Veruška. She longed to be healthy again, and I looked at her with eyes filled with tenderness, and the kisses I bestowed on her contained my very soul. We were happy, brimming with hope, and our kisses took us back to the earliest days of our marriage; everything else was forgotten. Once more that mighty fortress rose up, where I could lock myself away; I, the man and the artist—my home, my family...

If only Adelka would get well—I know that then our life would be revived. She is starting to understand me, and when my compositions appear in print, I shall make the rounds of our local *haute monde* and tell them how they arrived in Berlin with a foreign name attached—and then, if God so wills—via Berlin to Zagreb!...My hopes are returning, along with my will and momentum. —

*

I can't get any work done at all. My thoughts abide continually with Adelka. She wrote me from her bed, because she had not fared well with all that traveling. I was overcome by an awful, desperate dread, and it derailed my mind. My spirit is now continually at her bedside, and I take her hand, dry the perspiration on her brow, and tell her cute stories about our clever Veruška. Sometimes entire hours pass with me lost in these daydreams, and afterwards it is like I am truly returning from spending time with her.

*

Last night while dreaming I heard someone pronounce my name. I found myself—without waking up—beside Adelka's bed, in a little bedroom I had never seen before. Adelka lay on her back without moving, very soft and pale; her eyes were closed and her breathing was light and rapid. When she noticed me, she smiled endearingly and beckoned me to her. She wanted me to place my head on her pillow and to take her hand. When I did so, she uttered: "It's easier to die when you're with me like this..." There were two other women in the room, plus the doctor, an older gentleman who was assigning tasks to the women. Then a young man entered the room and showed the doctor a piece of paper. I couldn't read what was on it, even though the doctor and the young man were standing fairly close to me. So that's what I dreamt last night. And this morning when I walked out of church, I was met by the telegraph courier. I turned to ice. My hands were shaking. My intuition told me what was in the telegram. I opened the envelope and read it: "To Amadej Zlatanić in the city of — : Your wife is unwell. It would behoove you to come."

She will not die...What if she were to die?—It was all inconceivable to me, and I just couldn't think properly. It felt like the whole world was congealing around me, people, objects, and the air itself...A standstill occurred in the perpetual motion of bodies.

I am going to her. I must.

*

I was calm when I returned home. It's already been eight days since we buried her, and I still feel no grief for her; she is before my eyes every moment, lying there with her eyes closed, on the bier, pale and feminine, looking alive. On her delicate and somewhat elongated nose her two black nostrils were visible, and below them her lips clenched into a wisp of a smile. Her eyebrows extended in graceful arcs above her closed eyes. It was only on her hands that she looked like a corpse; they were an unseemly yellow color. Candles burned around her bier, their yellow flames giving off smoke that meandered through the room like a black veil. There was

peace all around her, and amidst that stillness I heard
the easy, regular beating of my heart. I felt in my breast
neither sorrow over her parting nor the need to pray for
her soul. I don't know how this could be, but I didn't
mourn for her then, and I'm not doing so now either.
But I would like to feel grief...then or now. I thought
back over our past, over the hours filled with naught but
our love, but it all seems so dead, so stiff, as if it were
winter. There is empty silence inside me. How much
sweeter it would have been if I'd been able to awaken
lamentation and love in my heart! If I force myself with
might and main to imagine what it is that could move
me to grief, my ears begin to ring with the gay sounds of
the dance music that I arranged for Berlin. I sprinkled
some holy water on her, as custom dictates, and I took
my farewell from her. I don't know why I said it, since
after all she couldn't hear me. I think maybe I wanted to
pretend that that goodbye was making me experience
sorrow. But it didn't. There is silence in me.

Thus we buried her—with no tears for me. I saw all
about me many unknown, tear-streaked faces, and certainly I also wanted to weep, but there was no way I
could. So I came back home free of sadness.

Our godmother runs the household for me and
watches over Veruška. The little girl is wearing black,
but even that doesn't touch me. True to form, I was not
even moved by her question: "Is it true, Daddy, that my
Mommy has gone to heaven?"

I am unable to sleep, so I spend half the night in the
pub. And even then I don't want to go home. Our
godmother carps at me endlessly about how scandalous

it is that I am already spending time at that inn, and she says that other people are taking offense at this. What do I care? The numb and awkward silence in this house is unbearable to me. When I lay down after midnight, I feel hale and fresh, as if I've already had a full night's sleep. Tonight I felt the urge to play the piano. And I got out of bed, took a seat at the keyboard in the pitch blackness, and improvised. So then in the morning our godmother greets me with this reproach:

"For heaven's sake, what will people think?"

What does she know, anyway?

*

Finally I burst out in tears. The night before I had been sitting at the piano. My fingers were flying over the keys and the despondent echo of a G-minor chord moaned through the darkness; I always recoiled from that chord like it was the desperate groan of mystical mythical creatures. My clogged-up emotions were beginning to loosen, and the sounds felt as though they were coming less from taut metallic strings than directly from my insides. And the darkness around me came to life. I closed my eyes and sensed the gloom around me gathering itself into folds, from which living creatures then sprang to listen to my fantasies on the piano. When the last chord receded, I felt as though I would cry. Life was palpable in that room. A silent shifting of darkness in the darkness.

"Adelka," I said softly, taking fright at the sound of my own voice.

Then stillness set in again, the deafening absolute silence in the gloom in which the gleam of the piano's white keyboard was barely perceptible.

Something changed in me, in my mind and in my breast. The rigidity of my inner life gave way and formless, imprecise, embryonic thoughts surfaced in my consciousness and then vanished swiftly into the dark where I could no longer lay my hands on them. I was wide awake in that room where I usually work, writing the figured bass notation for the concluding chords of my *fantasia* in G-minor and then added, in big letters on the outside, the title "Notturno." —After that I tiptoed into our bedroom and began to undress, very slowly and with no light, so that I wouldn't wake Adelka. She was breathing softly, and the sweet scent that belonged only to her body arose on the heat from her bed. Whenever I catch that smell, which is the same as the breath from a baby's mouth, I cannot refrain from touching her with my lips, quietly, so as not to wake her. So I moved towards the bed and discreetly bent over her. I inhaled the warm, sweet fragrance of her body and, fully inebriated with amorous joy, I leaned towards her face in order to kiss it. At first I felt her hair, and then the smooth, soft warmth of her forehead like velvet... Her eyelashes fluttered and brushed against my right temple.

"Aren't you sleeping, sweetheart?" I asked calmly.

Then she wrapped her long, loving arms around my neck and sought my mouth with hers.

I don't know how long it lasted, this embrace of ours. But then, precipitously, the opening chords of my G-minor *fantasia* could be heard from the piano. I was convinced that Jahoda was out there playing it—and a glacial dread of the music that I myself had created sent my soul reeling.

I opened my eyes. All was gloom and silence, and I was lying half-naked on Adelka's bed. She is dead...I thought. And that thought hurt me in a fearsome and inexplicable way. I stood up and walked back and forth in the room, calling out softly to her: "Adelka!... Adelka!.."

Then the old lady came into the room and said:

"Calm down, for God's sake. If you go on like this, you'll get sick, too."

I stayed in the room, seated on Adelka's bed, and wept softly till morning.

*

I am sitting at the organ, playing Mass, and all at once I feel Jahoda behind me. It seems odd. I mean, he's dead—and yet here he is! All at once it occurs to me: maybe he isn't dead, if he's here—and maybe Adelka didn't die, either? And right when I had started entertaining joyous thoughts, some bootmaker who attends Mass every day up here in the choir loft, began waving his hands at me to stop playing.

"Why don't you stop!" he shouted. His face was all red and full of fury and stupidity. "Why not stop when you see that the priest has been up there waiting to sing *Pax Domini sit semper vobiscum*?"

I stare right through the idiotic bootmaker and blurt out in his face, without waiting for the priest: *Et cum spiritu tuo*. Why'd I serenade him with that? Once more I miscalculated. He was not lame; as a matter of fact, he had two healthy legs. But there was no spirit in him, as if her were a pumpkin or a gourd. So why did I go and sing *"Et cum spiritu tuo"* to him?

*

This morning Jahoda got behind me once more and was telling me something about Adelka. I take my fingers off the keyboard so I could hear better. The bootmaker is yelling at me, asking why I haven't ceased playing. Jahoda disappears. My anger boils over and I leave the balcony. Let the idiotic bootmaker play the music. —I come home. Adelka is here somewhere. I can sense her, but she's hiding, right? I hunt for her, and our godmother asks me what I'm looking for. Nothing, godmother, nothing...Afterwards I lock myself in the bedroom with Veruška and inquire of her:

"Darling, do you know where Mama is?"

"In heaven."

"But haven't you seen her?"

"Yes, I have."

"Well, where?"

"Here. She was making this blue dress for me..."

The child will end up telling me everything.

*

I attached a rope to the window and was just about to string myself up (though now I can no longer recall why I wanted to do this) when my godmother walked into the room.

"What are you doing? For the love of God!" and she was looking at me as if she had lost her mind.

"I pray you," I told her calmly and earnestly, "not to meddle in my affairs."

But she took the rope and dragged it off somewhere and then returned with the mayor and a watchman. In a bit the old physician arrived, too. The mayor informed me that my compositions were in danger somehow.

"You, sir, are mad," I said to him, "for my compositions are in print in Berlin."

After that the doctor and the mayor left, but they left the watchman behind—to guard my compositions.

Why is he guarding them here, when they're in Berlin? I cannot make any sense of this.

*

The watchman is with me, and this makes me angry. I would be composing, and writing something new in my journal, but he is disturbing me!

But then, who knows. Maybe it will prove possible to have a conversation with him?

"Hey, friend. Do you know how much my compositions are worth?" I ask him.

And he gives me this moronic look, and says: "I dunno."

And his head almost touches the ceiling.

"You, my dear fellow, are every bit as stupid as that mayor of yours. Please be so kind as to leave. Here you go…"

The doors, however, were locked. We looked everywhere for the key, but it wasn't to be found. I pounded on the door with my hands and feet, and at last my old godmother came around. She says she has no key either…Why would they shut me in with this idiot of a watchman? They're playing some dishonorable game with me. So it is!

Now you, dimwit, whom stupidity has caused to grow roof-high, you make sure to retreat into that corner now, and be as meek as a lamb for me!

Then I put out the candle and waited for Adelka and Jahoda to arrive. If only they do not recoil from this imbecilic face that abides with me in this room. I try to come up with ways to compel him to quit the room—and finally I have the good fortune to hit upon something. I sit down at the piano and start to plunk out the little waltz that Rakovčić wrote for *tamburicas* and dedicated to our mayor's "noble and gracious wife."

"So, friend. Are you still here?"

"At your command," that thief answered.

So he will not flee, even from such music as this! I won't be able to forgive him for that very easily. Ultimately I'm going to have to grab him by the throat.

Our godmother brought us supper, and afterwards I elaborated my *notturno* in G minor until late in the night.

*

They have all convinced me that my Veruška looks like her mother. I take her onto my lap and look at her.

"Veruška, why are you all dressed in black?"

"Because my mother died."

"They are deceiving you. Your mother is here. I know she is. Let's go get rid of the mourning clothes. I'm afraid of them, just like I am of this G-minor *notturno*. —There we go, Veruška. Now look me in the eyes."

The child opened her eyes wide, looked at me for a long time, and then burst out in jarring laughter.

"Nope, Veruška. Those are my eyes...And you have my nose...my mouth and skin...So where is your mother's portion?"

Veruška just smiled.

"Give me your little hands. It might be that you have your mother's hands."

Veruška held out one soft, small hand and I placed it on my palm and studied it. At that point I experienced an uncomfortable emotion...Why, this hand is mine also, a hand with rather long, narrow fingers made for picking out notes. While her mother has round, plump hands. Her fingertips are the only thing—they are pink like yours. Therefore I gently kissed the pink tips of Veruška's little fingers, and she liked this. So she offered me her other hand for a kiss as well.

"I don't want your hand!...Give me what would be mama's, you little urchin!"

"Here you go," says Veruška, turning her lovely tender lips towards me so I'd kiss them.

I kissed her and smelled Adelka's living scent. How I loved that Veruška, pressing her to my breast with passionate force so that I could again merge with the sweet breath of Adelka's being. That, Veruška, is your mother! You see, Veruška, she is not dead, though they dressed you all in black. This is what the fragrance of her life was like...But the child started to shriek wildly, so she was cruelly torn from my embrace.

*

Today the parish priest had to sing a requiem, but he was celebrating Mass in golden robes. Therefore I sang "*Requiem aeternam...*" Now I am ultimately at fault for the errors he made.

*

The wagon has been waiting in front of my door. It's going to take me to the train station. We are going to seek justice in Berlin. That publisher is the slayer of my good name....I wander about the world without a name, and consequently no one can see me. Let him therefore give me back my name! At first they gave me that ridiculously gangly and imbecilic watchman as an escort. I asserted: "Pardon, gentlemen, but I am not traveling with him. We would bring disgrace upon the whole country of Croatia. The Germans would say, namely: Voilà! What people Croatia brings into the world—so huge, but so stupid!"

*

Now I realize at last that I have ended up in the company of lunatics. They are legion! We walk every day in the sprawling gardens, where I run into them. I talk to them. There's no end to the stupidity I encounter.

Nothing but lunatics! But ultimately everything I see is happening outside the walls of this sanatorium as well.

*

I am getting really fed up with being among these madmen. They flock constantly around the doctors: "Let me go home! You promised, you know, so why are you keeping me here?" And some of them ask nicely: "Oh kind, sweet, good doctor! Do let me go!"…And yet others scream at the physician: "You bloodsucker! Bandit! Thief!"

They do not believe they are mad.

And, in truth, I am deceived. When I got to this place, they told me that I'd only be staying a couple of weeks. But now I've already been here, surrounded by lunatics, for close to two months, and they will not allow me to go home. And I am starting to be gruff with my doctor.

"I beg you, allow me to leave. Can you not see that I am mentally and physically healthy?"

He shakes his head.

"So I am ill?"

"Yes."

"And what is wrong with me? I sleep well, my digestion is good, I have no pains to report anywhere; so how am I ill? And if I were mentally unwell, would it not be unlikely that I would be conversing so reasonably with you?"

"What is going on with your wife, the late Adelka?"

"How is it, Doctor, that I am unable to clear up your confusion on this one simple issue? If she were dead, how would I be able to kiss her, how would I be able to carry on conversations with her, how would it be possible for me to see her…and anyway, my darling, I would rather be holed up with these lunatics that in the company of Mesarić, Rakovčić, and the mayor. I have already told you so many times that I kiss Adelka. Tell me, how would I be in a position to kiss someone who isn't there? Who no longer exists? I assure you once more that she loves me and I love her—and how would that be feasible if she were dead? If it is true, then, that I killed her, then they should have taken me away to prison and not to an asylum."

Well, I can't show that man anything, not even something that simple. However…each and every day I am able to steal a furtive glance out the open gates of the garden, to where a broad plain can be seen, and a forest, and beyond it the blue and purple mountain range. Where Adelka and Veruška abide.

I laugh to myself, for I am hatching some plans…

PART THREE

Chapter One

Without a doubt, Amadej had found the beauty in women since his youth—beauty that caused his blood to boil, beauty from which his sound and vigorous temperament was unable to free itself, as befits the powerful laws of nature. But there was one emotion—one that was independent of physicality, remaining as pure as it was forceful and stormy even when his body sensed neither the motivation nor the occasion to crave the embrace of a woman—this one emotion was only awakened in him by Adelka. And she caused its appearance in him, even when he was still a child, when that which some see as the impulse to the higher sympathies of the human spirit was still asleep in the boy. It was an emotion for which the world of bodily creation was too crude; it felt the world's touch and perceived it as both painful and deadly; it longed for unknown fastnesses, distant beyond the point of access by the senses...These were the worlds whence Amadej's melodies came, penetrating, streaming through his entire spirit without need for recognition by his acoustic nerves.

But they told him that Adelka had died. How could she be dead? That emotion, still registering inside him, cannot die, and in the same way neither can the melody that arises from his soul and spreads out, and out, like light, not by means of material vibrations but through the vibrations of his thoughts coursing out to the place from which all conceptions of beauty and goodness, of faith in their endurance, take off and take their spot in the human intellect. All people can push that far when they rid themselves of the burden and torments of hunger for bread and the shackles of power and gold. Push to that place where there is neither hunger nor hierarchy. And so how could Adelka have died, when he'd been wedded to her spirit since their childhood in that realm where love is stronger than death? For there is no death! She has merely returned to that pure world, in her state of full beauty and as the creature of an angelic childhood, removing the bonds between Amadej and herself, incapable as they had been of completely and harmoniously enjoying a divine gift of the magnitude of love. And her organ of Corti, which was imperfect the way the world gave it to her, in the manner of all the fruits she bore—she returned it to the earth; and now she listens without hindrance and understands with her very essence every exceedingly tender quiver in Amadej's spirit, with its pure escaping melodies that seem to be urged forth by the hands of angels and fine golden rays of sunlight.

And she's dead? How can something that understands death itself die?

Why, wondered Amadej, had they then locked him up among madmen? Why had they separated him from Adelka and Veruška?

Yes, but they are the ones who think that Adelka has passed away...

But behold: the level earth stretches away towards freedom. Look at the trees beyond the fields, and at the purplish mountains pushing up into the clear blue sky. Look at how the clouds float about unencumbered, like a virgin's song soaring serenely into the heavens. Amadej's soul flows along with them, rushing abroad, passing over the plain and the forest and the tall purple mountains—rushing to Adelka...

Oh, come, come, Adelka!

Shapely but as delicate as a child, she approaches, and behold: with steps so timidly tiny and soft that she seems not even to touch the ground. Amadej opens his arms to her as she nimbly alights. Firmly in his grasp, she descends onto his bent knee with her scarcely perceptible weight.

Ah, Adelka, how I have been perishing from desire! How I have been craving this moment, when you would come to me and I could embrace you and feel your lips with my mouth. And now turn to me, Adelka, with those peaceful bright eyes of yours, the eyes into which the happiness of our entwined souls has sunk like in a bottomless sea. Do you hear how wondrous the melodies are that surround us? Do you feel how your heart trembles with beauty, and how we submerge with such sublime sensations into the vastness of Eden? Look at me, Adelka! Look at me with those eyes! I was perishing for the lack of them, for they inspired me with the delicious life that is childhood. We will die, Adelka, wrapped in this embrace, before the fiery poison of hunger for bread, gold, and power seeps into this paradise. But no! We will not die yet! Do you see the people, how they have forgotten their hunger and hierarchies, and how they take account of neither sadness at death nor joy at wealth?...We elevated them, bewitched, into our realm on the power of the elegant harmonies in our spirits. You will witness it: when the final chord of our song fades, they will start to weep; they will stomp on their money, trample their distinctions, and shout to the two of us: Glory! We shall prevail, Adelka. Therefore, let us go back out among people, return to life. This is our calling: to light an eternal flame for the people, so that their eyes will begin to see. Let us depart, Adelka! Do you see Jahoda calling to us, crowned with a wreath of moonbeams? Come! Don't you feel the way our conjoined souls ascend from the earth to the heavens, as if guided by mellifluous strings of bright rays of sunlight? Do you hear the way they shiver with our love, filling the space between heaven and earth with their brilliant harmonies? Adelka—let us be off! Behold the plain stretching untrammelled out before us, and beyond the plain the wood, and beyond the wood the mountains, pushing their violet crests into the serenity of the clear skies? Wait for me there, Adelka. Here I am drowning behind these walls. Their proximity is suffocating me, even as my heart reaches out from their midst, aching and yearning for you. Wait for me, Adelka! I shall come to you.

*

But how cunning I am! I retreat, quietly, carefully dragging my feet and telling them to their faces that I am as crazy as they are. And so, *voilà*, Adelka, I have already put the lunatic asylum behind me, while before me sprawls the plain, immeasurable, just as endless as my soulful longing for you. But be careful! It is possible that they have already remarked my flight and raised a posse to hunt for me. Have no fear, Adelka! There is thick brush along the river banks...I am choosing my steps carefully, but with urgency...Aha, I've reached the undergrowth. Just let them search for me now! —Hark— I hear their steps!...I crouch in the bushes, as I watch to see where they will strike. It's cold, and the water is freezing on the edges of the river, and a few random leaves are rustling in this stand of willows. Everything is dying. But if you come, Adelka, the world will be warmed by our kisses and spring will sprout and leaf. For did not the angel adorn Veruška's soul with our kisses?

But behold! It wasn't the inmates. Some little boy was driving his pony through the grove; the pony was hanging its head dejectedly.

The gray twilight is descending, full of tiny needles of cold that stick right through my asylum clothes. But in my heart: a flame!

But you know, Adelka, what it means to desire you in this way! And, oh, when I find you and pull you close, our kiss will be fierier than the sun.

Onward, onward! The distant plains again open up before me. Everything is as quiet as a grave. I can hear only the crackling of the river, where the water is freezing, but I think the heavens are igniting star by star. Far off before me the edge of the forest blackens...there's nothing for it but onward, and with dispatch, for the lunatics are persecuting me. I hear their servile voices, ill-tempered and bestial, gloating over their coming victim, but I too am wily. I mean, why was I once a man? I lowered myself to the ground and crawled along the frozen earth on my hands and knees...This is tiring, so tiring...I am covered in sweat and I must take a breather. I listen intently...once more I am mistaken. The belling of hounds reaches my ears from afar. They are barking at the moon that is just now coming up.

Stunning silvery light spills across the frozen landscape—just a bit further—aha, here I am in the copse. Now they may search for me as they will. I will laugh at them, out loud, and the satyr will respond from the other end of the forest and then they will seek me there, damning my existence, there, where I am not. And I daresay they did not understand my voice earlier. My soul was weeping melodies of joy—that part was you, Adelka—and of dolor, wherein the woes of the human race have slowly accumulated. But they did not comprehend these sounds; they knew neither what they were nor whence they came. But I loved those people anyhow. I was always daydreaming and planning ways I could protect them from misery and injustice...but, my Adelka, we were weak. Evil was stronger than the good. It was only our love that was strong, stronger than everything else...but that love was not of this world. And the stars have pulled it up to the heights with them.

Here I am in the wood. Now I am certain, Adelka, that I will make it to your side. Let them harry me all they wish! They will search for me and blunder about in the dark in vain, as they have been accustomed to doing since they were born. I would be glad for a rest, but I can't wait for the hour of my arrival at your side. You are sitting there in our humble room, with our little Vera on your lap, fallen asleep while waiting for me. Your beautiful eyes are filled with love and your face radiates sweet, smiling happiness like a clear sky at the precise break of day. Now I'm not tired any more, I am being transported by a pleasant lightness, as if I were being carried along by hands invisible yet powerful. It is an idea that is carrying me, a thought of yearning that is hurtling towards you. In this way I will lay my hands on your nubile body—a delicious idea and a hot desire— and bear you off through the peace and quiet of the brilliant, magical night. We will enter yonder forest like a great temple, with the bright moon pouring its soft, silvery light through the ebony branches. The night will be holy, and you and I and Veruška will bide beneath the wing of an exalted and godlike tree while we sing a hymn to love and peace.

I then left the forest and the gorgeous country in front of me quivered with life in a sea of moonlight. It is exquisite, Adelka! A valley opened up before me, with a stream winding along its bottom, illuminated in some areas like pure silver and dark in other places like velvet. In the brook is reflected a jittery image of the black undergrowth and cliffs rising up next to the water. Ice sparkles at the edge of the flow, like embroidery on vel-

vet framed by silver cords. Farther away, on the far side
of the valley, a mountain towers glorious and terrible in
its colossal shadowy stillness. When I make my way past
this mountain, Adelka, I will find you. This is what my
heart tells me...

I have reached the waters now. Quiet wavelets hurry
past, reflecting amidst their breath-taking play the beams
of moonlight. The mountain waits quietly, and everything around me is at peace, but I am listening to the
singing of the *vilas* rising into the cosmos from behind
the mountain. If I did not have to go to you, I would
remain here and inscribe their song on my soul so that
you would know what a splendid melody lies in the
murmuring of a stream, with every drop of water acting
like a silver-toned string, producing melodies altogether
more satisfying than any ever penned by Beethoven or
Chopin. I hearken as if this were the church-organ of
the spheres, used by the musical genius over all of nature to accompany the song of this enchanted night. If,
Adelka, I did not need to come to you, I would not step
forth from this holy spot.

I remember, you know, how I used to sit by the
brook that flowed near our hometown back in the first
days after I returned from Prague. People, houses, trees,
every little village, every stone—all of it, everything to
be found on that holy ground, my native soul, it all had
soul, goodness, gentleness, sincerity, and I loved this
soul and it loved me. I trembled and cried in front of
you at the feeling of magnificence, and it inhabited me
whenever I took my place on the banks of our little
stream on whose waters my childhood flowed. Seated

thus beside its course, I listened to its soft, mellifluous gurgling and felt that a good friend was reciting the poetry of childhood to me, from a time when my mother was still alive. The tiny little waves and low-hanging green branches bending their fresh, verdant boughs in the direction of the current; the oaks hovering above the waters like faithful sentinels, and the flattened far shore, with its white flocks of geese and ducks—the lot of it resolved itself into intimate shapes of affection, sincerity, and joyousness, everything yearned to give me its love; it was as if it had all joined in my deep emotion as if entering an ocean, and we merged into one being, soaring off to some place where there is nothing but love. And then I, like right now, listen, in the rhythms of the quiet murmur of the water, to a composition that I never wrote down but that I can still hear in my spirit now. This very evening, Adelka, I will play it for you on the harp; you will hear what a phenomenal piece it is that our little brook has narrated to me.

There is not a footbridge or a log anywhere. All the better! If those crazy people get the urge to chase me, they'll get this far and then turn around and go back. To that place where we will be, you and Veruška and I, people are not permitted to travel. I strode boldly into the water accompanied only by the thought of you: and that thought carried me, just as the sun elevates rivers and seas to the radiant heights.

Here I am now on the other side of the stream. Farewell, you folks over there—farewell! And then I was walking across ground that belonged to our love. I bowed down and kissed that ground. "The love through which this kiss speaks has no rival and flames without compare, but burns only at your altar…"

I waded into the water up to my belt, but I was even prepared to swim. Thank God this was the final hurdle. And, now, apace, to you, Adelka. To you, the longing of my life! The moon's light grows colder and colder, and my limbs shake with chill. Would that I had reached you, Adelka, so that I could take my warmth in our loving.

I entered a forest. The night is divine. Darkness and obscurity circle around me and in the crowns of the trees, high and thick, silvery points dance in the breeze like gleaming walnuts amidst the silently shaking branches. What difficult going it was! The deeper I went into the forest, the more my legs became entwined in the low-growing bushes and struck thick roots, fallen timbers, and stones. But my mind is carrying me towards you, Adelka, and by dint the thought of you I am made light and feel as though I were walking on clouds. But have I not already suffered more than this all the while that I, so very far from you, and hungry and humiliated by humanity, awaited the hour when I would step into your presence: *voilà*—you can be mine!

Again I am prey to that old human grief: my mind is conveying me to you but my body does not allow me to conquer the mountain and join you corporeally. Fatigue, pain, and cold afflict me, though my soul races on to abide with you, each and every moment without exception. For my whole life I have been split like this— strung between heaven and earth. My soul speeds like light through the dark trunks and crowns, into the serene illumination of the moon, and my body wanders on through the gloom, with rocks and undergrowth slicing my legs and sharp boughs poking my face and brow. I move forward on all fours. My palms and legs sink into the earth. A bitterness repellent to me permeates my soul: why should my weakness and physical pain manifest themselves at a time like this, as I am speeding into the distance, towards you. Once Mesarić gave me a book to read. It was called *Die monistische Seelenlehre.* I wish the philosopher who wrote that would come here; I wish he would find himself rushing urgently with desire and longing to his love, and that he would feel the weight of pain, fatigue, and cold forcing his body to the ground as if he were bound with chains. Let him have a taste of this and then assert that he doesn't sense himself in himself......

Behold—light! It was as if lights, calm white mystical lights with irregular outlines, were descending onto the thick black night of the forest. They seemed to be very far away, but, as I know from experience, that is an optical illusion. They must be close, approximately one hundred steps in front of me. I stood back up, since I had torn up my hands going on all fours. They hurt...This magical light I behold before me is reassuring and wondrous—and it proclaims your presence! Out there the forest comes to an end, and beyond it the beautiful plains unfold, where the dear town of our birth reposes. You'll see, Adelka—soon we will meet there and embrace standing by our Veruška's crib. My body aches and cold flows out of the moonlight into my limbs. The wet clothing on me has frozen in place like ice-bark, which the warmth of my blood cannot melt. And that means that the unbending shell of my body is constricting my soul, too.—But I can sense, Adelka, that you are close by, and then the fatigue and cold and physical pain yield to the feeling that we will soon be together, in an instant equal parts tenderness and grandeur.

I have come to the edge of the forest—and the first thought that settled on my mind, to my indescribable surprise, was you, Adelka, you. Adelka must be there! Before my eyes a shrine took shape, a splendid temple shot through with holiness, where colossal, sky-high statues and altars of granite, silver, and gold tremble soundlessly in their insides in the light of the eternal flame: here abides the mystery of the divinity. Is this place the creation of the human mind and spirit, a work conceived by a sumptuous Oriental imagination and realized with the hands and blood of thousands of slaves, at the cost of legendary sums of their sovereigns' money? Or is it a holy spot, safely sequestered far from everyday life, where no human may set foot? It seems to me that I can sense on the stone the steps of Svarog, and that from on high I detect the soft singing of a choir of *vilas*. Before the great altar a gray-bearded shaman, his face in the dust, whispers his prayers in the immediacy of the godhead; the euphonious murmur of water, flowing mysteriously down the walls of the shrine, is like the voice of legions of spirits from Svarog's retinue.

With sacred dread I enter the magnificent shrine. I anticipate that the spirits residing therein will resist my brazenness. With longing in my soul I tread across the reddish-white stone on which sizzle rays of moonlight and I feel myself melt away into nothingness amidst this vast splendor surrounded by walls that reach up to the heavens while giving off droplets of water like the fount of eternal life. A great black forest looms like a boundary marker at the opening of the depths of eternity, and in the crowns of the trees, interlaced with beams of moonlight, I hear through my soul's ear the magnificent hum of chords unknown in human music. Gradually I get my bearings in the temple, and my steps gain in boldness; I listen to the muffled tread of my feet on the shrine's floor and I am guiding you, Adelka, my arm around you, up to the huge altar that rises from the light in the bowels of the earth to the black obscurity of the grove, above which the moon is shining. We are just about to wed, Adelka, and Svarog, who will bless our marriage, awaits us. The wedding guests attend us. They are an army of spirits, and from the balcony echoes a nuptial song from the throats of the *vilas*. If you listen well, Adelka—it's my composition, "The Hymn to Love"! And there, in front of the choir, is an image of Jahoda's dear head and face, illuminated by a wreath of moonbeams. Blood! I was all atremble. Blood! Blood from my hands and knees was profaning the sacredness of this place. You see—wherever a human being turns up, there also appears that admixture of earthly dust, human blood, and personal tears! In this abominable compound human life on our planet wallows, while above it an evil spirit like a heavy cloud reveals itself and descends like black rain into human hearts as hunger for bread, for gold, and for power. Through the hulking black body of this evil spirit rays of light flash and ignite, and people fall to their knees in the nauseating mix of blood, tears, and dust, and they raise their hands towards the light, wailing despondently for justice...And the massive body of the evil spirit swells like the sea, shrouded in dusty obscurity, poisoning people with vicious cravings of self-love—and the millions fall once more hopelessly into that vile blend of earthly dust, tears from the soul, and blood of the heart...

I look at my own blood and feel myself once more on solid ground. In fact, fatigue, cold, and pain are driving me down into it. I quake from the chill and from the sight of my own blood. Is this truly the first time that this ground has been desecrated by human blood, this space where I could sense divinity just a few moments ago?—It seems to me that I can hear how centuries ago this peace and stillness heaved with the mad screams of warriors and the moans of wounded horsemen. I can hear war and killing, the curses and prayers of the dying, and the glorious jubilation of the victors. I observe the injured heroes as they drag themselves back to this spring, broken men looking to wash out their wounds and bring relief to their parched mouths. A red trail of blood is left where they have trodden. The pounding of drums, the jangle of weapons, the whistling of pan flutes, the thudding of horses and cheers from human throats grow ever more remote. Mute silence descends once more, and in come the mothers and wives, mixing the tears they shed over their dead heroes with the blood already lodged in the dust of the earth...

Adelka, why am I a poet, why do the strings of my soul groan with redoubled plaintiveness at the dolorous sounds of human sufferings? Why? And behold—they

have just now dressed me in the frozen suit of a madman, me, who has cried for all the miserable of the earth,
me, who you know could conduct by memory any one
of Beethoven's symphonies! Ah, what do they care
about the great Beethoven, whose soul contained in its
immensity and strength as much as the souls of Homer,
Sophocles, Dante, or Shakespeare? They find sublime
thoughts and transcendent emotion in Sophocles, Dante,
Shakespeare, Hugo and Tolstoy, but they cannot bring
themselves to explore the sonorous depths of Beethoven's soul, like a cork on the surface of the sea. They
swim about on the top, in superficial brilliance, where
prance like rays of sunlight on the water the blood-red
colors and aural rhythms. For what purpose was I born
among them as an artist and musician, if they cannot
fathom my soul? I have been left so alone. For a long
time, Adelka, I lived by deluding myself that they envied
me this power, and that they would bow before the
force that allowed me to plunge into the profundities
and poetry of notes, while all they could do was amuse
themselves with the rhythms of the waltz. How I deceived myself. Wild animals that live thousands of meters above the sea, or far down in the bowels of the
earth have, of course, a right to live...but they do not
covet the life of the creatures for whom the observation
of nature, irradiated by the light of the sun or moon, is
the chief joy of living. Thus it is that two men, born on
the same planet, can inhabit two worlds that do not
connect. Why are things this way? Who would have the
gall to answer that question? Is the apotheosis of life this
disjuncture from which so much painful dissonance is

born? Is this dissonance the *summum bonum* of human existence, beyond which it peters out into nothingness? No, Adelka, this is not how it ends! Life merely begins here, and then it flows into that capital state of concord that can only be perceived by select minds that thirst for it with an irrepressible need in their souls, which can never be allayed on this earth.

In the shrine the lights go out. Below me the night has begun to obscure the traces of my blood, and above me spreads the black air with the star-sewn sky behind it. The cold is painful and it gnaws on my body through the frozen lunatic's outfit they put on me. To a person suffering from unabated headaches it might seem that such an illness inhabits the head of every human being...Down with this kind of garb! It's undignified of me to be in this shrine with such clothes on my back!—A madman in a shrine...That'd be a first-rate subject for Byron!—Me, a madman? I, who understand every beat of the human heart, I am given the uniform of a crazy man? And how many people with rotten corrupted hearts, how many real crazies, go through life in the guise of worthy citizens? It's an old comedy, sometimes authored by stupidity and sometimes by injustice, but it contains ever the same substance; only the characters change from work to artistic work. No, no, I am not going to tolerate these clothes on me. Here, here you go, you real lunatics. Put it on. It becomes you.

In the shrine all the lights have gone out. All around me is aught but the chill of night. Then frenzied piping can be heard from afar, and clouds fly past above my head. They bring wild music with them, fierce, pos-

sessed, and they get tangled up in the hair of the Furies
seated atop the temple's entry-way. They have black hair,
huge as trees, and a gale wails around their heads with
dry, scraping sounds, like when leafless trees sway back
and forth in winter. Up high the cold is tremendous, and
I am supporting myself on the warm wall where lukewarm water tumbles down. A pleasant sensation of
tiredness overcomes me, and I feel the way I did in
childhood when my mother would tote me in her own
arms, clasping me firmly to her breast. The heat is luxurious and sweet in the icy atmosphere around me...On
the huge altar flame after flame comes to life, and heat
and light spread around the temple while people beyond
number flock to the solemn ceremony. And you enter,
Adelka, radiant with beauty and the loving eyes of an
angel, wearing your precious garment of satin, which is
replete with pearls like the clothes of a queen. How cold
your sweet, pallid hand is, and how hot my lips, as they,
burning with love, kiss it! Around us flow murmuring
voices, light, splendor, magnificence, and holiness;
above the shrine boom the thunderous and mellifluous
sounds of bells. The divine liturgy is underway. An elderly holy man with a white beard and golden robes takes
his place in front of the altar, and behind him are thousands of adults and children in white raiments holding lit
candles in their hands. Everything dances in the light.
Listen to the way that grand chord from the organ has
burst forth, as if the granite walls of the shrine themselves are ringing with this sound. With *motifs* and daring
combinations of harmonies like those in a fugue by Beethoven! How much imagination there is in this mysteri-

ous artist! I felt as though my soul was overflowing with the broad waves of these notes. Like a tempest in a deep gorge, the organ rumbles, and the temples' granite walls rock on their foundations...Then, darkness and silence once more. Under a fine rushlight of yellow a withered old man prostrates himself in front of the altar and utters a prayer of repentance for sins he committed in his youth. And I feel compunction, too—death draws back the drapes at the entrance to eternity...It's a majestic feeling, Adelka! With the light from my soul I pierce the black body of the evil spirit and hurtle, meteor-like, through the endless night. I speed as in a dream, as if I were sleeping on a soft, bright cloud. Fatigue, excruciatingly sweet, overcomes me, and I race through the night with a feeling at once indescribable and heavenly...I speed on as if on a weightless, bright cloud, under my own power, and you, Adelka, are close by. I sense you, and rush pell-mell towards you, urgently, gently, inaudibly, like a star.

Now I am five years old, and I am crying. I see around myself four of my classmates; a boy of about seven is standing there, too, out of breath and red in the face, as if he has worn himself out beating me for some unknown reason. A woman walks past and says to the boy, "Why did you thrash him so? He is a poor wretch with no mother or father. There is no one to defend him. Why don't you take pity on him?" And my eyes brimmed with tears all the more acrid.

And now I am ten. I'm sitting at an organ, and every touch of my little fingers on the keys sends indescribable delight through my heart...Jahoda is listening to me, his eyes laugh and cloud with tears and...then he kisses my brow.

And now I'm sitting in his room at the old piano, and you, Adelka, come in. To me it's like an angel just entered the room, the way your face flashes its beauty at me. I believe that you have descended from heaven, and that the wings that flew you here are clapped behind your back. In vain I seek on the piano the chord that will make your angelic appearance reverberate in my soul...Much later I did find precisely that chord in Chopin—and I laugh and cry with delight and pain...

Now I'm with Jahoda in his room: he is stretched out on the bed while around us spreads the silence of a chilly autumn evening. Jahoda relates to me a story about Mařenka, and a queer, unbidden warmth, both sweet and painful, cascades over my heart and floods my bloodstream. Something is roused in me, something that more than anything makes me want to weep. It awakens in me and extends over me, and in my isolation I weep, oh, Adelka, weep while looking at your beatific countenance. Through it my entire life is made holy, and through it are blessed every step I take on this earth and every contact I have with others. In my heart, love is born...

Now I am in Prague. You blaze high above me, star-like; my soul longs to rise up to your heights, but hunger wrestles me back to earth. Not a single night passes that I do not drench my pillow with tears. But my soul does not divert its eyes from you, or your world, built of the most wonderful melodies. I get them from your soul. I know that triumph and fame await us.

Vesely warns me away from you. I recoil at his close presence; I am afraid of his words and his eyes, and when he moves away from me, I feel sorry for him; I think he is a martyr and an innocent victim; a wave of compassion washes through me and I am drawn to him.

Now I am starting to live with the body of a child but the mind of a grown man. I am seated on a tall hill above the Vltava. Spring is kissing the earth, and flowers and love alike are born from these kisses. My eyes probe yearningly southward; my thoughts race to the place of my birth, where flowers are awakening this same way, and from the cozy lap of spring love is brought forth.

A terrible, unrestrained longing stirs in my chest, threatening to rip me asunder with its power; aches weigh me down; they prevent me from spreading like light and girding with my essence all of the planet and everything, too, that is between heaven and earth. But behold: now the tight shackles are bursting, and I expand, and rise up, feeling an inexplicable lightness and pleasure.

I return, crowned with a laurel wreath, from Prague to my homeland and to you, Adelka. Singers with beautiful, strong voices perform my composition "Hail, Homeland," which I had sketched out in the train car back then, to the rhythm of the wheels...On the train an elderly peasant woman had asked me, a look of intelligence on her compassionate face: why are you crying? Don't have any relatives there?—And I reply: "I have a fiancée, and I feel as though my world..."

We kissed for the first time. Our kiss took wing up into the heavens and switched on like a star. One night

an angel brought us Veruška in her arms, and I found
that same star in her eyes. Her light flashed in my soul,
and it brought my "Hymn to Love" to life. People did
not understand it; I sold my birthright; and, if you remember, Adelka, I wept...

How did this come to pass, Adelka—from your being my soul drank in its poetry, yet you did not understand it? How can that be? Aha! Now I understand! The
culprit is the organ of Corti in your ear. For how could
you fail to love me, honestly, with your soul, which I
love? Well, see here. Think of how much the country of
your affection and sensibilities influenced you in an effort to refine your ear. I mean spirit, Adelka, the poetry
of our souls, as well as that vulgar and unfair organ of
Corti. How many roadblocks, how much absurdity, was
there in this country's aspiration to be at the service of
the poetry of musical notes to which my soul is giving
birth, fructified by the touch of your angelic being! Give
it back, Adelka. Give back to this land its gift.

She will bury the gift in her poverty and assign it to
new progeny. Return it to her, even if it will decompose
and putrefy in her entrails. And our two souls will expand from star to star like two golden strings of sunlight
that intone, when strummed by our affections, the
melodies of the ages!

An mind-boggling sea of light, and beyond it, in the
darkness, next to a discarded straitjacket, a chunk of
black earth with a distorted shape that resembles me...
An ineffable sea of light...with the raw power of expo-
nentially magnified calm and sublime moonshine... Ah,
what kind of marvelous music over there is carrying

forth my "Hymn to Love"? It's perfect, the same way it was when it circulated through my soul after it was created there. Now it floats somewhere above the earth. I enter with a wondrous lightness the radiant light...as if I were being born...Aha, and there you are, Adelka...and Jahoda...

Afterword

John R. Palmer

The lives of Vjenceslav Novak and the two main characters of his *Dva svijeta*, Jan Jahoda and Amadej Zlatanić, span an era that encompassed sweeping changes in Slavic musical culture within the Hapsburg empire. However, because they are of different generations—Novak lived from 1859–1905, and he implies that Jahoda was born in 1822 and Zlatanić in 1862—the musical environments of Novak and his characters, particularly Jahoda, would have been of two worlds.[1] Jahoda, a Czech, is a contemporary of Bedřich Smetana (1824–84), whereas Zlatanić grew up at a time when the voices of both Czech and Croatian composers were heard with increasing frequency in their homelands.

[1] In Part One, Chapter Three we learn that Jahoda completed his studies at the Prague Conservatory in 1846, at the age of 24. Zlatanić's birth year I have based on Part One, Chapter Five, in which Zlatanić, aged 18, attends the première of Dvořák's *Stabat mater*, which took place in December of 1880. This does not jibe with Novak's description, in the first chapter, of Zlatanić as a boy of 12 when Jahoda is 60.

Zagreb and Prague, especially, afforded completely different musical landscapes for Novak's and Zlatanić's generation than they did for Jahoda's.

Jan Jahoda's Prague

Unlike Zlatanić, Jahoda could not have studied composition at the Prague Conservatory in the early 1840s, for although it was founded in 1811, the Conservatory did not establish a composition program until the late 19th century. Prior to that, the conservatory's sole purpose was to train performers in established repertory, primarily by German, Italian and French composers.[2] Furthermore, the first director of the conservatory, Bedřich Diviš Weber (1766–1842), was a conservative Mozartian, swept up in the Mozart craze stemming from the composer's triumphs in the city in the 1780s with *Le nozze di Figaro* and *Don Giovanni.* Thus, the Conservatory did not promote, and arguably hindered, the development of a Czech national style. Also a bastion of musical conservatism was Dvořák's *alma mater*, the Prague Organ School, established in 1830 and whose first director, Jan Vitásek, was another Mozartian.[3] The conservative atmosphere

[2] J. Bužga, Adrienne Simpson, "Prague," in *The New Grove Dictionary of Music and Musicians*, ed. Stanley Sadie , vol. XV (London: MacMillan, 1980), 195.

[3] By the time of Dvořák's matriculation, in 1857, some faculty members at the organ school had more modern interests, such as the music of Mendelssohn and Liszt. John Clapham, "Dvořák," in *New Grove*, vol. V, p. 765.

continued under Weber, who assumed the directorship in 1839.

Prague's first real opera house was established in 1783, but until 1861 only one performance per week was given in Czech. Italian repertoire dominated the opera house stage in its early years, and when this was displaced in the second decade of the 19th century, it was not by Czech works, but by German and French. Although a number of Czech folksong collections and patriotic songs were published in the 1830s, the will to create first-rate institutions dedicated to Czech concert music did not bear fruit until the early 1860s. Jahoda's Prague was thus very different from both Zlatanić's and Novak's.

Amadej Zlatanić's Prague

Novak began his study at the Prague Conservatory in 1884, but sets Zlatanić's arrival in the city four years earlier. In Part One, Chapter Five, one of the first things Zlatanić does after arriving in Prague is attend the première of Antonin Dvořák's *Stabat mater*, which took place on 23 December 1880. At the time, Dvořák was well known in his homeland, and was on the cusp of international fame. Such an event simply would not have occurred in Jahoda's Prague.

Many of the seeds that produced the vibrant Czech music culture in Zlatanić's Prague were sown in the 1860s, including the founding of the Prague Hlahol choral society (1861, all male until 1879) and the Umeľčcká

Beseda (Artistic Circle) (1863), and the opening of the
Provisional Theater (1862), built for the performance of
Czech opera, which found no place at the German-
dominated Estates Theater.[4] Smetana's conductorship of
the Hlahol and presidency at the Umelĕcká Beseda
promised greater exposure for Czech composers, but
Umelĕcká Beseda concerts featuring works by his Czech
contemporaries failed to attract audiences and lost
money.[5] More importantly, during Smetana's tenure at
the Provisional Theater (1866–74) he staged many of his
own operas on Czech subjects, inspiring other Czech
composers to create such works. More than any earlier
or contemporary composer, Smetana, from his *Braniboři
v Čecháh* (*The Brandenburgers in Bohemia*) of 1866 on, established a Czech musical voice. The growth of Czech nationalist stage works led to the opening in 1881 of the
Národni Divadlo (National Theater), the site of premières of operas by Smetana, Dvořák, and Fibich over
the next two decades. Inspired by Smetana's success,
and emboldened by political reforms, Czech artists took
the necessary steps to create a true Czech musical culture in Prague.

This would not be easy. New laws introduced in 1867
in the western Hapsburg realms guaranteed national
rights to all citizens and led, over the next few decades,
to universal, equal, male suffrage in 1906. This effec-

---

[4] The poor state of Czech musical theater at the time is evident
in the choice of work to open the new home of Czech opera:
Cherubini's *Les deux journées*.

[5] John Clapham, "Smetana," *New Grove* (1980), XVII/394.

tively put the Germans in their proper place in terms of proportion of the population, and there was a backlash against Czechs and Slavs of every stripe from which the world of music was not immune.[6] The case of Brahms and Dvořák will serve as a good example.

Brahms came to know Dvořák's work through the latter's application, each year between 1874 and 1878, for the Austrian State Stipendum, intended to support young, poor artists.[7] Brahms became an adjudicator in 1875, and in 1877 Dvořák submitted, among other works, his Moravian Duets. Brahms passed the score on to Berlin publisher Friedrich Simrock, a much larger firm than Dvořák's current publisher, Starý in Prague. When Eduard Hanslick, another adjudicator, later wrote to Dvořák concerning the Stipendum, he told Dvořák of Brahms's actions and suggested Dvořák provide "a good German translation," of the Duets, which Dvořák did two weeks later. "After all," Hanslick continued, "it would be advantageous for your things to become known beyond your narrow Czech fatherland, which in any case does not do much for you."

Hanslick's suggestion that Dvořák provide a German translation of his Czech texts was not unreasonable: it

[6] Brigitte Hamann, *Hitler's Vienna: A Dictator's Apprenticeship*, trans. Thomas Thornton (New York: Oxford University Press, 1999), 304–24 provides a summary of German reactions to the growth of Slavic, particularly Czech, political power.

[7] Dvořák won the Stipendum every year he applied. See Herman Krieger, "Antonin Dvořák: A Biographical Sketch," in *Dvořák and His World*, ed. Michael Beckerman (Princeton: Princeton University Press, 1993), 218, 228, n17.

was a matter of practicality that would increase sales. However, his assertion that Dvořák's "narrow Czech fatherland" had done little for Dvořák was untenable, as Dvořák, through Starý, had built a list of publications and had seen many performances in his homeland. The comment, particularly the use of the word "narrow," betrays a Germanocentrism that saw Bohemia an insignificant cultural backwater. Even after Dvořák had achieved international recognition, Simrock insisted on printing the titles of Dvořák's works, and the composer's first name, in German, including the Czech title parenthetically, if at all.[8]

Brahms's relationship with Dvořák evolved into a real friendship, and Brahms promoted Dvořák's music until the end of his life. Nevertheless, there is a hierarchy apparent in their correspondence, and Brahms's comments about Dvořák betray a common German perception of Czechs as unsophisticated. In his letters to Brahms, all in German, Dvořák's tone often approaches fawning. When describing Dvořák's music, Brahms applauds Dvořák's "natural" melody and says nothing about the "learned" aspects of his music. In a letter praising Dvořák's "New World" symphony, Brahms muses that he himself might have composed it "one day after breakfast." During commentary on Dvořák's

---

[8] For example, what is now referred to as Dvořák's Ninth Symphony, "From the New World," was first published by Simrock in 1894 as *Aus der neuen Welt. "Z nového světa."Symphonie (No. 5, E moll.) für grosses Orchester, Op. 95.* Aside from Brahms, Dvořák was arguably the most famous living composer at the time.

Eighth Symphony Brahms describes the composer as a "charming musician," who "fails to achieve anything great and comprehensive with his pure, individual ideas," unlike Bruckner, who knows how to create a solid structure.[9] Brahms's entrenched German nationalism most certainly colored his perceptions. Extant letters show that he expressed clear dislike for Dvořák's works that were overtly nationalistic or otherwise Czech-themed (*Te Deum, Hussite Overture, St. Ludmilla*).

It is no surprise that the German disregard for Czech music, and the resultant tension between the two cultures, arises several times in *Dva svijeta*. What is surprising is that, in the very first chapter, it becomes clear that Jahoda's estimation of Croatian musical ability parallels the German estimation of Czech musical ability.

In years nearer to Novak's writing of *Dva svijeta*, tensions between Czechs and Germans in the Empire increased. On 4 October 1897, Gustav Mahler conducted Bedřich Smetana's *Dalibor*, with a German translation by Max Kalbeck of the Czech libretto.[10] That Mahler, who had made his debut as a *Kapellmeister* only in May, should choose a Czech opera as his first new work for the Vienna Hofoper raised eyebrows and a few hackles, particularly on the backs of German nationalists in Vienna

[9] David Beveridge, "Dvořák and Brahms: A Chronicle, an Interpretation," in *Dvořák and His World*, 82.

[10] It is perhaps ironic that the libretto of *Dalibor*, one of Smetana's most nationalist operas, was written by Josef Wenzig in German and translated into Czech by Ervin Špindler before Smetana set it. Also, Smetana, a German speaker, could neither speak nor write Czech until his 30s.

who were unsettled by the recent granting of parity between the German and Czech languages in Bohemia and Moravia. Most reviewers commented, favorably, on the production itself, but politicization of the event was perhaps inevitable. Kalbeck's *Neues Wiener Tagblatt* reported that most of the audience consisted of Viennese Czechs, as well as "numerous spectators not usually in the habit of attending opera premières... Czech members of the Imperial Parliament."[11] A few weeks after the opening night of *Dalibor*, which was staged 13 times that season, Mahler received an anonymous letter, reading, in part, "So you insist on fraternizing with the anti-dynastic, inferior Czech nation which has been carrying out acts of violence against the German and Austrian states."[12]

Amadej Zlatanić's Zagreb

Spurred by the Illyrian movement (1835–48), development of a national musical voice occurred somewhat earlier in Zagreb than in Prague. As in the Czech lands, this development consisted, in part, of crawling out from under Hapsburg dominance, but in Croatia, some

[11] Kurt Blaukopf, *Mahler: A Documentary Study* (London: Thames and Hudson, 1976), 214. Also quoted in Henri-Louis de la Grange, *Gustav Mahler: The Years of Challenge (1897–1904)* (New York: Oxford University Press, 1995), 65.

[12] Anonymous letter of 7 November 1897. Österreichische Nationalbibliothek, Wien, Theatersammlung, Hofoper Archiv. Number of performances from Wilhelm Beetz, *Das Wiener Opernhaus: 1869 bis 1945* (Vienna: Panorama, 1949), 164–5.

reforms were met with local resistance as well. Nevertheless, assertions of Croatian musical independence occurred in Zagreb and other cities. Among these was the establishment of choral societies, such as the Zora Society in Karlova in 1858 and the Kolo Society, to which Zlatanić sends his "I love you, my ideal," in Zagreb in 1862.[13] In a move that was at first more political than musical, the Zagreb Musikverein, founded in 1827, shed its German name in 1851, when it became Društvo Prijatelja Glazbe (Amateur Music Association), and began receiving state funding ten years later. In Part Two, Chapter Three of *Dva svijeta*, Zlatanić name the two most important Croatian composers of the 19th century, Vatroslav Lisinski (1819–54) and Ivan Zajc (1832–1914). Separately, the two composers established a Croatian voice in stage and concert music and brought musical institutions in Zagreb into the modern era, raising the performance standards to those of major cities in Western Europe.

Zagreb's public theater opened in 1834, and in 1846 staged the première of *Ljubav i zloba*, (*Love and Malice*), by Lisinski, twenty years before Bedřich Smetana's *Braniboři v Čecháh* was heard in Prague. *Ljubav i zloba* was the first Croatian opera, and Lisinski, who drew on Croatian and Czech folk melodies, became generally accepted as the founder of modern Croatian music. A hero of the early

[13] "Croatia" at Oxford Music Online: http://0-www.oxfordmusiconline.com.iii.sonoma.edu/subscriber/article/grove/music/40473?q=Illyrian+movement&search=quick&pos=1&_start=1#firstht

Romantic era in Croatia, Lisinski was rejected by the Prague Conservatory in 1846 because of his age, changed his name from the Germanic Ignacije Fuchs after the politically pivotal year of 1848, ceased composing after 1853 because of political oppression, and composed his own funeral march.

Novak's model for Amadej Zlatanić is perhaps a composite of Vatroslav Lisinski and Ivan Zajc (1832–1914), a Croatian native who studied music in Milan and worked in Vienna before settling in Zagreb in 1870, accepting the post of Director of the Opera, a position he held nearly 20 years. While in Vienna, Zajc became the Director at the Carltheater, and the years 1862–70 saw about 140 performances of 11 of his works, all written under the name Giovanni von Zaytz. Adoption of such a pen-name by composers who were neither German nor Italian was not unusual, and it is no surprise that Novak's Zlatanić is asked by a publisher to do the same. (Novak, too, wrote some works anonymously or under a pseudonym.)

Although Zajc's success in Viennese operetta augured a European career, he elected to move to Zagreb in 1870 to revive the city's musical culture, which had grown stagnant after the death of Lisinski. Over the next three decades, Zajc's work at the newly founded Croatian National Opera (1870–89) and Glazbeni Zavod music school (1870–1904) transformed the provincial musical milieu into a formidable, modern culture with a large repertory. When Novak took up his post as music professor at the Zagreb Teachers' College in 1887, the state of musical culture in the city was at its height due to Zajc's efforts.

Although Zajc occasionally borrowed traits of Croatian folksong, he was a cosmopolitan composer open to musical developments throughout Europe. In his work at the Glazbeni Zavod music school he showed a determination to educate other Croatian musicians in the modern idioms that he knew his contemporaries would find unpalatable. Like Zlatanić in *Dva svijeta*, Zajc sought to establish a Croatian voice not solely by clinging to the nation's folk roots, but by incorporating modern European traits into a musical language that would be Croatian in origin and at the level of "high art." His struggle was primarily with his compatriots, not the Hapsburg regime. Unlike Zlatanić, Zajc succeeded.

Soon after Jahoda leaves his Czech homeland to work in a small, provincial Croatian town, he receives a long letter from Lipovský, who writes that "the literary revival of the Croatian people has scarcely gotten rolling." It is the late 1840s, and the Illyrian movement, which had begun only 13 years earlier, was about to end. Lisinski's *Ljubav i zloba* appeared in 1848, but Lisinski would disappear soon after, and most of Jahoda's life witnessed a lull in Croatian musical activity. By the time of Zlatanić's return to Croatia, musical culture in Zagreb had progressed to the point where he, as a Croatian, is able to speak with pride of ownership to his townsfolk of "...musical geniuses from *their* Scarlatti to *our* Lisinski and Zajc..." (italics mine). In terms of their art, Novak's Jahoda and Zlatanić lived in two, very different, worlds.